The
Honey Well

Other Books by the Author

Promises to Keep

Weeping Willows Dance

Shades of Jade

When We Practice to Deceive

GLORIA MALLETTE

The Honey Well

Dafina Books

KENSINGTON PUBLISHING CORP.
http://www.kensingtonbooks.com

DAFINA BOOKS are published by

Kensington Publishing Corp.
850 Third Avenue
New York, NY 10022

All Kensington titles, imprints and distributed lines are available at special quantity discounts for bulk purchases for sales promotion, premiums, fund-raising, educational or institutional use.

Special book excerpts or customized printings can also be created to fit specific needs. For details, write or phone the office of the Kensington Special Sales Manager: Kensington Publishing Corp., 850 Third Avenue, New York, NY 10022, Attn. Special Sales Department. Phone: 1-800-221-2647.

Dafina Books and the Dafina logo Reg. U.S. Pat. & TM Off.

ISBN 0-7582-0467-1

First Hardcover Printing: November 2003
First Trade Paperback Printing: September 2004
10 9 8 7 6 5 4 3 2 1

Printed in the United States of America

ACKNOWLEDGMENTS

I have been remiss in my acknowledgment of the Lord for blessing me with the skill and the ability to tell a story. All blessings come from the Lord, one must never forget that.

Much love and appreciation to Arnold, for being a wordsmith and for letting me bend his ear; and a big bear hug to our little boy, Jared, for saying to all, "Did you know that my mommie is a writer?"

Much appreciation to my sisters, Linda and Brenda Rudolph, and my aunt Jimmie L. Mosby, my niece Tracy Rudolph, my cousin Sheila Hall, and my brother, Early Rudolph, for telling their friends and coworkers about my tales.

A special thank-you to my editor, Karen Thomas, for letting me keep my voice, and my agent, Stacey Glick, for her skill and expertise. Thank you for addressing my concerns.

Much affection for my friends in prose—Mary B. Morrison, Karen E. Quinones Miller, Hope C. Clarke, Tracy Price-Thompson, Travis Hunter, Carl Weber, and Michael Presley—for sharing the experience. The journey is ongoing.

BABY GIRL

*Baby girl, baby girl, you're born into a world in which you are a
pearl.*

*You're precious, you're pure, you're lovely to behold, yet you're
ignorant to the world of troubles that shadow you.*

*If you are not protected, you will be used, abused, stolen and
misused, maybe your life taken to render you voiceless.*

*For you, baby girl, are born with something more precious than
the golden sweet honey made by the honey bees.*

*Kings have abdicated, battles have been fought once eyes
have set on your beauty and man has tasted of your honey.*

*Some men will not wait to be worthy, some men will seize
what is yours by right of birth.*

*You can choose, baby girl, you can decide—you have a will,
you have a voice, let no one take it from you.*

*Baby girl, baby girl, grow in mind, grow in body, grow in spirit,
and nurture your soul.*

*Protect yourself, respect yourself, and know that only you can lose
yourself.*

—Gloria Mallette

PROLOGUE

Esther put her arms around Arnell as they exited the subway on Nostrand Avenue and Fulton Street and began their five-block walk home to Dean Street. "Sweetie, we have a problem."

"I know, Mommy. We owe three months back rent."

"Yes, and I've been trying to find a job that pays a decent salary, but I can't seem to find one. My little clerical assistant job is never going to pay me more than two hundred and fifty dollars a week. The way things are going, I'll never be able to pay our rent and eat, too."

"I have that thirty-three dollars I've been saving to buy that dress for the school dance, but I really don't have to go, Mommy. You can have it for the rent."

"Thank you, sweetie, but I want you to have that dress. I want you to go to that party."

"But, Mommy, what are we gonna do about the rent?"

"Actually, I know a way we can wipe out what we owe and start fresh next month."

"Really? How?"

They stopped at the corner of Atlantic and Nostrand. Esther whispered, "Wait," to Arnell because a hoard of people were standing close around them, also waiting for the light to change. Esther wanted no one to hear what she was about to say.

As usual, the traffic on Atlantic Avenue was heavy. Overhead, the rumble of the Long Island Railroad coming into the station from downtown Brooklyn heading out to Long Island made Arnell look up. One day she wanted to take that train out to Long Island to see not only how far it went, but she also wanted to see the homes of the white faces and of the few black faces that looked out from the train windows down on the poor, hardworking black people of Bedford-Stuyvesant. The three-story brownstone she and her mother lived in on Dean Street was old, stuffy, and dark. They were behind on the rent, but no one should have to pay to live in a dilapidated, cramped, one bedroom apartment.

The traffic light turned green. With her arm still around Arnell, Esther began crossing Atlantic Avenue with the rest of the people.

"Arnell, I need you to do me a big favor."

"What do you want me to do, Mommy?"

"Before I tell you what it is, sweetie, I want you to know that we don't have any other way out. If we get put out of our apartment, we may not get another one for months. I just don't have the money."

"I know." Arnell was getting more frightened by the moment.

"That's why I need for you to do something for me. Sweetie, would you do anything for your mommy?"

"I'll do anything you want," she said. "What is it?"

"Arnell, our landlord, Mr. Hershfeld, said he'd forgive our past due rent if we gave him something he's been wanting for a long while."

"What can that be, Mommy? We don't have anything in our apartment that cost a lot of money."

"That's kind of true. What he wants is worth more than everything we own a million times over."

Arnell couldn't figure out what that could be.

Esther couldn't bring herself to say it. "Arnell, I want you to know that I wouldn't ask you to do this if there was another way out. I've begged Mr. Hershfeld to let me do what he wants, but he wasn't interested. I swear to you, Arnell, I'd do it myself except it's not me he wants."

She was confused. "Mommy, you're scaring me. What does he want from me?"

Esther swallowed hard. "Mr. Hershfeld wants you to have sex with him."

Arnell stopped walking. Dumbstruck, she gawked at her mother as people brushed past them on the busy sidewalk.

"Sweetie, if you don't do it, Mr. Hershfeld is going to evict us. We don't have anyone to turn to for help. I went down to welfare but they said I made too much money on my job. Can you believe that? Me? I make too much money."

Arnell began shaking her head, not to the question, but to what her mother wanted her to do.

Esther pulled Arnell into an empty doorway of a closed up, burned out storefront. "Please, Arnell, don't say no without thinking about it. We are in big trouble. Mr. Hershfeld won't hurt you, he promised me that he wouldn't."

Tears welled up in Arnell's eyes. "But, Mommy, I don't want that old smelly Jew touching me."

"Sweetie, he's really not all that old. He just looks old because of his clothes and because of the beard, but he's only forty-five years old."

"That's old! No, Mommy. I can't do it."

"Shh," Esther said, checking to see if anyone was looking at them. A down-home, sanctified-looking old woman was passing by and eyeballing Esther. Esther waited until the woman crept on by before she continued. "Arnell, Mr. Hershfeld said he'd forgive all of our past due rent, and if you did . . . it, you know, got with him once in a while, he'd discount our rent, maybe even let us keep the apartment for free."

"No, Mommy!" Arnell started crying. "I can't. I ain't never liked the way he looked at me. And, Mommy, you know that I've never had sex before. I'm a virgin. I can't do it. I can't." She started to walk away.

Esther pulled Arnell back to her. "You have to!" Tears rolled down Esther's own cheeks. "Arnell, you're my baby. I wouldn't ask you to do this unless it was life and death. Sweetie, our lives depend on this. I can't pay the four hundred and fifty dollar a month rent. We will be put out on the street.

"Arnell, I've been trying to find a better job for months. I can't find one, and you know this. With what little money I get, I feed you before I feed myself, and even then, we're eating oatmeal for dinner. I put clothes on your back before I even think about my own needs. I've been taking care of you by myself since you were three years old. I need you to help me take care of both of us for a little while. I promise you, I'll get it together. You won't have to do it for long. Please, baby, you have got to do this."

"Oh, Mommy," Arnell cried, "can't we call Uncle Matt?"

"No."

"But, Mommy, I know Uncle Matt will give us the money we need."

"I said, no."

Arnell didn't want to accept no. "Mommy, last year, Uncle Matt told me he'd always be there if we—"

"Not *we*, Arnell. He said you. My brother called me a whore. When you were three, he called child services on me. He tried to take you from me. As far as I'm concerned, he's dead. I don't have a brother. Arnell, we're on our own. Get use to it. We have to take care of each other. Since your father died, you and I are alone in this world and no one gives a damn about us."

It felt as if something had grabbed Arnell's belly button from the inside and was twisting it hard enough for her to clutch her stomach. "Mommy, please don't make me—"

Esther suddenly took Arnell's face in her hand. "Listen to me. All my jewelry is gone. I have nothing else to hock. Arnell, you have got to do this. We don't have a choice. Life isn't fair sometimes. Sometimes we have to do things we don't want to do, but we must do any- and everything to survive."

Arnell's tears flowed as she looked deep into her mother's eyes. The fear she saw there scared her all the more.

"Sweetie, I swear to you, I won't let him hurt you," Esther said, tearing. "I swear."

They both stood in the doorway crying. People walked by, curious, but no one stopped. Arnell fell into Esther's arms where she wanted to stay forever.

"You know I love you, don't you?" Esther asked, gently pushing Arnell off her.

Although she wondered about that love, Arnell nodded.

"Sweetie, if there was another way for me to get the money, I wouldn't ask you to do this. You know that, don't you?"

Although Arnell knew how close they were to losing their apartment, she would have never dreamed that her mother would ask her to have sex with their Jewish Orthodox landlord in order to keep a roof over their heads.

"Sweetie, will you do this for us?"

Crying and taking short gaspy breaths, Arnell nodded. Only then did Esther hold her again and let her cry herself out. Esther kept her arms around Arnell the rest of the way home, mostly to hold her up to keep her weak knees from deserting her. Beyond that, Arnell remembered little else about the rest of that day. All she knew was that Mr. Hershfeld was coming that Friday, a day away.

One

Misshapen, the stretched out wire clothes hanger, angrily flung across the large bathroom, hit the sandstone-colored tile floor with a tinny clank as it splattered specks of contaminated water on the wall and floor. The hanger bounced twice and vibrated before settling and lying still like a petrified, undernourished snake. For the last twenty minutes, Arnell had twisted and maneuvered the hanger in a myriad of different shapes trying to hook her diamond engagement ring and pull it out of the unflushed toilet bowl. She just couldn't seem to get the tip of the wire to slide under the ring so that she could hook it. Her futile efforts had only frustrated and nauseated her. Thank God she had eaten some time ago. Still, Arnell wretched time and again when the ring kept slipping and sliding on the porcelain on the bottom of the toilet bowl. Several times she had almost hooked her ring but it would slip into the narrow hole, completely out of sight, scaring her, making her work harder to pull it back into sight. In the end, the clothes hanger had only wasted Arnell's time, making her later than she already was. And that was just it, she was late. She hated being late for any appointment, but more than she hated being late, Esther was going to hate it even more. Esther—or Queen Esther, as she liked to be called by her girls or people that worked for her—didn't like anyone messing with her money, and Arnell being late was doing just that. But wait a minute. Arnell wasn't supposed to be one of Esther's girls anymore, and really, she wasn't supposed to be working for her in any capacity. Yet, she was stressing herself out trying to keep an appointment that she wanted nothing to do with.

The appointment with Mr. Woodruff Parker, from the upper west side of Manhattan, had been set up a week ago by Robert Morris, one of Esther's favorite clients; and Esther wanted Arnell to take care of him personally, which was the reason her ring was off her finger in the first place. She couldn't very well wear an engagement ring to meet a man that she had never laid eyes on and that she was going to take to bed. After she brushed her teeth, she had slipped the ring off her finger and set it on the back of the toilet tank. When she finished her business and stood, she must have bumped the tank because the ring slid off into the bowl before she could catch it. She had screamed, "No!" but that was about all she could do. She watched her beautiful three-carat marquis-cut diamond ring sparkle brilliantly just before it sank amid the putrid waste. For the first five minutes she had shouted, "Damn!" no less than ten times. She was angry at herself for taking the ring off in the bathroom and for putting it on top of the slippery smooth tank, but then she had cursed Esther for putting her in the position to have to take the ring off her finger in the first place.

Esther had promised Arnell she would not have to work after she got her B.A. in Fine Arts, which she got a year ago from Long Island University after attending classes part-time for six years and a day. Arnell's dream had been to teach high school English, but she was realistic. An ex-prostitute teaching a classroom full of sexually fertile minds was even too scandalous for her, so she let go of that dream real quick. Turns out though that she was a damn good editor. Arnell found that out by helping a classmate with her term papers. So she started working from home as a freelance copy editor. She made good money, but even so, her degree was thirteen years past due, and had been hard-earned, mainly because she had, in hindsight, stupidly continued living in Esther's house, at Esther's pleading, and servicing clients all the while she was in school busting her butt. One would think that Esther would respect Arnell's determination to stay in school and do well to boot. But no, Esther saw Arnell's education as a "foolish waste of time" when she already had a "God-given moneymaker—your vagina." This is why Esther disregarded her promise to let Arnell completely quit the business when important, free-spending clients like Woodruff Parker called. According to Robert Morris, Woodruff Parker, Wall Street maverick, had money to burn, and Esther intended to be the furnace. She ordered Arnell to be especially beguiling in order to entice Woodruff Parker into being overly generous. Esther didn't care what she had to do or whom she had to use to get what she figured was due her, and that was all the money she could get her hands on.

The money she hoarded was not from need but from greed. Esther had more money than she ever dreamed of, more than enough to keep her in the lifestyle of the grand madam she had set herself up to be. Besides her fancy cars and expensive clothes and jewelry, Esther lived in a sixteen-room mansion that she had moved heaven and earth to purchase. Esther would not be satisfied until she could afford to buy the century-old Victorian house, in the up-scale Ditmas Park area of Brooklyn, that was once owned by the very proper and very rich Mrs. Abigail Hawthorne, although Esther used the mansion, which her clients had dubbed The Honey Well, for a business that Mrs. Hawthorne, long dead, would never have approved of. But did Esther care? No. Esther planned on taking the hate she had for Mrs. Hawthorne to her grave.

Esther's mother, Alice Moore, had been Mrs. Hawthorne's housekeeper and cook for four years when Esther was a teenager. Esther said that Mrs. Hawthorne treated Alice like she was a slave, always yelling at her, demeaning her if the food wasn't cooked to her liking, ordering her to dust the furniture over if she saw a smudge, but worse than that, demanding that Alice wash and massage her feet every Friday afternoon. At times, Esther said she had to help her mother clean Mrs. Hawthorne's house and those were the times she saw how her mother was treated. Those were the times Esther wanted to punch Mrs. Hawthorne in the mouth, but her mother would always rein her in, stop her cold. Alice needed her job. There was nothing else she was qualified to do and Mrs. Hawthorne did pay better than most. But Esther, when she turned fourteen, after calling Mrs. Hawthorne a crotchety old bitch for calling her a pickaninny, refused to step foot inside Mrs. Hawthorne's house ever again. That is until Esther set her sights on buying the mansion. Her only regret was that Mrs. Hawthorne had to die before she could get her hands on that prize. But that didn't spoil the satisfaction for Esther. She was content thinking that Mrs. Hawthorne was turning over in her grave every time the doorbell rang. Esther thought that was really funny. For a time after she bought the house, Esther would ring the bell herself, tickling her own funny bone. Esther was very proud of what she was able to accomplish. Her money put her where she wanted to be and as long as she made the money, she would stay there. Nothing and no one would stand in the way of Esther making her money, including her one and only child, Arnell.

Which is why, until Arnell did what Esther wanted her to do, Arnell would have no peace.

"Arnell, there isn't anything I wouldn't do for you, and you know it. All you need to do is ask, and what I'm asking you to do for me, isn't anything you haven't done before."

"And that's exactly my point," Arnell said. "What I've done before, I've done too many damn times as it is. And I'm just not going to do it anymore."

"So this is how you show appreciation for the sacrifices I've made for you."

Arnell wanted to scream but she took a deep breath. "You know, Mother, I am tired of hearing about these so-called sacrifices you've made for me. What damn sacrifices? I'm the one that had to prostitute my body, not you!"

Esther cooly dragged on her cigarette. "And that's because youth is the most powerful aphrodisiac. You had it and I didn't. You're selfish, Arnell. I could have made a better life for myself without you, but I was determined to raise you on my own. After your father died, I could have put you up for adoption or in a foster home—lots of people told me that I ought to, but," Esther shook her head, "no, you were all I had, and I was all you had. There was no one to put a hand out to us. We had to take care of each other, but I would take the food from my own mouth to put in yours, if you didn't have enough to eat. So don't tell me about sacrifices."

Esther always had plenty of guilt to dump on Arnell's head, and as she had done in the past, Arnell tucked her tail and let Esther set her up with Mr. Parker, but still she couldn't bring herself to stick her hand down inside the toilet. She had been staring down at her own shit for damn near thirty minutes, trying to figure out how to get her diamond ring out. More than once she started to flush the toilet but she didn't know if the ring would stay put on the bottom when the water swirled and pushed the waste out, or if the rush of water and waste would push the brand new white diamond out into the city sewer. In fact, Arnell had foraged around so much in the toilet bowl with the clothes hanger that she couldn't even see the ring anymore, although she knew that it was there hiding underneath all that crap. The irony of it all was that this situation was so much like her own life. Underneath all the crap, there was another her, a better her, trying to get out. If only she could get Esther to release her hold on her.

Way off down the hall, the wall clock in the living room chimed. It was eight o'clock. Arnell was supposed to meet Mr. Parker at nine at the mansion. She wasn't even dressed yet. Ahead of her, from Garden City, Long Island, she had at least a forty-five minute drive into Brooklyn. Time was rushing by, but Arnell couldn't leave her ring to marinate in waste. While James might be understanding about the ring if she lost it, surely he would kill her if he ever found out about the life she once lived that he knew nothing of. He had given her the ring three months ago at the engagement party Esther had thrown for them at the mansion. Esther had been real proud when James slipped that expensive rock on her finger. The size alone impressed Esther. Hell, Esther might want to kill her, too, if she didn't get that damn ring out of the toilet. Come to think of it, if that had been Esther's ring, Esther would not have thought twice about sticking her hand in all that crap to retrieve it. Arnell was reminded that nothing would stand in Esther's way when she was going after what she wanted. That's how Esther faced life's problems—head-on. No matter how messy, how ugly, how difficult, the end result was all-important, and that was that she come out on top. At this moment, something she'd heard Esther say a long time ago was never truer—*Sometimes you have to stick your hand in a bowl of shit to get what you want.*

Outside the bathroom door, Arnell could hear the telephone

ringing. It would be no one else but Esther calling to see if she had left. The ringing was persistent.

Arnell looked back down into the toilet.

It was now or never.

As she bent over the bowl, Arnell held her breath and squeezed her eyes shut. Haltingly, she eased her hand down toward the murky water. She wretched. She stopped short, yanking her hand back. She couldn't do it. Gloves. She needed a pair of rubber gloves. Arnell threw open the vanity doors underneath the sink. Squatting, she looked inside and there, draped over the drain pipe, lay limply, a pair of yellow rubber gloves. She snatched them. She was about to close the doors when she glimpsed a bottle of green pine disinfectant. That, too, she took. She plugged up the sink and poured the whole bottle of disinfectant into it—the strong pine smell filled the room and Arnell's nostrils. Now she was ready.

Holding onto the cuff of the right glove, pulling and stretching the rubber as far up her arm as it would go, Arnell again closed her eyes and eased her hand down into the midst of her own waste. She grimaced when the coldness of the water reminded her that although her eyes didn't see it, there was more touching her gloved hand than water. Yuk! Disgusting. Again she wretched.

"Just do it!" Arnell eased her hand haltingly but gingerly to the bottom of the bowl. She pressed her fingers firmly against the porcelain, feeling for the roundness of the gold band or the rock-like feel of the diamond. Suddenly, she touched the hardness of the stone.

"Thank God!"

Arnell wasted no time pulling the ring and her hand out of the toilet. Immediately, she dropped the ring into the pine disinfectant. The ring was still sparkling. The gloves she pulled off inside out and dropped them into the wastebasket lined with plastic. The whole thing she would discard on her way out of the house. No matter what happened this evening, nothing would faze her. Not after what she just had to do. Although, as with sticking her hand in the toilet, Arnell was about to wade back into the cesspool of a life she wanted so badly to forget. After this one last time, nothing, not even Esther, as expert as she was with laying a guilt trip on her, was going to get her to step foot back inside The Honey Well. Mr. Parker had best enjoy what she was planning to lay on him; he would never have the pleasure again.

Arnell pushed down on the handle of the toilet and sent all the crap in her life on its way. Tomorrow was going to be a new day.

Two

Sixteen was a lousy age and Trena Gatlind couldn't wait to get out of her teens. It seemed that some adult always had something to say about what she did, especially her sister, Cheryl, who was older than her by eight years. Cheryl had her own car and a full-time job. Why Cheryl didn't get out and get her own apartment, Trena didn't know. If Trena was twenty-four, she would have been long gone, but not Cheryl. Cheryl didn't look like she was ever going to move out, which meant that she was always going to be there to keep bossing her around. Ever since their mother, Maxine, who was a nurse, started working the night shift at Kings County Hospital nine years ago, Cheryl had become a serious pain in the ass. Their dad, Joe, when he was home the last time, told Cheryl to ease up, but he wasn't home much to see that Cheryl did. Joe was a long-distance trucker, "pushing the big rigs," he called it. He had been "putting his foot in the floor and getting in the wind" way before Trena was born. Joe said, "The only thing that would pull me off the road is death—my own," and he meant it. His own mother died two years ago; he never made it to her funeral.

Trena heard her mother say every time she argued with her father, "You love the freedom of the road more than you love your family." Her father never denied that and thought electronically transferring large portions of his pay back home from wherever he was more than made up for his lack of presence at home. He made good money and supported them well, but Maxine still worked long hard hours all the same. At the end of the day, she barely had enough energy to climb into bed, which is why Cheryl pretty much did as she pleased. Since Cheryl stopped seeing Alex, she was always in a nasty mood. Cheryl wasn't going over to Alex's apartment anymore so she was always home to get on her case about every little thing. "Clean up your room, Trena. Have you done your homework, Trena?" Trena was beginning to hate to hear her own name said out loud, but that's all right. It's Friday night. She was going partying, and it was none of Cheryl's business where she was going. She was so damn nosy. Always sneaking around trying to catch her doing something so that she could snitch on her, especially after what happened two weeks ago.

Cheryl said she was going shopping after work with her girl-friend, Phyllis. If they did their usual dinner afterward, Trena figured Cheryl wouldn't be getting home until after ten o'clock. Breathing room—plenty of time for her to have some fun with Omar, her boyfriend of four months. But then, just as she and Omar were getting a good feel on down in the basement, Cheryl comes home—early.

"Trena, are you down there?"

Trena abruptly pushed Omar off top of her and scrambled to her feet.

"Damn!" Omar whispered. He had a hard-on that uncomfortably strained the skin it was in. Holding himself, he scrambled to find a place to hide in the wide-open basement. There was nowhere.

Trena quickly adjusted her breasts inside her bra and pulled down her oversize T-shirt. She hurriedly ran her hands down her thighs, smoothing out the wrinkles in her denim skirt.

"Trena, I hear you down there. What are you doing?"

"Nothing! Dang, Cheryl."

Omar shoved his hand inside his open fly and tried to adjust himself inside his loose-fitting boxer shorts. He kicked out his left leg.

"Trena! You got somebody down there?"

"No, I don't!" Trena looked over at Omar squeezed up in the far corner of the room trying to hold himself down. He started moving from foot to foot like he had to go to the bathroom. Trena covered her mouth and doubled over to keep from laughing out loud.

"I want you upstairs, Trena. Now!"

"Cheryl, will you leave me alone!" Trena could hear Cheryl overhead, walking around in the kitchen. Any minute she might rush down into the basement and neither Trena nor Omar wanted that. As funny as Omar looked, he had this panicked look in his eyes. He had cause to be scared—he had been jumped on by Cheryl once before. Trena wasn't supposed to have a boy over when no one was home, and Omar, in particular, wasn't suppose to be there— ever. A month after they started going together, Cheryl caught her and Omar in her bedroom and of all places, on her bed hugged up tight in a deep-throated kiss. After Cheryl had screamed on Omar and kicked him out, she called his mother.

"Mrs. Lester, I just pulled your son off top of my little sister. I suggest you buy Omar a boatload of condoms because he's going to get somebody pregnant and it had better not be my sister."

Omar's mother retorted, "I'll deal with my son when he gets home, but I suggest you put your little sister on the pill because she is obviously a fast one."

After calling Mrs. Lester an old bitch, Cheryl had slammed the telephone down in her ear and turned on Trena. The funny thing was, she was still a virgin. That didn't stop Cheryl, though. In the end, Trena and Omar were both grounded for two weeks and for- bidden to see each other ever again. Yeah, right. Cheryl and Mrs. Lester had better recognize.

"Trena, what's taking you so long to get up here? I want you to come upstairs right now and take out the garbage."

"Dang, Cheryl. How come you can't take out the garbage some- time?"

"Because that's your job."

Trena glanced at Omar. He was again shaking out his leg. Nothing dropped. His penis was hard and pressing into his gut. By the look on his face, he was hurting. Trena thought that was funny and began to giggle behind her hand.

"Trena, if I have to come down there to get you, I'm—"

"I'm coming! Dang."

The anxiety of being caught had finally softened Omar's penis.

He mouthed to Trena, "Stop provoking her." Trena disregarded what Omar was saying as she was only interested in getting him back on the bone. She pulled up her T-shirt and started rubbing her nipples through her bra while flicking her tongue at Omar. Right away, Omar began massaging himself through his unzipped fly. He had barely started when he was on the bone again. That excited Trena. She felt a warm tingle in the very spot where Omar had earlier been pressed up against her. She couldn't take her eyes off Omar's hand.

"Trena."

"Give me a minute, Cheryl. I'll be right up," she said, no longer shouting. "I thought you were going out after work."

"I did."

"Then why are you home so early? It's Friday night." Trena's heart was beating faster as Omar's hand massaged faster. His eyes rolled back in his head. He began to moan softly. There was a throbbing sensation between Trena's thighs. She wanted to touch herself. Her eyes stretched as Omar was about to get off right before her eyes. Intrigued, she giggled nervously.

"I have to get up in the morning, Trena. Now, get your behind up here and take out the garbage."

"Okay, I'm coming. I just wanna hear this last side." The music had been on, but all the CDs had played out when Trena and Omar had gotten hot and heavy.

"I don't hear any music," Cheryl said, starting down the stairs. "Trena, what are you up to?"

Omar made a headlong dive behind the sofa.

Trena sprinted softly to the bottom of the stairs. "Dang, Cheryl, why don't you stop trying to be my mother."

Cheryl stopped midway down. She studied Trena's flushed face. "You have a guilty look on your face."

"Cheryl, didn't Dad tell you to stop hounding me? I am not a kid, and specifically, I am not your kid."

"No, but you are my responsibility."

"No, I'm not. Why don't you go and make your own baby and leave me alone. You're such a pain. I can see why Alex dropped you for that other girl—you were probably trying to be his mother."

Cheryl blanched.

Trena immediately regretted her cutting words. Cheryl hadn't told her about Alex and the other girl; she had overheard her talking to him about it on the telephone. "See, Cheryl, you made me—"

"You know something, Trena? I don't like that I have to baby-sit you either. You're a selfish, mean-spirited little girl that has never appreciated the fact that I've missed out on a lot of good times with my own friends because I've had to be home taking care of you. Well, I tell you what. I don't care what you do anymore." She started back up the stairs.

"Cheryl, I didn't mean—"

"Yes, you did! But that's all right, Trena. You're free of me. You go ahead and do whatever the hell you feel like doing. I'm no longer your baby-sitter."

" 'Bout time." She and Omar both waited until they heard Cheryl walk across the kitchen floor toward the living room.

"Man, your sister is whack," Omar said, getting up from behind the sofa. "She be trippin'."

As glad as she was about finally getting Cheryl off of her back, Trena didn't take any pleasure in knowing that she had made her cry. She could hear Cheryl crying as Cheryl climbed the stairs to her bedroom on the second floor. Her crying was definitely a mood breaker. Plus Omar no longer had a hard-on but he was trying get it back by rubbing up against Trena.

She was no longer in the mood. "Cut it out, Omar. You got me in trouble."

"Your sister didn't even know I was down here."

"Just go home."

Trena sneaked Omar out of the house through the side door. Just like before, Cheryl had spoiled it for her. Sure, Trena had promised her mother that she'd stay a virgin until she was eighteen, but not getting her feel on wasn't part of that promise. She liked the feeling she got when Omar rubbed himself all into her, all in between her thighs, and the intensity of what she and Omar were both feeling might just have gotten him a taste of the sweet juice that was oozing from her just before Cheryl showed up. Dang. It was getting harder and harder to keep that promise.

With nothing else to do the rest of the evening, Trena took out the garbage, and when the pangs of guilt over making Cheryl cry crept up on her and wouldn't let up, she knocked twice at Cheryl's bedroom door to apologize, but Cheryl wouldn't answer. It was just as well. She wanted Cheryl to stay mad, maybe then she'd stay off of her back for real.

As strange as it was to not have Cheryl bitching at her, Trena missed talking to her, but she didn't miss her enough to try to apologize again. She was glad to be free of her mothering. Like she did two weeks before, Trena was going to hang out with her girl, Alyson. Afterward, she might go somewhere private with Omar.

Outside Cheryl's closed bedroom door, Trena taped her handwritten note. *I'm hanging out with Alyson. We're gonna catch a movie. I'll be back by two.* She was pushing the two in the morning part, but then, hey, her parents weren't home to tell her to make it back home by her midnight curfew. They were lucky she left a note at all. After all, she was almost grown.

Three

For the third time in the past half hour, Esther pressed hard on the talk button disconnecting the unanswered ringing at Arnell's house. "Damn it." Esther tossed the cordless phone onto her bed and turned her back when it bounced into the padded golden brocade headboard. Fresh out of the shower, she hadn't begun to dress, she was too nervous. She began to pace. If Arnell didn't get there soon, she was going to have a stroke. Esther went to her outer suite door; opening it, she stuck her head out. Saying nothing, she listened. The only thing she could hear was the orchestral sounds of Yanni making love to his piano. The melodiously grand music filled the first floor corridors.

Esther closed her eyes. *Relax. Take a deep breath. Feel the music. Arnell will be here. Just relax.* Doing just that, Esther felt better. Yanni's music always relaxed her. This is why, when she decided to run her business from her home, she had insisted on soft jazz and soothing classical music. After all, The Honey Well was a classy house, in a classy neighborhood. From her bedroom suite on the parlor floor in the back of the house, Esther could hear clearly the music played on that floor, so she was downright particular about the music and the musician. On the two floors above, she allowed the girls some leeway with the music; as long as it was easy-listening jazz or classical, she wasn't so picky about the musician. It helped that she couldn't hear much of anything from the individual rooms above—good solid doors and plush carpeting went a long way in keeping private sounds contained. In about a half hour, there would be more activity in the house, but that activity would be kept respectfully quiet. Even those less-cultured individuals who considered her establishment the oldest profession would have to agree that, at least, it was a classy establishment. Her four girls were attractive, well groomed, well polished, and had at least a high school diploma. Like Arnell, one even had a college degree. None had ever stood on a street corner, and none had ever used drugs. She made sure of that. Each was given a random drug test, and so far, she had to dismiss only three girls in the twelve years she had been in business. The one girl that she would never forget was Chyanne, a born loser. Chyanne was a closet crack user and when she was finally caught, she raised holy hell and threatened to expose Esther's business. In fact, Chyanne anonymously called the police. The police came. They found nothing. Esther pointed out that there was no law that said that a woman couldn't have a gentleman caller in her home. And that was what all the men were that called on her girls— gentlemen. Businessmen, one and all, who paid well to be with her girls. And her girls? They were all ladies. Each had at least a two-room suite or a large single room in the mansion and used the mansion address as their legal residence. There was no law against renting. Too bad Chyanne didn't know that before she made that call. After Big Walt got finished schooling Chyanne on the facts of life—specifically that she might not continue to have a life— Chyanne never made another call to the police about the house on Dorchester Road. Word was, Chyanne was walking the streets up in Hunts Point, an area of the Bronx many prostitutes frequented.

Esther closed her door to Yanni. She was definitely going to have a serious talk with Arnell. Woodruff Parker hadn't gotten there yet, but she wanted Arnell there before he arrived, as it was proper that a man willing to pay well for his pleasure be received by his lady of the evening. Robert had already told her that Woody wanted the best for his money, and the best he would get—Arnell, whether Arnell liked it or not. The truth was, Arnell was the best by default. In her day, there was none other better than Esther herself. She had been and still was the queen when it came to pleasing a man, then and now. It was her body, now, that was no longer pleasing to men who paid for tight, shapely, nubile young bodies. That's why time was running out for Arnell. In a few years, she would age out of the business. She needed to capitalize on her assets now.

In her bedroom, standing in front of her brass cheval mirror, Esther slowly untied her silk robe and let it drop to the floor at her feet. The naked body reflected in her mirror really wasn't all that hard on the eyes. Of course, it would do Esther's body good if she exercised more. She pulled in her stomach to make it flatter. She turned from side to side. For a sixty-two-year-old woman, she didn't look all that bad. The flesh on her thighs could be a little tighter, but they weren't so loose that they offended anyone's sense of beauty. The real problem was her breasts. They were no longer "plumpers," as Tony used to call them. Esther was still a thirty-six D, though it was more skin that filled that D cup than breast tissue. Without her bra, her breasts hung like deflated balloons. No paying man, drunk or sober, wanted to suck on a shriveled up balloon. This is why Esther loved Tony DiAngelo. He loved her body just as much as he did twelve years ago. She had thought about getting breast implants and Tony even offered to pay for the surgery—if that was what she really wanted for herself. Tony said that he didn't see the need. Arnell, on the other hand, thought it ludicrous that a sixty-two-year-old woman would want to walk around with firm round tits, defying gravity, sitting up to her neck. Arnell claimed that everyone would know they were implants, but, hell, what did Esther care? With her brown skin, everyone obviously knew that she had dyed her short, naturally curly hair blond and no one said anything about that. She saw nothing wrong with a woman up in age having nice tits, a nice ass, and a hellified sex life. As far as she was concerned, there wasn't much more to think about. Right now, the timing was wrong—there were only a few weeks to summer, and summer was a bad time for any kind of surgery—too hot. Come September, when the weather cooled, she'd get her implants.

Esther cupped each of her breasts and lifted them up to where they used to be—decades ago. Again, she turned from side to side. She wouldn't look bad at all.

"So what are you going to do about your face?" Arnell stood in Esther's bedroom door. "Get a facelift?"

Esther quickly covered and held her breasts with one arm while bending modestly and snatching her robe up off the floor. She turned her back to pull her robe on. "What have I told you about barging into my bedroom without knocking?"

"What have I told you about keeping your door locked? I think, secretly, you're hoping some fine young stud will wander in here and rock your world. What's wrong, Mother, is Tony not satisfying you?"

Esther tied her robe tightly around her body. "One of these days, Arnell, your smart mouth is going to write a check that your ass can't cash."

"No, Mother, it's not my mouth that's going to get me in trouble, it's you. I moved out of here three years ago because I was done with this business. But you won't let me stay gone. You keep manipulating me back into your decadent world. You promised me—"

"Yeah . . . yeah . . . yeah," Esther said, flipping her hand at Arnell. "We've had this conversation a million times. Why are you late?"

Arnell tossed her pocketbook onto Esther's bed. "You know something, *Mother*? It warms my heart to know how much you really care about me."

"Don't start with me, Arnell," Esther said, her voice low. She modestly turned her back to Arnell as she pulled on a clean pair of black lace panties. "I asked you to do me one little favor and you're making a federal case out of it. By the way, that wrap dress looks quite nice on you. Is it new?"

Arnell couldn't believe it. "Is that what you call it? One little favor? Mother, I've been doing these *little* favors for you since I was sixteen. Back then I trusted you, I didn't know any better."

"So now you're thirty-three and, supposedly, you know better. Don't you still trust your mother, sweetie?"

"Stop fucking with me, Esther. I am not a child anymore."

"Watch your mouth, sweetie, I am still your mother."

Amazed, Arnell paused. "I find it hard to believe that you actually know that. If only it meant something to you."

Esther exhaled her annoyance. "Oh, damn. I see you're in one of your 'put upon' moods again. Okay, Arnell, my back is strong. Place all the blame, for all the wrong ever done to you in life, on my back."

Arnell felt like screaming. "Here's a news flash for you, *Mother*. You turned me out. You pimped me. You—"

"No, I never pimped you. I couldn't possibly, I am not a man. Therefore, I am not a pimp."

"Humph! Let's call you what you are, *Mother*—a pimp. You are a pimp, you just wear lipstick and heels. You turned your own child into a prostitute."

"No, not prostitute, dear. I prefer to say that you are a lady of charm. You know, like a geisha girl or even the Mayflower Madam . . . oh, that's me." Pleased with herself, Esther smiled.

"You're sick," Arnell said. "In case you forgot, the Mayflower Madam was put out of business. She was arrested, you know."

"Her luck ran out; mine won't."

"You better hope that it doesn't, but you're not getting the point. You've made me ashamed of who I am."

"That's funny, Arnell, you don't seem to be ashamed of all that money you got socked away. You're not ashamed of that expensive house you bought out in Garden City with the money you made on your back, or of that college degree you paid for with that same money. Still, I'm the bad guy in all this, right?"

"Damn right you are. Like I said, you just don't get it. You're my mother. You schooled me in becoming a prostitute. Mothers don't do that. I don't know if I can ever forgive you for messing me up like that. And you know what goads me even more? You have the audacity to keep trying to make me continue to do this against my will. I don't know why, but it amazes me that you could care less about how I feel about it as long as you get paid. Well, here's another news flash for you, Mother. After tonight, this is it. Don't call me anymore. I am out of the family business, and this time, I mean it."

A trifling little smile curled Esther's full lips as she sauntered over to her overstuffed chair and slowly lowered herself. All the while holding Arnell's gaze, she took her time crossing her legs as she took a cigarette from her gold cigarette case.

Arnell felt the muscles tighten in her stomach. The only time Esther smoked was when she was trying to come up with some manipulative strategy or plotting some sort of revenge. The hard, cold twinkle in Esther's eyes was so familiar. It was a condescending *that's what you think* look that Esther gave Arnell every time she was about to force her to do what she wanted.

A blue flame leaped to life when Esther flicked her gold cigarette lighter. She lit her cigarette and closed the lighter with a snap. With her gaze still fixed on Arnell, Esther took a long slow drag and held her breath long enough to savor the nicotine that gave her a rush. She blew the smoke out through a soft whisper of her lips that turned into a taunting little kiss to Arnell.

"The hell with you." Arnell grabbed her pocketbook off the bed and headed for the door.

"I wonder if James is home at this hour?" Esther asked, loudly, with a sharp edge to her voice. "Or better still, where do you think his father, the Right Reverend James W. Stanton is?"

Arrested where she stood, Arnell glared at an invisible spot on the door. "I hate you."

"Is that a nice thing to say to your mother?" Esther flicked her cigarette ash into the ashtray.

Arnell growled her frustration.

"Sweetie, I don't like it when we fight."

"Then stop using me. You swore you'd leave me alone."

"I'll make a deal with you. You take care of Mr. Parker for me, I'll buy you that car you've been thinking about. My treat."

The only treat Arnell wanted was for Esther to drop dead, but with her luck, she knew that wouldn't happen anytime soon. She wondered, if she killed her own mother, what would her sentence be?

"Arnell, sweetie, do we have a deal?"

Buzzzz!

Esther immediately ground out her cigarette. "That's him. I have to get dressed. Arnell, I've already instructed Fawn to take Mr. Parker up to your old suite. I'm depending on you, sweetie. Don't let me down." Esther disappeared into her large walk-in closet. "Give them a minute to get upstairs."

Arnell angrily clinched her jaw. She forbade herself to cry. This just had to be the last time. She opened the door to the romantic mood-setting tones of Kenny G's heart soaring alto saxophone. This was not the music she wanted to hear. Not tonight.

Four

The burden of Arnell's anger and frustration rendered her legs heavy and her chest tight as she made her way slowly up the stairs to the third floor. What she expected when she entered her old suite, she didn't know. What she saw gave her a sense of relief. Woodruff Parker, standing at the mini bar in the living room, impeccably dressed in Armani, was a small man. He wasn't even taller than Arnell's own five-foot, five-inch frame, and if he weighed more than one hundred and forty pounds, he was fat. All in all, Woodruff Parker's name was bigger than he was. Although she knew better, she hoped that his sexual appetite was equal in stature. Then she would be home free.

"Mr. Parker, I'm Nell," Arnell said, slipping into her role. "I'll be your lady of charm this evening. May I fix you a drink?"

"Sure thing." He moved back a pace from the bar. "I'm a brandy man."

Arnell went to the bar and picked up, what she expected to be, the decanter of expensive brandy. Knowing Esther, she would have already found out what Mr. Parker's drink was. "Mr. Parker, say when," Arnell said, slowly pouring the brandy.

"I'm a friendly man," Mr. Parker said, pressing his body into Arnell from behind and slipping his arms around her waist. "You can call me Woody."

Arnell wanted to push Woody off her, but forced a strained smile instead. She reminded herself, *When with a client, as long as the client doesn't hit you, let him have his way.* Arnell offered the brandy to Woody.

He didn't take it. He tightened his hold on Arnell's waist with one hand, felt her breast with the other, all while nuzzling her neck. He began pressing himself harder into her behind, grinding himself against her, pushing her into the edge of the wooden mini bar.

Arnell pushed back against Woody to keep from falling over the bar. There was no doubt he was ready to do what he had come there for. Her skin began to crawl as fear crept up her spine.

"Mmm, you're so soft," Woody said huskily. He began kissing Arnell's bare shoulders and rubbing himself lewdly against her. "You smell good enough to eat."

Arnell was repulsed. It had been six months since she had been with a client. And before that, it had been four months. She wasn't ready. In fact, she was beginning to think that she wasn't going to be able to go through with it. As it was, each time she slept with a client, she couldn't be with James for days afterward.

"You certainly are an eager man, Woody," she said, holding the brandy up for him to see. "Why don't we take a minute to get to know each other."

Woody stopped kissing Arnell, but that's all he stopped. He continued to grind her even as he took the brandy.

Arnell tried to pull out of Woody's hold on her, but he held onto her with one arm still around her waist. It was quite apparent that although he was a small man, there was no doubt that he was a strong one. Arnell could feel the crushing hardness of the muscle in his arm against the side of her body. Woody was hurting her and his unrelenting hold on her was unnerving her.

She had to get control of the situation. "Woody, would you like to sit?"

Woody downed the brandy in one gulp. He put the snifter down on the bar with a thud. "Baby, I'm a busy man. I don't have time to sit." He again fully encircled Arnell's waist and with his body still pressed into her, he turned her away from the bar and walked her, step for step, over to the back of the sofa that sat in the center of the room.

What Woody had in mind wasn't Arnell's game. She tried harder to pull away. "Mr. Parker, please. We have a lovely bedroom with beautiful satin sheets that I know you will enjoy. And perhaps a nice massage before—"

"Baby, this is just fine for me." Woody pinned Arnell to the sofa with his upper body while he pulled back enough to unzip his trousers and free himself with one hand.

Arnell tried to turn around to face him. He held her firm. "Mr. Parker, you don't have to do it like this." With one hand Arnell braced herself against the back of the sofa to keep from falling over. With the other, she tried to pry Woody's arm from around her waist.

Her heart was racing. "Mr. Parker, please. Just wait a minute."

Woody wouldn't wait. He yanked the back of Arnell's dress up, throwing the skirt of the dress over her head.

Gasping, Arnell quickly snatched the dress off her head. She felt Woody's pipe-hard penis thrust between her buttocks, jabbing her, hurting her. Squeezing her buttocks tight, she tried to keep him from entering her from behind.

"Wait!" she shrieked. "Please. I have condoms. Please let me get you a condom."

Woody ignored her. He began feeling Arnell's butt for her panties. She was wearing a G-string. He caught hold of the string at Arnell's hip and ripped it from her body, stinging her skin.

Fear filled Arnell. She tried to pull away from Woody's assault but couldn't, the sofa was stopping her. With both hands and her body, she began trying to push the sofa. The thick carpet wouldn't give to let the heavy sofa easily slide. But it did move—a few inches. It moved enough for Woody to have the space to thrust his free hand down Arnell's front and grip her pubis. Tensing up even more, Arnell's thigh muscles were burning from squeezing them so tightly.

"That's right, baby, don't make it easy for me," Woody said, slobbering on Arnell's neck. He began to roughly burrow his hand between her thighs. To Arnell it felt as if his hand was made out of jagged rock instead of flesh and bones. Her thighs couldn't take the searing assault. In her silent struggle, Arnell's thighs weakened, but they wouldn't completely relent as Woody brutally rammed two fingers up into her vagina and began to roughly finger her.

"No! Not like this." Arnell reared back with her head, butting Woody in the face. He made not a sound. It was like he didn't even feel it. Arnell tried to push back with her body, but Woody only pushed harder with his upper and lower body while squeezing Arnell harder with his one muscular arm around her waist. It felt like his penis was stabbing her. She had to let up on pushing back into him.

"Please don't do this. Don't—"

"Baby, trust me. You're gonna like it," Woody said gruffly, slobbering on Arnell's back. He held his fingers inside her, ramming her until she cried out in pain. Using his knees, he roughly parted Arnell's thighs so that he could stand in between them.

"No!" Arnell clawed at the back of Woody's hand, but he seemed to not care that she was scratching him in her struggle to get him to release his death-like grip on her. Gasping for each breath she took, Arnell broke out in a cold sweat as her heart pounded in her own ears.

"Please! Stop!"

Suddenly, Woody yanked his fingers out of Arnell. He put his forearm on her upper back. He pushed her forward, forcing her downward until she was bent over the back of the sofa. Her face kissed the back cushion while the top of her head pressed into the seat.

"No . . . no . . . no!" She clawed frantically.

Woody was deaf to Arnell's cries. He held her down with one hand and with the other, he took his penis and rammed himself inside her vagina.

"Oh, God! Please. We need a condom!"

"I don't use condoms."

With each mighty thrust, Arnell cried out.

With each mighty thrust, Woody grew more powerful. He panted, "Oh, yes. You're worth my money. Oh, baby."

Five

The Brooklyn Café was jamming. The music was loud. The music was hot. Next to The Lab in Bedford-Stuyvesant, the Café in Flatbush was Trena's favorite spot to party. That was because there were always older guys hanging at the Café and they were as fine as they could be. Omar hadn't shown up yet, and really, he didn't have to. Trena wasn't having any trouble getting guys to dance with. She was having a good time. The music was tight! She hadn't been able to sit down longer than three minutes before the music and a fine brother took hold of her and pulled her back out onto the dance floor. Usher, with his fine self, was her favorite singer, but when it came to rap, Jay-Z was off the hook. His pulsating rap had the Café jumping.

Trena had danced so much, she was hot, sweaty, and dying of thirst. "I need something to drink!" she shouted to Malik, her tall dance partner. With him she had danced three times.

"Me, too!" Malik kept on dancing.

Trena stopped dancing. "Well! Ain't you gonna get me a wine cooler, a soda, a drop of water, something?"

"Baby," Malik said, slowing his roll, "I don't own no store. You want somethin' to drink, you better pull out some Lincolns." He danced away from Trena, leaving her in the middle of the dance floor with her jaw dropped.

"You cheap, scandalous punk!"

Dancing next to Trena, her main girl Alyson laughed. "Girl,

these fools ain't got no money. The truth is, they're hoping that you'll buy them a drink."

"I don't think so. My momma didn't raise no fool."

"Mine neither," Alyson said, raising her hand for a high five.

Trena acknowledged her friend with an enthusiastic high palm slap.

Alyson's forgotten dance partner pulled her back to him. She snatched her arm out of his grasp. "Hold up! You don't know me like that."

"Damn, baby," the tall, lanky boy said, "don't go postal. You dancin' or not?"

Flattening out her hand in his face, Alyson rolled her eyes. "Not. Come on, Trena, let's get something to drink." She linked arms with Trena, they started walking away.

The boy flipped them the bird. "Damn lezzies."

They both heard him. Trena turned back, pulling Alyson with her. Trena marched right up to the boy and boldly pressed her firm breast into his chest. She didn't have on a bra, just the tight midriff tube top that pushed her breasts up and gave her enough cleavage to make her feel sexy. The boy didn't back away. He waited for Trena to make her move.

Smiling mischievously, Trena teasingly began rubbing her breast on the boy. "Can you handle this?"

"Can you handle this?" he asked, thrusting his pelvis into her.

She pressed back. The boy took hold of Trena's hips and held her into his body. He slipped his thigh between her thighs. Ja Rule, with his raunchy, gravelly voice, was jamming with Ashanti on her new song, "Happy." Trena's blood was hot. It was on. In beat with the music, Trena and the smart-mouth boy both moved their hips. Trena felt his hardness on her thigh. With her arms hanging limply at her sides, she moved her hips in unison with his grinding. The boy, whose name Trena didn't even know, began to grind slower and more intensly, pressing harder in between her thighs. She matched his grind and pressed back even harder. They were both beginning to sweat. People were starting to look at them. Trena didn't care, she was going to make this fool eat his words.

A boy standing next to Alyson shouted, "Man, get that stuff!"

Alyson laughed nervously. "Girl, you so nasty."

"I'm real nasty, ain't I, baby?" Trena asked teasingly of her dance partner.

The boy could only groan. His eyes were closed. He licked his lips, wetting them. He gripped Trena's behind, holding her tighter against his body.

"Man, hit that shit," another boy said.

Girls were whispering to each other. Some giggled, while others frowned disapprovingly.

"Trena," Alyson said, "let's go." A boy standing next to Alyson palmed her butt. She punched him in the arm. "Get off me! Jerk!"

The boy laughed.

Dancers close by pressed in closer. In the low light, Trena saw the excited but curious faces around her. She had started this as a joke to show this fool that she was not a lesbian, but she was starting to enjoy not only the attention she was commanding, but the feeling she was getting in her body. She could feel herself juice. She found herself getting lost in the moment. This was the second time in a matter of hours that she had done this with a boy. Maybe she was ready to go all the way despite her promise. Where was Omar?

"Trena," Alyson said, pulling on Trena's arm, "this is real nasty, girl. You better come on."

Trena studied her partner's face. His eyes were still closed, his teeth were bared, sweat was beaded up on his forehead. His grinding, once in sync with the music, was now faster and more intense. She felt him beginning to tremble. She had him where she wanted him.

With both hands, Trena suddenly pushed really hard on the boy's chest. He tried to hold onto her. She punched him in the chest and then quickly jumped back when he let go of her completely.

"Come on, baby. How you gon do me like this?" Holding onto himself, the boy took a step toward Trena, but she put her hand up, stopping him.

She looked him up and down. "Oops. Did a lezzie do that?"

"Baby, I was just joking."

"No, you weren't, but I got your lezzie and then some," Trena said, proud of herself. Again, she and Alyson linked arms and walked off the dance floor.

"Oh, shit," a guy said, laughing. "That's cold."

"Man, you 'bout to explode!" another guy said.

The crowd laughed.

"Man, you better go beat your meat," the same guy said.

"Shut the fuck up!" the boy snapped.

The laughing continued.

Still holding on to himself, the boy searched the crowd. His eyes came to rest on a shapely, cleavage-exposed girl a few feet away.

"Don't even think about it," the girl warned, backing up. Along with her, several girls did the same, while others didn't move an inch.

One girl, standing her ground, dared, "You come near me, I'll take that thing off and feed it to my dog."

"I know that's right," another girl confirmed. "I got a pit bull at home and he loves fresh meat."

The crowd roared.

Embarrassed, the boy let go of himself. He squared his shoulders. "That bitch wasn't all that." He walked cooly through the crowd in the opposite direction of Trena. Behind him, the snickering and laughter continued.

Sitting at a table off in the corner, Trena and Alyson were having a good laugh of their own. Tears rolled down their cheeks.

A stylishly dressed young woman stopped at the table. "You girls having a good time?"

"Yep," Trena managed to say before she lost it, doubling over the table, laughing hard while Alyson, trying to catch her breath, sounded more like she was crying.

"Ladies, ladies, what you did wasn't all that funny."

"It was to us," Arnell said, still laughing.

"No doubt. Mind if I sit," the woman said, sitting before either Trena or Alyson gave her the okay. "What are you girls drinking?"

"Why? Are you buying?" Trena asked, suddenly serious.

"I might be, unless you rather I didn't."

Trena and Alyson exchanged suspicious glances. They looked the woman over.

"You a lezzie?" Alyson asked.

"If I were, neither one of you would be my type."

Alyson relaxed. "That's okay by me. I'll take a wine cooler. I'm thirsty."

"Me, too," Trena said.

"Jeanette," the woman said.

"Huh?" Alyson asked.

"My name is Jeanette."

"Oh. I'm Alyson. This is my girl, Trena."

"Trena, you're a nasty girl," Jeanette said, taking a ten-dollar bill from her wallet. She handed it to Alyson.

Taking the bill, Alyson stood. "See, I told you you was nasty."

"So. I got it that way."

"Hot mama, huh?" Jeanette asked, amused. "Alyson, I'll take a wine cooler, too. Strawberry."

Alyson strolled off, weaving through the dancers, to get to the bar.

Suspicious of Jeanette's generosity, Trena looked her over on the sly as best she could in the low candlelight there was on the table. The woman wasn't old, though she wasn't as young as she and Alyson. She had thick, long, black, straight hair—probably a weave—and she was pretty, in an overly made-up sort of way. If Trena could tell that in the dimly lit club, then homegirl was wearing way too much makeup. Maybe in the daylight she was a fright, but that wouldn't explain why she was buying them drinks.

"How come you buying us a drink?"

"Can't a sister buy a sister a drink?"

"Oh, it's a respect thang, huh?"

"Something like that. When I saw you on the dance floor, I thought to myself, 'that was me when I was a teenager.'"

"So you was a diva, huh?"

Smiling, Jeanette flipped her hair off her neck. "I guess I was. By the way, how old are you?"

"Eighteen," Trena lied. "How old are you?"

"Twenty-four."

"That's not so old. You can still hang."

Jeanette smiled. "Thanks."

"You here by yourself, Jeanette?"

"I'm with some friends, but I lost sight of them. We'll hook up before we leave."

Trena began bobbing her head to the music. For a minute she and Jeanette watched the dancers do their thang. "Jeanette, can I ask you a question?"

"Sure."

"Did I really look nasty when I was . . . you know . . . doing that to that boy?"

Jeanette nodded.

"Well, he asked for it. He called me and Alyson lesbians."

"You're still a virgin, aren't you?"

That question surprised Trena. "No . . . maybe."

"Honey, either you're a virgin or you're not."

"Well, I'm—"

"If you weren't a virgin, Trena, you would have never played with that boy like that. Girls that know better, don't play with fire. You got that boy hot to the point of boiling, and then you, literally, pushed him out. If you hadn't been in a public place, that boy would have never let you walk away. The worst case scenario, you would have been raped."

Trena sassily shook her head. "I don't think so. I would have whipped his ass."

"How old did you say you were?"

"Eighteen."

Jeanette looked Trena dead in the eye. "Say again."

"Well, I'll be eighteen in July," she said, sticking with her lie.

"Seeing what I saw you do, how did you manage to keep your virginity?"

"I promised my mother I would keep my legs closed until after I graduated high school, which is in three weeks."

"Having a hard time, aren't you?"

Trena rolled her eyes. "It's a damn pain. Actually, I'm thinking about leaving home after graduation and shacking up with a friend of mine. Then I'll be able to do anything I want. My sister won't be on my back all the time."

"Where's your mother?"

"I guess she's home by now."

"Won't she have something to say about you leaving home?"

"Look, Jeanette, I'm not a little girl anymore. I can make my own decisions."

"Then why are you still a virgin?"

"Hey, I can give up my virginity whenever I feel like it. It's mine to give and nobody's to take."

"I hear you, Miss Thang, don't go gettin' huffy." Jeanette smirked in her amusement of Trena. "Just a word of advice—when you do give it up, don't waste it on these little boys. You need to be with a man who knows how to treat a pretty girl."

Trena smiled. "I know that's right." She liked that Jeanette thought she was pretty. "The guy I was dancing with wouldn't even buy me a bottle of water."

"That's my point. Don't give anything away for free—not a feel, not a shaft-rubbing grind. Even that has a price. But more importantly, Trena, check yourself. Nobody likes a tease. Don't be advertising something you're not prepared to sell."

"But I—"

"Jeanette, we've been looking all over for you," a woman said as she and two well-dressed men approached the table.

"I've been sitting right here. Did you find Lenard?"

"No, he's not here. Look, we're ready to go."

Standing, Jeanette looked at Trena. "Maybe we'll bump into each other again. You remember what I told you."

"I will. But what about your drink and your change?"

"You and your friend can keep the money and share the cooler. Next time, you can treat me." That said, Jeanette was gone.

Left alone, Trena thought about what Jeanette had said. Not that she'd said anything new, but Jeanette confirmed for her that a boy was not what she wanted. As much as she liked Omar, she had to admit that it irked her that he was always asking her to lend him money. She had lent him enough to buy the leather jacket that he wanted but couldn't afford. He was forever saying that he was going to pay her back but that day hadn't come yet. Maybe she had better rethink losing her virginity to his cheap behind. Not to mention that Omar had long ago lost his virginity so he wasn't giving her anything special in return. If anything, if she did have sex with him, he had better be able to give her something special like a gold bracelet.

"Hey, baby, wanna dance?"

Trena cut her eyes up at the fine-looking Hispanic boy that had snuck up on her. "You got any money?"

"What?" he asked, frowning. "You gold-diggin'?"

"Yep."

He flipped his hand at her disgustedly and walked away.

"Same to you, brother," Trena flipped her hand back at him. At least she didn't waste her time on him. From now on, she wasn't wasting her time on any broke brothers. If a brother didn't step up to her right, his feelings were going to get hurt, for real.

Six

Arnell wrapped herself tightly in the red silk kimono taken from the bedroom closet. She sat with her legs tucked under her ravaged body across from the sofa that she would never sit on again. She felt like nothing. She felt dirty. Tears flowed endlessly from her, although, aloud, she was not crying. Never in a million years would she have believed that something like that would have happened to her. Even when, in her heart, she didn't want to have sex, she had always given her body without resistance to the many men she had slept with over the years. None had ever had to take her by force and make her feel like she was a nobody.

Woodruff Parker, with all his success, with all of his wealth, proved to be the lowest of bastards. The five-hundred-dollar tip he left on the bar after he downed two more brandies could never make up for what he did to her.

"My time is valuable," he had said. He'd wiped himself off with the linen napkin from the bar and left Arnell bent over the back of the sofa, angry, humiliated, and sore. When she could, she straightened her sore back and made it into the shower to scrub away the evidence of the rape that seeped down her thighs. She was hurting and she was scared. Not of pregnancy, she was on the pill. Disease. What if she got something from him? Oh, God. If James ever found out about tonight or about any part of her past, he would never marry her. Just this past November he had been elected councilman for central Brooklyn. Secretly, Arnell had prayed that James would lose. When he won, she cried, but James had taken her tears for tears of joy. His budding political career would never tolerate a wife who had worked as a prostitute in a brothel, no matter how fancy the establishment. James could lose his elected office as well as his standing in his father's church. And, oh, Lord, what about Reverend Stanton? What wouldn't he do to save his son from her? It was all too draining. Arnell didn't want to think about it. She could make her life so much easier if she broke off the engagement, but how could she? James was her salvation. If he didn't marry her and get her away from Esther, she'd lose her mind. Which is why there could never be another night like this one. Arnell had to make sure of that.

"You decent?" Esther asked, smiling broadly as she entered the room.

Arnell dried her face with the pink tissue she held.

"Sweetie, you did yourself proud," Esther said, sitting on the sofa. "Woody was *very* pleased. He gushed all over himself about you. Not to mention the fact that he paid double the fee for you. I'd say you've done yourself real proud. He wants to see you again."

Cringing in the pit of her stomach, Arnell slowly shook her head.

"Oh, not to worry, sweetie. No time soon. Woody will be away on business until the end of the month. He wants to see you the last Friday in June. That's three weeks."

Again, Arnell shook her head.

"Oh, come on, Arnell. It couldn't've been that bad. The man wasn't up here that long."

He was up here long enough to rape me.

"Hell, he didn't have time to smoke a cigarette? Arnell, how much easier could that have been for you? The man left happy. You really oughta be happy, too—you still got it. A girl could get rusty laying off the job. See, I think you should—"

"Shut up!"

Stunned, Esther stared at Arnell.

"Just shut up," Arnell said softly. She really hated her life. The tears came again.

"Well, I be damned," Esther said. "Arnell, what the hell are you

crying for? I just can't figure you out. This was *the* perfect job for
you. Why are you crying?"

"He raped me!" Esther and Arnell locked eyes. "He raped me,"
she said again.

Esther looked around the room. Nothing was out of place. She
studied Arnell's face. There were no bruises. "You look fine."

"Don't you believe what I'm telling you? That *bastard* raped me!
He treated me like I was a guinea pig, like he could do anything he
wanted to me and I had no say."

"But . . . sweetie . . . did he hurt you?"

"Yes! He hurt me. He almost broke my damn back!"

Esther considered the way Arnell was sitting. She wasn't sitting
stiff or ramrod straight as if her back was hurting, and she was
moving her head and neck just fine. "Sweetie, do you wanna go to
the doctor?"

"No, I do not want to go to the doctor! Mother, the man shamed
me. I hate myself, but I hate you more. Do you understand that,
Mother? I hate you."

"You need to calm down, Arnell. You're too upset."

"Well, excuse the hell out of me for being so upset!"

"I just meant—"

"I hate you for making me come here tonight!"

Esther saw the look of scorn in Arnell's eyes. She had never seen
that dreadful look so clearly before. She needed a drink. She went to
the bar. As she reached for a glass, she saw the stack of one hundred
dollar bills. She counted them.

"I see Mr. Woodruff Parker is a very generous man."

"He's a goddamn rapist. What he did to me, he could have done
to a dog."

Esther lay the bills back on the bar. "In a way, dear, all men are
rapists." Esther poured herself a shot of brandy.

"How can you say such a thing?"

"Because I know what I'm talking about. Arnell, did I ever tell
you about my Uncle Kevin?"

"I've never met the man, so I don't give a damn about—"

"Now, sweetie, hear me out. You might find this interesting."

"I doubt it."

"Everyone called Uncle Kevin, Slick. And believe you me, he was that and more." Esther sat again on the sofa.

"Slick was my father's youngest brother. You never met him because he was in jail by the time you were two. I suppose he's dead by now. I never heard from him or about him after he went to jail. For all I know, he's been dancing with the devil for years."

Arnell wanted to scream. "What the hell does your jailbird uncle have to do with what just happened to me? Are you so damn cold that you don't understand that I've been raped?"

Esther raised the snifter to her nose. She inhaled the strong nutty flavor of the brandy. Brandy wasn't her drink. It was too strong. She could never drink enough to get her head where she wanted it to be. When she was relaxing, a dry sherry was her preference. When she was partying, when she was fired up, a gin straight up was her poison. She could use a shot of gin right now, but it was a waste to break the seal on an unopened bottle in the suite when there was no client to appreciate it. Not to mention that Arnell wouldn't share the bottle with her. Arnell never drank anything stronger than flat ass white wine.

"I want out," Arnell declared, standing. "I'm getting dressed. I'm not ever coming back here."

Esther changed her mind about drinking the brandy. She held onto it. "Arnell, I do understand rape."

"You could have fooled me." Arnell started for the bedroom.

"I was raped," Esther said quickly.

Arnell stopped. Although skeptical, she turned back. "You'd say anything to—"

"I was."

"Yeah? When?"

"When I was a child. Slick raped me."

That Arnell didn't believe. "What are you talking about? Slick was your uncle . . . my grand-uncle."

"Family ties mean nothing to a rapist, Arnell. Slick was a man before he was my uncle. I was eleven when he raped me."

Arnell narrowed her gaze skeptically.

"As God is my witness." Briefly, Esther held up her right hand. "I was home alone. I let him in, he was no stranger, he was my uncle. He raped me. It's as simple as that."

"What the hell is simple about rape?"

"It's simple if you accept that certain ugly things are going to happen to a woman, and rape is one of them."

Disagreeing, Arnell shook her head. "Rape is something that should never happen to any woman."

"Says you, but you've never been a realist, Arnell."

"Says you."

"And who would know better? Look, this is nothing for us to argue about. As long as there are men on this earth, women will be raped. I was raped. Yes, my rapist was my uncle and maybe it shouldn't have happened, but it did. I let my uncle into the house when I had been told to not open the door to anyone. So in a way, the first time he raped me, I brought it on myself. He was—"

"The first time?"

"It happened twice more when Slick caught me alone."

Feeling sick to her stomach, Arnell sat again. She was blown away. "He raped you three times?"

Esther nodded. "The first time, he messed up my face something awful. I looked like a monster."

"Mother, if he messed up your face, your parents had to have noticed. You told them, didn't you?"

"Nope."

"Why the hell not? How did you explain your bruises?"

"I told them I was in a fight."

"Are you crazy? You should have told your father. He would have killed Slick."

"Arnell, I never told anyone. I kept my dirty little secret to myself."

"Why didn't you tell Uncle Matt? He would have helped you."

"Are you serious?" Esther sucked her teeth. "Shoot. Big brother Matt was born a punk. He was a wimp then, and I guarantee you, he's a wimp now."

"You haven't seen your brother in almost twenty years. You don't know how he is."

"I don't have to see Matt to know what I know."

"God forbid that you should be wrong."

"Arnell, I grew up with Matt. You only saw him twice in your life and the first time you wouldn't remember because you were only three. You didn't see him again until you were fifteen. You were never in his company long enough to shit out a good meal."

"That's because you kept him away. I never got a chance to get to know him. Your parents were already dead by the time I was born. I should have been able to have a relationship with your brother and his kids, my cousins."

"Well, I disagree. You were better off not knowing Matt. He was such a punk."

What Esther wasn't telling Arnell was that Matt had an annoying habit of pointing the finger of condemnation at her. Whenever she did anything at all that he thought was wrong, he'd lecture her like their father used to do.

"When we were kids, Matt was scared to go trick-or-treating—everything scared him. He use to get beat up in the school yard all through elementary and junior high school. Hell, if I had told him what Slick had done to me, he would have hid from Slick just in case Slick had ideas about touching him up."

"Was Slick into boys, too?"

"I don't know anything about what Slick was doing to other people, I had my own worries."

"I'm sure you did, but I still say that you should have told someone."

"Well, I didn't, okay? Back then, no one would have believed me. In fact, Slick convinced me that my parents would never believe me over him. He was an adult—my uncle, for God sake. I was a child."

"Oh, come on, Esther, you didn't buy that."

About now, the brandy was inviting. Esther turned the snifter up to her lips and eased her head back. She downed the shot without letting much of it touch her tongue. The brandy opened up her sinuses. She batted her eyes.

Arnell didn't know if she should believe Esther or not. But why would she lie? Esther had nothing to gain by lying—or did she?

"Esther, what's the real reason you didn't tell?"

Seven

Esther set the empty glass on the coffee table. "Let me enlighten you, sweetie. In my day, a child stayed in a child's place. A child never disputed an adult. And mind you, what also made me keep my mouth shut about the rape was my own fault. I've told you before, I was no angel. The first time Slick raped me, earlier in that week, I had gotten into trouble in school for stealing a girl's cheap ass plastic bracelet. I lied about stealing it, and got caught with it when the teacher searched everyone's desk."

"Damn. You were stupid."

Esther chuckled. "For a little while, anyway."

In that dry chuckle, Arnell could hear her mother's pain. "How come you never told me this story before?"

"Well, it's not the kind of story a woman likes to talk about over tea and biscuits, especially with her daughter."

"Are you kidding? After the life I've had with you, that's a story you should have told me instead of prostituting me."

"Don't start that again, Arnell. And why should I have told you something like that? So you can feel sorry for me? Don't. Pity is a wasted sentiment. Besides, shit happens to the best of people."

"What was I thinking?" Arnell asked, annoyed. "I forgot to whom I was speaking—a woman who thinks that rape is a daughter's legacy."

"I'm just facing an ugly fact of life. I believe what I believe and nothing can change that."

"If that's the case, Mother, I can't begin to understand why you would ever be a mother to a daughter, or to a son for that matter?"

Esther chuckled sourly. "Sweetie, life plays tricks on all of us. I had you. No regrets. I love you more than I love myself."

"Yeah, right." That was the biggest lie Arnell had heard all night.

"I know you don't believe me, but it's true. And I know you might not agree, Arnell, but I didn't tell you about being raped because I want my past to remain just that, my past. I've lived it, I've put it behind me. I'd be lying if I said that at the time of the rape I wasn't traumatized, but I learned early in life that what happened to me wasn't that unique."

"That's where you're wrong. Esther, you are my mother. Whatever happened to you, good or bad, is unique to me. If you don't understand that, then I need to stop bashing my head against the wall trying to make you understand me. It's too tiring."

"I think that's probably for the best."

"Fine. So, in the end, what happened to Slick?"

"Let's just say, I got my satisfaction."

Arnell knew perfectly well what that possibly meant, but she asked anyway, "So he didn't get away with raping you?"

"Oh, at the time, he thought he did," Esther said, crossing her legs. "Actually, I *let* him think he had gotten away with it. But you know your mother, don't you, sweetie? I learned early how to bide my time. I don't let anyone get over—"

"Esther, stop beating around the bush. What did you do?"

A low rumble of a laugh rose from Esther's throat.

It was that throaty laugh that chilled Arnell. She remembered Esther laughing like that when one of her clients refused to pay after having partied for four hours with two girls, and guzzling bottles of expensive liquor. By the time Big Walt hemmed the guy up against the wall and Esther got a vicious claw lock on his balls, the guy couldn't rattle off the names and telephone numbers of his employer, his wife, and his parents fast enough.

While Esther had the guy's balls, she remarked, "This might be The Honey Well, baby, but stinging bees make up this hive and I am the queen bee—Queen Esther, to be exact, and my sting is vicious. Don't fuck with my money."

Esther not only got paid in full, she got a shipment of top sirloin and a boatload of shrimp and lobster tails—all free. That was one client who never patronized the mansion again. The funny thing is, Esther had laughed then also.

"Would you please tell me what the hell you did?" Arnell asked impatiently.

"Damn, you're like a pit bull. If you must know, some years later, when I was about thirty or so, I scored two kilo of uncut cocaine along with some other dubious paraphernalia and I—"

"You set him up?"

Esther leveled a calm *damn right* look on Arnell.

"Where did you get the money to make a score like that? When I was a kid, you were always broke."

"By the time you were three, things changed."

"But what did it change from?"

"Suffice it to say that I once knew a fella who had lots of money."

"Another secret? That *fella* is someone you've never spoken about. Who was he?"

The devilishly handsome young face of Kesley Hayden flashed before Esther's eyes. She could almost see the jet black curls that she loved to play with framing his face like each had been individually placed. She closed her eyes and imagined she felt his succulent lips on hers.

"Look at you," Arnell said, amazed at the dream-like look on Esther's face. "You're thinking about him, aren't you? Tell me about him."

Esther opened her eyes. "My past, remember?"

"Mother, who was he?"

"Leave it alone, Arnell."

"I don't get this," Arnell said. "You once told me that no man was worth protecting, and that's what you're doing by not telling me about him."

"For all you know, smarty, I could be protecting myself. But I'll tell you his name—he's probably dead by now anyway. It's been almost thirty years since I heard anything about him. His name was Kesley Hayden and he was a mistake. My mistake," Esther said. "That's all you need to know."

"Did you know this Kesley Hayden before you met my father or afterward?"

"Leave this one alone, Arnell. Trust me, you don't want to know about that part of my life."

"Could it be any worse than this part of your life?"

"Sweetie, things can always be worse."

"But damn, Mother, was your past that bad? Besides Slick, is there something more?"

"There is always more, Arnell, but my past, no matter how bad, is responsible for who I am today. I have no problem with who I am—I like me, but some things are best left in the past."

"Like what?"

"I said, leave it alone." For a second, Esther felt as she did when she had to reprimand Arnell when she was a child. "Damn, you're stubborn. All you need to know is that by the time I was twenty-two, I knew more than some fifty year olds. Like I said, I was no angel, and, yes, I had my connections, which I won't go into, so don't ask. Suffice it to say, a friend got the stuff for me. I got a couple of guns, I planted everything under Slick's bed while he was asleep, and then called the cops. In court, he cried like a baby, just like I did when he raped me. He was a three-time loser, so he got twenty years." Esther shrugged casually. "Just desserts."

"Did he know that it was you that set him up?"

"Hell, if he didn't, he was stupid. When they were taking him away after the sentencing, I got as close to him as I could. I shouted, 'Payback's a bitch, isn't it, Uncle?' Slick looked at me like I had shot him between the eyes."

Ever so slightly shaking her head, Arnell almost felt sorry for Slick. He was a rapist so he would never get her sympathy, but he sure as hell was stupid if he didn't know that one day there would be a reckoning for raping Esther.

"I know you're not feeling sorry for the bastard," Esther said.

"Do I look like I'm feeling sorry for him?"

"Just making sure. Slick raped me for a minute of satisfaction, I got him back for a lifetime of satisfaction. You know how I feel about getting—"

"I know—your satisfaction," Arnell said, finishing Esther's sentence.

"That's right. I can't sleep until any debt owed me is paid."

Arnell felt like a train had rolled over her—she felt crushed.

Esther never ceased to amaze and shock her. What would she not do to get even? Esther was her mother, the queen of all nightmare mothers. Hell, why didn't someone just drop her ass out a window when she was born? She was already doomed. A rapist for an uncle, a cold-hearted, conniving, manipulative shrew for a mother. Arnell never had a chance.

"I need a real drink," Esther said, going back to the bar. She tore the seal from the bottle of gin. "Sweetie, can I get you a glass of wine?"

Wine would mellow her out but Arnell didn't want to feel mellow. She wanted to feel the anger that was hers to savor. Her anger was going to help her find a way out.

Esther poured herself a stiff drink. Again, she sat. The gin hit the spot.

"Look, Arnell, I told you about Slick raping me so that you would know that you are not alone. True, I was a child. I couldn't defend myself. I don't think I need to tell you that what Woody did was different."

Arnell raised her brow. "I know you're not serious. That man—"

"For one thing, you are not a kid, and you were entertaining the man."

"That bastard entertained himself!" But then realization dawned. "You don't believe me, do you?"

Esther studied the angry glare in Arnell's puffy eyes. "You've never been a liar, Arnell. I believe that Woody Parker may have raped you, but . . ."

"May have?"

". . . Woody paid well for the privilege."

Arnell sucked her lungs full of air. She sprang up and pounded menacingly toward Esther.

Esther sat cooly. Her eyes never left Arnell's.

Arnell stopped inches from Esther. She wanted to slap her, but a little voice said, *She's your mother. No matter what she does, she's still your mother.* But Arnell was fuming. "I can't believe you said that! How many times do I have to remind you, Esther, that I am your daughter? Your flesh and blood?"

Unfazed, Esther eyed Arnell cooly. "I don't know why you're so upset. I only meant that, at the time, maybe Woody didn't think he was raping you. And, maybe, if he thought he was a little rough, that's why he left you that money, as sort of an apology."

"That's how you see it, huh? Well, let me show you what I think of his so-called apology." Arnell rushed to the bar and snatched up the money.

Esther stood. "What are you going to do?"

Arnell brushed past Esther on her way to the fireplace.

"Don't do that." Esther tried to beat Arnell to the fireplace. "Arnell, you earned that money." She tried to take the money from Arnell's hand.

Arnell slapped Esther's hand away, stinging her.

Esther pulled back. "You hit me!" She rubbed her hand.

The money, Arnell threw into the fireplace. From the mantel above, she snatched a box of matches.

"I can't believe you hit me."

"You think I earned this money, *Mother*? How? By putting myself in a position to be raped? You are truly sick. I don't want this money. It's filthy. This money is not an even exchange for my dignity."

"You've always been so dramatic, Arnell. If anything, that money gives you dignity."

"You are seriously warped." Arnell struck a match. She flung it on top of the money. The flame went out.

"See, it's not meant to be burned. Sweetie, you're upset. Take a minute to calm down."

Arnell struck another match.

"Arnell, please, let me hold onto the money until you calm down." Esther again reached for the money.

Arnell roughly elbowed Esther aside, surprising them both.

"Excuse you, Arnell! You're getting a bit too physical with me, aren't you?"

"If you touch that money, I'll throw this match on you." Arnell's hand shook.

Somewhat amused, Esther smirked. She stepped back. "Sweetie, you're getting to be pretty nasty, aren't you?"

Arnell glared at Esther. "I've come by it honestly, Mother."

Esther began patting her hips. Her cigarettes weren't there, she had no pockets. She had left them downstairs. "If it'll make you feel better, go ahead, burn the damn money. I don't need it and apparently neither do you."

"I wasn't asking for your permission." Arnell retrieved one of the bills and lit the edge. It caught. She lay it underneath the edge of the other bills. They all caught. Arnell stood back, staring at the small fast-burning fire.

"Feel better?" Esther asked.

Arnell tossed the box of matches back atop the mantel. "Don't ever call me about your business again." She went into the bedroom to get dressed.

Esther glanced at the black ashes that remained from the burned one hundred dollar bills. She cut her eyes toward the bedroom. "Small battle, big war." She reached for the telephone sitting on the end table. She dialed.

Eight

"James!" Esther said loud enough for Arnell to hear her in the bedroom.

"Yes?"

"Hi. How are you, *James*?"

Arnell came running. She was half dressed with only her bra on and the kimono wrapped around her waist. She gawked at Esther.

"Who is this?"

"It's me, James, Esther," she said pleasantly, looking at her irate daughter. "Arnell's mother."

Arnell's heart almost stopped beating.

"Mrs. Rayford, how are you?"

Esther and Arnell were locked in an icy glare. "James, dear, I'm just fine. It's been a while since we talked. In fact, it's been a while since I've seen you. I almost feel like Arnell is keeping you from me."

"Oh, no, that's not the case. I've just been very busy."

"Well, James, don't work yourself to death. How are you otherwise?"

Esther's syrupy sweet voice sickened Arnell. She wanted to throw up. More than that, she really wanted to hurt her mother.

"I'm just fine."

"Good. Good. Arnell and I were just sitting around talking. I was telling her that it's been a while since we've all gone out to dinner."

Arnell's pulse began to race. Finally able to move, she rushed over to Esther. She grabbed for the telephone.

Esther yanked the telephone out of Arnell's reach. "Oh, Arnell, you can talk to James anytime you want. I made the call. Let me talk to him."

Stop it! Arnell mouthed, angrily.

"James, you should see your fiancée trying to take this phone from me. She must really love you."

"I love her, too."

"Sweetie, he loves you, too."

Stop it! Arnell again mouthed.

"It's good to hear from you, Mrs. Rayford."

"Oh, that's so nice. See, Arnell, I told you James wouldn't mind my calling and inviting him out to dinner. Am I right, James?"

"It has been a while. As I said earlier, I've been very busy. I—"

"I'm sure you have been, dear, but I'm also sure that you can find a few hours for your future mother-in-law."

You are such a bitch, Arnell mouthed, abruptly unwrapping the kimono from around her waist and pulling it on over her body.

"Oh, Arnell says hi."

"Hey, baby."

"He says, 'Hey, baby,'" Esther said sultrily to Arnell. "He's so sweet."

Heat seemed to rise from Arnell's chest up her neck, onto her face. She balled up her fists.

"Tell her I'll see her in a few hours."

"He says that he'll see you in a few hours."

Screw you, Arnell mouthed.

Esther smirked. "She says, she can't wait. Oh, James, you two are so sweet together. Arnell is so lucky she met such a wonderful young man. Tell me, James, how is it that you and Arnell met again?"

"I was working on a major fund-raising campaign at the United Negro College Fund—probably the most important of my career—and I wanted the proposal to be as tight as possible. See, I'm a pretty good writer, but this was a multimillion-dollar campaign. I went in search of a copy editor."

"And you found Arnell."

"*Yes. I saw her ad in the* Park Slope Press. *I called her. She took on the project. She did a superb job.*"

"And, as they say," Esther said, looking at Arnell, "the rest is history."

"*Yes, indeed. I'm glad she agreed to go out to dinner with me six weeks later. I was running out of proposals for her to edit.*"

Arnell stood with her hand over her closed eyes. She was picturing herself jumping off a building.

"Oh, how romantic," Esther said. "Arnell, James is a sweetie pie."

Go to hell, Arnell mouthed.

"*About dinner, Esther. How about Sunday? Arnell and I will pick you up around six.*"

"Oh, *you'll* pick me up?" Esther asked, looking pointedly at Arnell. "How nice, but I have my own car. In fact, I'd like to bring my dear friend Tony along. You two need to meet since we're all going to be family."

"*I look forward to it.*"

"Don't do this," Arnell pleaded softly. "I'm begging you."

"James, dear, would you hold on a minute?" Esther asked sweetly.

"*Sure.*"

Covering the mouthpiece with her hand, Esther narrowed her eyes threateningly at Arnell. "Say you're going to be a good girl."

Arnell was breathing so hard her parched throat hurt. Her chest heaved. She glared hatefully at Esther.

"Say it," Esther ordered, threatening to take her hand off the mouthpiece.

Arnell folded her arms. Her right foot went to tapping. All the hate she was feeling for Esther was choking her.

"Sweetie, I love you to death, but you really don't wanna try me."

Again their eyes locked in a battle of wills and control, which Arnell was losing. The knot in her stomach was so tight, she cramped. She knew that this wasn't a fight she could win. Her lips began to tremble. She dropped her arms. She dropped her eyes.

"That's better," Esther said, feeling victorious.

Defeated, Arnell went to stand in front of the fireplace. With her back to Esther, she began kneading the cramp in her stomach as she stared hopelessly down at the expensive ashes. She wondered what her life might have been, if she had burned every tainted dollar she'd ever received in payment for spreading her thighs. Would Esther have gotten such a stranglehold on her life without the money?

"James," Esther said in her sweetest voice, "I am so sorry for having kept you waiting. I had to straighten out the details with Arnell. She wants Tony and I to meet you and her at Fiorentino's. I love Italian food. How about you?"

"Love it."

"Good, it'll be my and Tony's treat," Esther said.

"No, you'll be my guests."

"James, don't debate me on this one, you won't win. Taking you and Arnell out to dinner will truly be my treat and, most definitely, my pleasure."

James chuckled. "I concede."

Arnell didn't think she could hate Esther any more than she did at that very moment. How much time could she get for killing her own mother?

"Thank you, James. I'll see you Sunday. I'll say good night now. Oh, and James, please, give your parents my regards."

"I will. Good night."

Smugly self-satisfied, Esther hung up the telephone. "James is such a sweet man. Arnell, you're so lucky to be marrying a man like him. I think he'll make a wonderful husband. Have you started planning your wedding, yet?"

Arnell didn't answer.

"Oh, sweetie, don't pout. Let's not fight anymore," Esther said, going to Arnell. She embraced her, hugging her close. "Arnell, I really do hate it when we fight."

A creepy feeling came over Arnell. There was a time a long time ago, when Esther's arms around her made her feel safe. But that was when she was a child, before she was sixteen. Since she was sixteen, Esther's motherly embrace only meant trouble for her.

Seventeen years later, thoughts of that long-ago Friday when Arnell had to suffer the touch of Mr. Hershfeld in order to keep a roof over her and Esther's heads still haunted her, which is why Esther's arms around her disgusted her. Esther wouldn't allow her to stop having sex with Mr. Hershfeld until they moved out of his apartment, but then, there were a whole host of Mr. Hershfelds to service that had nothing to do with keeping a roof over their heads. Scornfully, Arnell pulled herself free of Esther's venomous embrace.

"Sweetie, I hate it when we fight."

Knock . . . knock . . . knock.

Esther glanced at the door. "I'll get rid of whoever it is."

"It doesn't matter, I'm not staying."

"Okay, sweetie, I understand if you're still upset. I'll leave. Stay up here as long as you want. You don't have to rush, Woody more than paid for the room."

"Damn," Arnell said, totally disgusted by Esther's callousness. She bustled off into the bedroom to finish dressing.

"Now what did I say?" Esther asked on her way to answer the knocking. She opened the door. It was Iris, one of her girls. "What is it?"

"Queen Esther, we have a problem."

"What now?"

"Kitt's pregnant."

"Damn. As if I don't have enough problems on my plate."

Back in the bedroom, Arnell heard the door close. She sat on the side of the bed. She felt just as she did—defeated, ashamed, dirty— after Mr. Hershfeld had his way with her young, inexperienced body. And here she was, yet again, seventeen years later, still letting Esther orchestrate the rape of her mind and body. Why in the world was she so weak?

Arnell stared at herself in one of the wall panels of mirrors that surrounded the bed. The woman that stared back at her looked angry, defiant. That woman didn't look the way Arnell felt inside— weak, defeated. That woman on the outside didn't look like she'd let anyone use or abuse her. Maybe it was time she let that angry woman take control of the weak woman inside her. It was time to take her life out of Esther's hands.

Nine

Unannounced, Esther barged into Kitt's room. "How can you be so stupid?"

Kitt had been lying down on the bed. She sat up immediately.

Esther tramped right up to the bed. "Have I been talking to myself about how you girls are supposed to protect yourselves from disease *and* pregnancy? Did I speak another language?"

Kitt's lips were trembling as she stared dumbly at Esther.

"Damn it, Kitt, I can't believe how stupid you are. I bet you don't even have a clue about what to do. What *are* you going to do?"

"I . . . I—"

"Just like I thought," Esther said disgustedly, turning away from Kitt. She looked around the room, tastefully decorated in deep burgundy and soft pink tones. She had picked the colors because Kitt said they were her favorites, which was key in making a girl feel like the room was hers. If the girls were comfortable in their rooms, then they'd treat their clients more like lovers than johns—lovers are more generous. In hindsight, perhaps she had made Kitt's room too comfortable when she allowed her to put stuffed animals and pictures of her family on the dresser. Maybe it was her fault for being compassionate.

"How far gone are you?"

"Huh?"

"Huh?" Esther mimicked Kitt. She suddenly got up close on

Kitt, making her push farther back on the bed. "Kitt, you are testing my patience. I told you when you came here that I wasn't running a nursery. How many months pregnant are you?"

"I . . . I think . . . I'm—"

"Spit it out!" Esther shouted. "How many months?"

Kitt jumped. "Four months, Queen Esther. Queen Esther, I didn't mean to get pregnant. I swear. It was Andrew Peebles who got me pregnant. He said he didn't like to wear condoms and he wouldn't do nothing with me if I tried to make him wear one. He said if I got pregnant, he'd take care of the baby."

"Stupid, what did I tell you about letting clients talk their way out of using condoms?"

"You said, don't let them."

"So why are we having this dumb ass conversation? Why are you pregnant?"

"I . . . I—"

Esther plucked Kitt hard on the side of her head.

Kitt gasped aloud as she brought her hand to her head to still the painful stinging.

"And that's another thing," Esther said. "Kitt, you were supposed to be on the pill."

"I ran out, Queen Esther."

Esther stood over Kitt with her hands planted on her hips. "I can't believe how stupid you are. You have got to get up out of here. I cannot abide stupid people."

"But, Queen Esther, I can't leave here. I—"

"Oh, yes. You can leave here quite easily, and you will."

"I'm sorry," Kitt whined. "Please, Queen Esther."

"Sorry doesn't work for me, Kitt, especially when I laid out the rules when you came in the door. Rule one," Esther said, beginning to check off each rule on her fingers. "Do not fuck with my money. Rule two: No drugs. Rule three: Do not get pregnant. Rule Four: Never call a client outside of this house. Rule Five: Act like a lady at all times. Rule Six: Don't mess up my damn house. And Rule Seven: I reiterate, Do not fuck with my money."

"But, Queen Esther, I wasn't trying to get pregnant."

"You weren't trying to use your brain, either, were you? Kitt, you stupidly broke rules one, three and seven. You have got to get the hell out of my house."

Kitt slid quickly off the bed and grabbed onto Esther's arm. "Please, Queen Esther, please give me another chance. I don't have anywhere to go. My mother moved back to Georgia. She lives in a two bedroom trailer with my little sister and brother. She don't have room for me. I have got to stay here, Queen Esther. Please, let me stay."

"Kitt, you're twenty-one years old," Esther said, roughly knocking Kitt's hands off her arm. "You're old enough to get your own place. I hope you saved some of your money—you're going to need it. And if you don't have any money, I hope you have comfortable walking shoes, sidewalks are hard on feet in stilettos."

"Please don't put me on the street, Queen Esther. I can't walk the streets. Please."

Esther surveyed the room. Besides a thorough cleaning, nothing major had to be done. Kitt had only been with her a year so she wasn't about to redo the room this soon. Her biggest problem was going to be in getting a replacement for Kitt at such short notice, a headache she didn't need.

"Queen Esther, I'll get an abortion. Please, can I stay?"

"No," Esther said flatly as she went to the door. "Start packing. Big Walt will be up in thirty minutes to help you move out."

Sinking down onto the bed, Kitt began to cry. "Please, Queen Esther. Please don't put me out."

Esther opened the door. "Kitt, you put your own self out. You broke the rules, and there are consequences for people who break rules. Oh, and by the way, do not even think about breaking Rule Four. Because if I find out that you called Andrew Peebles, you will be sorry."

Throwing herself onto her side on the bed, Kitt sobbed hard and loud.

Disgusted, Esther slammed the door and closed her ears to Kitt's pitiful cries. She'd had high hopes for Kitt. She was a slim, long-legged, pretty young girl whose insatiable appetite for sex bordered on nymphomania. The fact that she was twenty-one was Kitt's biggest asset—old men in particular and young men, too, lined up for her, especially Andrew Peebles, the twenty-five year-old wanna-be rap singer turned producer. He couldn't get enough of Kitt. If Esther had known that he had not been using a condom, she would have gotten on his ass right away. She certainly had an earful for him when she saw him again.

Esther took the back stairs down to the kitchen on the parlor floor where she was certain that she'd find Big Walt. Big Walt sat at the large kitchen table in the center of the huge room chowing down on a large piece of fried chicken and a plate of macaroni and cheese which Melvina made especially for him. At the stove, Melvina stirred a large pot. Arnell suddenly came through the same door behind Esther.

"Hey, Arnell," Big Walt said, surprised to see her. "I didn't know you were here."

Arnell continued on through the kitchen but she waved half-heartedly at Big Walt. He had always been cool with her.

"Are you all right, Arnell? Need me for anything?"

"She's fine, Big Walt," Esther said. "Aren't you, sweetie?"

Ignoring Esther, Arnell turned back to Big Walt. "What's up?"

"I have that CD I mixed for you. I'll get it for you." Big Walt started to get up.

"I'll get it later," Arnell said. She went quickly to the back door.

"Sweetie, you leaving now?" Esther asked. "Can we talk a minute?"

Arnell didn't answer Esther as she went out the back door.

Esther rushed to the open door. "Arnell, can I speak to you a minute?"

Stopping at the top of the short stairs that led down into the backyard, Arnell looked yearningly at her car. She wanted so badly to run to it, to drive it so far away that she wouldn't know herself where she was.

"Sweetie," Esther said, speaking in a low voice, "I thought about what happened to you tonight."

Arnell looked longingly at her car.

"I just want you to know that Tony and I will take care of it."

That got Arnell's attention. "I don't know exactly what that means, and, really, I don't care. Just leave me alone about it."

"Arnell—"

"Mother, I have to go." She started to leave.

"Arnell, I'm in a jam. Kitt's pregnant."

"No."

"Oh, I'm not asking you to replace her, but I do need you to help me find and screen her replacement."

Arnell said quietly, "I can't help you."

Realizing that the door was open behind her, Esther glanced back inside the kitchen. Both Big Walt and Melvina were looking at her. Esther pulled the door in.

A car cruised to a stop in the driveway. Arnell continued on down the stairs.

"Arnell, I have a schedule to maintain," Esther said, stopping Arnell again. "If I don't get someone in here and trained right away to take care of Kitt's clients, I might lose them."

"That's not my problem," Arnell said, watching Jeanette get out of her car. "Speak to Jeanette. She thinks more like you than I do. I'm sure you two will come up with a solution."

"You're my daughter, Arnell. You—"

"I have to go," Arnell said, passing Jeanette without giving her the time of day.

"Hi, Arnell," Jeanette said, the gaiety in her voice quite unlike the deadpan look on her face. She went straightaway up the stairs to Esther. "She have a bad night?"

"Leave Arnell alone. What time is your next client?"

"Twelve-thirty."

"Good. I need you to do something for me," Esther said, going back into the house.

"Name it."

"Big Walt, go up to Kitt's room and give her a helping hand. I want her out of here in twenty-five minutes flat. Take her to that motel over on Pennsylvania Avenue in Canarsie. I'll give you enough to pay for two weeks. After that, she's on her own."

Big Walt pushed his half-eaten plate of food away. There would be a fresh plate of food waiting for him when he got back. He was a big man. Six foot four, two hundred and sixty pounds of hard, rippling muscles that he fine-tuned in the gym two hours a day, five days a week. His arms were as big as most men's thighs. His sheer bulk alone stopped many would-be incidents in the mansion the minute he appeared. His job was easy and he got paid well for it and that's all that mattered. He needed lots of money to finish producing his first rap artist. He figured another year ought to do it and he could say good-bye to being Esther's flunky. Right now, he had a job to do.

"What did Kitt do?" Jeanette asked eagerly. "Which rule did she break?"

Melvina turned away from her pot and waited for Esther to answer.

"Melvina, please fix me a chicken salad," Esther said. "I haven't eaten all evening."

"Right away. Do you want it in your room?"

"No," she said, sitting. "I'll eat it here. Jeanette, I want you to take Kitt's eleven-thirty appointment. I'll make it worth your while."

"Okay, Queen Esther. Anything for you."

"Good girl. Now you go on and get ready, I have to brainstorm with Melvina on replacing Kitt."

"Yes, ma'am," Jeanette said, about to leave when she had a brainstorm of her own. "Queen Esther, maybe I can help. I met a girl tonight at the club. I think you might like her. She's a hot young thing ready to leave home and everything."

Esther's curiosity was instantly piqued. "Tell me more."

Ten

Arnell considered calling Sharise but dismissed the thought as quickly as it came into her head. The minute Sharise heard her voice she would know something was wrong and that that something more than likely involved Esther and the mansion. Sharise would not want to hear that Arnell had gone back and had gotten raped to boot, especially after spending long, emotionally upsetting hours holding her hand, listening to her gripe about the life she wanted to escape from just as Sharise had done. This time, Sharise might not lend a sympathetic ear. Sharise had implored Arnell to get as far away from Esther as she could. The problem was, Esther was first and foremost Arnell's mother and it wasn't as easy to escape a mother as it was to escape a boss—as it had been in Sharise's case. Sharise had never agreed with Arnell's reasoning.

Sharise had been living on the streets since she was seventeen. At nineteen, Esther cleaned Sharise up and took her in. For a while, Sharise was fine with living and working at the mansion, but after a bad night with an old geezer who had downed Viagra and screwed her raw, Sharise realized that prostituting her body was not something she wanted to do rest of her life. When she announced she was quitting, Esther had a fit, but she couldn't make Sharise stay. Sharise left the business five years ago, when she was twenty-six, while she was still young and pretty enough to catch the eye of the right man. That man was Michael Simon. He knew all about Sharise's past life at the mansion; Sharise had told him about it herself. Michael had blinked, but he didn't stop loving her. That's how much he cared. They had two adorable children and a life in Baldwin, Long Island, that Arnell had only dreamed about.

As much as she needed to talk to Sharise, Arnell didn't have the courage to call her. As always, Arnell was on her own and consoling herself was something she was use to. She headed home because that's where she needed to be to lick her wounds and talk herself into doing what she needed to do to straighten out her life. Forty minutes later, halfway into her block, Arnell could see James sitting, under the light, on her front steps waiting for her. She wasn't ready to see him, she felt too dirty. She stopped her car in the shadows of the trees that lined her street three doors away from her house. She parked and shut off the lights. She had never given James the keys to her house, Esther had strongly advised against that. *No man should have a key to a woman's home until he's paying the bills, and even then, only if he lives there.* Some of Esther's teachings were well ingrained in Arnell's psyche. James wasn't paying Arnell's bills, and neither was he living with her. She hadn't asked him on either account and he hadn't offered. It was just as well, she didn't want James to take care of her, she could take care of herself. She had stayed on track in going for her degree even while Esther tried everything in her vast storehouse of manipulative mind games to dissuade her. Arnell stayed the course, determined to prepare herself for a life outside of The Honey Well.

But to be fair, The Honey Well had given Arnell her one true friend in life—she had met Sharise there, and she had managed to save over two hundred thousand dollars in cash over the years from selling her body. She would have had more if she had not paid off her house and paid cash for her tuition. But that was all right, she was debt-free and well invested in stocks and mutual funds. She liked living that way. Of course, she could never let James know how much money she had—a man should never know a woman's worth, à la Mommy Dearest. That made sense to Arnell, especially since the money was ill gained. James accepted her lie that her father, who she didn't even remember, had died in a horrible car accident and that she and her mother had received compensation from a life insurance policy, an auto insurance policy, and from her father's employee benefits package. Her part-time job from home as a copy editor would have never justified her lifestyle. So many lies, so much to fear.

Arnell took out her cell phone and realized at once that it was turned off. Turning it on, she ignored the flashing signal that she had voice mail. In the darkness, she knew by heart which buttons to press to call James.

"James, hi," she said to his answering machine. "I'm sitting in my car outside your apartment. Where are you? It's twelve-thirty. I'll wait a little while longer and then I'll head home. Call me later." She shut off her phone. It disturbed Arnell that she could lie so easily, but the truth was, she had been living a lie as far back as she remembered. It's all she really knew. This, too, like everything else she was forced to do or be was Esther's fault.

Checking his watch for the time, James stood. He stretched. He looked first one way up the block and then the other. Arnell sank ever so slightly in her seat even though she was sure James couldn't see her in the darkness. She hated standing him up, but she couldn't be with him tonight. More than likely, he would want to make love. She just couldn't. As painful as it was to admit to herself, Arnell didn't feel worthy of James's touch or of his love. In fact, she wasn't worthy of becoming his wife. He deserved better.

Arnell watched James make a call on his cell phone. He appeared to be listening. He ended that call and made another. He seemed to be waiting. He spoke briefly before he snapped his cell phone closed. She could tell by the way he snapped the phone shut and shoved it back inside it's belt holder that he was angry. Probably at her. He took long strides to his car sitting in her driveway and yanked the door open. Sadly, she watched him hurriedly back out and turn his car in her direction. Again, sure that he couldn't see her, she didn't move as he sped past, headed she didn't know where. James's time was valuable and what he hated worst of all was wasting a minute of it. Maybe this was as good a time as any to end the engagement. It could never work between them. Her past would never allow it.

Arnell didn't bother to turn on her headlights as she slowly pulled out and drove right up into her own driveway. Using her automatic garage opener, she opened the garage door and drove inside. If James came back, she didn't want him to see that she was home. She didn't want to see him until Sunday at dinner with Esther and Tony. She couldn't wait to see the sick look on Esther's face when she broke the engagement to James. Esther's hold over her would no longer carry weight. If that look was the only satisfaction Arnell got, it would be well worth it.

Eleven

The door started opening even before Trena's key touched the keyhole.

Oh, shit. My ass is grass. She had a light buzz on from drinking three strawberry wine coolers and smoking half a joint, but her mind was clear enough to know that it was three o'clock in the morning.

In the doorway, Maxine stood with one hand on her hip. "Do you know what time it is, Trena? Where have you been?"

None of your business. Playing it cool, her head down, Trena tried to slip into the house past her mother.

"Oh, no you don't." Maxine blocked Trena from entering the house with her body.

Trena quickly made up her mind, she was going to stay cool. She wasn't about to blow her high behind a war of words.

Maxine stepped back and looked Trena over. "Trena Marie Gatlind, where do you get off dressing like this? Where did you get that short behind skirt? I didn't buy that for you."

"Mom, I dress like all the girls dress." Trena went around Maxine on into the house. "It's no big deal."

Closing the door, Maxine skimmed Trena, head to toe. "Trena, I can damn near see your tail."

So. Don't look.

"Child, if you bend over too far, your tail will drop out and your breasts will pop out."

Good. What the hell I got them for if I can't show them.

"Trena, where do you get off going outside this house dressed like that?"

Trena sucked her teeth. *I'll dress any way I damn well please.*

Near the top of the stairs, Cheryl stood in her nightgown. "She looks like a whore."

Poof! Trena's high was gone. "Screw you, Cheryl!"

Maxine slapped Trena on the upper arm. "Trena! Watch your mouth!"

"What you hittin' on me for? You didn't say nothin' to Cheryl. She called me a hoe."

"I said you look like one."

"You wish you could look this good."

"I look better."

"Your sister's right," Maxine said, "Trena, you look cheap. You get your fresh behind up those stairs and take those trashy clothes off. I don't want to ever see you looking like this again."

"Mom, Alyson and Bebe's mothers don't say nothin' about the way they dress. There's nothing wrong with the way we dress."

"If your friends' mothers want their daughters to look like tramps, that's on them. I'm your mother and I refuse to let you dis-respect me by the way you dress."

"I ain't dissin' you! I'm just tryin' to do my own thang."

"Well, Miss Trena, you do your own *thang* when you get your own *thang*. This is *my* house, and you will do what I say and dress the way I say."

Trena began stomping up the stairs. "Then I'm gettin' out of *your* house."

"You keep talking to me like that, you'll be leaving here on a stretcher. And don't be walking away from me, young lady, I'm talking to you."

Trena stopped climbing the stairs. Her bottom lip shot out.

"Mom, I told you how she was acting," Cheryl said.

"See, Mom," Trena said, "you getting on me because of Cheryl. She's . . ."

"Don't even put me in it."

". . . tellin' you lies about me!"

"Trena, you're the one that messed up," Cheryl said. "You stayed out late. You—"

"Cheryl, I got this," Maxine said. "Trena, my mother, God bless the dead, would say that you're smelling your own musk and she'd be right. You're still a child, but you think you're grown. When you start thinking that you're grown, you need to be out on your own."

"Are you puttin' me out? You're putting me out, aren't you?"

"That's not what she said," Cheryl said. "She said—"

"Mind your business, Cheryl!"

"Trena," Maxine said, pulling Trena around to face her, "if you don't live by my rules I will put you out."

Trena stared in disbelief at her mother. If her mother could even say out loud that she would put her out, then she didn't care about her. She didn't love her. "That's all right. I can make it on my own," she said, continuing on up the stairs.

"You think you can, Miss Smart Behind." Maxine followed close behind Trena. "I promise you, everything's not as easy as you think. You got it good here, Trena, you just don't know it. You're rushing to be grown and on your own, but one day you're going to wish to God that you could be a child again."

"No, I'm not. I'm—"

"Oh, yes you will. Mark my word, Trena, you will. And don't think you're not on punishment for coming home at three in the morning. You will not go out of this house for one month, except to go to school or with me or your sister. You are confined to your room. Do you understand me?"

Trena stopped three steps below Cheryl. She glared up at her. "You can't make me stay in the house, that's child abuse."

Stepping up on the same step alongside Trena, Maxine again pulled Trena around to face her, but Trena wouldn't look at her. It was Cheryl she glared at.

"I am *your* mother, Trena. You are not mine. I know you're not telling me what I can't do to you. If you think punishing you is child abuse, then you don't know very much at all."

Defiant, Trena said under her breath to Cheryl, "I hate you."

"Trena, Mom's not beating you or depriving you of food. She's punishing you for being delinquent. You—"

"Shut up, Cheryl! Leave me alone!"

"Cheryl, I'm handling your sister," Maxine said.

"Fine. I'm out of this."

"It's about time," Trena snapped. She started to go around Cheryl, but Maxine stopped her.

"Trena, you're out of control. In my heart, I know you're headed for trouble. Maybe it's partly my fault. I haven't been home much because of my hours, but I've always done the best I could by you, and so has your sister. But I see what the problem is. You're beginning to smell your own tail."

"My tail don't stink," Trena sniped, rolling her eyes.

"Child," Maxine said, hitting Trena on the hip, "you better watch your tone and hold those eyes still in your head or you will be sorry."

Trena again rolled her eyes.

Maxine again hit Trena on the hip. "Okay, I see what I need to do. I need to see about changing my hours so that I can be home to neutralize your fresh behind. Your sister told me what you've been up to with Omar. I'm not having it. You will not behave like a slut in my house."

"So now I'm a slut?"

"Trena, don't be putting words in my mouth. The bottom line is, you had best get your act together, young lady. Do you understand me?"

Without even giving her mother the courtesy of a glance, Trena pushed roughly past Cheryl, shoving her into the banister.

"Hey!" Cheryl gripped the banister to keep from tumbling down the stairs.

"Trena!" Maxine raced up the stairs behind her. At the door to Trena's bedroom, Maxine caught up with her. She snatched Trena around. "You—"

"Let go of me!" Trena jerked hard enough to pull herself out of Maxine's grasp.

"Trena! You talking to me like this? You really are out of control. You almost knocked your sister down the stairs, and now you think you're grown enough to sass me?"

Cheryl rushed up the stairs to stand beside Maxine. She jabbed her finger at Trena. "I'm gonna kick your ass!"

"Go for it!" Trena shoved Cheryl's hand out of her face. They started to tussle.

"Both of you, stop it!" Maxine grabbed Cheryl by the waist and yanked her back. Trena advanced on Cheryl. Maxine shoved her hard into the wall. "Trena! Stop it! Now!"

Trena was breathing hard. "She put her hand in my face! You didn't say nothin' to her!"

"Trena, you almost knocked your sister down the stairs."

"I could've been killed!"

"I wish you had broken your damn neck!" Trena started to push past Maxine to get into her room.

Maxine grabbed onto Trena's shoulders, holding her against her will. "Have you lost your damn mind?"

"Get offa me!"

"Trena, you don't talk to me like that!" Maxine's spittle sprayed Trena's face.

Trena strained to pull back as far from Maxine as possible. "You're talking to me like you want to."

"See, Mom," Cheryl said. "See how fresh she is. I told you. This is how she's been acting."

Trena tried twisting herself free. "Shut the fuck up, Cheryl, and get the hell—"

Slap! The hard, stinging slap caught Trena across the mouth, silencing her words. Trena gulped in air as she brought her hand to her cheek. Tears sprang up in her eyes.

Maxine grabbed a chunk of Trena's arm and pinched her.

"Ouch!"

"Trena, you don't curse anyone in this house! You are not supposed to be cursing any goddamn way."

"How come you don't ever hit Cheryl?" Trena asked, rubbing her bruised arm.

"Because Cheryl hasn't done anything wrong, Trena! You're the one that's showing your ass. And I am telling you right now, I will not put up with you cursing, coming in this house whenever the hell you feel like it, or with you wearing skirts up your fresh ass or blouses barely covering your breasts. In other words, Trena, you are not going to run wild in my house!"

Tears rushed down Trena's cheeks. "You're always taking

Cheryl's side against me." Trena rammed her body up against her bedroom door, shoving it open. She barreled inside.

Maxine stayed on Trena's heels. "No, Trena, it's not about taking sides. I'm trying to get you to see that you don't call the shots. You are not the adult in this house. You've always been spoiled. It's my fault for giving you too much. When I couldn't be here for you, your sister has been here doing for you like you were her own. You should be grateful to have a sister like Cheryl."

"I hate Cheryl!" Trena flopped down on her bed.

"Fine, you can hate me all you want," Cheryl said, her voice sounding hoarse. "I don't care."

"Good! Because I'm gonna always hate you."

"That's it!" Maxine stuck her finger in Trena's face, touching the tip of her nose. "Not another word out of your mouth, young lady! Not another damn word."

Holding her head stiffly, Trena poutingly folded her arms across her chest, pushing her breasts up higher, exposing her cleavage more.

"Trena, your nasty ass attitude and your foul ass mouth has gotten your tail in serious trouble. You will *not* step foot out of this room until Monday morning to go to school. You will *not* use the telephone or the television. In fact, Cheryl, get that television and that telephone out of here."

"Whatever. I don't care," Trena mumbled.

Cheryl went for the telephone.

Maxine hovered above Trena. "You will care when you have to come straight home from school each and every day, and when school is over in three weeks for all of your friends, you will still be going to school. Your grades aren't that good, young lady. You could benefit from summer school."

"I don't care."

"Oh, by the time I finish with you, miss, you will care. I guarantee you that."

Cheryl wrapped the cord around the base of the telephone. "Mom, you're wasting your breath. Trena doesn't care about anything. And that's her problem."

"You just wait, Cheryl, I'm gonna kick your behind!"

"Trena! You will not touch your sister. Do you hear me?"

"Well, she keep botherin' me. I am gonna kick her butt."

Maxine flat-palmed Trena on the forehead, snapping her head back.

"Ow!" Trena was getting tired of being hit.

"You're not going to do any such thing," Maxine said. "You hear me?"

"How come you keep hittin' me?" Trena's eyes watered.

"Because your tail is out of control. But that's all right, Miss Trena, I know what to do with you. These clothes you're wearing, they're going out with the trash. You will throw out, this night, every piece of rag you bought behind my back that I . . . In fact, I'm going to throw them out myself."

Maxine went to the closet. She began pulling clothes hangers apart one by one, inspecting the clothes that hung from them. A short black leather skirt she yanked off its hanger and tossed onto the floor.

"No!" Trena sprang off the bed. She snatched the skirt off the floor. "Mom, please don't throw away my leather!"

Maxine tried to snatch the skirt out of Trena's clutches. Trena held onto the skirt for dear life.

"Let go, Trena. This is not a game. I am not playing with you. You've lost all privileges in this house. And if you don't get your act together, I will call the juvenile division of social services or the Department of Corrections, or whatever agency that has jurisdiction over bad ass, delinquent kids, and have them put your tail in a disciplinary school until your age catches up with your attitude."

Sullen and defiant, Trena set her jaw. *I'm not going nowhere.*

"I promise you, Trena, you will not stay under my roof and make my life a living hell. Maybe a boot camp is the place for you."

Trena stopped tugging on the skirt. The threat of being sent to a boot camp was not an idle one because her mother knew about Kathy Bailey and had applauded Kathy's parents for "doing the right thing." Kathy lived across the street and was a friend since seventh grade. Last year, Kathy's parents put her away for six months. Kathy said she was treated like a convict. Worst of all, the counselors were up in her face, bad breath and all, screaming on her, threatening her all the time. Kathy said that the food was nasty, the clothes were ugly, and that she had to go to bed every night at eight o'clock sharp and get up every morning at five. Kathy couldn't even go to the bathroom without permission.

No, Trena wasn't about to let her mother put her away. She let go of the skirt. She went back to the bed and sat. She no longer cared that Cheryl had disconnected her telephone, or that her mother was emptying her closet. She wasn't planning on being here.

"You will not spend my hard-earned money on garbage that would shame a harlot. Do you understand me, Trena? You will not walk around here dressed like some tramp in heat. I will take you shopping myself from now on, and if I have to dress your fresh behind every morning myself, I will.

No, you won't.

"I guarantee you, Trena, you will leave this house looking like a vestal virgin."

No, I won't.

"And if you think you're going to sneak and change your clothes after you leave this house, think again. I will be checking on you when you least expect it. You won't know when or where, but I will know what you are wearing every minute of the day. Whether you want to or not, you will get your act together, young lady, or you will answer to me."

I ain't scared of you. You can't do a damn thing to me. Trena rolled her eyes just as Maxine looked back at her.

"Trena, you roll your eyes at me one more time," Maxine said, pointing her finger, "I am going to slap your head right off your neck."

Try it. I'll call the cops on you.

"That's your problem, you're too damn fresh." Maxine continued to pull clothes from the closet. "You need to be concentrating on your schoolwork and what the hell you wanna do in life, instead of thinking about those knuckleheaded young hugger-muggers out there. That's another thing, the next time you call yourself dating, you will be as old as I am."

That's what you think.

"And keep looking at me like that, hear? I'll pluck your eyes right out of your head."

Cutting her eyes away, Trena fixed her eyes on the doorknob. She closed her ears, she closed her mind to all that was coming out of her mother's mouth. She knew what she had to do. She had to bide her time until she could sneak out of the house. Hopefully, that would be tomorrow. She was going to run away. She couldn't wait to get the hell away from Cheryl. Cheryl and her mother both were going to be sorry for the way they treated her. They were going to be real sorry.

Twelve

Standing at the window, just out of sight behind the partially opened blinds, Trena watched Maxine and Cheryl get into the car. They were probably going food shopping as was their usual Saturday morning routine. When they left the house, they probably thought she was asleep. She wasn't. In fact, she hadn't been to sleep at all. Although she had lain down, she had been too upset to sleep. Her mind had been in overdrive trying to figure out where she was going to go. She could hide out at Alyson's for the weekend, but Alyson's mother knew her mother and would question her staying past Sunday afternoon. Besides, Alyson's apartment would be the first place her mother would call. If she hooked up with Bebe, Bebe's mother and father might wonder why she was there past Sunday also, but she had to go somewhere.

Maxine and Cheryl drove off.

Figuring that they would be gone at least two hours, Trena began to quickly pack a bag. The first thing she grabbed was her telephone book. She wasn't about to help Cheryl or her mother find her. Since her mother had taken her favorite outfits out of her closet, and even the outfit she had on last night, Trena was left only with jeans, slacks, and long skirts. But that was all right, she looked good in all her clothes. Sure that she had just what she needed, Trena stuffed, squeezed, and zipped everything inside the bag.

She didn't waste a sentimental moment looking over her room or waste any brain cells trying to compose a good-bye note. Her father she would miss, but he was rarely home anyway. He never seemed to miss her. Her mother and, in particular, Cheryl, she hoped to never see again in life. They were both trying to keep her from becoming a woman. Well, no more. Her life was her own. Twenty-three dollars and eighty-seven cents wasn't much to start out on, but it would have to do. Trena threw her heavy, overstuffed bag over her shoulder, grabbed her denim jacket, and walked out of her mother and Cheryl's house.

Thirteen

Saturday night was *the* night to be at The Brooklyn Café. Not that the music was any better, any louder than it was at the Lab, the music was just more static. The pulsating beat enticed many more hot, sweaty bodies onto the dance floor, making each dancer gyrate raunchily until, as a crowd, they climaxed into a multitude of passionately rhythmic organisms. As bad as she was feeling, Trena couldn't help but pop her fingers and wiggle in her seat to the heart thumping music. She had hidden out in Alyson's room all day, jumping into the closet if Alyson's mother came within two feet of Alyson's bedroom door. Luckily, Mrs. Hicks didn't usually trespass in Alyson's space so for the most part Trena was safe from detection. That is, except for the seven or eight times her own mother called looking for her. Mrs. Hicks called Alyson to the telephone each time, but Alyson never gave her up. It took a minute for Trena to figure out that her mother was getting her friends' telephone numbers from the memory on her cordless telephone.

How long she was going to be able to hide in Alyson's closet, Trena wasn't sure. As it was, she had to wait until Mr. And Mrs. Hicks went out before she and Alyson could sneak out of the apartment and make their way to the Café.

"Trena! Guurl," Bebe dragged a chair from another table to the table where Trena and Alyson were sitting, "your mother called my house five times today looking for you. I think she called the police. You are in a shitload of trouble."

"Did you tell her anything?" Trena practically shouted. The booming music wouldn't allow her to whisper.

"Hell, no! I told her I hadn't heard from you. I put on a real good act, too. I acted like I was worried about you."

"Good, 'cause I ain't never going back home."

Alyson puffed once on her cigarette. "You'd be crazy if you did. Your moms is talking like she's gonna lock you up in the G Building at Kings County."

"After what you told me about what happened last night," Bebe said, "I know that's right."

Trena took the cigarette out of Alyson's hand. "I have got to find a place to hide out." She puffed on the cigarette. She had tried to smoke twice before and had never taken to it. She handed the cigarette back to Alyson. What she needed was a joint but she couldn't spend what little money she had.

Alyson wistfully flicked her cigarette into her empty glass. "You haven't spoken to Omar, yet, huh?"

"I told you, every time I call him, his mother says he's not home."

"What's up with that?" Bebe asked. "Has your mother been calling there?"

"I wouldn't know," Trena said. "I didn't tell Omar's mother that it was me. I changed my voice and told her that my name was Debbie."

"That was smart." Bebe searched the crowd. "Maybe he'll show up here tonight."

"I hope so," Trena said. "I need to get some cash off of him. I'm real low. Bebe, you got any money?"

"At home, I got about fifteen dollars. On me," she said, sliding her hand inside the pocket of her tight jeans, "I got twelve dollars."

"Man, Bebe, you more broke than me," Alyson said. "We don't even have enough to score some serious weed."

Bebe pulled her hand out of her pocket. "Hey, my daddy ain't rich. Just 'cause he's from Detroit and his last name is Ford don't mean that Henry was his daddy."

Alyson and Trena both laughed. "Girl, you so crazy," Trena said.

"She's sick." Alyson chuckled. She dropped her burned out cigarette into her glass. "But seriously, Trena. What you goin' do?"

Trena shrugged. "I guess I'm gonna have to live on the streets. Kids do it every day."

"Oh, boo." Bebe scooted closer to Trena and put her arm around her. "You can't live on the street. You don't even like using a public toilet."

Trena frowned. "Girl, those things are nasty."

Alyson raised her hand to Trena for a high five. "I know that's right."

Trena obliged her friend with an enthusiastic high five, although inside she quivered fretfully. She couldn't let on how scared she really was. There was nowhere for her to go that she wouldn't, in the end, be returned to her mother, or worse, be put away. At least for tonight, she prayed that she could sneak back into Alyson's room without getting caught.

"Okay," Alyson said, "let's put our heads together. We're your girls, Trena, we got your back. We'll come up with something."

The three of them put their fingertips to their temples, trying to think, but the music wouldn't let them concentrate. The pulsating beat took hold of them. One by one they started to pop their fingers and sway to the music. They went with the beat.

"Ha . . . a!" Bebe sang, really getting into the music.

"Par . . . ta!" Alyson shouted.

Getting into the groove, Trena laughed. It was party time. "Let's dance." She'd worry about her problem later. "Where're the boys?"

Alyson and Bebe stood also.

Someone tapped Trena on the shoulder just as she was about to dance away from the table. She looked back. She smiled. It was her new friend.

"Jeanette, what's up?"

"You. I've been looking for you all evening. How's it going?"

"Just partyin' with my girls."

"Hey, Jeanette," Alyson said.

"I don't know you," Bebe said, "but hey, Jeanette."

"Hi, girls." Jeanette smiled, but it was Trena she was there to see. "Trena, you got a minute? I'd like to talk to you—alone."

"Me? What about?"

"What we talked about last night. You got a minute?"

Trena looked at Alyson and Bebe. Alyson shrugged. Bebe finger waved at Trena and danced away. Alyson followed.

Jeanette saw no need to small talk. "How's it going at home?"

"How come you asked me that?"

"Just something I picked up on last night. I was worried about you."

"Why?"

"It's pretty bad for you at home, right?"

"Yeah, I ran away this morning."

Jeanette leaned closer to Trena, their shoulders touched. "I'm not surprised."

"Well, I couldn't take it anymore. My mother always sides with my sister, and last night, they ganged up on me. I ain't never goin' back there."

"I've been in your shoes," Jeanette said. "I left home when I was seventeen and I've never looked back."

"Did you have to live on the street?"

"Puleeze. Do I look like I ever lived on the street? Girl, I went to live in a place better than the apartment I lived in with my parents. I still live there. It's a mansion. It's gorgeous."

Trena's eyes stretched. "For real?"

"For real. Trena, where are you staying?"

"I hid out in Alyson's bedroom today, but I'm not going to be able to stay there for long."

Jeanette casually flipped her hand. "Don't worry. I can hook you up."

"For real? You'd do that for me?"

"Of course I would. I came looking for you tonight because I felt that you might need a friend. If you want, you can come home with me tonight."

"Oh, man, that would be great, but I left my things at Alyson's."

"No problem. We can get those things tomorrow."

"Jeanette, I really appreciate this. I just need to stay until I can get a job and get myself an apartment, but I'll pay my—"

"Trena, please, don't worry about it. I know what it is to be in need of a place to crash. Look, I've had enough of this music. I'm ready to leave if you are."

Trena felt like jumping up and down. "Sure. But I need to tell

Alyson and Bebe that I'm jettin'." Trena began to search the faces in the dancing crowd. She didn't see either Alyson or Bebe. "Damn, where did they go?"

"You can call them tomorrow. We have to get your things from Alyson anyway."

"True," Trena said, hating that she wasn't going to be able to tell her girls until tomorrow that she had a place to stay. Things were going to work out after all. When Jeanette slipped her arm through Trena's, and they threaded their way through the crowd toward the exit, Trena was glad that she had let Jeanette sit at the table with her and Alyson the night before. Tonight, Jeanette was saving her life.

Fourteen

Arnell was in a deep, dreamless sleep. She didn't hear the doorbell chimes the first time they rang, nor the second time. The third time she did hear them, but even then to her ears the chimes sounded far, far away, when in fact the bell was mounted high on the wall only twenty feet from where Arnell lay zonked out on the living room sofa still unable to open her eyes. They felt glued shut. After she got in last night, she had taken a long, hot bath which didn't relax her enough to put her to sleep. At two in the morning, she found herself sitting on the sofa stuffing her face with tablespoon-size doses of Haagen Däzs vanilla Swiss almond ice cream. She ate the whole pint along with a large bag of cheese twists and half a box of soft, gooey double chocolate chip cookies while watching *Police Academy* ten or something. The movie, however, wasn't funny enough or silly enough to keep Arnell from crying about what Woodruff Parker had done to her. The truth of it was, her tears weren't all about what had happened last night, they were about the many men that had used her body as a sperm receptacle. She felt like she had never had any say about how her body was to be used or about the path in life on which she walked, and it angered her. That's when her four throw pillows became exactly that— throw pillows. Arnell angrily threw them across the room, but she felt no better. Then she cursed Esther for ever giving birth to her. She was mad as hell about being born to Esther Rayford. Arnell gave herself permission to wallow in her anger like she'd never done before. She allowed herself to cry without shame and it was cathartic—she felt like a thousand pounds had been lifted off her chest. Now she had to find a way to remain unburdened. Since coming home Friday night, she had ignored the ringing telephone. She listened only to the recorded voices that spoke to her on her answering machine—Esther begging her to return her calls, and when she didn't, said finally that she would see her at dinner on Sunday. James's message was a demand to know where Arnell was. He had called three times.

By five in the morning, while nibbling on a bag of salty potato chips and drinking a second glass of sweet iced tea, she had begun watching another comedy that she again couldn't focus on, so she didn't have a clue as to why Ben Stiller was climbing out onto the roof of a house. He wasn't funny, either, but he did finally help her drop off to sleep.

The bell chimed a fourth time. Arnell lay still. It was probably a pair of persistent Jehovah's Witnesses hoping to convert her, or some salesman trying to sell her a bronze-tipped dipstick or something. Whoever it was, Arnell had no intention of answering the door. She turned onto her side and curled up; she was going back to sleep.

Suddenly, there was a loud banging at the front door. "Arnell!"

Her eyes popped open. *Oh, shit!* It was James. She sat right up. The VCR clock illuminated the time in amber—12:17 P.M.

James banged again. "Arnell!"

Arnell hurriedly pried herself out of the sunken spot her body had made in the sofa cushion and rushed to the front door. With her hand on the doorknob, she glanced back at the remnants of her disgustingly gluttonous binge on the coffee table—an empty bag of cheese twists, two dirty drinking glasses, a dried-out milky container of Haagen Däzs vanilla Swiss almond ice cream, a half a bag of potato chips, and a box of Entenmann's double chocolate chip cookies with only two cookies inside. It was going to take her a month to lose the pounds she'd packed onto her hips. Oh well, too late to worry about that now. It was also too late to do anything about the wrinkled fleece shorts and cotton T-shirt she was wearing. She took a deep breath and opened the door.

James all but pushed Arnell out of the way in his agitated haste to bustle into the house. "Isn't your bell working?"

Arnell closed the door just in case James decided to test the doorbell.

"Didn't you hear me banging and screaming out there?" James looked suspiciously around the dark room. The blinds and curtains in the living room were drawn tight. "Were you still in bed?"

Arnell's reply was a wide-mouthed yawn. She quickly covered her mouth with her hand and got an unexpected, unpleasant whiff of her own foul morning breath. She headed straight for the bathroom.

"Where are you going?" James was right on Arnell's heels.

"Do you mind if I go to the bathroom?"

"I need to talk to you."

"James, whatever you have to say can wait five minutes."

"Why are you talking to me like this? Are you angry with me for some reason?"

Arnell stopped walking but she kept her back to James. She didn't want him to see that she was close to tearing. "James, I may look awake, but believe me, I am the walking dead. At this moment, I can only handle one or two very mundane chores, and those are peeing and brushing my teeth."

James still tried to follow Arnell into the bathroom. "Damn. What did you do last night?"

She ignored James's question. Just inside the bathroom, Arnell abruptly turned on him. "I *can* do this alone."

"It's not like I haven't seen you sit on the toilet before."

Arnell snipped, "Like that's something to boast about."

James leveled a perplexed look on Arnell.

"I'm sorry, but I am not feeling too well right now."

"Which is why I asked, what's wrong?"

Huffing her impatience and annoyance, Arnell put her hand on the door to close it. "Can we talk when I get out of the bathroom—please?"

"Fine, fine." James stepped back so that Arnell could close the door.

Inside, Arnell fell back against the door. She could slap her own face for answering James's knock. She should have just pretended that she wasn't home. She was in no condition to deal with him. It wasn't fair to him that she was in such a foul mood. He didn't deserve to be treated so irritably, not to mention deceptively.

James tapped softly on the door. "What happened to you last night? "

Arnell dropped her chin to her chest. *Please leave me alone.*

"Arnell, did you hear me?" James tapped at the door again. "I came by like *we* planned. I waited for you for quite a while. Where were you?"

"James, I left you a message that I stayed with my mother later than I intended and then, I guess, we must have passed each other on the road."

"I called your mother. She said you'd left soon after she and I spoke. It wasn't that late, Arnell."

With the bathroom door still between them, Arnell clinched her jaw and her fists. *Damn Esther!* If Arnell didn't know better, which she did, she'd swear that Esther was trying to ruin any chance she'd ever have at happiness.

"Look, James, I was exhausted. I would not have been good company."

"Is that what we are to each other? Company?"

"I just meant that I would have bored you."

"Baby, we wouldn't be getting married if either one of us bored the other."

Arnell felt terrible. What James said was true. There were times when they just sat and read books with no music, no television, no words spoken, yet, it was as if their sheer silence and an occasional glance was all the communication they needed.

"I worried about you all night," James said. "Why didn't you call me when you got home?"

Arnell went to the sink and turned on the water. She and James were great together, but he was acting like he was already her husband—demanding that she account for every minute she wasn't in his sight. God, he'd lose his mind if he ever found out what she had done last night and what had been done to her.

James hit the door hard. "Damn it, Arnell! Will you answer me?"

Arnell turned the cold water on full force. With her hands cupped, she splashed handfuls of cold water on her face.

"Fine!" James tramped away from the door into the living room. He flipped on the light switch. He gawked at the mess on the coffee table. "Damn! Did you have a party last night?"

Even with the water running, Arnell could hear James's question. No doubt he had seen the mess she'd made. *What the hell.* Taking her time, Arnell dried her face and brushed her teeth. She thought she had to use the toilet but didn't. Her hair looked a mess, but she didn't really care. It was time to face James and looking good was the least of her concerns. Arnell took a deep breath and exhaled a belch. Boy, was she going to pay for eating all of that junk. She felt like she was stuffed up to her nose. After James left, she'd take a laxative, but for now, she patted her full stomach as she left the bathroom.

James was still staring at the mess on the living room table.

"No party," she said, "just me being a pig."

"I know it's not your time of the month, so you couldn't have eaten all this junk because of hormones."

"Oh, you know that, do you?" Usually, it didn't bother her that James knew her cycle better than she did. At that moment it did. After all this time, it was still strange to be with a man who was not just about screwing her and going on about his business. James stayed with her even when she doubled over from the cramps that came with her period, and he never balked about having to run out to get a bottle of Midol or a bottle of Motrin, whichever she had need of and was out of. Yes, James was a special man—the kind Arnell thought would never cross her path.

The first time they were together James didn't get out of the bed to leave minutes after he'd shot his wad. For quite a while he'd lain in bed holding her, kissing her, whispering sweet nothings into her ear until his whisperings became light snoring. Throughout the night she kept waking to see if he was still there. He was, and the next morning he had breakfast with her. She had never had that kind of relationship before, which meant that she'd never had a man make love to her and care whether she'd been satisfied or not. It had been obvious that James had held back until she was ready to climax with him and, oh boy, did she ever. It was an orgasmic awakening for her. She had gripped James with every ounce of her being, not wanting to let him pull out of her. She soon learned that her orgasm was as intensely emotional as it was physical. She was in love with James. That's all there was to it, and now with Esther holding her past over her head, she could lose him.

"Arnell, are you going to talk to me or not?"

She began snatching the garbage from the table.

"Don't play this goddamn game with me, Arnell. Something's wrong. It's evident by your nasty attitude and it's, for damn sure, written all over your face. You look terrible."

That comment didn't bother Arnell in the least. "Yeah, well, I'm not posing for pictures today." She took the garbage to the wastebasket in the kitchen and dumped it before she thought to take the spoon out of the empty ice-cream container. She quickly retrieved the spoon and flung it into the sink. It clanked loudly. She turned to leave the kitchen and bumped right into James.

He put his arms around her. "Baby, talk to me."

She tried to pull away. James held her fast.

"James, I'm trying to clean up."

"It can wait."

"No it can't. I—"

"Cut the crap, Arnell. Something happened last night and I—"

Arnell abruptly pulled herself free of James's hold. She was too scared to give herself up. "James, you're trying to make something out of nothing. Nothing happened last night. So I had a vicious sweet tooth, so what? I'm entitled—I am a woman, and that's not to say that I have a problem. I just felt like eating pure, sugar-laden, heart-clogging junk. That's my prerogative." Arnell's lies were making her just as queasy as the case of indigestion she had. She went back into the living room. She flopped down on the sofa.

"Okay, fine, so nothing's wrong? Then why do I feel like you went out of your way to avoid me last night."

Arnell lowered her eyes.

James sat in the armchair across from Arnell. "Baby, our evenings together are too few and far between as it is for—"

"That's not my fault, James. You're the one that's so damn busy. I'm always here. I work from home, remember?"

"That may be true, but you know what my schedule is like. The City Council has stepped up its meetings on the Brooklyn Navy Yard referendum. We're trying to stop the mayor from using the yard as a waste disposal site. We're hoping to get condominiums built down there. The meetings have been exhausting. Baby, I am wiped out by the time—"

"So, this is why I figured that you could use this weekend to get some rest. In fact, maybe we should postpone dinner tomorrow."

"Nope," James said, shaking his head. "I'm looking forward to having dinner with your mother. Baby, it's so rare that I get to see my future mother-in-law. We need to get to know each other. Plus, I get to meet that Italian lover of hers you've told me about."

Damn! He's not giving me any kind of break. "Fine, but don't blame me when you need toothpicks to prop your eyes open at your next council meeting."

"Baby, my position on the City Council is an important job—I won't be falling asleep. This job is an important step for me—for us, Arnell. The time I'm putting in now is insurance—"

"Yes, I know—toward our future. James, you've told me a million times."

"Then you should know that our time together—"

"Look, last night couldn't be helped, okay?"

"And why not? Did something happen that—"

Arnell suddenly rose to her feet. "Will you please stop interrogating me and leave me the hell alone. I—"

"Hey!" James shouted. "Why are you talking to me like this? What's going on?"

Arnell stared blankly at James. She tried to tell herself to calm down. She was messing up big time.

James glared at her. "I have not raised my voice or disrespected you."

No he hadn't, but Arnell couldn't take another minute of his inquisition. *God, what am I supposed to do?* Arnell began to rub the tenseness out of her forehead.

"Arnell." James leaned forward in his chair. "I was worried about you last night. If you have a problem with that, sue me, because I will worry about you when I can't reach you."

Arnell stood mute. *I can't keep living this lie.*

"I know you think I'm checking up on you, but you're wrong. I had reason to worry. I called Sharise—she hadn't heard from you . . . "

Arnell fixed her eyes on James's mouth. She watched his teeth appear and disappear behind his lips as he spoke.

". . . You weren't at your mother's like you said. You ignored my calls. Are you seeing someone else? Is that it?"

"Of course not!" She could not pull her eyes from James's mouth. "I don't want anyone else." Arnell's own lips quivered. That was the truth. She wasn't seeing Woodruff Parker—he was business. "You don't trust me?"

"Baby, we're getting married next year. I think by now we're supposed to be trusting each other."

Arnell sank slowly back onto the sofa. She felt lousy. She didn't deserve James, and if he didn't stop talking, she feared she would blab everything right then and there, but then a bolt of realization. Telling James the truth without Esther being present wouldn't carry as much weight if Arnell couldn't see the look of defeat in Esther's eyes.

"Arnell, you shouldn't be afraid to tell me what's bothering you."

"I am not afraid." *I am petrified.* "I just have nothing to tell."

James threw up his arms. "I'm done. I guess I'm just reading you wrong, or maybe I'm just stupid."

"Would you please stop browbeating me?" She was sick to her stomach with this conversation. "You want to know what's wrong? I'll tell you. I'm sick and tired of the third degree."

"That's obvious," James said drily. "The question is why?"

Arnell again stood. "Damn it, James! You're acting like I committed a crime. So what. I didn't see you last night. Big deal! It was not an act of treason, nor was it a sin against God Almighty. Geez, let it go. Stop haranguing me."

James slumped back and crossed his legs. He looked away.

Arnell felt like an emotional yo-yo—angry, unworthy, remorseful, bitter, then angry again. Now she was back to being remorseful. She knew she had hurt James's feelings. She went to him.

"I'm sorry."

He still wouldn't look at her.

"Can we get past this?" she asked. "Last night was my fault. I admit that. I am really sorry."

Reluctant to accept her apology, James said nothing. He and Arnell locked eyes. He saw the tears beading up in her eyes. She saw the hurt in his eyes. *Dear Lord, please don't let me lose this man.*

Arnell lowered herself to her knees in front of James. He uncrossed his legs. Arnell eased up between his thighs. She slipped her arms around his waist and lay her head on James's chest. She closed her eyes and nestled against James as he wrapped his strong arms around her.

"We're okay, aren't we?" James asked.

James was breaking her heart. She had already broken his, he just hadn't felt it yet.

"Arnell, you'd tell me if we weren't okay, wouldn't you?"

The word *yes* caught in Arnell's throat. A yes would have perpetuated the lie. In hindsight, she had never been fair to James. She had robbed him of his choices the moment they met. He had a right to decide if he wanted to be in a relationship with a woman like her. He had a right to know who he was really marrying, and he should have known this before either one of them was emotionally invested. Now she dreaded the look of disgust that would surely replace the look of concern, of love, in his eyes. Yet, Arnell saw no other way out. She was going to have to tell. It was the only way to free herself of Esther's control. As long as she kept the lie going, Esther was going to keep calling her back. The truth had to be told.

"Arnell, baby—"

"I love the way you feel," she said.

"Mmm," James said, moving his hands sensually up and down Arnell's back. "You feel mighty good yourself."

Lifting her head, Arnell raised up to touch James's lips. They kissed deep and long, their passion for each other instantly magnetic. She let James help her up off the floor. She let him take her hand and lead her into her bedroom. While Arnell's mind wouldn't let her forget that another man had touched her last night, she told herself that making love to James was far removed from that incident and that bastard of a man. But the truth was, this might be her last chance to make love to James without him looking at her like she was a tramp, because tomorrow at dinner, she was going to tell him the truth in front of Esther. Tomorrow was going to be the start of a new life. The question was, was James going to be a part of it?

Fifteen

The late afternoon sun nearly blinded Arnell as she climbed out of James's car in front of Fiorentino's Ristorante. She had forgotten her sunglasses, but not her engagement ring—it weighed heavily on her finger as she walked into the restaurant on James's arm. She felt like she was walking the plank. Following behind the maitre d' Arnell said a silent prayer—*Lord, give me the strength to get through this*. Right away she saw that her prayer wasn't strong enough. Esther was wearing a low-cut, cleavage-revealing pale pink blouse that was far from classy. Tony was sitting back from the table as usual because his rather large belly wouldn't allow him to get closer. Esther and Tony both were sipping wine.

"Well, it's about time," Esther said. "I gave you two up for lost."

The maitre d' placed two menus on the table and walked away.

"Mrs. Rayford, good to see you again," James said.

"Yes, James, it's good to finally see you again."

Tony stood—all five foot ten, two hundred and thirty-five pounds of him. He opened his arms and Arnell stepped into his familiar embrace. She kissed him on the cheek. He kissed her back—on both cheeks.

"How's my girl?" Tony asked.

"I'm fine." Arnell stepped out of his arms. "Tony DiAngelo, this is my fiancé, James Stanton, whom you would have met six months ago if you had made it to my engagement party."

"Arnell, *il mio amore*—my love—you know I would have made it if I could have. My business stranded me in Italy longer than I expected."

"*Le scuse*—excuses," Arnell teased, knowing that the truth was that Tony's wife had gone to Italy with him and made him stay with her family longer than he wanted to.

"Arnell," James said, "did you just speak Italian?"

"Of course she did," Tony answered for Arnell. "Arnell speaks fluent Italian."

"Really? I didn't know." James looked questioningly at Arnell.

"It's no big deal," Arnell said, realizing she had never told James she spoke Italian. It was a subject that had never worked its way into their conversations.

Esther smiled a secret little smile to herself.

"Sure it is," Tony said. "To speak Italian well when you're not Italian, *è una cosa grande*—is a big thing. I'm very proud of Arnell. I taught her well."

"Yes, you did," Arnell agreed. "The language courses alone would not have been as authentic, but moving on, James Stanton, Tony DiAngelo."

Tony extended his hand. "Glad to finally meet the man that won Arnell's heart."

James took Tony's hand. "It's a pleasure to meet you too, sir. Arnell speaks very fondly of you."

Arnell sat in the chair she had been standing behind, which happened to be next to Esther. "Mother."

"Hi, sweetie. You okay?"

Arnell gave Esther a *What do you think?* look.

"Why didn't you return my calls?" Esther asked in a low voice.

"Need you ask?" She cut her eyes away from Esther and looked at James. Tony was still holding onto James's hand.

"I love Arnell like she's my own. James, I trust that you'll take good care of her."

Arnell could see James sucking in his breath. Tony was crushing James's fingers into each other. While Esther smiled, Arnell shook her head. Tony was such a bully. She had known he was going to do this even before he did it. He had done it with the only other man—Calvin—she had introduced him to. She hadn't warned James because the truth was, she got a sick little kick out of Tony's obvious challenge of strength and character in a man. Being Italian, Tony said it was a tradition in his family that every man brought into his family be challenged by the man of the household to see if he had *le palle*—balls. If a man made a noise or commented about the vise-like grip that assaulted him, then he was *un ragazzo di pasta*—a dough boy. If he kept his mouth shut and challenged back, then he was a man worthy of the woman he courted. Some time ago, Calvin, Arnell's date, had grimaced and made a grunting sound. He did not challenge Tony, perhaps because the assault was so sudden, there was no time to fight back before his poor hand was crushed. Even if Calvin had been able to present some sort of attempt at a challenge, he probably would not have won. Tony was sixty-four years old, but in his day, for twenty years, he had been a national arm wrestling champ. His grip and his arms were still powerful.

At first alarmed, James had indeed sucked in his breath, but he quickly tightened his grip on Tony's hand and squeezed back. He set his jaw and locked eyes with Tony, who was shorter by four inches and outweighed James by at least fifty pounds, but James's strength was more than equal. He hadn't been pumping iron three days a week for the last five years for nothing. He and Tony both clamped their teeth behind lips that smiled falsely.

"Okay, boys," Esther said. "It's a draw. Can we get this dinner started?"

Until Tony let up, James wouldn't.

"Tony, you're upsetting me." Esther sipped on her wine.

Letting up, Tony cracked a smile. *"Buon uomo*—good man." He gave James a hearty slap on the back. "Arnell, I like your young man. *Ha cuore*—he has heart. *Ha delle palle forti*—he has strong balls."

James looked puzzled.

"He says that you're a good man and that you have heart," Arnell translated with discretion, although it mattered not to her whether Tony liked James or vice versa. It was too late.

Smiling, Tony winked at Arnell.

"Thank you," James said.

Tony sat. "James, you're marrying a princess."

"That, I know," James said smoothly as he eased his sore hand under the table and began to slowly flex it to get the blood flowing and to stretch out the pain in his bones.

"Now that we all love each other," Esther said, "can we please get the waiter over here before I faint? It's been hours since I ate anything."

Arnell picked up her menu. "If you were so hungry, Mother, you should have asked for the bread basket."

"I could have, but it's not very good manners to eat before all the dinner guests are seated. I thought I taught you that. Where is that waiter?"

Arnell dropped her menu back onto the table. She looked at James. He didn't seem to be fazed. He knew how contentious Esther was, she had told him so. She had also told him that their relationship was not the typical mother/daughter relationship, that they had their problems and, specifically, that Esther could be a bitch. But it didn't make Arnell feel any better that James was seeing Esther in action.

"Esther, be an angel," Tony said. "Let's just have a nice evening. You wouldn't want Arnell's young man to get the wrong impression, would you?"

"James, am I offending you?"

"Not at all."

"See, Tony, I don't know what you're talking about."

"Esther—"

"Tony, don't waste your breath," Arnell said, annoyed. "We both know what she's doing."

"What am I doing?" Esther asked, feigning ignorance. "James, they're ganging up on me when . . ."

Arnell sighed impatiently.

". . . they know I hate to be kept waiting. Especially when I'm hungry." Esther lay her hand gently on Arnell's shoulder. "I'm sorry if I'm embarrassing you, sweetie."

Arnell leaned into Esther. She lowered her voice. "Stop it."

"What?" Esther asked, this time feigning innocence.

Arnell wanted to scream, *Stop acting like you have to have all of the attention.*

James could see that Arnell was upset, but he found the banter between her and Esther amusing. He wanted to laugh but stifled the urge. He cleared his throat.

"Sweetie, you have no sense of humor. I was teasing you. You are always so serious. Isn't she, Tony?"

"Esther, you know that Arnell has always been a very serious young lady. I can remember when she was in her early twenties and she got her first car."

Esther smiled. "Now, that was a scream."

"Tony, please," Arnell said, "do not tell that story."

Tony rubbed his fingertips with his thumb. *"Il mio silenzio non viene economico*—my silence doesn't come cheap."

Arnell smiled in spite of herself. Tony had a way of making her smile. That was his special talent from the moment he became Esther's special friend. Tony came into their life three months after Esther opened the mansion for business. That was twelve years ago. After meeting Esther, Tony didn't want the young girls she offered him. Thankfully, he didn't even want Esther's daughter. It was Esther that turned Tony on. At the time, Esther was fifty years old, had a body that rivaled any young woman, and when she worked her magic, Tony was a goner. Their first night together was a marathon of sex and God knew what else. Tony ended up spending the night, which was against Esther's own rules. Tony paid well that night and would pay well this night. Except now, neither he nor Esther viewed the money as payment, but a gift. Either way, money was never an issue for Tony—he owned a very profitable floor and wall tile business. Contractors and homeowners came from all over the tristate area to buy from him. No, Tony wasn't hurting for cash. He was able to take care of Esther just as well as he took care of his wife and his five grandchildren. His three children were all in their forties. His eldest son was his partner.

"I'd like to hear about Arnell getting her first car," James said. "Especially if it's funny."

"Good, because Arnell was a hoot."

"Traitor," Arnell said to James.

"Tell it, Tony," Esther encouraged.

"James, I took Arnell to pick out her new car. See, I have a friend who has a Honda dealership so I knew we could get a good deal. Well, Arnell picks out this silver Camry. Hot little number. My friend tells Arnell that she should take the car for a test drive. Now, I noticed that Arnell was a little nervous. I didn't think much of it. It was her first car. I figured she was a little excited, you know, a little nervous. She only just got her driver's license a few months before."

Arnell dropped her head forward. She realized she would never ever live down that day.

Esther prompted, "Get to the good part, Tony."

"Okay . . . okay. James, you gotta picture this," Tony said, beginning to talk with his hands. "Arnell is driving. She's nervous. She's gripping the steering wheel with both hands so tight, her knuckles are sticking out. You ever see a little old man or a little old woman behind the wheel of a big car?"

Smiling broadly, James had been listening intently. "Yeah, they drive hunched over the steering wheel."

"Exactly. They have this stern look on their faces yet they look like they're about to kiss the wheel."

"Thanks a lot, Tony," Arnell said. "It was the first time I had ever driven in rush hour traffic."

"Rush hour? Arnell, it was two in the afternoon."

James laughed.

"Go on, Tony, finish the story," Esther prompted again.

"Well, we're driving, real slow mind you, down Fourth Avenue in Bay Ridge. *Real slow.* Other drivers were blowing their horns at Arnell to get out of their way. I'm trying to get Arnell to put her foot in the floor and she finally gets the car up to about thirty, when a couple of cop cars come roaring up our ass. Arnell panics. She speeds up. I tell her to pull over. She screams, 'I can't! I can't!' Everyone is pulling over, except for Arnell. She's about to cause an accident. A cop car is on her ass, pushing her. She's screaming, the cop car is screaming, hell, I'm screaming. I think my ass is about to be split in two."

Tony starts laughing. Esther is chuckling. James is cracking up.

Although she is embarrassed, Arnell is snickering softly behind her hand.

Catching his breath, Tony continues. "This cop shouts at Arnell on his PA system. 'Pull over! Pull over, now!' Arnell really starts screaming then. She jams her foot into the brake. The car fishtails before it screeches to a halt, narrowly missing about ten other cars."

"Tony, stop lying. It was not ten cars."

"You're right—it was nine." Tony howled.

Esther and James both laughed.

"I know who my friends are not," Arnell said, trying to not laugh herself, but failing. She went with it. It felt good to be laughing.

Again, Tony had to catch his breath. "Get this, James. The cops were on their way to an emergency. The second car forgets about the emergency and screeches to a halt next to us. These two cops, mad as hell, jump out of their car with their guns drawn, shouting at Arnell, and me, to get out of the car. One is pulling on Arnell's door, which is locked. Arnell is . . ."

"Still screaming," Esther said, laughing. Tears were streaming down her face.

". . . still screaming." Tony wiped at his own eyes. "When I release the lock so that the cop could open the door, Arnell screams, 'I didn't steal this car! I'm not in the mob! He is!'"

Esther doubled over with laughter. Tony laughed so hard he began coughing.

Remembering the whole fiasco, Arnell laughed pretty hard herself. At the time she couldn't laugh, she had been scared out of her mind. The police made her and Tony raise their arms above their heads and stand spread-eagle. They were patted down and questioned right out there on Fourth Avenue in broad daylight. It was truly an embarrassing situation.

"Oh, no she didn't," James said, laughing. "Don't tell me she thought the cops were after her because you were Italian."

Nodding, Tony kept coughing and laughing. He tried to drink some water.

"Arnell thought Tony's friend was a mob connection," Esther explained.

"Hey," Arnell said, "I was young. I didn't know. I had just seen *The Godfather*."

"Yeah, that Italian classic," James quipped.

"We're all in the mob, right?" Tony chuckled. "Arnell thought the cops were on to us. It took me damn near twenty minutes to explain that Arnell was a new driver and that she was out test driving her new car."

"Did they give her a summons or threaten to pull her in for failure to yield?" James asked.

Tony waved his hand. "Naw. They were my *fratelli*."

"Brothers," Arnell translated for James before he asked.

"Oh, shit," James said, laughing.

"Hey, we look out for each other."

"Yeah, that Italian thing," Arnell said, feeling somewhat vindicated. "That's why I panicked. I don't look Italian."

"No, Arnell," Tony said, disagreeing. "You panicked because those cops had you driving like a bat out of hell and you thought that car was going to take flight and leave earth. I think you aged ten years in two minutes that day. I don't think you drove that car for a month after that."

"Two months," Esther corrected, smiling at Arnell.

"Even then it took a while before I could hear a siren without my heart pounding. But, hey, at least we get a good laugh out of it every now and then." And indeed, to Arnell, it felt good to laugh again.

Sixteen

Tony and James were still laughing when the waiter appeared.

"Before we order," Tony said. "*Porti un'altra bottiglia di* chianti—bring another bottle of chianti," Tony said. "James, what are you drinking?"

"Does anyone care that I'm hungry?" Esther asked.

Arnell's heart sank. The moment of laughter and frivolous chatter was gone.

"Ma'am, I could bring you the bread basket."

"That would be *really* nice."

Arnell closed her eyes. If only she could twitch her nose and disappear.

After looking at Arnell, James ordered, "Two white zinfandels."

"*Porti la bottiglia*—bring the bottle." Tony said.

"Right away, sir. And, ma'am, I'll bring that bread immediately."

"Thank you." But then Esther mumbled, "Someone seems to care."

Arnell cut her eyes at Esther. "Why are you so petty?"

Esther smirked. "People do say that we are very much alike, sweetie."

"In your dreams."

"*Signore*—ladies," Tony said, "Let's play nice."

Arnell felt like she was being wrongly chastised. She pouted. James began to rub Arnell's back in a slow circular motion.

Arnell stilled her tongue. She folded her arms and looked across the room.

Esther sipped her wine.

"Mrs. Rayford—"

"James, we're not strangers. It's Esther, dear, or I won't speak to you anymore."

Closing her eyes briefly, Arnell knew she was not going to make it through dinner. She had to put an end to the phoniness. "Wouldn't you rather he called you Queen Esther, Mother?"

Esther leveled a reproachful look at Arnell. "Esther will do just fine."

James glanced at Tony. Tony nodded, giving his approval, so James looked again at Esther. "Esther, Arnell and I sat out in the car talking for a minute. I apologize for keeping you waiting."

Arnell could feel her blood pressure rise. "Don't apologize to her. We were on time."

"Perhaps, sweetie, but we did wait twenty minutes."

"Esther, let it go," Tony advised. "You really can't fault others for making you wait if you come early."

"Fine." Esther mimed zipping her lips.

Arnell shook her head. Esther was always difficult, but tonight, she was worse than ever. It was like she was challenging her as Tony had challenged James.

James was determined to be the peacemaker. "Tony, I must say, waiting becomes Esther. She looks great. She must have had Arnell when she was a teenager."

Smiling, Esther lifted her glass to James, but it was Arnell she spoke to. "Sweetie, if you weren't my daughter, I'd steal this handsome, charming young man from you."

"Excuse me, Mother, but I believe I'd have something to say about that, and so would Tony."

"Oh, Arnell, lighten up. Tony's not a stuffy old prude like you. Are you, Tony?"

"I've never been accused of being a prude, though I have been accused of being naughty." He winked at Esther.

Esther blew Tony a kiss. "James, I hope you're not an old stick in the mud like Arnell. You weren't offended by what I said, were you?"

Under the table, James nudged Arnell on the thigh. "Esther, I like your style. If Arnell wasn't your daughter, and Tony wasn't such a big, strong man, I just might let you steal me."

Arnell sucked her teeth hard. Now she wanted to slap James.

Esther giggled. "Oh, James, you're just as naughty as Tony."

Smiling, Tony drank a hearty swig of wine.

Again, James nudged Arnell. He smiled at her and Esther both.

James's nudging told Arnell that he believed he was winning Esther over, but she was disgusted all the same. Their flirting was nauseating her. She hated the stupid grin on James's face. She hated that he was taken in by Esther's obvious flirting, or if he wasn't, that he had to play Esther's game to impress her. But Arnell wasn't stupid. She knew that Esther wasn't playing the game James thought she was—a little tease, a little taunt. Esther was playing the "fuck with Arnell game." The object—to break her will. Esther was the innovator and creator of that game. The flirting, however, was new to the game. Never had Esther been this blatant before with any of her few male friends, but then again, she had never been engaged before.

"Tony, maybe you and I should leave these two to eat alone," Arnell said.

"Arnell, what I tell you about life?"

She hoped that her blank, disinterested look told Tony she didn't know or care which little pearl he was referring to.

"If you keep taking people and life so seriously, you will end up having a heart attack on a merry-go-round."

Arnell smirked. "Maybe the merry-go-round I'm on has runaway horses that can't be reined in."

"Sweetie, all horses can, eventually, be reined in," Esther said, winking at James.

Arnell had had enough. "James, I'm leaving."

"Baby, your mother is only playing with you," James said.

"You're too serious, Arnell," Tony said.

Esther again lay her hand on Arnell's arm. "Don't be silly, sweetie. Dinner wouldn't be any fun and certainly the food won't taste good without you."

"Well, Mother," Arnell said, brushing Esther's hand off her arm as if she were brushing off an annoying fly, "you have so much sugar on your tongue you won't be able to appreciate the taste of the food anyway."

Esther brought her hand to her chest. "My, but I do think that my baby girl is a wee bit jealous." She winked at Tony.

Tony simply shook his head. "James, I'm use to these two going at it. I've learned to stand back out of the line of fire."

"I can see why." James opened his menu. "Where are those drinks?"

Arnell wanted—no, needed—to wipe the smirk off of Esther's face. "Mother, since I'm getting ready to marry James, shouldn't he know everything about our family business?"

James was only half listening, he was studying the menu.

"Everything like what, sweetie?" Esther glanced at Tony and back at Arnell. A knowing little smile crept onto her lips.

"Oh, you know, Mother. I think James should—"

The waiter appeared. He set a basket of steaming-hot, sliced garlic bread on the table. "Are you ready to order?"

"*Avrò mio usuale*—I'll have my usual," Tony said, not wasting time on the menu.

James and Tony both took a piece of buttery garlic bread.

Esther didn't even glance at the bread. She was looking at Arnell.

A wineglass was placed in front of Arnell. While the waiter set James's glass in front of him and began working at uncorking the bottle of zinfandel, Arnell locked eyes with Esther. Not surprising, there was a devilish glint in Esther's eyes and a mischievous smirk on her lips. Arnell knew that look well. When she was a little girl, Esther taught her how to play poker. For the longest time, Esther always beat her because Arnell could not read the look on Esther's face. After losing more times than she could keep count of, Arnell learned that an easy little smile meant that Esther had an okay hand, while a mischievous smirk along with a devilish glint meant that Esther had a fabulous hand, that she was holding all the right cards. And that's what Esther thought she had now—all the right cards. Normally, Arnell would have tossed in her hand. Not this time. There was too much at stake. Besides, she had learned a thing or two about poker herself.

The waiter filled Arnell and James's glasses with the caramel-colored wine.

James tasted his wine. It was good. "I'm ready to order," he said, studying his menu. "You ladies ready? I'm thinking about having the veal scaloppine."

Esther never opened her menu. She continued looking at Arnell. "Veal sounds good. I'll start with the melon prosciutto and then I'll have the veal parmesan with spaghetti. Go light on the sauce. What about you, sweetie? You love veal parmesan. But, waiter, tell the chef to go light on the cheese. My daughter can take just so much cheese. Isn't that right, sweetie?"

Esther's audacity amazed Arnell. This was a high-stakes game and Esther was daring Arnell to trump her.

The waiter held his pen ready to continue writing.

"Arnell, are you having the veal parmesan?" James asked.

She dragged her eyes off Esther. The waiter was looking at her, and so were James and Tony.

Esther solicitously lay her hand on Arnell's hand. "Are you all right, sweetie?"

There it was again. That creepy feeling she got whenever Esther touched her. Arnell pulled her hand away. "I hate it when you call yourself humoring me."

"Sweetie, I'm not doing any such thing. Boy, are you sensitive."

In that instant, Arnell made up her mind to do what she had come there to do. She eased her hand from under Esther's.

"Waiter, I will not be having the veal parmesan. In fact, I won't be ordering."

"What?" James closed his menu. "You're not eating?"

"Arnell," Tony said, "*guardarme*—look at me."

She did because Tony's face was the only face that she could look into and not be afraid.

"*Non lei me fida di, fa lei*—you trust me, don't you?"

Arnell didn't know where Tony was trying to take her but she did not want to be led away from what she was about to do. She didn't answer him.

Quietly, Esther sat back. She crossed her legs and folded her hands neatly in her lap.

"You do trust me, don't you?" Tony asked.

Finally, "Yeah. And?"

"You know there is nothing I wouldn't do for you."

"I know that, Tony. So what are you trying to say?"

The waiter cleared his throat.

It was Tony that the waiter was looking at. It was Tony who said, "*Lo chiameremo quando siamo pronti*—we'll call you when we're ready."

The waiter immediately walked off.

"What's going on?" James asked.

Tony took Arnell's hand. "You're like my own daughter, *il mio sangue*—my blood. You know that I will take care of anything or anyone that causes you unhappiness."

"Arnell, has someone done something to you?" James asked. "Is this about Friday night?"

It was as if James hadn't spoken. Tony held Arnell's gaze. "I know what happened. I'm sorry."

Arnell teared.

"What happened?" James asked, clearly frustrated. No one was answering him.

Esther busied herself with folding her napkin.

"I've never let you down before, have I?"

Arnell barely shook her head.

"Well, then. Trust me. Everything is going to be just fine—in three weeks when that problem comes back to town. I promise you."

"Okay," James said, looking at Tony. "I feel like an outsider here. Arnell, what is this about?"

She finally looked at James. "Actually, James, something quite ugly happened to me."

Esther cleared her throat. "I don't think you should speak about this."

"I don't care what you think. James, I have to tell you something."

"I'm listening, baby."

"Sweetie, I know you're upset, but—"

"Sweetie! Baby! Don't you people know my damn name? I'm a grown woman. For God sake, call me by my damn name!"

James was dumbstruck.

Outwardly, Esther was cool—it was her mind that was frantically searching for a way to stop Arnell.

Diners around Arnell were looking at her, talking about her. As angry as she was, she had enough sense to be embarrassed by her big mouth.

Tony gulped down his wine, emptying his glass. He glanced over Arnell's shoulder at the couple sitting with their two young sons at the next table. They had overheard Arnell and were looking at her. The woman was frowning disapprovingly, the kids looked just as shell-shocked as James, but the man never stopped eating. Tony liked that—this was not a man's argument. He looked at Esther. Her eyes looked pained. She had her hand over her heart. She was pressing her fingers into her skin, trying to massage her heart.

"Esther, are you all right?"

"How can I be all right? My daughter hates me."

"No, she doesn't. Arnell, you don't hate your mother, do you?"

"Tony, I can't do this anymore."

"Do what?" James asked.

Again, Tony ignored James. "Arnell, let me talk to you in private."

"No, Tony, this has to be done here, out in public. Oh"—she chuckled dryly—"Tony, this is too funny. You're the one that told me that 'things done in the dark will come out in the light.'"

"Yes, but—"

"Don't . . . waste . . . your breath, Tony," Esther said, sounding out of breath. "Let Arnell . . . ruin her . . . life if . . . if—"

"I think you did that when I was sixteen. Mother, do you have any remorse for what you've done to me?"

Esther began to slowly knead the left side of her chest.

James slapped the table. "I'm two seconds from walking out of this restaurant."

"Esther"—Tony was gently patting Esther's hand—"here, drink some water." He held the glass to Esther's lips. Esther did not drink.

"Well, James, " Arnell looked at Esther. She saw how Esther was beginning to take long, labored breaths.

James's attention was divided between Esther and Arnell. He didn't know what was going on, he just knew that he didn't like it.

"This is about who I am," Arnell explained. "It's about the lie I've lived all my adult life. If we are to have a future—"

"Wait a minute, Arnell," James said. "Your mother looks pretty ill."

Esther's eyes closed. Her breathing became labored gasps, alarming Tony. "Esther, are you all right?" He got up and gestured to the waiter to come.

James also rose from his chair.

Esther's arms dropped and dangled at her side. "I . . . pain." Grimacing, Esther dropped her head back.

Arnell flipped her hand. "There's nothing wrong with her. She's faking."

James went to help Tony with Esther. "Arnell, your mother is sick!"

The waiter rushed over.

"*Chiamare 911*—call 911!" Tony ordered.

The waiter rushed off.

Tony began fanning Esther with his hand. "Arnell, check your mother's bag for her medicine."

"What medicine?"

"Arnell, check her bag!" Tony ordered.

"Tony, she's faking. I'm telling you. She's faking."

"Arnell!" James exploded. "Your mother has a bad heart. Look at her!"

Esther's face was contorted into a mask of anguish. Her eyes were closed. Her mouth was open as she gasped for air, but still, Arnell couldn't believe that Esther had a bad heart. It was a manipulative lie. If Esther was sick, she would have told her a thousand times over by now. For one thing, Esther was always scheming for sympathy and a bad heart would have given her a huge leg up. No, this was just Esther manipulating the situation. Esther knew that if she told James about her life, James would leave her and Esther would lose her power over her. That's what this bad acting was all about.

Refusing to be drawn into Esther's game, Arnell watched Tony grab Esther's pocketbook off her lap. "She has both of you fooled."

James held Esther's head up. "Arnell, what's wrong with you? How can you be so cold?" He grabbed the napkin Esther had been folding and shook it out with a pop. He dabbed Esther's forehead with it as Tony began rummaging around inside Esther's pocketbook.

Watching the two of them fuss over Esther, Arnell began to feel less certain that Esther was faking. Esther had broken out in a cold sweat and she couldn't seem to catch her breath. Her face was strained and ashen. Fine veins had popped up around her eyes. Esther looked startlingly old.

"I can't find her pills," Tony announced anxiously. "She was supposed to carry them at all times."

Arnell couldn't believe it. "She really has pills prescribed by a medical doctor?"

"Esther didn't want you worrying about her. She's been keeping her illness from you. She has angina."

"Since when?"

"About a year now, and stressing her out isn't helping."

"But she drinks alcohol. And, Tony, you know she smokes."

"You know your mother, Arnell. She's stubborn. She does what she wants." Tony still rummaged for Esther's medicine. "I can't find a damn thing in this bag."

Arnell shot out of her chair. She grabbed the pocketbook from Tony. Expertly, she went right to the bottom. She swept her hand from one side to the other until she thought she found what Tony had been looking for. She pulled out a small brown plastic bottle with a white cap. She read it—*Nitroglycerine*. Arnell's own heart pulsed hard.

Tony snatched the bottle from Arnell's hand. He poured all of the tiny white pills into his powerful hand. He took one pill and stuck it under Esther's tongue. The rest he poured back into the bottle, dropping a few onto the floor.

A sick feeling slammed Arnell in the pit of her stomach. Could it be true that her mother really had heart trouble? Esther should have told her. But no, Esther had to play games and wait to use it to her advantage. Always, Esther had to have her way.

Arnell was pushed aside as paramedics began working on Esther. Helplessly, she watched as an oxygen mask was strapped onto Esther's face and her blood pressure taken. It was Tony who told the paramedics about Esther's heart condition and that he had given her a nitroglycerine tablet. Esther was laid out on a stretcher and wheeled out of the restaurant. Still unable to move on her own, Arnell was aware that it was Tony and not James that took her by the waist and walked her outside and put her in his car for the ride to the hospital. She didn't know if James was following behind them or not; she hadn't heard a word that had been spoken between he and Tony. She hadn't heard much of anything except the sound of the siren screaming as it rushed her mother to the hospital.

Seventeen

Just as Arnell had suspected, Esther had been faking. The heart specialist gave Esther a thorough exam and deemed her well enough to go home after spending one night in the hospital for observation. He said that she must've been overly excited, to which Esther said, "I was a little upset."

Yeah, right. Arnell watched quietly on the sideline to keep from saying anything to *upset* Esther further, as well as to allay the stern, disapproving looks James and Tony were both giving her. Neither seemed to realize that Esther was acting, and that was because neither one caught the gloatingly sick smile that crept onto Esther's lips when only Arnell was looking at her.

You get that one, Mother. Arnell turned her back on Esther as the nurse checked Esther's vital signs. *Two can play this game.*

In the hospital emergency room Tony became a player also. He urged James to go on home since he had a breakfast meeting with the City Council. James didn't balk at that. He said his good nights and out of earshot of Tony asked, "What the hell happened back at the restaurant? What was that crap that Tony said he'd take care of for you?"

"James—"

"And what the hell is this cryptic shit that's going on between you and your mother?"

Arnell could feel the eyes of onlookers on her. "Would you please lower your voice," she said.

James's eyes widened. "Damn it, Arnell, tell me something!"

Oh, she wanted to tell James more than just something. However, the question was, did she want to stand in a busy corridor in Coney Island Hospital, with the ears and eyes of nosy people on her while she laid the ugliness of her life on the table. *I don't think so!*

"Well!" James said impatiently.

"I'm not a child, James."

"Arnell, don't play with me. I feel like I was a pawn in a game of chess with you and your mother jostling all around me. She was flirting with me while fencing with you. What was that all about?"

"My mother was being her usual, cantankerous old self."

"No, Arnell, there was something more going on between you two. When your mother got sick, you would not lift a finger to help her. How could you be like that?"

"Oh, I don't know, James. I guess I'm just too use to my mother's games," Arnell said, thinking that it was probably best that she hadn't had a chance to expose herself to James. He might not believe that Esther had turned her out.

"Arnell, you only have one mother. You should treat her with more respect."

Arnell could feel her lips tighten. She narrowed her eyes. "I see you've really been suckered in."

"Oh, I see we're not getting anywhere," James said. "Forget about your mother. What about this thing with Tony? Are you in some sort of trouble?"

"No."

"Then what is Tony supposed to take care of for you?"

"What do you want to hear, James, that someone has done me a wrong and that I need Tony to rub that person out? Or that—"

"Damn it, Arnell!" James turned away. He was oblivious to the curious onlookers, but Arnell was not. Nor was she blind to the reproachful look Tony was giving her from the doorway of the room that Esther was in. His frame filled the doorway. Tony was being every bit the doting lover and the hulking bodyguard to Esther.

"James, please, just go on home. I'll tell you everything, just not tonight and not in this place."

Arnell walked away from James, leaving him with unanswered questions and a frown on his face. And from the sour look on Tony's face, he was just as disappointed with her, but Arnell wasn't about to keep her mouth shut about her life with Esther. She was telling James, no matter how much Esther or Tony made her feel like the bad guy.

The bad guy was Esther and she was wallowing in the attention she was getting from both James and Tony. The very next morning, Monday, James sent Esther an expensive floral arrangement, Tony sent a dozen pink roses, and Arnell sent nothing. Esther was discharged from the hospital before the flowers had a chance to fill her room with their fragrance. Home less than twenty minutes, Esther slipped into her grande dame role, which was one minute after Tony left. Arnell slipped out into the kitchen while Esther was in the bathroom.

Melvina left the pot she had been stirring. "Is Queen Esther goin' to be okay?"

"She's fine. When you get a chance, make her a cup of that Red Zinger tea she's so crazy about."

"I already got a pot brewin'. You think her will eat somethin'? I made she my nice thick vegetable soup. I throw in some water chestnuts like her like it."

"It smells good, Melvina, but isn't it a little warm to be making soup?"

"Soup is good all year round. Queen Esther like soup even in hot weather."

That Arnell did know about her mother. "She'll eat. Believe me, I don't think she's sick enough to forego your soup, Melvina. Look, I have to run. When you take her the soup, tell her that I had to leave."

Melvina went back to stirring her pot of soup. "There's plenty soup here for you, too, Arnell. Why you not stay and eat withcha mother?"

"Because I just don't have the stomach for it."

"Do not disrespect your mother, Arnell. Queen Esther a good woman. She done more for me than my own family done did. If it not for Queen Esther, I never woulda got my son in this country. No tellin' what become of he in Jamaica. He could be dead. And . . ."

"I'm glad—"

". . . look at all the girls she help. You lucky child to have such a good mother, Arnell."

"Melvina, it's nice that you feel that my mother has done a world of good for you, but I doubt seriously that pimping young girls is a great help to them. Now, until you've walked in my shoes, you cannot tell me a thing about my mother. What's gone on between my mother and I, I alone can attest to and it isn't pretty. So, if you don't mind, please, don't ever try to sell me on my mother or chide me for disrespecting her. I know my mother better than anyone on earth."

"I know she better than you think." Melvina began to ladle out steaming vegetable soup into a bowl.

Arnell couldn't care less that Melvina might be upset with her—that was her problem. She wasn't telling Melvina that she couldn't appreciate what Esther had done for her, that was between them. Esther was paying Melvina well not just for her cooking talents, but for her silence—Esther demanded that no one speak outside of the mansion about what went on inside. Melvina proved that she was loyal to a fault, not to mention that she spied for Esther and told her everything that went on when she wasn't around. Melvina acted as if Esther was her savior, especially when Esther gave her the apartment over the garage to live in and paid to have Melvina's only son, Hubert, brought over from Jamaica. Esther even vouched for him on his visa and got Tony to give him a job, which really cemented Melvina's devotion to Esther.

"What if Queen Esther ask me where you go?"

"She won't."

"What if she get sick again?"

Arnell stopped at the back door. "Call Tony."

Trena burst into the kitchen. "Melvina, I'm starving! Whatever you're cookin', I want some. It smells awesome."

"Get yaself a bowl, girl," Melvina said. "I glad somebody want to eat my food."

Arnell ignored Melvina's remark as she watched Trena take a bowl off the counter. She had never seen Trena before and was struck by how young she looked. Arnell moved away from the door.

"Mmm." Trena inhaled the aroma of the vegetable soup Melvina was ladling into her bowl. "You got some meat to eat with this vegetable, right?"

"Sure do," Melvina said, removing foil from atop a pan of short ribs of beef drowning in their own oily juices. "These melt in ya mouth, girl."

"Mmm," Trena said again. "I could eat all of them."

"Excuse me," Arnell said, feeling like she had been ignored. Melvina and Trena both looked at her. "Who are you?"

"'Scuse me," Trena said snidely. "I don't know you."

"Trena," Melvina said, "this is Arnell, Queen Esther's daughter."

"Oh." Trena hurriedly set her bowl on the table. "I thought you—"

"Trena," Arnell said, "how old are you?"

"I'm old enough. That's all anybody gots to know."

"Not really." Arnell approached the table. "Trena, if you're younger than eighteen, you cannot be living or working in this house. So, how old are you?"

"I look young, but I am eighteen. Queen Esther don't have no problem with me looking young, she already said I can live here."

"Do you know what goes on here?"

"Yeah, and?" Trena asked with attitude.

Arnell critically scrutinized Trena. Trena had the tight boyish figure of a girl who had yet to lose her virginity—her breasts were small, her hips were slim, the only roundness evident were her cheeks. After Arnell started having sex when she was sixteen, Esther had pointed out how her breasts had filled out, how her hips had gotten rounder, how her face had taken on the look of a woman and not a baby-faced little girl. Esther had to see that Trena was old if she was sixteen. If what went on in the mansion was ever exposed, they would all go to jail, but if it was learned that Esther was pimping out a sixteen-year-old, Esther would have hell to pay.

"My mother must not have gotten a good look at you, Trena. I think I had better have a few words with her."

"What Trena say is true, Arnell," Melvina defended. "Queen Esther say Trena could have Kitt's room. She been here since Saturday night."

"Two days too long," Arnell concluded. "Melvina, this child is not eighteen. If—"

"Arnell, Queen Esther say it be all right."

Fear gripped Trena. Was Arnell going to get her thrown out? "I am eighteen! Queen Esther said I could stay here. You can't make her put me out, I ain't done nothin' to you or nobody." Trena was near tears. "I live here now! I'm stayin'!"

Arnell could hear the desperation in Trena's voice and see the anxiousness in her eyes. "You know something, Trena? This is none of my business. You wanna live here? Fine. Live here. Have a ball. I'm out of here."

"Arnell," Esther stepped into the kitchen, "I was hoping you were still here. I need to talk to you."

Arnell pointed at Trena. "Mother, you know this is wrong."

"What's the problem, Arnell? The girl says she's eighteen. I—"

"And you believe that? You know what? I really can't do this anymore. I won't stay around to witness this little girl's degradation, I've already witnessed my own." Arnell yanked open the door. "By the way," she said, suddenly remembering that Tony said he would take care of Woodruff Parker for raping her, "tell Tony to forget about my little problem from last week. I'll live with it."

"But, Arnell, if you were . . . you know . . . hurt, then we—"

"Do you ever listen to me, Mother? I said, tell Tony to leave it alone." Arnell stormed out.

"Arnell!" Esther rushed to the back door. "Arnell!"

Arnell never turned back. She got in her car and sped away.

"What's her problem?" Trena asked no one in particular. "Sister got issues."

Esther gave Trena a searing look that stilled her tongue. "If you want to stay in my home, I suggest you not say a damn thing against or about my daughter."

Trena glanced at Melvina, but Melvina was busy cutting on a piece of short rib.

"Do you understand me?" Esther asked.

"Yes, ma'am," Trena said just above a whisper. She didn't dare move as Queen Esther left the kitchen. Trena's own mother had given her all kinds of evil, threatening looks and had beaten her, yet she had stood defiant against her; but the look that Queen Esther gave her scared her and weakened her knees.

"Sit, child." Melvina set a plate with short ribs on the table next to the bowl of soup Trena had forgotten about.

"I ain't hungry no more."

Eighteen

Trena was awake. She just hadn't opened her eyes. The bed wouldn't let her. From the first night, six days ago, when she lay on the red satin sheets in the firm but lusciously soft king-size bed, it had embraced her in its cushiony cocoon of comfort and lulled her into a deep sleep like a newborn baby. If she didn't have to, she wouldn't get up at all. Yesterday she had slept well past ten o'clock, and then she had taken a long, relaxing candlelit bubble bath scented with the sweetest smelling rose crystals she had ever smelled—which she had never smelled before. It was the label that told her the crystals were rose scented. By the time she left her room it was one in the afternoon, and that was only because she was hungry.

Trena liked Melvina and Queen Esther, too, when Arnell wasn't around. Thank goodness Arnell hadn't been around. Arnell's nastiness reminded Trena of Cheryl and she didn't need Cheryl's twin on her back in Queen Esther's house. For a hot minute, Trena had been scared when Queen Esther gave her that look, but they were cool now. They talked about a lot of things. They talked about sex and about what a man wanted. None of that was new to Trena, but what was, was the many ways a woman could satisfy a man. The things Queen Esther showed her—how to give a man a good massage, how to wash a man down when he's in the tub, how to tongue a man's body, and how to tongue his penis and his balls—was unbelievable. She had never done any of that stuff with Omar or anyone and now Queen Esther was saying that she could have a man up in her room to try those things on, was just too cool. Man, her mother would have a stroke—big time. Never in a million years would she let her do anything like that. But Queen Esther said, whatever Trena did up in her room with a man was her business but that she had to always act like a lady. No sweat. Trena could handle that because she was a lady and not a kid. It was only Arnell that thought she was sixteen. No one else bothered Trena about how young she looked. Jeanette gave her some makeup and in her room, she experimented with different looks. Nope. She didn't look sixteen anymore. She was a grown-up with her own room in a fabulous mansion.

And her room? It was the bomb. It was big and it was sort of pretty in an old-fashioned kind of way. For sure, the pink, green, and white flowery wallpaper that covered the wall behind the bed and wrapped around on both its sides definitely would not have been Trena's choice, but when she awakened the first morning, surrounded by full-blooming flowers, it sort of grew on her. She found it rather cool.

What Trena liked most about her room—it didn't feel like a bedroom. It felt like a living room. There was a sofa and a coffee table, a thirty-two-inch television, and an entertainment center. It was bad! There were plenty of CDs. Just that there was not one CD she could stomach. They were all old people's music—violins and piano and stuff. She couldn't get with that, but she wasn't about to sweat it. The music was a little thing, besides, there was a radio. The room was the big thing and overall this room was far better than the one she had at home. Not to mention that if she didn't feel like lying in the bed or sitting on the sofa, she could lie on the ultra thick burgundy carpet that her feet sank in. This room was slammin'! And best of all, Queen Esther said it was her room—just take good care of it. That was never going to be a problem, because Trena wanted to stay there forever. If she ever saw her mother and Cheryl again, it would be too soon.

Admittedly, the first morning Trena did feel a little conflicted. On one hand she felt a tiny bit homesick. On the other, she was still so mad at her mother and Cheryl that she could spit fire. She would never forgive her mother for beating up on her and for always taking Cheryl's side. She wasn't about to ever forgive either one of them for throwing out her clothes. Alyson said that her mother was crying a lot. Trena didn't believe that. Her mother didn't act like she was going to miss her when she was threatening to put her away. Alyson had also said that Cheryl, talking all tight-assed, had called her house every day demanding that she tell her where she was. Alyson was her girl. She still hadn't given her up and never would.

The police had her down as a runaway and her mother had taken time off from work to try to find her, but Trena wasn't tripping. Her mother would never find her in Ditmas Park. Brooklyn was a big, wide, spread-out borough and although Bushwick wasn't all that far away, Ditmas Park was like another world. It was an upper-class, mixed-race neighborhood on the far side of Prospect Park. It wasn't a neighborhood that anyone she knew would just happen to walk through, and it was definitely the last place her mother would think to look for her. They may as well get use to it, she was gone for good.

Arching her back, Trena spread her arms wide, and opening her mouth just as wide, she yawned, stretching out her slumbering body, waking it. Her eyes popped open. She had to get up. Jeanette was taking her shopping. The clothes she had taken from home, Queen Esther said weren't sophisticated enough.

"You're a very pretty girl," Queen Esther said. "You should dress like a pretty girl, and not like a hip-hop waif."

At first Trena wasn't about to hear anything about the way she dressed; she had heard enough from her mother, but then Queen Esther had said Jeanette could take her shopping. Now, that, Trena could get with. Jeanette was hot. Last night Jeanette had on a purple leather bustier, and a short black leather skin-tight skirt. Even the ankle-high leather boots were kicking. Hot! Now, if Jeanette was going to buy clothes like that for her, then Trena was game. She was liking Queen Esther more and more. Queen Esther was cool for an old lady. In fact, Queen Esther dressed kind of cool herself—for an old lady. Thursday night, Queen Esther had on a straight, knee-length, red, matte jersey skirt with a scoop-neck, fitted, red sleeveless sweater. Queen Esther was *wearing* that outfit. Queen Esther must have been a "babe" when she was young, because she wasn't bad-looking now—for an old lady. She was even wearing her hair short as a minute and blond as a Barbie. Yeah, Queen Esther was cool, and actually, the old lady was a real diva to call herself Queen Esther. But that was her b . . . i . . . z. No one had a problem with Latifah calling herself Queen, either.

There was a soft tapping at Trena's door.

Trena sprang up off the bed. "One minute!" She flung the covers over the bed and rushed to open the door.

Jeanette looked Trena over. "You planning on wearing your panties and that funky T-shirt to Manhattan?"

"No! I'll be dressed in five minutes." Filled with excitement, Trena ran off to her own private bathroom to wash up.

Nineteen

Sharise was shaking her head. "I don't get it, Arnell. You say you want completely out of the business, yet you let your mother browbeat you into turning one last trick. One of these days, that one last trick is going to be the death of you. You—"

"Sharise," Arnell said, annoyed, "please. You're not telling me anything that I don't already know." *Never mind what has already happened.* "Don't you think I hate myself for allowing my mother to dictate the path of my life? I get sick just opening my eyes every morning knowing that she'll call me. I know I have to get far, far away from her, but—"

"That's just it, Arnell. You should be able to live right next door to your mother and not take her shit or jump whenever she cracks the whip."

"I don't jump every time she—"

"Oh, yes, you do. No matter how pissed off you are with your mother, she calls you, you go running. I'm beginning to wonder about you. Are you scared of your mother?"

"Am I scared of you?"

"I don't know, maybe you are, I just don't know it."

"Sharise, get serious."

"I'm serious, Arnell. I think you're scared of Queen Esther because she got something on you. Does she?"

"I know you're not asking me that question."

"Okay," Sharise said. "I know about James, and I know that he doesn't know about your past, but it's not that deep. I have the same past. You act like there's something more." Sharise popped her fingers. "That's it, isn't it? Your mother is blackmailing you into doing what she wants, isn't she?"

Arnell said nothing—she was too ashamed.

"What else does your mother have on you?"

Sighing heavily, Arnell got up from the window seat. She didn't move away, she just stood looking out the window as the sun began to set on Sharise's beautifully landscaped garden. The winding path of slate-gray cobblestones enhanced the beauty of the array of flowering plants, variegated shrubbery, and trees spaced throughout the large backyard. Sharise had at least an acre of land surrounding her colonial style house, which wasn't too shabby in the shadow of the small mansion across the way.

Sharise stood next to Arnell.

"Your garden gets prettier every year," Arnell said.

Sharise sat on the window seat with her back to the garden. "Arnell, I know you're tired of hearing me bitch about your mother, but I know there's something—"

"What you don't understand, Sharise, is that a lot has gone on between me and my mother. Much of it you know about, but there are things that sicken me to dredge up in my own mind, much less talk about out loud." Tears started to roll down her cheeks.

Sharise took Arnell's left arm and pulled her down to sit next to her. "Arnell, I would never betray—"

"I can *never* talk about it." Arnell looked down at her diamond. Its sparkle was too brilliant, too effervescent, too pure for her hand. She twisted the ring until the diamond was on the underside of her finger.

"That's bad luck," Sharise said.

"I should worry about that, huh? Humph. Once James knows the truth, he will not only never marry me, he will damn my soul to hell."

"My God, Arnell. Is it that bad?"

"I'm ending the engagement."

"But you love James, and he loves you."

"Perhaps, but I should have never gotten together with James, that was a mistake."

"You're wrong. Falling in love is never a mistake."

"It is when telling the truth can destroy that love." Arnell was suddenly very tired. In the last week, she'd gotten very little sleep. "Look, Sharise, I have no choice. If I want my mother to stop blackmailing me, to stop using me, I have to end it with James."

"Yeah, but . . . damn, Arnell, maybe you're wrong about James. Maybe you're not giving him enough credit. Remember how scared I was to tell Michael about my past? He surprised me—he didn't leave me, and he's never thrown any of it in my face."

"I hope he never does."

"He won't, Michael loves me. That's all there is. I think you should take a chance and tell James the truth. He might surprise you."

Arnell began to laugh softly, but then her laughter turned to weeping. "If . . . anything, Sharise, I'll surprise . . . the hell . . . out of James."

"Oh, Arnell," Sharise said, hugging her friend. "You don't have to suffer like this."

"That's true, I don't," she said, wiping her eyes. "I'm ending it with James." Arnell eased back against the ledge of the window.

Sharise suddenly stood. "You need to kick that bitch's ass!"

"Whatever Esther is, she's still my mother."

"Hell, the queen's not my damn mother. I'll kick that bitch's ass for you!"

"Sharise, you better calm down. My godchildren are upstairs."

"They're sleeping. At least, they better be." Sharise rushed out into the foyer to the bottom of the staircase. She tilted her head to listen for any sounds of two-year-old Alise or three-year-old Michael Jr. stirring above in their bedrooms. Hearing nothing, Sharise returned to the sun porch.

"Arnell, let's take a very real look at Queen Esther. The way I see her, she's mean, she's cannibalistic . . ."

"Cannibalistic? Sharise, what the hell does that mean?"

"She's been eating your ass, alive at that, since the day she prostituted you for rent money, and she's a vulture because she's still picking your bones."

Arnell had to agree that no truer words had been spoken about her mother.

"Just think about it, Arnell. Queen Esther really isn't your mother. Sure, she gave birth to you, but she isn't your mother. No mother would do what she's doing to you—not her own child."

Pensively, Arnell wiped at the tears that began to flow again. She knew what Sharise was saying was true, but too much time and too many things—ugly things that maybe God could never even forgive her for—had gone on between her and Esther to easily break away from her.

Sharise again took Arnell's hand. "Okay. Arnell, if it's like bad, break it off with James, because your mother will always know how to fuck with you. Then break away from her. Move. Leave the country. As long as you're in shouting distance, you will always be in contact with her. Change your name. Hell, get plastic surgery if you have to. Just get the hell away from the queen bitch before you lose your mind or worse, lose your life."

Arnell knew there was no simple solution for dissolving her relationship with her mother—they only had each other. "I am not leaving the country, Sharise. I will not scurry away like some small animal that's afraid of the big bad wolf."

"Okay, maybe that suggestion was a bit much, but I do have another," Sharise said. "You should move in here with me and Michael until you know what it is you're going to do."

"I can't do that. Besides, I do have my own house, remember?"

"So, you could still stay with us for a while."

Arnell shook her head. She didn't want to hide behind anyone or anything anymore.

"Arnell, look at yourself—you're crying. You need to get as far away from Esther as you can. Come. Stay here. Esther won't bother you here. She knows better than to call my house. I'm not afraid of her or big ass Walt."

Arnell couldn't help but chuckle. The day that Sharise walked out on Esther, she had warned Sharise to keep her mouth shut about the mansion and what went on inside or she'd get hurt. Sharise told Esther, "I have a videotape of your sex den, and so does my lawyer and certain members of my family. And for good measure, there are backup copies in safe deposit boxes at two different banks. So fuck with me, and you'll be the one that gets hurt."

Esther had found herself at an impasse and neither she nor

Sharise had spoken to each other since that day. Esther hated that Arnell was still friends with Sharise but Arnell didn't care. Sharise was the first real friend she'd ever had.

"So, will you move in?"

"No."

"Will you think about it?"

"Sharise, my mother will never let me go without making me and everyone around me miserable. I do not want anyone, especially you, caught up in my mess. Give me a moment, I'll handle this on my own. Who knows, I may have to relocate to do that, but it will be my choice. Where? I don't know, but I won't be leaving any unfinished business behind. I will end it with my mother, and I will end it with James."

"Damn, Arnell, I really don't envy you."

Arnell wiped her face completely dry. "Hey, I don't envy myself. I've been messed up for a lot of years. I know I won't be able to slay the mighty demon that stalks me, overnight."

"Well, sis, I'm here for you. You don't have to do it alone."

Arnell and Sharise held onto each other's hand.

"So," Sharise said, covering Arnell's hand with her other hand, "what do you have in mind for your mother?"

"I'm going to close her down."

"Wow! You would go that far?"

"It's time. Sharise, I've seen to what lengths my mother is willing to go to keep me an emotional and psychological prisoner, and what's worse, I saw the new girl she found to replace Kitt, who, by the way, was kicked out because she got pregnant."

"Kitt was always an airhead."

"This is true, but my concern is for the new girl. She can't be older than sixteen—the same age I was when Esther turned me out."

"Damn, that's foul. Arnell, we have *got* to stop your mother."

Arnell smiled to herself. She heard the *we* that rolled off Sharise's tongue. It wasn't true anymore that she only had Esther. She had Sharise and Sharise had never let her down and even now, was willing to stand shoulder to shoulder with her in her fight against Esther. This was a good thing because she was going to need all the emotional support she could get. Esther was not going to go down easily. She would fight until her tongue was hanging from her mouth and she was lame and dragging her foot behind her. That kind of adversary Arnell wasn't prepared for, although she well knew Esther's weaknesses. She needed to get away and ready herself for the fight of her life.

"So where do we start?" Sharise asked eagerly. "I've got the evidence. I'm ready for the queen's ass. All we have to do is call the district attorney. We could—"

Arnell's stomach flipped. She cringed at the thought of her mother going to jail. "No."

"But you said you wanted to close her down. By going to the DA, we could shut Queen Esther down for good."

"Sharise, I cannot put my mother in prison. I could never live with that."

"Hell, I could live with it."

"I know, but prison is not an option, so forget it. This fight is between me and my mother. I can close her down without going to the DA."

"How?"

"My mother has personal information on every client that steps through the door of the mansion. I have a duplicate copy."

"Oh, I get it," Sharise said, liking the idea. "Cut Esther off at the knees by stopping guys from patronizing The Honey Well. In other words, threaten to expose the men."

"Their families, their business associates, any sensitive area there is."

"That would do it."

"Without a doubt," Arnell said. "But before I declare all-out war against my mother, because war is what it will be once she figures out what I'm doing, I have to get my head ready. I think I'll head upstate to the Catskills."

"You're going to that health spa? Are you kidding?"

"Nope."

"Girl, this is no time for a beauty makeover."

Arnell pulled her shoulder-length hair up off of her neck and twisted it into a bun. "Did you ever read *The Stand* by Stephen King?"

"What the hell does *The Stand* have to do with you going away to a health spa? There was no health spa in *The Stand*."

"No, but if you remember, *The Stand* is about the forces of good and evil. As I see it, in this case, that's me and my mother."

"No argument there, but the health spa, Arnell? What the hell does the health spa have to do with anything?"

"Do you remember when Mother Abagail told Stu, Ralph, and Glen about going west to fight the evil one that was trying to take over the world?"

"And?" Sharise was impatient.

"Well, Mother Abagail impressed upon them that while they were on their journey west, they were not to eat any food or drink any water. That's what God—"

"Arnell, you're not journeying west, you're going three hours north of the city. So—"

"Sharise, Mother Abagail was telling Stu that this is what God wanted them to do. Not eating or drinking would make them stronger. I'm going to the spa to fast. I'll drink but I won't eat any solid foods, especially after all the junk I ate a week ago. I haven't felt well since. I'm going to cleanse my body, clear my mind, and get ready to do battle with my mother—the evil one."

"Well, I guess I can understand that."

Arnell was pensive. "Damn, Sharise. Doesn't that sound terrible?'. . . do battle with my mother—the evil one'?"

"Yeah, well, isn't it just as terrible that your mother chose to pimp you out when you were sixteen, instead of standing on the corner her damn self?"

There was no need for Arnell to answer that question. She hated dredging up thoughts of her early years prostituting to keep a roof over her and her mother's heads. For one whole year, twice a week, she had sex with Mr. Hershfeld, who never took off a stitch of his black clothes, and for one whole year, twice a week, she threw up afterward. It never got any easier to open her thighs to a man that rammed himself inside her and grunted his release like a braying donkey. When it first started, when Mr. Hershfeld was done, he'd get up quickly and leave. After a few months, he started lingering several minutes too long, and saying annoyingly nice things like, "thank you," and "I enjoy you." His words didn't make Arnell feel any better, nor did the presents of expensive jewelry left behind on the dresser—which Esther took. The rent payments were never mentioned again. By the end of the year, Esther had figured out how to use other girls who needed a place to lay their heads, to make money. That was a lot of years ago, but Arnell felt so tense inside, it was like it had happened yesterday.

At the time, Arnell did what she thought she had to do, what her mother told her to do. Sure, she had regrets, but she learned early in life that she could never go back and put her life on a different path. What was done was done. It's what she had yet to do that was of concern to her now. Going up against her mother was not a task she looked forward to.

Twenty

Jeanette had been right about Trena, she was itching to lose her virginity. Esther watched Trena and Andrew Peebles barely move their feet as they called themselves dancing to Grover Washington's passionate rendition of the "Flower Duet." Even from where she was sitting, Esther could see Andrew pressing his hard-on into Trena's hot triangular patch and Trena wasn't pulling away. A week's training was about to pay off. Trena was grinding Andrew just as hard as he was grinding her. Yep, Trena was a hot little miss who was still claiming that she was not a virgin and thought she was fooling people about her age. Eighteen. Ha! She was sixteen if she was a day, and probably a runaway, but Esther was desperate to replace Kitt and didn't have the time to look around. If anyone ever accused her of pimping a minor, she could say, honestly, that Trena swore she was eighteen.

As she had done with all her girls, Esther schooled Trena on how to take care of herself—condoms, whether it was the mouth or the vagina—condoms. Hopefully, Trena wasn't as stupid as Kitt. But just in case, so that there would be no more mistakes, Esther took Andrew Peebles aside and warned him about not using condoms in her establishment. He swore that he wouldn't mess up again and Esther let it go at that. When she saw him whisper something into Trena's ear and Trena giggled and started toward the stairs, Esther knew that Trena would get a nice tip before the night was over. Andrew had paid to be with her for the rest of the evening.

*   *   *

Sitting on the edge of her bed in a skimpy bra and G-string, her arms crossed tightly across her chest, Trena froze as Andrew Pebbles, butt-naked, walked right up to her, straddled her thighs, and stuck his huge erect penis barely six inches from her face. Giggling nervously, Trena kept looking bashfully away as Andrew unlocked her arms and took her right hand and kept trying to get her to take hold of his penis. The first time she touched it, its heat and its heaviness startled her, unnerving her. She yanked her hand away. As many times as she had touched Omar through his pants, she never imagined that his penis was that hot or that heavy.

Andrew squeezed his buttocks in and pushed forward, touching Trena's right cheek with his penis. "Baby, I'm ready for you."

Aghast, Trena lurched sideways away from the hot, jerky penis. "Don't do that!" She wiped hard at her cheek.

"Then hold it," Andrew said, again trying to put his penis into Trena's hand. "Come on, baby girl, hold on to your lollipop. I want you to lick it and suck it like it's your favorite flavor."

Trena giggled. "That's nasty."

"No, baby, this is good. Here, hold it." Andrew roughly took hold of Trena's hand and shoved his penis into it. She tried to pull away but Andrew held her hand around the shaft so that she couldn't move. Squirming, Trena tried to open her hand. Andrew wouldn't let her as he slid his penis against her soft palm. Closing his eyes, Andrew began sucking in his breath between his teeth.

"Come on, baby, just touch the tip of your tongue to the head. It's soft, you'll like it."

Trena tried harder to pull away from Andrew's iron hold on her hand and arm. "Wait. I ain't never done nothing like this before."

"That's okay, baby, you got the best teacher in the world." He took ahold of the back of Trena's head and pulled her into his penis. She squeezed her eyes shut. She pressed her lips tightly together as the warm flesh slid alongside her left cheek. "Open your mouth," Andrew said in a hoarse whisper.

Trena started pushing hard against Andrew's stomach and pelvis. "No! No! I don't wanna do this. Stop!"

The more Trena pushed, the firmer Andrew's hold was on her head. "Aah, c'mon, baby. Don't do me like this. When we was dancin', you was rubbin' your hot little body all up against me. I been on the bone for you for damn near an hour. I gots to get me some of this sweet honey tonight."

Trena started to cry. "But I ain't never did this before. I can't."

"Yes, you can, baby. I won't hurt you. I promise. Queen Esther said to be real gentle with you because this is your first time."

"But . . . but . . . I'm scared!"

Andrew suddenly released his hold on Trena's head. "Okay, okay. I tell you what."

Trena tried to get up but Andrew held onto her as he sat down next to her and tightly wrapped his arms around her. She couldn't stop crying.

"Okay, Trena, baby, stop crying. You don't have to give me no head, okay? Let's forget about that. I won't make you do nothing you don't wanna do, okay?"

Trena's whole body heaved from her gasps for air as she sobbed.

"Are you listening to me? No dick sucking, okay? I know you're all right with that, ain't ya?"

Nodding, Trena stopped struggling to get away. She felt Andrew's tight embrace loosen as she lay against his muscular chest. He began to gently rub her arm, moving up to her shoulder and then across to her breasts. That didn't feel so bad so she let him finger her nipples until they were tight. Before Trena realized it, Andrew had pulled her breasts out of her bra and had begun to tongue her nipples. She closed her eyes as she felt his hand slide down her stomach to her triangular patch. Trena's thighs were close together but she didn't resist when Andrew pulled her thighs apart and slid his hand under the side of her G-string and his finger found her slit and he began to finger her. Omar had never actually touched her naked clitoris, he had always massaged her through her panties. Oh, but she was liking it this way much, much better. There was a tingly sensation in the pit of Trena's stomach. She felt her clitoris throbbing. Tensing up, she clasped her thighs tight around Andrew's hand and began to grind herself into his hand.

"Yeah, baby, you're hot. Daddy got something that'll put out that fire."

Trena moaned. With her eyes still closed, she let Andrew lay her back on the bed. She felt like she was floating. She felt him pull her

G-string off. She felt him pull her thighs farther apart, and she felt him stretch out alongside her. She felt his hardness on her thigh.

Although she felt like she was in a dream, Trena opened her eyes. "Queen Esther said you have to use a condom. I got some in the top draw," she said, pointing to the night table.

Andrew rested on his left elbow. "I will, baby, in a minute. Right now, I'm just gonna use my finger for a while. See?" He held up his long thick middle finger and showed it to Trena. She saw the finger and watched as he began to gently push it into her vagina.

"Damn, baby, you're tight. You're genuine, ain't ya?"

Because she was so wet, Andrew's finger finally slipped right in. Trena shifted her hips.

"Close your eyes," he said, moving his finger slowly in and out of Trena. "Man, this is gonna be some good shit."

This is what Trena had been wanting for a very long time. She closed her eyes and opened her thighs even wider. Arching her back and gyrating her hips, she let Andrew have his way. He wasn't hurting her and when the hardness of his finger filled her vagina and pushed harder and farther up into her, the little pain that came barely made her gasp; it was feeling too good to hurt. Trena squeezed her eyes tighter. But then Andrew's finger seem to push all the way to her back. She was moving with him until he lifted her hips up off the bed and then she wondered how he could do that if he was resting on his elbow and fingering her with his free hand. She opened her eyes and saw Andrew above her, his eyes were closed, his teeth were bared, and his head was back. Trena looked down and saw the shaft of Andrew's thick, wet penis gliding smoothly in and out of her vagina. She gasped from the sight and from the orgasm that snuck up on her and made her scream. It had yet to register that she had lost her virginity to a man she had just met and he wasn't even wearing a condom.

Twenty-One

Every time her bath water seemed to cool, Trena drained some of it out and ran fresh scalding water back into the tub. She had done that several times. It didn't matter that it was three in the morning, she was in no hurry to get out of the water. She felt like she had to soak. Andrew Pebbles didn't leave until two-fifteen. He said he couldn't get enough of her "sweet pussy," and he meant that. Between eating and sleeping, he had sex with her five different times. By the time he was finished, she was sore and scared out of her mind. Not one of those five times did Andrew use a single condom. What if she got pregnant? What if she got VD? Queen Esther must have told her ten times to make sure Andrew used a condom. What was she supposed to do when he wouldn't?

"Please, Andrew, put a condom on this time." Trena held the condom in her hand. He wouldn't take it.

"I don't like those things. They dull the feeling."

"But, Andrew, Queen Esther is gonna be mad at me if you don't use a condom."

"She won't be mad if you don't tell her."

"But, what if I get pregnant?"

"You won't. I just busted you for the first time. Virgins can't get pregnant when they're first busted, their eggs ain't ready to be fertilized until they've had their tenth orgasm. How many did you have?"

Trena started to count in her head how many orgasms she'd

had. "I think I had . . . Wait a minute! I ain't never heard that before. I learned in biology that I could get pregnant from the time I started getting my period. Having my period means that I was ovulating and that meant that I could get pregnant."

Andrew back-flipped his hand at Trena. "That's not true for everybody. Besides, that's old biology. It's like old math."

"No, my doctor told me—"

"Look, if you get pregnant, don't worry about it. I'll be there for you."

"But I don't wanna get pregnant and Queen Esther—"

"Trena, if you tell Queen Esther that we did it without a condom, she'll put you out of here like she did Kitt, the girl before you."

That was the last thing Trena wanted.

"You don't wanna be put out do you?"

She shook her head.

"Then, don't tell. It'll be our little secret. Here." Andrew peeled off a single fifty-dollar bill. "Go buy yourself something pretty and wear it for me next week. I gotta jet."

Trena took the money and at the door, puckered her lips to kiss Andrew on his lips. He pulled back.

"Naw, baby, I don't kiss no hoes. Y'all tongue too many dudes. Besides, little girl, this ain't about a love thang, it's about the booty."

Minutes after Andrew was gone, Trena still stood looking at the door he had gone through. Andrew was the first man she had gone all the way with and he had called her a whore. She hated him. She was never going to have sex with him again. He made her feel nasty and worst of all, he was going to get her in trouble with Queen Esther. She couldn't tell Queen Esther about Andrew not using a condom, she would put her out for sure. And what if she got pregnant? Her mother would kill her if she got pregnant, and Cheryl would get a kick out of being proved right. She'd call her a whore, and this time, she'd be right.

Trena covered her face with her washcloth and cried.

Twenty-Two

If there was a heaven on earth, it was being stroked and rubbed down by a masseuse. Arnell had yet to find anything more divine. As she had done every day for the past week, Arnell immediately began to doze under the strong, soothingly soft hands of Helga. The first thing she did after she registered at the New Age Health Spa was sign up for daily massages with Helga as she had done every one of the four other times she had been at the spa. After she'd done thirty minutes of aerobics, an hour of yoga, which truly stretched her out and relaxed her, Arnell sweated thirty minutes in the sauna, and then she ended her day with a massage. If only her life in the real world was this pleasurable.

Arnell had left all thoughts of Esther and James behind her on the other side of the Hudson River when she crossed the George Washington Bridge. The farther she traveled along Route 17 up into the Catskills, the better she began to feel. She had turned off her cell phone before she left home and was even tempted to toss it out the window but changed her mind when she remembered the time she got a flat tire on the Southern State Parkway. The lug nuts were literally welded on so she couldn't change the tire herself. Her cell phone battery was low and she hadn't yet purchased a car adapter, but there was enough energy in the battery to call AAA. Having a cell phone was a good thing, especially when she could simply turn it off, and that she did.

A phone wasn't needed up in the mountains where fresh air

filled Arnell's lungs and long three-mile walks from the spa down to the Neversink Reservoir tested her legs and her will. Pounding down those narrow, steep sloping roads at a quick pace wasn't so much the problem as trudging back up those same long, roller coaster–like roads was. Arnell's calf muscles burned. There was no question that she was a city girl spoiled by the four-wheel lazy boy she drove every day, but she was determined to not let anything get the best of her. At the crack of dawn the first day, Arnell had ventured out on her own. It was fine going down to the reservoir, not too strenuous. The lush countryside made her feel one with nature. However, on the way back to the spa, Arnell found herself down on all fours trying to crawl the last two hills. And she thought she was in great shape! Hell, she was so exhausted after that walk, she fell out on her bed and blacked out. She missed her breakfast of fresh-juiced, muddy-looking, room temperature apple juice. Something as putrid-looking as that could only taste good when a person hadn't eaten solid food for a while. By lunchtime, that apple juice looked and tasted like fine wine. When Arnell went out on her walk the next morning, she walked with two other brave souls who, in the end, locked arms with her and they helped each other climb the last two monstrous hills.

Seven days into her ten-day stay, Arnell was feeling strong. She wasn't hungry. All the kinks in her brain and in her muscles were worked out, an enema a day and one high colonic had cleansed her colon. She'd had a pedicure, a manicure, and two facials—mud and oatmeal. Tomorrow, she was getting her hair done in Woodstock. She was readying herself to go up against Queen Esther, the mighty queen bee. Arnell knew just what she had to do about Esther. Yes, she would first take away Esther's trump card—she would indeed tell James the ugly truth about her life. Then she'd scare Esther's clients away, and in the end, simply walk away herself. In time, Esther's greed would be her own undoing, that is, if it was ever true that one reaps what one sows.

The one bitter truth that Arnell came to understand while her mind and body were being purged of toxic waste, was that it wasn't Esther that was holding her prisoner to Esther's demands, it was Arnell herself. All these years, she was afraid to be alone. With no other family to fall back on, she had always been afraid of losing

Esther. But it was Esther who was hurting her most, and the truth was, she would have done better in life without Esther picking away at her flesh.

"Miss Rayford, you have a telephone call in the office," Mia, the receptionist, said from the doorway.

It could only be Sharise wanting to know how she was doing. Arnell refused to open her eyes. "I'm not taking any calls."

"It's a Mrs. Sharise Simon. She says it's urgent."

Still, Arnell wouldn't open her eyes. "Helga, how much time do I have left?"

"Ten minutes."

Arnell wasn't about to give up a minute of her massage time. "Mia, please tell Mrs. Simon that I'll call her back in twenty minutes."

"Yes, ma'am." Mia closed the door and left.

Arnell didn't even want to begin to think about what the urgency could be. If it had anything to do with Esther, she didn't want to know. Sharise and James were the only ones that knew that she was at the health spa, and she had sworn Sharise to secrecy just in case Esther lost her mind and called looking for her. James, she didn't expect to hear from. Time would come soon enough when she would have to face him.

A quick cool shower refreshed Arnell while her dinner of a glass of fresh, murky green spinach and carrot juice energized her. Using her cell phone, she placed a call to Sharise.

"Sharise, it had better be life or death."

"*It is.*"

Arnell's heart skipped a beat. Sharise never joked about such things. "Is something wrong with the kids?"

"*Thank God, no. It's your mother. She's been calling for three days leaving messages.*"

"She must be desperate."

"*I thought she had lost her damn mind. In fact, I ignored the first two messages for you to call her—I was screening my calls—but today, she's been calling since early this morning. I finally took her call and I was about to tell her about herself, when—*"

"You mean you didn't?"

"*Arnell, the queen was crying.*"

"Boy, was she running a serious game on you."

"Not this time." Sharise paused. *"Arnell . . . Tony's dead."*

Arnell inhaled sharply.

"It's true, Tony's dead. I'm sorry, Arnell. I know you liked him a lot."

Not Tony. Tony really was one of the nicest people Arnell had met in the mansion besides Sharise. God, Esther must be devastated. If Esther could have truly loved any man, it would have been Tony.

"Arnell, I thought I'd never live to see the day that Queen Esther would shed a tear."

"Oh, my God. Do you know what happened?"

"Queen Esther didn't say. She just kept saying that she needed you."

"Damn." Arnell checked her watch. It was three forty-five. It would take her almost three hours to drive down from the Catskills. "Okay, I'll call her."

"Arnell, don't let that woman sucker you in. You know how manipulative she is."

"I know," Arnell said, going to the closet and pulling out her suitcase. "Sharise, I'll call you as soon as I know anything."

"You better. Drive carefully."

When she pressed the *end* button on her cell phone, Arnell saw that her hands were shaking. She pushed the *recall* button and zero-one to instantly call Esther but ended the connection after the first ring. She wasn't ready to talk to Esther. Not yet. Besides, talking to Esther would hold her up from packing and getting on the road. She never did like driving on the roads in upstate New York after dark—too dark, too scary. They were not lit up like in the city. She could drive off the road and not even know it until she landed at the bottom of a cliff.

Arnell packed quickly and was on the road by five-thirty. Her drive home would not be leisurely as she had planned. Now she was in a hurry to find out how Tony died.

Twenty-Three

As she had always done since she moved out, Arnell entered the mansion through the kitchen door. At first it was because it was convenient, now it was to avoid bumping into any of her old clients. She didn't want any of them seeing her and maybe propositioning her.

Melvina was in the kitchen. As was her norm, Melvina was cooking or baking—the baked goods being for the clients who were not in a hurry to leave after being with their lady of the evening. There was always something deliciously sinful to eat but the girls were forbidden to indulge as Esther had strict rules about gaining weight.

"Arnell, where ya been, girl? How ya stay gone and not call ya own mother?" Melvina scolded, her hands on her hips.

Taken aback by Melvina's scolding, Arnell almost laughed at how Melvina's accent had thickened, but she saw the anguish in Melvina's eyes. "My goodness, are things that bad around here?"

"Yes, girl. Your mother need ya. Her heart broke. Her hurtin' somethin' awful."

"So it's true. Tony is really dead?"

"Dead and gone. Three days now."

The thought of Tony being dead had filled her thoughts all the way back into the city, but that optimistic side of her had hoped. She thought that maybe Esther had made it up to get her to come running. It was an awful thing to think that Esther would be that cruel, but she could never say what Esther wouldn't do to get her to jump through hoops.

"Don't ya stand there, girl, ya mother need ya with her," Melvina said. "Queen Esther take not a bite of food into her mouth in three whole days. I make her drink water and tea. She paining real bad. Go to ya mother, Arnell, she waitin' on ya."

If what Melvina was saying was true, then Esther was taking Tony's death hard but Arnell wasn't in a hurry to see Esther. "How did Tony die?

"It's not for me to say, girl. Go let cha mother tell ya." Melvina picked up the large spoon she had been using to stir the bowl of yellow cake batter.

Arnell just looked at Melvina. By now, she should have been used to Melvina treating her like Esther's wayward child. Esther had told her once that Melvina thought her an ungrateful daughter.

"Go," Melvina said, shooing Arnell with the large spoon dripping with batter.

"You've dropped batter on the floor."

"I can see. I not blind, girl. You just go on and see about cha mother."

"Goddamn it, Melvina! Would you *please* stop pushing me. I am not a child, nor am I my mother's keeper."

"You her child, Arnell! Her only child and ya desert her when she needcha most."

"I assure you, Melvina, my mother needs no one. Oh, don't get me wrong, she loved Tony, but she didn't need him. She—"

"You cold in ya heart to say such about cha darlin' mother. Her—"

"Melvina!" Arnell said strongly. "Mind your business. Keep your damn nose in the kitchen."

Huffing loudly, Melvina puffed herself up. "You cannot talk to me in this way. Queen Esther will—"

"Queen Esther isn't going to do a damn thing in defense of you. I'm her daughter, remember? So, I'd appreciate it if you'd keep your surly attitude, your smart mouth, and your inappropriate opinions to yourself." Arnell didn't wait for any back talk. She left the kitchen—a bit more ticked off than when she had arrived. At Esther's suite door she grabbed the doorknob—it wouldn't turn.

She stood back and looked at the door. It was locked. Maybe Esther was as messed up as Sharise had said. Arnell started to knock hard on the door, but thought better of it. She knocked softly—three times. There was no answer. She knocked again. "Mother, it's me. Open the door." Arnell listened at the door. She heard nothing and was about to knock again when she heard first one lock then a second lock being turned. She waited, but the door didn't open. She grasped the doorknob. This time it turned. She opened the door. The room was dimly lit. Esther was lowering herself in her chair.

Closing the door, Arnell turned on the ceiling light. She was stunned by the sight before her. Esther's hair looked like crows had been picking at it—it was a mess of prickly blond straw. It was a fright. Esther's face was worse—her cheeks were tear-streaked with old and fresh tears. Deep, long worry lines straddled her red, bloated nose, and what little Arnell could see of Esther's puffy eyes was sunken and red.

"My God, Mother. What happened?" Arnell saw Esther's chin quiver as her face morphed into an ugly frown just before a flood of tears gushed from her. Esther covered her face with her hands and wailed. Seeing her mother cry so painfully tore at Arnell. She was uncertain as to what to do. For an uncomfortably awkward moment she watched Esther cry, but then her own sadness at Tony's death claimed her. She fell down onto her knees before Esther and pulled her into her arms, holding her and holding onto her tightly while both their bodies were racked with grief. Arnell's tears were not just for Tony, they were also for Esther. This was the first time Esther allowed herself to be comforted by anyone.

Twenty-Four

When Arnell could get Esther to stop crying, she ran her a hot bath and ended up practically bathing Esther and dressing her in the silky, pastel blue lounging pajamas she loved so much. She brushed Esther's hair until her tiny blond curls were shiny and hugged her skull. No words passed between them as Esther let herself be led to her bed. She got under the covers up to her waist but she didn't lie down because Arnell had propped three pillows up against the headboard for her to sit back against. Even when Arnell left the room, Esther didn't move. She sat staring down at her hands, wondering what she was going to do without Tony.

In the kitchen, Arnell and Melvina moved stiffly around each other in a sullen waltz of silence, never looking at each other while going about their business of getting something for Esther to eat. Although unspoken, Melvina knew that Arnell was getting food for Esther so she filled a soup bowl with homemade chicken noodle soup. She placed it on a tray with a saucer of Saltine crackers. Arnell saw the tray that Melvina was preparing, but she thought Esther needed more sustenance. She made a thick ham sandwich with lots of mustard and a slice of Swiss cheese. That went on the tray, too. She and Melvina both agreed without words on the tea although it was Melvina who put a small pot of it on the tray along with a cup. Arnell left the kitchen carrying the heavy tray, while Melvina quietly sucked her teeth at Arnell's back.

Half expecting Esther to reject the food, Arnell set the tray on the dresser. "I think you should eat something."

"Yes, I am hungry," Esther said quietly.

First removing the teapot, Arnell carefully carried the tray to the bed and set it on Esther's lap. Esther took a moment to check out the food on the tray before picking up half the ham sandwich. A dab of mustard was left in the corner of Esther's mouth. Arnell quickly handed her a napkin.

"Thank you."

"You're welcome." Arnell was secretly quite pleased that Esther chose her sandwich over Melvina's soup, yet she was feeling ill at ease. She didn't know if she wanted to sit on the bed or in the chair, but she knew she couldn't just keep hovering.

"Sit on the bed," Esther said, as if reading Arnell's mind. Arnell did, facing Esther.

Esther took another small bite of her sandwich. She chewed slowly. The sandwich was probably very tasty but she truly couldn't tell if she was eating ham or steamed cauliflower. Despite that, she ate the whole half of sandwich to please Arnell.

"You always made the best ham sandwiches," Esther said, feeling quite full.

Arnell smiled the weakest of smiles. "That's the way you taught me to make them."

"I did, didn't I?"

For an awkward moment, Arnell and Esther couldn't look at each other. Finally, Esther pushed the tray an inch away, indicating to Arnell that she was finished. Arnell immediately picked up the tray and took it back to the dresser. That's when she saw the teapot.

"Would you like a cup of tea, Mother?"

"Yes, thank you."

Esther took the cup of tea Arnell handed her and placed it on the night table. She would wait until the tea cooled. She nestled back into her cloud of pillows and closed her eyes.

The moment was still, yet Arnell had questions that were shouting in her head. They had to be asked. "Mother, we've avoided talking about Tony all evening. What happened? How did he die?"

When Esther looked up, fresh tears filled her eyes. "I don't know."

Sitting again on the bed, Arnell asked, "How can you not know? Haven't you spoken to Tony's brother yet?"

"Peter said that Tony fell down the stairs and hit his head on the marble floor in his house, but I don't believe that, Arnell. Tony wasn't a clumsy oaf; he knew how to walk up and down a flight of damn stairs and chew gum at the same time."

"Mother, maybe he blacked out and—"

"No!" Esther sat forward. "Tony did not black out and fall down the stairs and bust open his head. No way will I ever believe that. I believe—"

"You weren't there."

"No, I wasn't, but Wednesday night before Tony died, he called me an hour earlier. He told me that he and Sal had had a big fight."

"Was Sal at the house?"

"He wasn't supposed to be there, was he?" Esther started to cry again.

Arnell didn't know what to think. Sal was Tony's youngest son and he had almost come to blows with him once before over Tony seeing Esther. Tony had put Sal out of his house. "Mother, do you believe that Sal had something to do with Tony's death?"

"I know he did," Esther sobbed. "Sal always hated that me and Tony were together."

"Yes, but he wouldn't kill Tony to break you two up."

"Yes, he would!" Esther said adamantly. "Don't you remember the time he followed Tony here and he told Tony that he would kill him for disrespecting his mother by sleeping with a black whore?"

Arnell remembered. It was a Saturday night, five years ago. She had been upstairs in her room and could hear Sal shouting above the music. She had raced downstairs to see what was going on and right away she could see the explosive anger in Tony's eyes. Tony charged at Sal like he was a tortured bull. He shoved Sal up against the wall in the parlor and grabbed him up by the lapels of his jacket and literally lifted him off the floor. Sal wasn't that small of a man himself, but he could not break Tony's hold on him.

"*Lei non insolentirà una signora nella sua casa*—You will not disrespect a lady in her home," Tony said through clinched teeth. "*Esther è una donna buona. È un amico buono a me. Lei l'onorerà o porterò di nuovo la vita che io'il ve dato lei*—Esther is a good woman. She is a good friend to me. You will honor her or I will take back the life that I've given you." Tony's fists were up in Sal's throat and he was choking the breath from him. Sal was gasping. His eyes were bulging, his face was scarlet, his veins pulsed at his temples.

Esther stepped in. "Let him go, Tony. You're choking him."

Tony, contemptuously, released Sal with a thrust.

Sal held himself up against the wall. When he could catch his breath, Sal straightened his back and glared at his father. "*Lei minaccerebbe la mia vita ed umilia mia madre negli occhi della nostra famiglia sopra un*—You'd threaten my life and humiliate my mother in the eyes of our family over a—"

With his fists clinched, Tony again charged at Sal. Sal tried to press his body into the wall, but he was trapped. Tony got up in Sal's face with his fist at his temple.

"*Lei ha chiuso la sua bocca di filty, Salvatore. L'ho insegnato rispetta—* You shut your filthy mouth, Salvatore. I taught you respect."

"*Lei me, come suo figlio, ha insegnato rispettare sua moglie, mia madre. Ma lei, lei farebbe il mancanza di rispetto lei da scegliere il suo mistress sopra lei, suo figlio—la sua famiglia*—You taught me, as your son, to respect your wife, my mother. But you, you would disrespect her by choosing your mistress over her, your son—your family?"

"*Scelgo, sempre, la mia famiglia. L'Esther è la famiglia a me*—I choose, always, my family. Esther is family to me."

"*Poi sono non più suo figlio*—Then I am no longer your son."

The flicker of hurt that Arnell had seen in Tony's eyes tore at her heart. She knew how much Tony loved his children. Especially Sal, who was so much his father's son. Tony always said that. Anthony, Tony's oldest son, cared not at all that Tony visited Esther—he was a visitor, every now and then, to The Honey Well himself. As hurt as Tony was by Sal's words, he wouldn't back down. He gave Sal a hard fist up in the air.

"*Poi prendere l'inferno fuori della mia casa! Andare vivere nella strada dove lei appartiene*—Then get the hell out of my house! Go live in the street where you belong."

The look that passed between Tony and Sal was one of defiance. Neither would give an inch. Both were breathing hard, glaring at each other, telegraphing thoughts that only they could discern. Every person that witnessed their fight could feel the bitter rage that flowed between them. Their words had not been understood, but their anger had been. A father and son's love had been torn asunder by their love for two different women—Sal, his mother, and Tony, his mistress.

At the door Sal turned back. *"Lei sono straniero a me*—You're a stranger to me," Sal said to Tony. *"L'ucciderò se lei mai ha messo le sue mani su me ancora*—I'll kill you if you ever put your hands on me again."

Tony growled and started after Sal. Esther quickly threw herself in front of Tony and pushed with all her might to keep him from going after Sal. "Let him go, Tony!"

Tony stayed with Esther for four nights before he went home. Arnell found out later that he was waiting for Sal to move out. Sal was twenty-four then. Tony said that it was about time Sal stopped standing on his feet and stood up on his own. How Tony's wife felt about Sal moving out or the reason behind it, Tony never said. Tony and his wife stayed together under the same roof, their marriage chiseled in stone. She was going nowhere. As well, Esther was a permanent part of Tony's life and his wife had no choice but to accept it. She had too much to lose if she divorced Tony. That, Tony was sure of.

Rarely did Arnell hear Tony speak at length of Sal or any of his other two children again, so she was surprised when Esther said that the day Tony died, he and Sal had fought.

"Mother, was Sal in the house when Tony fell down the stairs?"

"Peter wouldn't tell me that. I asked him, but he wouldn't say, he kept avoiding the question. He wouldn't even look me in the eye. So I know what the answer is. Sal was in the house. He wasn't supposed to be in there. Arnell, Tony put him out."

"Yes, he did, Mother, but Sal probably came back to see his mother. Tony knew about that. He even told you he knew Sal was coming to the house when he wasn't home."

"But Sal was there Wednesday when Tony was home. Arnell, Sal pushed Tony down those stairs. I know it as sure as I'm breathing. Sal killed Tony. He said he would, and Arnell, Sal is trying to keep me from going to the funeral home to see Tony."

"Mother, maybe it's for the best. Tony's family—"

"Peter told me that mouse, Sal, hired guards to keep me away."

Esther slammed her fist into the mattress. "Can you believe that shit? Arnell, I can't even say good-bye to Tony. After all these years, he's going to be put in the ground and covered up for all eternity and I can't even see him one last time and tell him how much I loved him." Esther's voice broke. "My God, Arnell, that's so insane."

Again Esther gave in to her despair and sobbed. Arnell could only sit and watch her mother grieve. What Esther believed about how Tony died Arnell could neither dispute nor confirm, though as she sat holding Esther's hand, she wondered whether it could be true that Sal pushed Tony down the stairs.

Twenty-Five

The loud knock at the door to Esther's suite awakened Arnell. She opened her eyes and looked right at the back of Esther's head. Esther hadn't stirred. She was sleeping soundly. It was probably the first sound sleep she'd had since Tony died. Arnell raised her head and looked down at herself fully clothed. She remembered stretching out on the bed around two-fifteen after Esther had cried herself hoarse and after Esther had asked her to stay a little longer. Arnell fell asleep listening to Esther talk about all the good times she'd had with Tony.

The knock came again.

Arnell quickly rolled off the bed and rushed into the front room to the door. She opened it just enough to see that it was Jeanette, whose eyes showed her surprise at seeing Arnell.

"Arnell, what are you doing here?"

None of your damn business was on the tip of Arnell's tongue, but she was too tired and sleepy to get into it with Jeanette. "What do you want, Jeanette?"

"I need to speak to Queen Esther."

"She's sleeping."

"Can you wake her up? This is really important."

"No."

"But there's a problem upstairs with one of the girls that Queen Esther needs to take care of."

"Jeanette, I am not waking my mother. Whatever the problem is, it will have to wait, or better still, you take care of it." Arnell started to close the door. Jeanette wouldn't let her. She pushed back against the closing door.

"Arnell, I already tried. Trena won't come out of the bathroom. She locked herself in."

"Trena?" That name got Arnell's attention. "Is that the new girl?"

"Yes."

"What's wrong with her?"

"She says that she's not going to have sex with any more clients. Andrew Peebles has been waiting to get with her for more than twenty minutes and he's pissed. He came late tonight because he was in the studio and Trena had already been with four other clients."

"Who were the clients?"

"I don't know all of them but Larry Bradley and Woodruff Parker were the last two."

"Oh, God," Arnell said, remembering her scary night with Woodruff Parker.

"What's wrong?" Jeanette asked.

"Did Trena say if anything unusual happened with Woodruff Parker?"

"No. But after he left, she did say that she wasn't ever doing it with him or Andrew Peebles again. Then she got hysterical and started crying and saying she wasn't doing it with anyone ever again. Arnell, she's acting like a child. Queen Esther needs to talk to that little girl."

"Jeanette, Trena's acting like a child because maybe she is a child, but my mother won't be talking to her tonight." Arnell glanced over her shoulder at the bedroom door. Even if Esther were awake, she wouldn't be up to overseeing the running of her house. Which was probably a good thing. She'd only pressure Trena into having sex with several more men before the night was over. "Let me get my shoes. I'll talk to her."

"Fine, she's up in Kitt's room."

"I'll be up in five minutes."

This time Jeanette let Arnell close the door. Arnell hurried to Esther's bedroom to make sure she was still asleep. Arnell didn't need Esther to wake up and find out Trena wasn't putting out. Arnell swept up her shoes and quickly retreated. In less than five minutes, she was knocking at the bathroom door in Trena's room.

"Trena, it's me, Arnell, Queen Esther's daughter. We met a few weeks ago down in the kitchen, remember? May I speak to you a minute?"

"Go away. I don't wanna talk to you."

"Well, Trena, there's a problem, then. If you don't speak to me, no one else will be able to help you with whatever it is that's bothering you."

"Nobody is gonna help me," Trena sobbed.

"You don't know that, Trena. If you'll tell me what's wrong, I might be the one person that can help you. Trust me. Open the door." Arnell listened to the soft sobbing on the other side of the door. Although she wanted Trena to open the door, Arnell really didn't need Trena to tell her what the problem was. She already knew. Trena had been hit hard with the reality of what she was doing. Having sex with a lot of men wasn't as easy as she thought it would be. She might have even opened her eyes and realized that she was prostituting herself.

"Trena, I know what you're feeling," Arnell said. "I've been there. It's not a good place to be."

"You're just saying that. You don't really know."

"Oh, honey, I can tell you stories that would fry your brain. Believe you me, I can testify to all that I've done and all that's been done to me. I can tell you what's going to happen to you even before it happens. I guarantee you, it won't be pretty. And I'll tell you something else, I know exactly how you feel."

Trena's sobs did not let up.

"You feel dirty, don't you, Trena? You feel used and mostly, you feel ashamed."

The deep down in the belly crying that erupted from Trena, Arnell had done so many times in the early years; she felt like she was transported back to her own teen years. She could feel herself cringe from the touch of strange men three times her age entering her body and claiming for themselves what God had given her at birth. So many, including Esther, had tried to make her believe that her vagina belonged to them and not to her. She had never wanted any part of that life and was angry at herself for letting herself be manipulated into being used like that. That's where she was different from Trena, who had thought that she could handle that sordid world—Arnell never thought such a thing and was, certainly, never that curious about sex.

"Trena, I know that you were with Woodruff Parker. He's not a very nice man, is he?"

"I hate him!"

"I do, too. He did the same thing to me that he did to you."

Trena's crying got louder.

"Trena, if you open the door, you'll see that you're not alone. I will help you. I promise."

The door suddenly opened and Trena threw herself into Arnell's arms, crying hard, her body shaking. Arnell gathered Trena in her arms and walked her over to the sofa and sat her down. She noticed immediately the ugly bruise on Trena's right cheek. She'd ask about that when Trena was ready to talk, because if Woodruff Parker was hitting—then . . . Arnell went back to the bathroom. She got a washcloth, which she rinsed in cold water. Mindful of being careful of Trena's bruised cheek, Arnell wiped Trena's face with the washcloth even while Trena continued to cry. Twice more she rinsed the washcloth in cold water. She kept wiping Trena's face until the coolness of the damp cloth calmed Trena and got her to stop crying.

"Trena, tell me what it is that you want."

"I wanna go home. I wanna go home to my mother. I don't wanna be here. I don't wanna do this no more. I don't like men doing it to me. I don't like it . . . I don't like it . . . I don't like it." Trena again fell into Arnell's arms, crying.

Arnell liked the words that were coming from this frightened, contrite Trena better than the words that came from the sassy Trena she had first met. Arnell gently pushed Trena off her and again dried her face. "Did Mr. Parker hurt you?"

Trena gingerly touched her sore cheek. "That old bastard smashed my face up against the wall and rammed his nasty dick up in me."

"I should have stopped that rapist weeks ago." Arnell knew for sure she had the ammunition to stop Woodruff Parker from visiting

The Honey Well. "Trena, I think you do need to go home. Where does your mother live?"

"On Pilling Street in Bushwick."

"Did you run away from home?"

Trena dropped her eyes ashamedly.

"How long ago?"

"Three weeks ago," Trena said softly.

"Have you spoken to anyone in your family since then?"

Trena shook her head. "Just my friends, Alyson and Bebe."

Arnell pushed Trena's hair back off her face. She really was a pretty girl. "Trena, I'm thinking it might be a good idea to call your mother and let her know you're all right and that you wanna come home."

The tears emptied again. "But what if my mother and my sister find out what I've been doing; they'll never let me come back."

"Trena, if your sister and mother love you, and I believe they do, they will be ecstatic to have you back home. I'm sure they've been looking for you."

"But my mother was so mad at me when I left, and my sister . . . my sister," Trena cried, "oh man, I treated my sister so bad. I know she hates me. She'll never forgive me, and she's the one that said that I was acting like a hoe and now . . . and now I am one."

"Trena . . . Trena," Arnell said, patting her on the back, trying to quiet her. "You're a whore only if you believe that you are. Do you believe that you are a whore?"

Trena looked tearfully up at the ceiling. "I didn't use to think so, but I think I am now. Andrew Peebles said so."

Arnell grabbed Trena's chin and pulled her face to her, but Trena averted her eyes. "Trena, look at me. Look at me."

As hard as it was, Trena forced herself to look into Arnell's eyes.

"What I'm about to tell you, Trena, is what I've taught myself in an effort to hold onto a good part of my self-esteem.

"Trena, do not ever listen to a man who barely knows your name, who screws you, empties the fluids from his body into your body that may either cause life to grow inside you or death to your life, and then calls you a whore either because he has nothing better to say, or maybe because he doesn't feel good about himself for what he's done. If anything, that man is the whore who does not have respect for you, himself, or his own mama. But don't get me wrong, Trena, you will be a whore if you stay in this house of your own free will when you know better, and keep allowing yourself to be used and abused. Do you understand me, Trena?"

Trena blinked tearfully in response.

"Okay, then. Why don't we do this? Why don't I call your mother and tell her that you're all right?"

Trena suddenly dried her face. She asked hopefully, "Would you call her for me?"

"Yes."

But then Trena thought about it. "Arnell, suppose . . . suppose my mother wants to know where I am? What will you tell her? Will you tell her what I've been doing?"

"Of course not," Arnell said, meaning it. "I plan on telling her that you're staying with me and that you're all right. Is that all right with you?"

Uncertain, Trena nodded slowly. "Will you ask her if I can come home? Tell her I'll be good. Tell her I promise I'll be good."

"I'll tell her." Arnell glanced at her watch. It was definitely too late, or rather too early in the morning to call anyone respectable. "Trena, it's pretty late. Why don't you go to bed? I'll get rid of Andrew Peebles. You get a good night's sleep and I'll come up and see you tomorrow afternoon."

"But what if—"

"You'll be fine. There are no clients allowed in the house on Sunday, remember? It's rest day. I don't know what time I'll see you because my mother isn't feeling well, but I will see you. We'll call your mother then."

"You won't forget, will you?" Trena asked anxiously. "You'll come back?"

"You have my word." Arnell gently touched Trena's cheek. "Trena, there is a big bad world out here—even for us adults. Take your time growing into it. You're a teenager, be one. You'll never know such innocence or freedom again."

Trena gave Arnell a cynical look. "Innocence?"

"Yes, Trena, innocence. You're still innocent, believe it or not. You may have lost your sexual innocence, but that's only a scratch on the surface of life," Arnell explained. "There's a lot more to the ugliness of this world that you haven't even begun to experience. Like I said, take your time growing up, don't go searching for trouble, trouble will find you. That's trouble's job."

Trena thought about that. She was the one that had gone looking for trouble, and, boy, was trouble waiting to kick her ass.

"Arnell, what if I got HIV from somebody?"

"I hope not, Trena, but I'll take you to get tested. Try not to worry." Arnell knew that it was an easy thing to say, "don't worry," but she had shared similar fears herself over the years. Hopefully, the only concern Trena would have, if any, would be a mild case of chlamydia.

Saying, "Good night," Arnell left after Trena had gotten into bed. Poor kid. Maybe there was a chance she could help Trena reclaim her dignity, something they both had to do.

Twenty-Six

Tony was going to be buried in four hours. Esther had been screaming at Peter on the telephone about Sal since six in the morning.

"First that son of a bitch kept me from viewing Tony's body, now he's trying to keep me from attending his funeral. That vicious bastard can't do this to me, Peter. I'm telling you, you better do something about that fool. He's not God, and he doesn't own the damn funeral home or the cemetery. They are both public places. I'm going to Tony's funeral and if Sal comes within spitting distance of me, I'm gonna shove a goddamn rusty butcher knife through his black heart! Do you hear me, Peter! You better buy that stupid ass nephew of yours a fucking clue. He's playing with the wrong woman. I'll fuck him up so bad, he'll wish he had driven up to my door and picked me up in a goddamn stretch limousine!"

Esther slammed the cordless telephone down on the end table. "I got something for that bastard." She then turned around and snatched the telephone up again and punched in a series of numbers.

"Mother, you need to calm—"

"Hell, no! I am not about to calm down to let that mouse-face son of a bitch tell me what I can and can't do."

"Mother—"

"Big Walt!"

"No, Mother," Arnell said, grabbing Esther's arm and pulling the telephone away from her ear. "Mother, don't put Big Walt in the middle of this. This is his day off—let him have his day."

Esther snatched her arm free. She ignored Arnell. "You there, Big Walt? It's me, Queen Esther. I know it's your day off, but I need you here right away."

"What's wrong?"

"I'll tell you when you get here. Big Walt, don't let me down. Please come. Oh, and Big Walt, bring a few of your friends, you might need backup."

Esther quickly disconnected the call, not giving Big Walt the opportunity to balk or to question.

"Now you know that's wrong." Arnell sat and crossed her legs. "You shouldn't be involving Big Walt or anyone else in this mess."

"Arnell, that asshole has forced my hand. I'm doing what I have to to kick his ass. As for Big Walt, I pay him a fortune. He can give me one Sunday afternoon out of his damn life."

"I see you're about having your way, no matter what."

"I'll show that pie-face son of a bitch." Esther went to her large closet and started rummaging through the many outfits that hung there. She was looking for the perfect black suit. She began snatching one outfit after another out of her closet.

"Mother, what do you expect Big Walt and his boys to do—slap Sal upside his head and tell him to behave and he'll quietly oblige? Because if you do—"

"Arnell, if you don't have anything constructive to say, leave me the hell alone."

Feeling insulted, Arnell started out of the bedroom.

"Sweetie, wait a minute," Esther said hurriedly. "I'm sorry."

Arnell waited.

"Please try to understand how important this is to me. Tony was a very special person in my life, just like I was in his. He would never forgive me if I didn't say good-bye to him. That's why I have got to go to his funeral."

"But, Mother, Tony's wife, his children, his family, his friends, everyone he's ever known will be at his funeral. You cannot disrespect his wife and his children like that. That's unconscionable."

Standing still for the first time since she opened her eyes at five A.M., Esther gave little thought to Tony's family. She thought only about the last time she was with him. They had made love and Tony had promised to take her to Italy next Easter. They had gone many places and seen many things, but Italy was a place that Tony had not taken her because of his family. Esther understood that and never forced the issue. It was Tony who decided it was time she see the country he was born in and loved as much as he loved America. But now there would be no trip to Italy—Tony was gone and she wasn't even permitted to pay her respects to him. Arnell might have been correct in what she said about respect, but Tony always said she was family to him also. Esther lifted the black dress her hand rested on out of the closet and inspected it. It was sleeveless and the hem fell just below her knees. This one would do just fine.

"Mother, please, don't go to that funeral."

With the dress draped across her arm, Esther slowly turned to Arnell. "Sweetie," she said softly, "twelve years ago, Tony, himself, set the bar for the level of respect his wife and children were to receive from me. The ultimate level of respect for them was supposed to come from him, and Tony chose, not me, to not respect the sanctity of his marriage or his family. He came here, to my home, to my bed. I didn't go to him."

"No you didn't, but—"

"There is no *but*, Arnell. It's simple. For twelve years, Tony was my man. I was his woman. His wife knew and stayed in that marriage under those terms. Now, I am going to Tony's funeral. His wife and his children will have to accept my presence as they have done for the past twelve years. And that's all I have to say about it."

Arnell watched as Esther walked off into the bathroom. What was there left to say? Nothing and nobody was going to stop Esther from doing what she had set her mind to. The question was, what was she prepared to do to make sure that Esther didn't get killed on the day of Tony's funeral?

Twenty-Seven

No matter how many times Arnell asked herself, *What the hell am I doing here?* the answer was always the same—*I don't even know.* It wasn't lost on Arnell that, yet again, she was doing something that she didn't want to do, but what Esther wanted her to do. Sure, she wanted to pay her respects to Tony just as much as Esther did, but they had no place at his funeral. It simply wasn't right. Yet, Arnell found herself, mad as hell, sitting in the backseat of Esther's Lincoln between two scowling, big ass, roughneck-looking men with cartoon character names—The Hammer and Ace—dressed in jeans and sports jackets that were bulging at the biceps, that Arnell would have been afraid of if she were walking down the street alone at night. Big Walt had introduced them as *his boys,* and she just looked at him when he said those stupid names.

Big Walt took Arnell aside. "Work with me, Arnell. If something goes down, we can't use real names. We got to protect ourselves."

Arnell walked away from Big Walt then because even that was really more than she needed to know. If something ugly did go down, she didn't want to know a damn thing about anyone. Yet, again, she was in the car on her way into Bay Ridge because she had stupidly, and impulsively, jumped into the backseat, at the very last minute, when no amount of reasoning would stop Esther from going to Tony's funeral. For some godforsaken reason, Arnell felt that she had to protect her mother, and that was so ironic—her mother hadn't protected her.

Big Walt triple-parked the Lincoln around the corner from the Bay Ridge Funeral Home. There wasn't a free parking space in sight. If the number of cars parked outside the funeral home was any indication of the size of Tony's funeral, then the funeral home was packed. As Arnell started to climb out of the backseat, a rather large hand reached in to help her. That hand belonged to Ace. His manners surprised Arnell—she didn't think of roughnecks as being gentlemen.

"Thank you," she said graciously, but she couldn't look Ace in the eye. He was a roughneck after all.

Big Walt spoke in a hushed voice to Arnell. "Stick close to Ace. You'll be fine."

That's when Ace took Arnell's arm and walked alongside her as they rounded the corner onto Fourth Avenue on the heels of Esther, Big Walt, and The Hammer. Arnell's eyes were immediately drawn to the two tall white men dressed in black suits standing guard outside the funeral home door. Their presence was ominous.

Arnell scampered to catch up to Esther. "Mother, this is really not a good idea."

Esther didn't acknowledge Arnell, she was focused only on the doors of the funeral home. Big Walt matched Esther's stride as they marched the short distance to the funeral home. Arnell's heart was fluttering as she climbed the few steps to the door. The two men in black stepped in front of the door. Big Walt, Ace, and The Hammer quickly stepped in front of Arnell and Esther. Arnell took Esther by the arm. What little she could see of one of the men, she saw in the narrow gap between the broad shoulders of Big Walt and The Hammer.

"This is a closed funeral," one of the men in black said sternly.

Big Walt and The Hammer each got right up in the face of each of the men in black. Their height was equal but the men in black in no way matched the brawn of Big Walt and The Hammer.

"We can do this the hard way or the ass-kicking way," Big Walt said menacingly. "Either way, you won't be left standing."

The two men in black opened their jackets and revealed their guns tucked in holsters under their arms. The one in front of Big Walt ordered, "Leave. Now."

"Mother." Arnell felt like she was about to pee on herself. "Mother, we can't do this."

Esther would not let Arnell pull her an inch away from where she was standing.

Big Walt, Ace, and The Hammer all opened up their jackets, exposing their guns.

Arnell couldn't see the guns or where they were tucked, but she looked down and saw The Hammer's fingers on his left hand fluttering anxiously. "Mother, please."

The two men in black were determined to stand their ground. They didn't budge.

"Move!" Big Walt growled.

It was a warm day, but Arnell felt like it was a swelteringly sweaty August night. The air was heavy and still. Beads of sweat popped out on her forehead. Arnell could feel her knees about to give way. She slipped her arm through Esther's and held onto her. Esther took Arnell's hand and steadied her.

"I say we fuck them up right now," The Hammer said. "I got people waiting on me."

"Let's do it," Big Walt said, putting his hand on his gun.

The two men exchanged worried glances. The Hammer took a menacing step forward. The two men quickly fell back and then stepped aside.

Big Walt and The Hammer each pulled open one of the double doors and stepped inside the vestibule. Ace let Esther and Arnell pass before he took up the rear. It was not difficult to locate the chapel in which Tony's service was held—it was the one where a sea of mourners all dressed in black spilled over into the hall. The service was well under way and was, in fact, about to end. Tony's casket was being opened for final viewing. Big Walt and The Hammer didn't stop walking. Arnell tried to hold Esther fast, but Esther pulled Arnell along as she followed Big Walt and The Hammer straight down the aisle toward Tony. Every head turned as Esther's tight little entourage paraded down the aisle. Gasps of surprise rose throughout the chapel and a chorus of hushed whispers floated on the air.

Arnell felt faint. "Oh, God." She glimpsed Esther's stoic profile.

Esther's head was held high, her jaw set, her eyes saw no one but Tony.

Twenty feet from the casket, Sal leaped out of his chair at the front of the chapel. The sheer look of outrage on his face chilled Arnell.

Sal screamed at Esther, "*Uscire!*—Get out! You are not welcome here." Others around Sal began to stand.

Arnell watched in horror as Sal rushed up the aisle toward them.

"Get the fuck out of here!"

Big Walt and The Hammer barreled through Sal, knocking him aside. Sal quickly regained his footing and rushed at Esther. Big Walt turned and grabbed Sal up by the lapels, just as Tony had done years before. And just as Sal couldn't do then with Tony, Sal couldn't free himself of Big Walt's pit bull–like hold.

The priest stepped forward. "*Fermarlo! Fermarlo! Fare non Tony disonori in questa maniera!*—Stop it! Stop it! Don't dishonor Tony in this way!"

No one seemed to hear the priest.

"Take your filthy black hands off me!"

"I'm gonna give you that, boy, because my hands *are* black," Big Walt said, "but you best calm your white ass down unless you wanna die today."

Sal was defiant. "I want you people out of here."

"Us people ain't goin' nowhere," Big Walt said. "The quicker you understand that, the quicker the lady can pay her respects. *Capite?*"

"Michael, Vincent! *Prendere questo bastardo via da di me!*—Get this bastard off of me!" Sal ordered.

"You best not be talkin' 'bout my mama," Big Walt said.

Two men started to charge at them. Big Walt didn't appear the least bit worried. He didn't take his eyes off Sal, while The Hammer wasted no time pulling out his gun and brandishing it about. Women shrieked, men drew back. Arnell tried to shrink back, but Esther was holding her firm and Ace was up against Arnell's back.

"Stay where you are," Ace said. "I got your back."

Arnell didn't know if she felt good about that or not. What the hell was she doing there in the first place?

"Don't make this harder than it has to be," The Hammer said, holding his gun firm but threateningly.

"Oh, God, Mother, this is so bad," Arnell said, trembling. "Tony wouldn't—"

"Shhh," Esther said softly. "This is what Tony would want me to do."

Esther started walking forward, taking Arnell with her. The path they set their feet upon began to clear as men backed off and away. An eerie hush fell over the room as if someone had demanded instant silence. Every head was turned toward Esther and Arnell. Arnell nervously scanned the faces of those who looked perplexed and those that looked scornfully at her and Esther. The only two people who weren't glaring at them were Peter and Anthony Jr.— Peter was sadly shaking his head, Anthony kept his eyes on the floor.

Esther looked neither right nor left as she passed Tony's family on her way to look upon his face. And when she did finally see Tony, a long, mournful gasp tore from her. Tony was truly gone. His naturally tanned complexion was no more—he was chalky white. Although Esther had told herself she wouldn't cry in front of all these people, tears rolled down her cheeks.

Arnell saw Esther's tears and she, too, welled up. It was still so strange to see Esther cry.

"Good-bye, Tony. I will always love you," Esther whispered so that only Arnell could hear her. Esther reached out to lay her hand on top of Tony's overlapped hands.

"*Toccarlo non lei*—Don't you touch him!" a woman's voice shrieked.

Esther's hand hung above Tony's. She held it there for what seemed like a heart-pounding eternity.

Arnell put her lips to Esther's ear. "She said, don't touch him."

Esther didn't turn around to see who had ordered her to not touch Tony, she already knew. It was Isabella, Tony's wife. But Esther didn't care. Ever defiant, she brought her hand gently down atop Tony's.

Isabella pulled away from Anthony's hold on her. "How dare you show your face here, in front of my family and my friends. What kind of cold-hearted woman are you?"

"You have no respect for anyone, do you?" Sal asked angrily. "*Sputo su lei, lei la femmina!*—I spit on you, you bitch!"

Scowling, Big Walt asked, "What did he say?"

"He said something about spit," Arnell said, not wanting to translate the word bitch for fear that all hell would break loose. She wanted to get out of there alive.

"You better keep that spit in your mouth," Big Walt warned. He tightened his grip on Sal, almost choking him. "Or I'll shove your tongue down your throat."

Sal quickly closed his mouth.

Behind her, Arnell could hear people stirring. They had found their voices and had begun to question what was going on. She heard one woman ask, "*Il Tony ha avuto un mistress nero?*—Tony had a black mistress?" She heard another say, "*Nessuno prodigio che non era mai la casa*—No wonder he was never home." The gossip mill was turning—viciously.

"Mother, you've done what you set out to do—you've seen Tony. Let's get the hell out of here."

Esther had closed her eyes and seemed to be praying.

"How can you disrespect my mother like this?" a woman's voice asked. "My father disrespected her all of his life, why must you carry on his legacy of disrespect to my mother in front of her family and friends?"

Arnell had never seen Tony's daughter. She wanted to turn and look at her but Esther's hold was still firm on Arnell's arm. Arnell couldn't look around comfortably without disturbing Esther in her stolen moment with Tony.

"Do you hear me talking to you!" Tony's daughter screamed. "*Lei il whore sporco*—You filthy whore . . ."

Arnell bristled. The word whore was understandable in any language, but *filthy* whore?

A chorus of gasps rose up from mourners who had no idea about Tony's other life.

". . . You should be stoned in the streets like the harlots of old.

You laid with my father for money and destroyed his family without a care in the world . . ."

Arnell felt Tony's daughter getting closer to her and Esther. Arnell's spine stiffened. She felt her heart race.

". . . You tricked and deceived my father with your gutter sex and vicious lies. He never saw through you, but I did. You're the *regina di whores*—queen of whores, and—"

Slap!

Arnell's slap caught Tony's daughter so by surprise, her head snapped back but her mouth continued to hang open in a startled gasp as she brought her hand to her stinging cheek.

Just as surprised was Arnell. She could not believe that she had slapped Tony's daughter, but she couldn't stand there and let her call Esther all those names. Not when it felt to Arnell as if those same names were being hurled at her.

Tony's large family started to lunge forward but The Hammer quickly fired once up at the ceiling. The loud report shocked all the mourners and everyone fell back with a shriek. That is, except for Tony's daughter. She clawed out for Arnell but Ace blocked her attack.

Now Arnell felt as if she had to protect herself as well. She faced Tony's daughter. "*La Femmina, lei farebbe il dorsa migliore via da*— Bitch, you'd better back off! "

Tony's daughter appeared to be more stunned by Arnell speaking Italian than by the slap. She stared, wide-eyed and open mouthed at Arnell.

"*Femmina*, I'm a half second from kicking *il suo grasso come ovunque questa cappella*—your fat ass all over this chapel."

"How dare you—"

"No! How dare you! You called my mother one too many goddamn whores, bitch, or would you prefer *femmina*? Your daddy taught me well, didn't he? But I'm telling you in English, call my mother just one more whore, and it'll be the last time you ever say that word to anyone."

Tony's daughter's eyes were wide with fear. "Who . . . who do you think you are?"

"I'm your worst nightmare, bitch. I'm the daughter of the

woman that your daddy preferred to be with. Understand this, my mother didn't come into Bay Ridge looking for Tony, Tony found his own way out of Bay Ridge, on his own, three days a week for twelve long years, looking for my mother. There was a reason why Tony stepped outside his marriage to your mother, but my mother had nothing to do with it. You, your brothers, and your mother have always known about his affair, you should have confronted him on that. But then again, I know that you did, and I also know that he told all of you to go fuck yourselves. If you didn't like it, you should have walked away from him, but you couldn't and you didn't. So deal with what Tony wanted. He would have wanted my mother to be here. I don't agree, but Tony would if he could. Now, we've paid our respects, so we're leaving. Tony was a good man. Too bad none of you were good enough for him to want to stay true to his family.

"Come, Mother, we've overstayed our welcome."

Esther opened her eyes and the tears she had been holding back flowed. She then bent down and kissed Tony on the lips.

Isabella swooned and was quickly pulled back to her seat where she slumped heavily in her chair, her eyes closed. No one fanned her, the chapel was air-conditioned.

With her arm around Esther's waist, Arnell rolled her eyes at Tony's daughter and led Esther past her.

Big Walt let go of Sal and graciously brushed off his lapels. The Hammer, still holding his gun, began to lead the way out while Big Walt and Ace brought up the rear. Esther still did not look at anyone as she raised her chin and allowed Arnell to take her out of the chapel. She had gotten her satisfaction.

Twenty-Eight

Forty-five minutes had passed since Esther's goon squad returned Arnell and Esther to the mansion. Arnell was still shaking. She had been sitting alone in the backseat of Esther's Lincoln parked in the driveway all of those forty-five minutes, too afraid to go inside the house for fear that she might kill Esther. All the way back, Arnell avoided looking at the back of Esther's head—she was afraid she would take her pocketbook and whack Esther with it. That's how pissed off she was. If Esther had been so desperate to see Tony, she should have gotten Big Walt and his boys to mount an attack on the funeral director last night or early this morning before all those people were in attendance—especially Tony's family. Oh, but that would have been too easy, too much like the right thing to do—if anything—compared to the near disaster they'd had this morning with guns drawn.

Arnell wondered what she had done in a past life to deserve the anguish of this life. Her life was a living nightmare. Arnell glimpsed her face in the rearview mirror. Boy, did she look bitter. And the truth was, she wasn't a bitter person. Of course, she wouldn't dispute anyone who said she was an angry person. Nothing truer could be said about her, but she had just cause to be angry. Nothing in her life had ever gone right and the ugliness of the last two months confirmed that.

For the umpteenth time, Arnell had let herself be blackmailed by Esther into servicing a client and that bastard of a client, Woodruff

Parker, had shown his gratitude by raping her. Then she had tried
to end Esther's hold over her by telling James the truth about her
life, but, oh no, Esther had to fake a heart attack and forestall her.
Then she had gone away to get her mind and body ready to go up
against Esther, but then Esther's frantic calls to Sharise about Tony's
death had put an end to her retreat and she had to rush back to
stand by Esther's side only to strong-arm their way into Tony's funeral with all the finesse of a pack of gangbangers at a debutante
ball.

Each and every one of these incidents, singly, was enough to
work Arnell's last nerve, but all of these incidents happening in
such a short period of time was more than enough to send her over
the edge, which is where she now tottered. All of her life Esther had
been the bane of her existence. Any trouble that found its way to her
always emanated from Esther directly. But, damn, was there ever to
be an end to the madness? Hadn't she, just a few days ago up at the
health spa, come to the realization that she, not Esther, was in control of her life? Hadn't she better start acting like it? Wasn't it time
she freed herself of Esther's jugular-sucking control? Whether or
not she ended up alone in the world, in order to survive Esther with
her sanity intact, short of being reborn outside of Esther's womb,
Arnell was going to have to put Esther out of her life—permanently.

Tap . . . tap . . . tap!

Arnell snapped out of her introspective trance and looked out
the car window into the tired, doleful eyes of young Trena. *Oh,
damn! I forgot all about this poor child.* Arnell quickly opened the door.

"Are you still gonna help me?" Trena asked anxiously. "Are you
still gonna call my mother?"

Damn, she had forgotten. "Of course, I'm still gonna help you,"
Arnell said, climbing out of the car. "Did you get any sleep last
night?"

"Not much. I kept having bad dreams. Can you call my mother
now?"

"Sure. Let's go up to your room where we can have some privacy. What is your mother's name?"

"Maxine Gatlind," Trena answered as she followed Arnell back
into the house. Together they hurried through the kitchen—Trena
with her head down.

Melvina looked up just as Trena and Arnell exited the kitchen. "Trena! Trena, you want something to eat, child?"

Trena didn't answer. She and Arnell both scampered up the back stairs to her room.

Down in the kitchen, Melvina was suspicious of Arnell being with Trena. When their being together crossed her mind twice, she was sure something wasn't right. Melvina headed for Esther's suite.

Upstairs, Trena dialed her mother and quickly handed the telephone to Arnell as soon as the first ring sounded in her ear. Then she began to nibble on her already gnawed fingernails.

"Hello?"

"Yes. Hello. May I speak with Mrs. Maxine Gatlind?"

"Who's calling?"

"My name is Arnell. I'm a friend of Trena Gatlind."

"That's my sister. Do you know where she is?"

"Excuse me, but what is your name?" Arnell asked to make sure that what the woman said was true.

"Cheryl."

"Yes, Cheryl, Trena has mentioned you," Arnell said, looking at Trena for confirmation.

In a hushed voice, Trena said, "Don't talk to her. Talk to my mother."

"What do you know about Trena?"

"Trena is fine, Cheryl, but I really need to speak with your mother. May I?"

The other end of the telephone was silent. Then, *"Mom! Telephone! It's about Trena."*

There was the sound of quick moving footfalls and then, *"Who is it."*

"I don't know. Some woman name Arnell. She wants to speak to you."

"Who is this?"

"Mrs. Gatlind, my name is Arnell and I'm calling on Trena's behalf."

Wanting to hear her mother's voice and what she was about to say, Trena pressed her head to Arnell's, trying to share the receiver.

"What the hell do you mean, on Trena's behalf? Where is she? I want to speak to my daughter."

"Who is it, Maxine? What are they saying about Trena?"

"Joe, wait a minute, the woman hasn't said much of anything yet."

"Goddamn it, ask her where Trena is."

Trena muffled her urge to cry but the tears came anyway. Her father was home.

"Miss, if this is a joke, I'll have your number traced and you'll be locked up so fast—"

"Mrs. Gatlind, this is not a joke. I do know where Trena is," Arnell said, realizing that there might have been many crank calls about Trena since she left home. "Mrs. Gatlind, you will be able to speak to Trena, but I just wanted to first put your mind at ease that she is all right. I've spoken to Trena and she tells me that she regrets running away and she wants to return home."

"That's fine. Tell me where she is and her father and I will come and get her."

Trena's eyes widened. She shook her head frantically.

"No," Arnell said quickly. "I'll get her back home to you. I just wanted to make sure she was welcome."

"Miss, I don't know what Trena has told you, but she has never been an abused child. Her father, her sister, and I love her and miss her. We want Trena back home, today. Is she there with you?"

Arnell pulled back from Trena and looked at her. Trena's face was wet with tears. Arnell handed her the telephone.

"Mom," Trena said, her voice sounding so much like that of a little girl.

"Trena! Oh, my God. Trena, where are you? Baby, where are you?"

Sobbing openly, Trena clutched the telephone. "I'm sorry, Mommy. Mommy, I'm so sorry."

Feeling weepy herself, Arnell slipped from the room, but she didn't go far—she waited outside in the hallway. She figured what Trena had to say to her mother from this point on was private.

"Arnell."

Because of the carpeted stairs, Arnell had not heard Esther come up the back stairs.

"What are you doing up here, sweetie?"

That damn nosy ass Melvina. "I could ask the same question of you. I thought you were resting."

"I was until I heard you were still here. Are you all right?"

"I'm fine." Arnell moved away from Trena's door. "I'm going home in a little while and I'm taking Trena with me."

"And why would you do that?"

"This one you don't get."

Esther daintily clasped her hands to keep from slapping Arnell. "I've invested a lot of money in this girl," she said, her voice low and steady, "and, you know me, sweetie. I don't ever put good money on bad investments. Trena lives here now."

"Not anymore," Arnell said, her voice just as steady. "Trena is going home to her parents, and I'm taking her. Now, Mother, if you're saying that you forbid Trena to leave this house, then you're saying that you're holding her against her will. My, what do you think the police will call that?"

Esther slowly raised her brow. "Are you threatening me?"

"Actually, I am strongly suggesting that you will not contribute to the ruination of this particular teenager, and that I am about to do for Trena what I couldn't do for myself."

"And what would that be?" Esther asked cooly.

"Save her from you." The stricken look that Esther leveled on Arnell lasted but a few seconds and was quickly replaced by a bitter scowl.

"Oh, don't look at me that way, Mother, I might think that you didn't love me."

Esther put her hands on her hips. "You're my daughter, Arnell, but I'll fuck you up just as sure as I'm standing here. You know better than to mess with my money, and Trena is my money."

Reminding herself to remain calm and to not let Esther intimidate her, Arnell stepped within two feet of Esther and boldly put her hands on her hips. A heavy hush filled Arnell's ears as she and Esther looked dead into each other's eyes. Arnell saw a cruel, selfish woman who would destroy anyone that got in her way. Esther saw a rebellious daughter who needed to be taught a lesson.

"It's your move, *Mother.* Do your best."

This was one of those times that Esther hated when Arnell called her mother. Arnell had a way of making the word mother sound like a filthy curse word. Hearing it made Esther recoil in her skin.

Even more than this, she hated, of late, that Arnell showed no fear in going up against her.

"One day, sweetie, you're going to push me too far."

"Well, Mother, I guess I could say the same about you, but I think this should be where we part company before things get a bit too ugly. I can't say it was wonderful knowing you, but I will say, always remember, I am *your* daughter. Whatever you think about doing to me, I will definitely make it my business to do ten times worse to you. If you know like I know, you'll let Trena go in peace and chalk this one up as a giveaway."

"I don't think so, sweetie," Esther said coldly. "I give nothing away that's mine, not even you."

"See, that's your problem, Mother, you think you own people. Get over it—slavery ended."

At that moment, Trena rushed out into the hall. Smiling broadly, she ran to Arnell, embracing her excitedly. "Thank you, thank you. Arnell, I'm going home. My parents want me back. They said they missed me."

Arnell's eyes never left Esther's. "That's so wonderful." Arnell slowly peeled Trena off her body. "Trena, I need you to do something right now, without question."

"Sure."

"Go outside, *right now*, to my car. It's the champagne-colored Camry. The door is open. Get inside and lock yourself in."

"But I have to pack—"

"You take nothing, Trena. You leave now." Keeping her eyes on Esther, Arnell shoved Trena toward the back staircase. "Go."

Esther started to reach for Trena. Arnell quickly sidled in front of Esther, blocking her from going after Trena, who bounded down the stairs. Neither Arnell nor Esther said anything but their glaring anger sent sparks of disdain through each of them.

"I'll get her back," Esther said confidently. "I do know where her parents live."

"I swear before God, Mother, if you do not leave that child alone, you will regret it. Like me, Trena was raped by Woodruff Parker. I will not leave her here to endure another rape at his hands. If you try to go after her, I promise you, I will destroy you and this business."

Esther's chest was heaving. She weighed her options. Arnell was privy to everything about the business from the start and could very well destroy her. Esther couldn't allow that. She sized up Arnell. Physically, she was no match for Arnell. She had youth and strength over her. There were other ways to hurt Arnell that were far worse than any punch or slap. She knew what she had to do. Miming a kiss, Esther blew the kiss at Arnell just as she turned and headed for the back staircase.

Arnell breathed a deep sigh of relief. For a minute there, she thought she was going to have to fight her own mother. That would have been a mind-blowing trip. Damn, how much worse could her day get? That blown kiss made Arnell more angry, but she could waste no time going after Esther when she had to get Trena home. She wasn't worried about Esther stopping Trena outside, she couldn't. If Big Walt was working this afternoon, then there might have been a problem, but Big Walt had gone home right after bringing them back from the funeral. Thank God for small favors. Gratefully, Arnell's only worry was in keeping her word to Trena and to Mrs. Gatlind. Unlike Arnell, Trena had a real home to go back to. In a strange way, Arnell felt by helping Trena, she was somehow saving her own life. Screw Esther; it was high time she learned that she owned no one. Not even her own child.

Twenty-Nine

"Queen Esther, you look hot, lady," Melvina said, admiring Esther in her low-cut, long, white, form-fitting dress slit up the front to the top of her thighs. "Where you goin'?"

Esther smoothed her hair back on the sides. "Nowhere, I'm staying in. Which is why I'd like for you to fix some simple but elegant hors d'oeuvres. Some brie and crackers, and maybe some of that shrimp dip might be nice. Enough for two, okay? Oh, and do serve some of that fine white wine that Arnell likes so much. For me, my usual."

"I thought I saw Arnell leave?"

"You did. She's not here."

"Yes, mon, I saw her leave in a mighty huff."

Esther sighed. "Lately, that's the only way she ever leaves."

"Maybe this time, she stay gone," Melvina said. "She had that kind of look in she eyes."

"Arnell will never stay away for good." Esther smoothed her dress down over his hips. "I assure you, she'll be back. How do I look?"

Melvina raised her brow. "You havin' special man company, Queen Esther?"

"Of course not, Melvina. What kind of woman do you think I am? Tony just died."

"I beg ya pardon, Queen Esther."

"You certainly should," Esther said haughtily. "Now, Arnell's fiancé is coming over to talk about his surprise honeymoon trip for Arnell, which I'm paying for. I'm helping him to plan it."

"That child do not know how lucky she is. You are such a good mother to she, Queen Esther."

"I wish you'd tell Arnell that."

"You want me to? I will, you know."

"That's all right, Melvina, you'll just piss Arnell off."

"It do not take much to do that."

Bzzzz!

Esther quickly smoothed down her dress over her flat stomach and round hips. She liked that James was right on time. "Melvina, don't bring the hors d'oeuvres and wine in until I call you. And don't let anyone disturb us. I mean no one."

"Yes, ma'am." Melvina smiled knowingly as Esther hurried off to answer the front doorbell.

Opening the door, Esther liked, too, that James was dressed to impress in his tan, short-sleeve, linen walking suit. "James, I'm so glad you had a little time to spare. Thank you for coming over."

"No, thank you for helping me out with this. Even though Arnell and I won't be getting married until next June, it is best to start planning the honeymoon now so that we can get the best accommodations."

"This is why I never do anything last minute."

"I need some improvement in that area," James said, admiring the original detail of the moldings over the doorways of the house. "This house is really great. I love old houses."

"They don't make them like this anymore." Esther led James into her suite. "Oh, that's right. This is only the second time you've been in my home, isn't it?"

"Yes,"

"Arnell should bring you around more often." Esther closed the door.

James admired the Italian provincial decor. "This is very nice, Esther. It's quite elegant."

"Yes, and quite cozy." Esther sat on the ivory white love seat and indicated for James to join her. "Have you spoken to Arnell since she's been back?"

"She's back?" James asked, surprised. "I thought she was still up at the health spa."

"No, actually, she came back a few days ago."

"And she didn't call me?"

"Don't be upset, dear. Arnell rushed back to be by my side." Esther sniffled. She drew on the image of Tony lying in his casket. Her eyes instantly watered.

James scooted closer to Esther. "What's wrong? Are you all right?"

Dabbing at her eyes, Esther shook her head. She crossed her legs at the knees, exposing her shapely legs through the sexy slit in her dress.

"Is there anything I can do for you, Esther? Anything at all?"

Esther began to weep openly. Distraught, she fell against James's shoulder. He put his arms around her.

"My God, Esther, what is it?"

"It's Tony. He was buried this morning."

"Buried? Tony's dead?"

Clinging to James, Esther cried harder.

Tightening his embrace, James tried to comfort Esther. "I am so sorry, Esther, I didn't know. Where's Arnell? She should be here with you. My God."

Esther stopped crying but she continued to nestle in the warmth of James's embrace. "Arnell left this afternoon. I think she might be driving back up to the spa."

"Are you kidding? Her place is here with you." James checked his watch. "What time did she leave? I'll try to reach her and get her back here."

"No." Esther sat up, but she didn't move completely out of James's embrace. She pressed her breast into James's side. Every time Esther moved just a little, her breast rubbed against him. "Let Arnell go. She was terribly broken up by Tony's death. She was with me for two days. I'm the one that told her to go back up to the spa to rest."

"That was considerate of you, Esther, but Arnell really should be here. Why didn't she call me? I would have been here for you both."

"I don't know, James. Arnell was acting so funny." It was but a featherlight touch but Esther rubbed her leg against James's leg. If he noticed, James gave no indication that he was uncomfortable with the touch or Esther's closeness.

"What do you mean, Arnell's acting funny? How was she acting?"

"Withdrawn. Sullen. Which is why I called you, James. I figure if we start planning the wedding and the honeymoon, we can surprise Arnell and cheer her up."

"I see your point," James said. "I'm sure she's just upset about Tony."

Esther sniffled. "Yes, I'm sure that's it."

"If you don't mind my asking, Esther, what happened to Tony?"

The tears flowed. "They said he fell down a flight of stairs. My poor Tony, I can't believe he's gone." Esther pressed into James again. This time when his arm tightened around her shoulder, she turned her body toward him. She lay her face in the crook of his neck and slipped her arm around the other side of his neck. Her tears were real; she truly missed Tony, so she didn't have to fake that, but her moves on James weren't supposed to be exciting her. She was trying to seduce him to get back at Arnell, but she was enjoying the feel of James's arms around her, not to mention how she was starting to feel in between her thighs. Too bad she would never be able to boast about this seduction to Arnell. This was going to have to be her little secret—Arnell didn't have to ever know for Esther to feel satisfied.

"Esther, I know it's hard right now, but you'll be fine." James began to rub Esther's back. "I only met Tony that one time, but he seemed to be a good man."

"Yes, he was," she said, making sure that her lips lightly touched James's neck every time she spoke. "Tony stood by me during some of the roughest times of my life." Esther let her arm slip lazily down from around James's neck onto his chest. It rested there. "Tony was like a father to Arnell and she was just as special to him." Esther's arm slid ever so slowly down onto James's stomach and then down onto his crotch, where she would have sworn she felt a hardness, but she did not let her arm rest there for she felt James's body stiffen. She eased her arm on down atop James's left thigh. There it rested.

James removed his arm from around Esther. "Ah, Esther, can I get you something? Some water?" He crossed his left leg over the right.

Inside, Esther smiled. She hadn't lost a bit of her skill. "Actually, James, I am thirsty and perhaps a little hungry. Let me see what Melvina has in the kitchen." She went to the suite door and stuck her head out into the hallway, and at the same time, stuck her butt in James's direction.

"Melvina!" Esther called loud enough to be heard back in the kitchen, but not loud enough to be crass or to break the mood she was setting. She bent her right leg at the knee and leaned farther out the door.

"Yes, Queen Esther."

"Melvina, please see if you can put together some of those left-over noshes from Tony's wake for me and James. Nothing fancy, okay?"

"Tony's wake?" Melvina asked quietly.

Esther mouthed, *Shhh.*

"Right away, Queen Esther," Melvina said.

Esther turned around just in time to catch James looking at her butt before he looked away. Again Esther smiled to herself. This was going to be easy. She closed the door and was about to walk away when Melvina knocked. Esther opened the door straightaway.

"Melvina, you're a saint. You're so fast."

"Thank you, Queen Esther." Melvina pushed the serving cart in and while she busied herself uncovering the two plates of hors d'oeuvres, she got her fill of James sitting with his hands clasped over his crotch. On the way out of the suite, she raised her brow slyly. Esther did the same.

"Melvina's the best." Esther picked up the plate of brie and crackers and held it out to James. "It's not much, but it satisfies the appetite."

"This is fine, I'm not that hungry." James took a cracker with a wad of brie on it and ate it immediately.

"Take another," Esther insisted.

James took three more crackers. Esther poured him a glass of wine. After James drank half the glass Esther refilled it. She took her gin and sat again on the sofa, this time a few inches separated them. She didn't want to scare James away.

"So, James, what kind of honeymoon do you have in mind?"

He cleared his throat. "I guess I'm like everyone else—the beach, the ocean, the sun."

"James, I'm surprised at you," Esther cooed. "I took you for a real romantic—a cold weather man."

James grinned like a schoolboy. "That's how you see me, huh?"

"Sure. You look like a man who likes to cuddle up in front of a burning fireplace on a bearskin rug with the wind howling outside and snow coming down nonstop. Arnell likes that sort of thing, you know."

"She never mentioned it."

"Sure, when she was a kid, we had a fireplace. Arnell used to love to stretch out on the floor in front of the fireplace butt-naked."

James laughed. "You're kidding. Where did she get that from?"

Smiling coyly, Esther offered James the shrimp dip. "From her mother, of course. I love stretching out in front of a fireplace with nothing on but the beautiful, baby soft skin I was born in."

Staring at Esther, James sat with the cracker in his hand.

Esther teased, "If you'd like something other than the dip, James, you're welcome to it." She slowly recrossed her legs, lifting them higher so that more thigh showed. James's eyes followed her every move. "James."

"This is just fine." He dipped his cracker.

Like a waking cat, Esther slowly stretched her body out. "Really, James, there is nothing like a cold day and heat from a hot fireplace. I can almost feel the heat on my body." Closing her eyes, Esther let her hands glide smoothly and slowly across her breast, down her body, over her pubis onto her thighs and back up to her breasts. "James, if you have never laid before a fire, you really must try it one day." Opening her eyes, Esther rubbed one leg atop the other, lifting her thigh higher so that the slit fell open all the way. "Nothing feels as good as heat on a naked body."

Mesmerized, James watched the movement of Esther's hands. His eyes shifted from her hands on top of her breasts down to her naked thigh. Again he was holding an uneaten cracker.

"Sex is even better in front of a fire. Did you know that James?"

Blushing, James lay his left arm across his erect penis. He popped the cracker in his mouth and quickly downed his glass of wine. "So you think we should plan a winter wedding?"

"If it were my wedding, I would." Esther refilled James's glass. "In fact, James, if it were cold outside right now, I'd have me a fire going. I have a fireplace—back there in my bedroom. Now that I'm thinking about it, when you leave, I just might start me a little fire."

"Esther, it's almost eighty degrees outside."

"So, I have an air-conditioner."

James chuckled nervously.

"I know it sounds stupid," she said, "but a fire totally relaxes me." Again closing her eyes, Esther began rubbing the back of her neck. "I've been so tense since Tony died."

James watched as Esther massaged her neck and moved her chest at the same time. He could see the top of her breast and leaned an inch closer to see if he could see farther down in her dress.

"James, would you mind massaging my neck and shoulders, I'm really not too good at massaging myself."

"Ah . . . sure."

Esther turned her back to James so that he could massage her better. Her butt was touching his thigh. James was having a hard time massaging Esther's neck, she was too close, but he was also uncomfortable because his penis was pushing against his underwear. He wanted to adjust himself, but he couldn't do it without being obvious. After a minute of massaging with Esther too close and his arms held up in an awkward position, James's fingers began cramping. "Ah, Esther, if you'd—"

"Oh, this isn't a good position, is it? Maybe I should face you." Esther started to get up.

"No! Maybe I should stand on the side of the chair." James started to get up, but Esther quickly pulled him back down.

"James, why should you stand and be uncomfortable. Wait, I can make this comfortable for both of us." Standing in front of James, Esther suddenly hiked the skirt of her dress above her thighs—startling James. His mouth dropped—Esther wasn't wearing any panties—he looked straight at her hairy mound. His nostrils inhaled her perfumed essence and something more naturally fragranced. Esther sat quickly on James's lap, straddling him, her knees on either side of his thighs. She shifted her hips so that her pubis was right on top of James's erect penis.

James stiffened. "Oh, my . . . my God. Esther . . . wait . . . wait a minute. You . . . we . . . I . . . I can't—"

"James, don't get yourself so worked up," Esther said innocently. She was quite aware that he wasn't trying to get up. "You're just going to massage my neck. That's all. Here, put your hands on my shoulders and massage—here."

"But—"

Esther took James's hands and placed them on her shoulders. "You can do it better this way." She arched her back, pressing herself into James's penis.

James was having a hard time breathing quietly. "Esther, what are you doing?"

"Nothing, dear, I'm just making it easier for you to massage me."

"Esther, I can't—"

"James, you're just massaging my neck. It's such an innocent little thing. Please, I'm so tense." She put her hands on top of her own thighs and, sitting straight, threw her head back and began to roll it from side to side. "Just for a minute, please."

Almost afraid to move, James sat frozen, staring at Esther's breasts inches from his face and feeling the heat from her vagina through his pants. His penis was rock-hard. Beads of sweat popped out above his upper lip.

"James, please, massage me."

Gingerly, James began to move his fingers. As he kneaded her neck, Esther began to slowly gyrate her hips, pressing herself more and more into James. "Oh, yes, that feels better. Ooo, yes, this is just what I needed." And she meant that in more ways than one. She was throbbing. Despite the fabric between them, she could feel James's penis hard and strong at the mouth of her vagina. With her eyes closed, she could hear him breathing and gasping softly. He was lightly but firmly pushing up on her. She began to ride him a little harder. His fingers were no longer moving on her shoulders. They were moving down the front of her dress onto her breasts where he palmed them. But he didn't stay there, he dropped his hands onto her behind and squeezed her naked buttocks. He pulled her even tighter onto his groin.

Esther needed to feel James's flesh up inside her. She fell into James and started to kiss him deep and long. He was no slouch. He returned the kisses with as much fervor and passion as her. Working quickly, Esther unbuckled James's belt, unsnapped and unzipped his pants, and reached in and pulled his hot, throbbing penis out of its cloth prison. In that same instant, she slipped it inside her and forgot that she even had a daughter, much less a daughter who was engaged to the man she was riding.

Riiiing! It was James's cell phone, but it was not going to be answered.

Thirty

Trena was hiding in her room, too afraid to venture out again to be with her family. She stood in front of her mirror in her bra and a pair of cotton panties, wondering if there was anything visibly different about her face, about her body, or even about the way she walked since she left home. If she wasn't mistaken, her bra was fitting a bit tighter. She tried to adjust herself inside the not-quite-fitting-right B cup. She wondered if her mother or father could tell by looking at her that she had lost her virginity, that she had been having sex with men she didn't even know. She could never let them find out she had prostituted her body and worse for money that she was never given—Queen Esther said that her money went toward the clothes she bought for her and for her room and board. When Trena's mother hounded her about where she had been staying for almost four weeks, she lied and said that she stayed in a homeless shelter in Bedford-Stuyvesant. Then they wanted to know who Arnell was, and again Trena lied. She told them that Arnell was a social worker at the homeless shelter. Her parents didn't question her further but told her those shelters were dangerous places.

Before Trena escaped to the solitude of her bedroom, her mother said she forgave her for running away and that she had really missed her. That was all good, but Trena didn't know if she could forgive herself for almost ruining her own life. She had missed the last three weeks of school and the first weeks of summer school, which she needed in order to qualify to take her finals. She had a lot of catching up to do. The tears came. This wasn't what Trena had planned for her summer, but she didn't want to cry anymore. She was too tired. She had been crying since she got home, and had only stopped crying long enough to blow her nose. Her mother had cried along with her while begging her to never scare her like that again, yet, her mother wasn't so heartbroken that she didn't bitch.

"Young lady, you still will not run wild in this house. You will still live by the rules or you will pay the consequences."

Her father, Joe, had held her close while telling her, "Trena, there are bad people out there who will take advantage of a pretty young girl like you. You were lucky this time that no one bothered you, but I wouldn't try my luck again, if I were you. Now, I got to get back on the road. You make me miss another run, you're going to wish you ran all the way to Timbuktu." Tomorrow, he was flying to Dallas where he'd left his truck.

Knock . . . knock . . . knock.

"Who is—"

The door opened before Trena could finish her question. In walked Cheryl.

Trena quickly grabbed her oversize T-shirt and covered her breasts.

"Little sister. So, you've gone out and seen the world. Did you have any fun?"

Cheryl hadn't said much of anything the whole evening. At times Trena only knew that Cheryl was close by, listening, when she'd hear her clear her throat. Whether Cheryl's clearing of her throat was intentional or not, it made Trena nervous. She had the feeling that Cheryl wasn't being fooled by anything she said.

Trying her best to avoid an argument, Trena climbed into her bed and turned her back to Cheryl.

"Fine, you don't wanna talk to me? That's okay, I understand. We hadn't been getting along for a very long time before you left. Anyway, I came to tell you that I'm glad you're home." Cheryl started out of the room. "Oh, by the way, I'm getting married."

Trena sat up. "For real?"

Cheryl smiled. "Alex and I are back together. We're getting married in December."

"What happened to the other girl?"

"He said it was a mistake."

"Wow," was all Trena could say.

"There's a spot open for a maid of honor, if you want it."

Again, those darn tears threatened. "But I was so mean to you."

Cheryl's own eyes watered. "That's behind us, isn't it?"

Trena nodded.

Cheryl pulled the door closed, leaving Trena alone to think about what was behind her and what might be ahead of her. Lying down again, she stuck her head under her pillow and cried. She was happy for Cheryl, but she had a dirty little secret that would spoil Cheryl's wedding and hurt her parents deeply. It was a secret she could never tell anyone, not even Alyson and Bebe. They knew that she was staying at the mansion, but she never told them about the sex. No one could ever know about that. When Arnell dropped her off, she had offered her telephone number, "In case you ever need to talk to someone." Trena didn't think she'd ever have to call on Arnell again, but Arnell was the only person that might understand how she was feeling. Yes, she would call Arnell tomorrow when she was alone at home.

Thirty-One

Long after Arnell dropped Trena off and late into the evening Sunday night, Arnell tried, several times, to get in touch with James. She'd left messages for him to call her on his home answering machine and on his cell phone voice mail. She even called his office on the off chance that he might be there. He wasn't. The more time passed, the more worried Arnell became. It had never been this difficult to reach James. How cruel a joke was that? Of all the times for James to come up missing, this was not the optimum. After facing off with Esther, after rescuing Trena from the mansion, Arnell was determined to move on with her life with no ball and chain holding her down. And that meant telling James the truth. But where in the world was he? When she told him that she was going away to the spa for ten days, he never mentioned that he was going anywhere.

Arnell didn't dare call James's parents' home—she wasn't comfortable speaking with his mother or his father. Mrs. Stanton was such a pompous phony. At their first meeting, Mrs. Stanton remarked, "James comes from a long, distinguished line of ministers. We were hoping that he'd enter the ministry also, but he had a more worldly calling—he wanted to be a businessman."

James had, in fact, become a nonprofit fund-raiser. He had worked as the director of development at the Brooklyn Museum for three years and was now working part-time as the capital campaign director for the United Negro College Fund while he pursued his interest in politics. To Mrs. Stanton, Arnell had said what she thought was safe—"He could change his mind one day." That's when Mrs. Stanton asked, "What do you do for a living? What does your mother do?"

Arnell had said she was a freelance copy editor, which she was when she felt like it, and that her mother had retired early from teaching. That was almost the truth. Esther had retired from servicing the clients herself, but she was still teaching girls how to satisfy men.

But it was when Mrs. Stanton asked, "Who were your people?" that Arnell knew for sure she wasn't going to be sitting tea with her. Damn, the woman was only a minister's wife, and a minister, as quiet as it was kept, who wasn't very righteous. Mrs. Stanton was not the wife of some blue blood who boasted ancestors who came over on some boat. James said his parents were from Mississippi, which meant that the boat their ancestors came over on was a far cry from the *QE II*. If Esther was ever right about anything, she was right when she said that a lot of church folk who, supposedly, claimed a *personal* relationship with God, were the biggest hypocrites in the world. What Mrs. Stanton didn't know that Arnell knew, was that James had told her that before his mother met his father, she had worked in a chicken plant pulling the innards out of assholes in South Carolina before moving to New York. As far as Arnell was concerned, there was nothing wrong with the work Mrs. Stanton had done—it was an honest living—but there was definitely something wrong with Mrs. Stanton forgetting where she came from and who her people were.

That's why Arnell's answer to that stupid-ass question, "Who were your people?" was, "Slaves."

Of course, the dead silence told Arnell that she had been a bit too insolent but she wasn't regretful. "Perhaps I've gone too far back," she said. "Actually, my family were just typical working Americans." Mrs. Stanton never asked Arnell another thing about her family.

Now, Reverand Stanton, the Right Reverend, as Esther liked to call him, was no different from his wife in church, but he was a hell of a lot different from her outside of church and away from his congregation. Before Arnell had even met James, she had met the Right Reverend and didn't connect the two when, five years later, she started editing for James. For five years, the Right Reverend was one of The Honey Well's most ardent clients and for a long time Arnell had pondered how Reverend Stanton had come to know about The Honey Well and finally got up the nerve to ask him.

He replied, "All things good or bad that happen in the world come to be known by word of mouth. One of my deacons told me."

The only thing Arnell could say behind that was, "Oh." Wasn't anyone righteous? Certainly not the Right Reverend or his deacon. With his starched collars and his hearty laugh, the Right Reverend's passionate delivery of his sermons were no match for his passion for hot and heavy sex. That's something James didn't know about his father, or if he did, he never mentioned it. The Right Reverend, this so-called man of God, spent plenty of his congregation's tithes and offerings satisfying his lustful appetite for women who, if they stepped inside the church, might catch fire and burn. The one and only time Arnell went to the Right Reverend's church with James, she cowered inside. Her faltering footfalls were obvious as James escorted her into the church.

"What's wrong?" James asked.

She shook her head and forced her feet to move. She knew that God was glaring fire and brimstone at her and at any minute she expected to spontaneously combust. When she didn't, she remembered Esther's words, "The church is full of hypocrites." Looking up at the Right Reverend sitting pompously in his pulpit looking down upon his congregation, Arnell figured if he was not on fire, then she wouldn't catch fire either. When the Right Reverend looked down and saw her sitting next to James, his mocha complexion ashened before Arnell's eyes, and once he got over the shock, a look of pure lividity shot from his eyes. After church, she didn't wait around to shake his hand. She rushed James out of there with the excuse that she had to go to the bathroom in the worst way.

The very next morning, the Right Reverend stormed into the mansion. "Stop seeing my son or I will tell him what you are."

Arnell had been about to respond when Esther stepped in. "Well, tell me Reverend. What is she?"

"She's a . . . she's an unclean woman of ill repute. I raised my son to marry a clean woman of the highest caliber."

"That's all well and good, Reverend," Esther said, "because the highest caliber is what Arnell is. Now, if you're saying that she's not, and I think that's what you're trying to say, and that you intend to tell your son that she's not, then I think I will march every girl you have fucked in the name of the Holy Ghost into your church, and we will all stand before your congregation, your wife, your son, and God Almighty and testify to the great whore that you are."

The Right Reverend then pointed at Esther. "You will reap the evil that you sow. You're both lowly women, Jezebels, that are be-neath—"

"Hold the fuck up!" Esther shouted. "You arrogant, pompous, son of a bitch! You've been coming in here for five years sticking your holy rod in any and every female in the house, including me. How dare you call us names and point your finger of damnation and indignation—which has been up inside the holes of many so-called righteous and unrighteous women, in and out of your church—in our faces when you're the greatest hypocrite in the eyes of your God there is. You brazen bastard! What do you think your God is saying to Jesus about your extracurricular activities, Right Reverend Stanton?"

The Right Reverend hauled ass out of The Honey Well as if a castrating lioness was on his tail. He never stepped inside the man-sion again, not even to attend his son's engagement party—he was away on "church" business. A likely excuse, but one that Arnell ap-plauded. She didn't know if she would have been able to enjoy her own party with him around. The few times she and the Right Reverend had been in each other's company since, their eyes never met and words were never exchanged.

Despite what she knew about James's father and the unforgiv-able deeds that she herself had done, Arnell had recklessly planned on marrying James, but she had been fooling herself. It would never work. There were too many secrets.

Again, Arnell dialed James. She had to tell him and soon.

Thirty-Two

Esther was feeling absolutely divine. While drying herself off with an oversize fluffy white towel after a cool, invigorating shower, she hummed the theme from *Love Story*, that's how good she was feeling. As much as she missed Tony, even he had never made love to her the way James did. Lord, he rocked her world and if she must say so herself, she had done the same for him. She had left James snoring, on his back with his arms spread out and his face pointing straight up at the ceiling. That was the only thing pointing up at the ceiling—the man was plumb tuckered out. It was well past midnight. James had been insatiable once he and Esther sparked that first fire in the front room, and moved back to the bedroom to set the fire ablaze in the fireplace. As warm as it was, they had laid out butt naked in front of the fireplace and made mad passionate love until they were drained from sweating, and exhausted from going at it nonstop like they were teenagers just discovering that sex could clear up their acne and give them the best high in the world. The air in Esther's bedroom was prime for an atmospheric collision of hot air from the fireplace and cold air from the air conditioner, but the air conditioner did very little to cool her and James down; they were making more heat than the flames in the fireplace.

Esther slipped on her robe and was about to wrap it around her body when she looked at herself in the full-length mirror on the back of the bathroom door. She opened the robe. Since Tony died, she had lost five pounds from not eating. That would not have been the way she would have chosen to lose weight, but she was glad all the same. Even without the five pound weight loss, the years had been kind to her, and what James had filled her with time and again was akin to the sweet nectar of youth. She felt like she was twenty years old, and indeed, she had made love to James like she wasn't a day over twenty. Esther smiled to herself. *Not bad for an old girl.* She slipped the robe off and sauntered into the bedroom, dragging the bathrobe behind her and wearing only a seductive smile. James was still snoring. Curious, Esther gingerly lifted the sheet off him and peeked. Oh, yes, he was ready for more. Again, she climbed on top of him. He fit inside her like a hand inside a lambskin leather glove. She didn't need James awake to get what she needed from him. She dug her knees into the mattress, closed her eyes and, taking her own sweet time, began her sensual ride in slow motion. After a few minutes, she felt James responding. When his hands gripped her buttocks, she knew that it was a matter of time before he would flip her over and take charge. She had no problem with that—she liked a man who took charge in bed. The flip was sudden. Esther lay back and was about to wrap her legs around James's back when he suddenly uncorked her. Her eyes popped open.

"Where are you going?" she asked.

James grumbled, "To the bathroom."

"You're just going to leave me like this?" she said, glancing down at herself spread wide open.

"You were screwing a pee-hard." James strolled off into the bathroom, closing the door behind him.

"Damn." While Esther eased her thighs closed, she didn't cover her nakedness. That pee-hard was feeling mighty good to end so abruptly. Arnell was a lucky girl. James was, supposedly, in love with Arnell, so his making love to Arnell had to be hellified. This man certainly had it going on.

James came back into the room. He had wrapped a towel around his waist, covering himself up.

"Did everything come out all right?" Esther asked teasingly.

James scratched his head. He sat on the edge of the bed, his back to Esther. He glanced at the clock on the night table—1:00 A.M. "Damn." Yet, he made no move to dress and leave.

"Why don't you climb back in here with me." Esther patted the bed next to her.

James began to slowly and firmly rub his hands together.

Esther rested her elbow on her pillow and her head in her hand. "So how are you feeling?"

James exhaled heavily. "I guess how I feel is indescribable. How about you? How do you feel?"

"Hungry," Esther replied, but food wasn't what she had in mind. However, she was beginning to wonder what James had on his mind. She noticed that he hadn't turned to face her. "You're a great lover, James. One of the best I've ever had."

Still rubbing his hands, James bowed his head. "We should not've done this."

"Perhaps not, but we did. If you're worried about Arnell, she doesn't have to know."

At that, James did turn to Esther. But seeing her naked, he immediately turned away. "And how do you propose we keep this from her? We're not the only ones that know. Melvina knows and no telling who she tells."

"If it's Melvina you're worried about, don't. Melvina will tell no one."

"That doesn't make me feel any better."

"I'm telling you, James, we have nothing to worry about. Arnell will never know. She rarely comes here anymore. You could come here—"

"No!" James stood. He started to walk toward the bathroom but turned back. "You can't mean—" He again turned away from Esther. His mouth moved but the words he spoke were without sound.

"James, you're not a choirboy. You—"

"No, I am not a goddamn choirboy." This time he faced Esther. He gripped the foot railing of the brass bed. "But I am engaged to your daughter! Look, I know what happened was just as much my fault as yours, we were both weak. But that's no excuse. We were both irresponsible."

"Perhaps, but we're both adults." Esther wasn't about to let James's guilt spoil her euphoria. "And adults are prone to being weak. It's how we handle this situation that attests to our maturity."

James frowned. "I don't feel very mature right now. In fact, I feel like the kid who peed on himself in front of his classmates. I feel terribly ashamed."

"It's too bad you feel that way," Esther said, sitting up. "I don't." She wasn't liking the way James was talking one bit. She pulled the sheet across her breasts and hips. "Personally, I don't think you have anything to be ashamed of. And by the way, I hope making love to me wasn't that disgusting."

"Goddamn it, Esther, you're not getting it! I spent half the night screwing my fiancée's mother, my future mother-in-law. Do you understand how despicably wrong that is?"

"You tell me, James," Esther said, feeling quite irked, "how wrong is it?"

"I see you're not taking this serious, but I am." James rubbed his temple hard. "You should consider how devastated Arnell will be when she . . ."

"If she—"

". . . finds out. Do you realize that what we did smacks of Oedipal betrayal?"

Esther drew back. "I don't know how the hell that is, I am not your mother." James was *really* pissing her off. "And you certainly didn't kill my husband to sleep with me, someone else did that."

"You . . . What?" James was stumped.

"Never mind," Esther said, flipping her hand at James. "Look, if you're so disgusted with what we did, why don't you just leave."

"No, Esther, we need to talk about this. You may not be my biological mother, but you'd be close enough, being my mother-in-law. And no, I may not have killed my father or your husband to sleep with you, but I feel like I've stuck a knife in Arnell's heart."

All that youthful energy and intoxicating zeal that Esther had been feeling since her and James's first kiss, which pumped up her ego and put a song in her heart, suddenly went *poof!* Esther felt her chest deflate.

"Esther, this should have never happened." James felt like he wanted to cry. "We were godawful wrong."

"Leave God out of this." In that moment, Esther became aware of her nakedness under the sheet. Holding onto the sheet to keep from exposing herself, she retrieved her bathrobe from the foot of the bed and modestly pulled it on, tying it tight around her body. She felt like a fool.

"Esther, we were never supposed to let such a thing cross our minds, much less get so weak that we couldn't stop what we ended up doing."

"Yeah, well, shit happens—oh, but you know that, don't you, James?"

"Not like this!" James threw out his hands. "You're Arnell's mother, for God sake! You will be the grandmother of our children."

"Grandmother? I don't think so. But I do see that you're not mature enough to know that all kinds of shit happens in this world." Esther was trying hard to remain calm, though James was making her angrier. She felt rotten—not for what she had done, but because of how James was feeling about her and how he was making her feel about herself—old. "James, what we did was what any two normal, sexual beings would do when they are attracted to each other. And what we did was good, damn good. I have no regrets. In fact, if you laid your hard ass down on this bed, right now, I'd make love to you all over again—with no regrets."

James clutched his head and walked away from the bed. He began to pace. "Oh, God. I can't believe this. Damn it!" He punched himself in the chest. "What the hell did I do?"

Esther felt like he had punched her, too. That good feeling she'd had all night and all morning vanished completely. "Excuse the hell out of me, but am I to understand that you're totally disgusted with yourself for making love to me?"

Rushing back at the bed, James gripped the brass foot railing. "Esther, wake the fuck up! We did not make love. We fucked, we humped, we screwed, we banged! I make love to Arnell. Why can't you understand that I love Arnell?" He shook the bed. "Don't you get it? I am going to marry Arnell, your daughter! So how the hell am I supposed to feel about what we did?"

"James, I think you're getting yourself all worked up over nothing. We—"

"Nothing!" James shook the bed again. "Esther, I love Arnell! If she even had a clue that we did what we did, she'd never, in a million years, marry me."

"Oh, I'm sure Arnell will still marry you—if you keep your mouth shut."

"Is that right? All I have to do is keep my mouth shut?"

"It's as simple as that," Esther said, totally disgusted with James. He wasn't acting all scared and worried last night when he thrust himself inside her too many times to count, or when he looked upon her face and knew who it was that he was making love to, who it was that he was lapping and devouring with his tongue.

James shook his head. "Well, I can't do that. This is a heavy thing to have to live with."

Scratching her nose, Esther smirked. "With such high morals, it must be tough to have a penis that has a mind of its own."

"Damn, Esther! Doesn't it bother you that we've betrayed Arnell whether she ever finds out about us or not? Don't you care that I may have lost the woman I love?"

"Poor you." Esther was disgusted. "James, why don't you go home? I hate having weak men who whine after the fact in my presence."

"If that's how you see me, fine. I don't have a problem with that, but I think you'd better put on a pair of bifocals and see clearly that we have a serious problem here."

Sitting at her makeup table, Esther began powdering her nose. It still irked her that James had called her old. "I told you, we have no problem if you keep your mouth shut."

"But Arnell and I have a trusting relationship. She would have never done anything like this to me. She—"

Esther started laughing.

"I don't see what the hell is so funny. Maybe you've never had the kind of respect and trust that Arnell and I share."

"You're wrong there—I've had that kind of respect and trust from men who are now dead. You're the one that's living in a fantasy world."

"Arnell and—"

"Save it!" Esther spun around to face James. "Boy, I could tell you things about Arnell that would have you singing a different song about trust and losing the woman you love. In fact, I should tell you the truth about Arnell so that I can relieve you of that 'terrible' shame you're feeling."

James was at rapt attention. "What truth? What are you talking about?"

Buzzzz! The front doorbell rang, drawing Esther's attention. On a Sunday night, she wasn't expecting anyone and by now, all the girls were probably still out visiting friends and family. Sunday and Monday were their days off and Melvina might have gone to her apartment.

"Esther, what truth about Arnell?"

Buzzz!

"I have to get that." Esther hurried out of the bedroom and quickly opened the door to her suite.

"I'll get it!" Melvina said, hurrying past Esther to the front door.

Esther closed her door and saw right away that James had followed her out of the bedroom. His face was strained, his eyes were angry.

"What do you know about Arnell?"

There was a knock at the suite door. Esther opened the door to Melvina.

"Sorry to disturb you, Queen Esther," Melvina said, craning her neck around Esther to get a look at James, "but there is a man here to see you."

"Who?"

"He say he a old friend."

"I don't have any old friends," Esther said, pulling her robe tighter. "Tell him to write a note." She started to close the door.

"So you're disowning me, are you?" The man stood in the dining room doorway.

Esther looked around Melvina into the face of the stranger and into the face of her past. Although he was a few years younger than she, his curly hair was already heavily streaked with gray. His naturally tanned skin was tanned even deeper, and it was obvious that he worked out—his muscular arms were nicely chiseled in his short-sleeve polo shirt. He came closer. He smiled, showing all his white teeth and the one gold tooth that Esther had no trouble remembering.

"My God," she said, her eyes widening. Her heart thumped. The face was older, but so much else was the same. "Kesley?"

"For a minute there, Esther, I thought you might've forgotten about me. How's my sweetheart?" Kesley embraced Esther.

Esther's jaw dropped. She also remembered that Arnell had forced her to mention Kesley Hayden's name just weeks ago. She had put his name out there and now the man that was so long ago her lover, the man that so long ago killed Arnell's father, was here in the flesh.

Thirty-Three

"I see you still like your men young," Kesley said, looking at James who had backed up to the bedroom door. "Nothing much has changed in thirty years, huh Esther?"

Esther couldn't answer Kesley's snide question—she was too awestruck—she thought him long dead, rotting in his grave.

James, feeling quite exposed, crossed his hands atop his groin, although the towel covered his nakedness. "I'm not her man," he protested angrily. "I'm . . . I'm a friend of the family."

Esther cut her eyes at James. *That was a stupid thing to say.*

"Yeah?" Kesley raised his brow. "That's cool. I hope you don't have to explain to anyone in the family why you're dressed only in a towel in Esther's room and she only in a flimsy robe."

"Look, man—"

"Let it go," Esther said, finding her voice. "You don't owe him or *anyone* any explanation."

"I don't like what he's implying," James said, filled with guilt.

"Ignore him." Esther glared at Kesley but she saw past him to Melvina, whose eyes twinkled with excitement.

"Melvina, don't you have something to do?"

"Oh! Sure do." Melvina scurried back to the kitchen.

Esther suspected that Melvina would be lurking close enough to eavesdrop. "Kesley, have some class. Come inside if you must speak to me at all."

Once inside, Kesley took his time looking around. "Esther,

you're indeed the queen. I figured your place would look like this. Nice. Real nice."

"What are you doing here, Kesley?"

Smirking, Kesley looked at James. "You'd think after thirty years, she'd ask me how I was doing? After all, I did go to prison for her."

"Goddamn it, Kesley, don't be saying no shit like that! You did what you did on your own. I had nothing to do with it."

Kesley sat in Esther's favorite chair and looked at James. "See, women have selective memory. Esther seems to have forgotten that she wanted to get rid of her husband—"

"That's a damn lie! Don't you dare lie on me, Kesley Hayden! You beat Bryant to death. You—"

"I don't need to hear any of this shit!" James abruptly went back into the bedroom and slammed the door.

Esther needed a cigarette bad. Her day was going from worse to downright disastrous.

Looking at the hatred in Esther's eyes, Kesley began chuckling. Esther started looking around for her cigarettes. They were on the end table. She quickly got one and lit it. She took a long deep drag, filling her lungs completely before she exhaled.

"Those things will kill you," Kesley said.

"Shut the fuck up!" Esther sank down onto the love seat, where she had initiated and succeeded in her seduction of James. She could almost feel the heat of the passion they'd emitted on the cushion. She crossed her legs to still the little throb that yearned for more.

"Is that any way to talk to an old friend?"

"Kesley, what are you doing here? I heard that after you got out of prison, you slipped out of the country and went back to Trinidad."

"I did—for about two weeks. It wasn't worth the hassle. I was trying to avoid dealing with the parole board for six more years of my life, but I realized leaving the States would land me in worse trouble if they ever caught up with me. So I snuck back into the country. America is my home anyway. I've been living in Jacksonville for the past ten years. I'm done with the parole board. I don't have to deal with the system anymore."

That surprised Esther. If Kesley was living in the States, she would have thought he would have come looking for her a long time ago. She again dragged deep and long on her cigarette.

Kesley smiled. "I know what you're thinking. Why now?"

With the hand holding her cigarette, Esther motioned for Kesley to go ahead and answer his own question.

"The time's right. I'm just now getting over being mad at you."

"Don't do me any favors, Kesley. Stay mad at me, I like you best that way."

Kesley looked pointedly at Esther. "If anyone should be mad, it's me. I was locked up for nineteen years; I'm lucky I got out when I did. Woman, I took a second-degree manslaughter conviction for you."

Esther angrily stubbed out her cigarette. "No! You did nineteen years for beating Bryant to death and . . ."

"Over you."

". . . for all that money and drugs that was found on you. You were a criminal anyway, you were a numbers banker."

"Which you reaped the benefits of!" Kesley blasted back.

"No, no! You—"

The bedroom door suddenly opened. James was fully dressed. He had heard their conversation and he chided himself for stupidly getting involved with Esther. He wondered if Arnell knew any of this stuff about her mother's past—she had never mentioned this Kesley person before.

Esther and Kesley both stared at James. It was as if they were both asking, *So what are you standing there for?*

"We have to talk—later," James said to Esther. He quickly left the suite.

"Damn, Esther, I'm eight years younger than you. This boy got to be what? Thirty years younger?"

"Twenty-seven," she said, insulted. "But that's none of your business. What are you doing here?"

Kesley sat back. "Visiting. Something you didn't do when I was locked up."

Esther lit another cigarette. She had visited Kesley the first three months he was up in Sing Sing, but stopped when she could no longer afford the trip up to Ossining and pay to have someone baby-sit Arnell, too. Things got real bad for her with Bryant dead and Kesley in prison. Plus, all her friends were telling her that it didn't look good for her to be visiting the man who had beat her husband to death. For a few months more she had written Kesley but even that stopped when he kept demanding she visit him. It had finally sank in that she was consorting with the killer of Arnell's father.

Kesley suddenly stood. "Why did you stop visiting, Esther? Was it because I couldn't give you any more money? Or was it because we couldn't sneak behind your husband's back anymore and fuck anywhere we could find some privacy?"

Esther had a sour taste in her mouth and it didn't help much that she was smoking on an empty stomach. She had never wanted to relive the night that Bryant came home early and caught her and Kesley in the garage making love in the backseat of Kesley's car. Kesley had never been to her house before and had stopped by, impulsively, after being out of town for a week. They didn't hear the garage door open—they had been engrossed in their lovemaking and the loud music from the car radio filled their ears along with their own breathless panting.

Bryant yanked open the car door. "What the—"

Sweaty, breathing hard with Kesley still inside her, Esther had started to say, stupidly, "It's not what you—"

Bryant snatched Kesley out of her with one mighty tug on Kesley's collar. Kesley had fallen onto the garage floor but he was younger, faster and bigger than Bryant. While Kesley zipped up his pants, Bryant had called him all kinds of lowlife bastards. If Kesley hated anything, he hated being cursed. His fist was lightning fast. The punch in the face slammed Bryant back into the car. It was on. Bryant charged at Kesley. They started to fight and Kesley's martial arts skills were immediately apparent, but Bryant was so angry, he wasn't letting Kesley's deadly blows stop him. Every time Kesley kicked or knocked Bryant down, he'd get back up on wobbly legs and lunge. Esther tried to catch hold of Kesley's arm to stop him from hitting Bryant, but in his rage, Kesley flipped his arm and fist back and slammed her in the forehead, knocking her out cold. When Esther came to, Bryant was sprawled out on the garage floor. Blood oozed from his mouth. He was barely alive. Kesley was sitting on the floor with his back against the car—his head was in his hands.

Bryant died in the ambulance on the way to the hospital. Esther had a knot the size of an egg on her forehead so it looked to the police like Kesley had attacked her also. She said nothing to dispute that belief or to defend Kesley, choosing instead to say that she couldn't recall anything. It helped that she had been knocked out. Kesley's attorney brought up their affair, which she didn't deny, but she let the prosecutor insinuate that she was trying to break it off. If anything, her testimony neither hurt nor helped Kesley. In the end, Kesley's defense meant nothing—a search of his car at the scene that day uncovered a gym bag of illegal numbers money and a plastic food bag full of marijuana—he was going to prison no matter what.

Remembering that day still saddened Esther. Bryant had been a good man. He was only thirty-seven when he died. He was trying to give her and Arnell a good life. She was the one that didn't think that all he did was good enough, not to mention that she was more into partying than being a good wife and mother. Partying is how she met Kesley in the first place—at a club one Saturday night. She had told Kesley that she had a husband and a four-month-old baby at home, but he didn't care and after they drank and danced all night, she didn't care either. Neither did she care that he was younger than her and that he was a known numbers banker. He always had money, he was always collecting money, and he was always willing to give her some. She would have left Bryant for Kesley, except she knew Bryant would never let her take Arnell from him. He loved Arnell to death. She was his sweetie pie. Esther continued to see Kesley three and four days a week. Bryant never suspected and never questioned the money she had to buy the clothes and jewelry she openly wore. After all, she did have a part-time job as a secretary and her money was hers to do with what she wanted. She had been seeing Kesley for three years when she got careless and got caught that fateful day in the garage.

"What do you want with me, Kesley? If you're trying to use me as a front to sell drugs or to set up a numbers operation, you can't. I won't allow it. I allow no hustling of any kind in my house."

"You don't think very much of me, Esther. I gave up numbers and dabbling in drugs when I went to prison. A man can't trust people handling his money on the outside when he's locked up on the inside. Besides, I've been walking the straight and narrow since I got out of jail."

Esther gave Kesley a skeptical look.

"It's true. I have ways to make money, maybe not as much as in the old days, but I make enough to get by on."

"I'm happy for you." Esther lit another cigarette. Kesley wanted something from her and she knew it.

Kesley glanced around the room. "I see you've found a way to make money for yourself, too, huh?"

Esther blew smoke in Kesley's direction.

"I think running a classy joint like this is smart. Do the cops bother you?"

Holding her cigarette, Esther glared at Kesley. She clinched her jaw. She wasn't about to dignify his question with an answer. Her business was none of his.

"Aren't you curious about how I know what you've been up to or even about how I found you?"

Esther didn't bat an eye. She spread her left hand out and pretended to study her well-manicured nails. Yes, she was curious, but she would never let him know that.

"Fine," Kesley said casually. "Then I won't tell you, but in the future, if you don't want to be found, tell your clients to keep their mouths shut. Word of mouth travels with people who travel and seek the same pleasures in other states."

Damn! It must have been that big-mouth, horny toad Garrett. He said he was going to Jacksonville a month ago. Esther again blew smoke in Kesley's direction.

Kesley went and sat next to Esther. "I've been wanting to see you for a long time." He put his arm around her. "You got a real nice place here."

Warning bells were sounding in Esther's head. She pulled back from Kesley. "Don't fuck with me, Kesley. Whatever reason you're here, forget it. I have nothing to give you. It took me a long time to get on my feet after you took my child's father from me. I will never forgive you for that."

"So how is your daughter? Does she know how her daddy died?" Kesley asked. "What was her name again?"

Esther narrowed her gaze.

"By the way you're looking at me, Esther, I'm beginning to think you've never told your daughter all there is to tell about that day."

Esther stubbed out her second cigarette. *What the hell is this? Is Kesley here to blackmail me?* She took hold of his hand and removed his arm from around her shoulders. She had always heard it said that bad things happened in threes. Well, her three was now four and the fourth had barreled in too fast and too furious for her to see him coming. Tony was dead, Arnell had stolen Trena away, James had punked out on her, and now, Kesley had risen up from the bowels of hell to make her pay for deserting him. If Arnell ever found out about Kesley being her lover and that he'd killed her daddy—

"Tell the truth, Esther. Does your daughter know about me?" Kesley suddenly snapped his fingers. "I can answer that. She doesn't. A mother wouldn't tell her little girl about her lover or that her lover killed her daddy."

Esther's sour stomach quivered. "Leave my daughter out of this, Kesley."

"Esther, what kind of mother—"

"Cut the bullshit!" Esther sprang up. She took her cigarettes with her. "I don't know what you want from me, Kesley, but threatening me with my daughter won't get it for you."

"You got me wrong, Esther. I'm not trying to threaten you or use your daughter to get anything from you. I know how to get what I want without standing on your daughter's shoulders."

"So if that's the case, what the hell do you want?"

"A place to stay," Kesley answered. "Just for a little while."

"I have no room."

"In this big house, you have no room? I can't believe that."

Esther said coldly, "I'm all rented out."

Kesley looked around Esther's suite. "Seems like plenty of room in here."

"Plenty enough for me and me alone." Esther lit another cigarette.

"Come on, Esther. I'm an old friend, an old, intimate friend at that. You can put me up for a few weeks, can't you?"

"Not even for an hour."

"I see." Kesley stood. He began to amble slowly around the room, looking at trinkets, looking at pictures. He stopped in front of a ten-inch picture of Arnell taken ten years back. "I guess this is that pretty little girl all grown up?" He touched Arnell's nose with his fingertip. "This picture doesn't do her justice."

Inside Esther bristled. "How would you know?"

"I saw her yesterday, before and after you came back from that funeral."

A chill ran down Esther's spine. "You were here yesterday?"

"Your daughter sat out in the car, all by herself, for quite a while after you got back. She must have been really upset."

"You've been spying on me?"

"Just getting a lay of the land. I flew into town Saturday and came by yesterday but I saw you were busy." Kesley picked up the picture of Arnell.

Esther rushed at him and snatched the picture from his hand. "I don't want you here! Get out."

Kesley grinned knowingly. "You were always so crazy about that daughter of yours," he said, ignoring Esther's demand that he leave. He sat on the arm of the love seat. "I guess you're pretty close to her, huh?"

Esther put Arnell's picture back on the table with a firm thud. "Kesley, if you think you know me well enough to fuck with my daughter, then you don't know me at all."

"Damn, Esther," he said, pulling back, feigning fear. "You sound like I oughta be afraid of you."

Cooly, Esther took a slow drag on her cigarette. "I think, perhaps, you should consider it."

"I guess I should. But then, I think you should consider what your baby girl would think of her mommy if she knew her daddy was killed by her mommy's lover."

Esther's thoughts turned to Tony. *What would Tony do in this situation?*

Thirty-Four

Seven days passed and James still had not returned Arnell's calls, whereas Esther had been calling ceaselessly to the point of ad nauseam. Arnell let her answering machine screen her calls—she wasn't taking any of Esther's calls no matter how desperate she sounded—and she wasn't the least bit concerned that Esther would show up on her doorstep—Esther rarely left The Honey Well—she was a micromanager. The only calls Arnell took were from Sharise and Trena. Sharise, Arnell spoke to every day and, in fact, she had just ended a two-hour conversation with her about James's mysterious disappearance. She had not been able to find out a thing about his whereabouts. If he was going to work, she wasn't able to catch him there. Sharise had called James's mother, pretending to be on the City Council, and was told that James was away on business. What business? Where? No one seemed to know.

Arnell couldn't understand why James had not called her, had not written her, or even sent word to her by carrier pigeon. She found herself worrying whether he had found out about her past. That would explain his not wanting to talk to her, but she needed to talk to him to explain why her life had taken that path through the doors of The Honey Well.

Stretching, Arnell tried to relieve the achiness in her neck and shoulders. She needed a speakerphone in the kitchen. That two-hour conversation with Sharise with the telephone held in the crook of her neck while preparing a dinner of fried flounder fillets and steamed broccoli for herself and Trena had been brutal on her neck. Trena had called, just before Sharise, asking if she could come by—all the way from Brooklyn—to talk. Arnell didn't want to tell Trena not to come—she knew how it was when she was sixteen and wanted to talk to someone about what she was going through, and there was no one. She'd invited Trena to dinner.

Trena said very little as she picked at her broccoli. The most she'd said in the thirty minutes she'd been there was, "This fish is good." Arnell agreed. The flounder was tender, sweet and, best of all, boneless, which was why flounder was Arnell's favorite fish. She hated picking the bones out of fish. There was just something so barbaric about picking bones out of a carcass. Trena said that she liked the flounder, but Arnell noticed she was not eating it. Arnell devoured her meal. She was hungry. She loved going to the health spa, but for weeks afterward, she could never get enough to eat so she countered her ravenous appetite by trying to eat right. Of course, drowning her steamed broccoli in thick, creamy French dressing wasn't exactly eating right, but it certainly tasted good. She offered the bottle of French dressing to Trena.

Trena didn't take the salad dressing. Even before Arnell saw the first tear drop from Trena's cheek onto her plate, she sensed that Trena was crying. The tears didn't surprise her: Trena had looked like she'd been crying when she got there.

Arnell decided to not try to console Trena with the lie that everything was going to be all right, because it would be a while before Trena got to a place where she could get over the shame of prostituting herself. She handed Trena a napkin. "Has it been rough at home?"

Drying her eyes, Trena shook her head.

"That's good. How are you and your sister getting along?"

Trena blew her nose and pulled a line of snot away with the tissue, skeezing Arnell out, but she said nothing. She just pushed her plate away.

"She don't bother me," Trena said, wiping her nose. "She's getting married."

"That's nice." A feeling of sadness suddenly rushed over Arnell.

It was her own wedding that would not come to pass that she was thinking about. Well, it was too late to dwell on that now. She watched Trena put her wadded-up napkin in her plate on top of her uneaten flounder. "So, how's summer school?"

Trena shrugged. "I couldn't get in, I was too late. But I'm glad."

"Understandable." Arnell took both their plates to the sink. She dumped Trena's uneaten food and snotty napkin in the garbage. She almost wanted to dump the plate but didn't.

"Trena, I have raspberry sherbet, would you like some?" From the freezer, Arnell took the container of sherbet she had bought earlier in the day. She was taking her large coffee mug down from the cabinet when she realized that Trena hadn't answered. Trena was again crying.

Arnell went to Trena and gently pulled her head up against her stomach. "It'll get easier," she said. "You'll see."

"No it won't," Trena cried. "I'm pregnant." She threw her arms around Arnell's waist and buried her face in Arnell's stomach.

"Oh, God."

Trena cried harder. "I can't have this baby, Arnell. I can't."

"This may sound stupid, Trena, but are you sure you're pregnant?"

"This morning I took a home pregnancy test. It was positive."

"Oh, boy," Arnell said. When she was sixteen and seventeen she had gotten pregnant twice herself. Esther had gotten her abortions right away with no admonishments except, "Make those fools use condoms," and "take your pill on time." Thoughts of those days sickened Arnell. "Trena, you may have to tell your parents. You—"

"I can't!" Trena pulled away from Arnell. "Arnell, if my mother found out I was pregnant, she would kill me. This morning she said last night she dreamed about catching fish. Do you know what that means?"

"The question is, Trena, do you know what that means?"

"I do now. My mother said dreams about fish meant that somebody was pregnant. Arnell, she asked me if I was pregnant. I almost died. I had just finished throwing up in the bathroom before I came downstairs."

"So what did you say?"

"I denied I was pregnant. I couldn't tell her I was."

"That had to be scary."

"It was. And what about my father, Arnell? He'll hate me . . . he'll hate me."

"Oh, honey, he won't hate you."

"Yes, he will! He told me before he left that I better not make him have to come off the road again. He'll hate me for that. Arnell, I can't have this baby!"

"Trena, your parents might surprise you again. They didn't scream at you when you went back home, right?"

"No, but this is different. If I tell them that Andrew Peebles got me pregnant, they'll have a stroke. They'll want to know who he is. I can never let them know who he is. I can't have his baby. If I do, my parents will find out I was living in that mansion and that I was having sex with different men. Arnell, I can't tell them that. I can't. And what about my sister? Cheryl will never let me live this down. Oh, God," Trena cried.

Trena's crying shook Arnell's body. She understood the dilemma Trena was in, but she didn't know how she could help her beyond trying to speak to her parents for her. But who was she to speak for anyone when she had lived the life she lived? Then it came to her.

"Trena, stop crying. Maybe we can take care of this problem ourselves." She gently pushed Trena off her. "I'll help you."

Hopeful, Trena asked, "How?"

"I'm not quite sure—yet. You're not that far gone, but too far gone for the Morning After pill. Of course, an abortion is the ultimate solution, but we'll need your parents' permission and medical insurance for that."

No longer hopeful, Trena fell onto her folded arms and cried.

Arnell let her cry. There wasn't much she could say or do. Unfortunately, she wasn't having any insightful flashes of brilliance to remedy Trena's problem. Arnell went back to the counter and began scooping out big spoonfuls of frosty raspberry sherbet into her oversize coffee mug trimmed with colorful hearts. James had given her the mug last Valentine's Day with a tiny white teddy bear sitting inside holding an armful of chocolate kisses. That day seemed a lifetime ago, but she liked the mug and enjoyed eating sherbet out of it. When the sherbet melted, she drank it. Too bad Trena's pregnancy wasn't going to simply melt away. Maybe she should not've offered to help Trena until she knew for a fact that she could. Unless . . . maybe she could pass Trena off as her daughter and pay for the abortion herself, with cash.

Arnell returned to the table. "There may be a way out," she said, sitting.

"I have to run away from home," Trena cried. "I can't stay—"

"Trena, I think you've been down that road before." Arnell stirred her sherbet to soften it.

"But I—"

"How would you like to be my daughter?" Arnell asked.

"Huh?"

"If you were my daughter, I could take you for an abortion."

"You're not old enough to be my mother."

"I am, if I had you at sixteen. I'm thirty-three. Happens every-day, including to you."

Trena's tears dried up. "Can we get away with it?"

"I think we can. We can't use my gynecologist, she knows I've never had children. I'll have to find a new gyn."

"Not in Brooklyn," Trena said. "It's too close to home."

"I'm thinking Queens." Arnell ate a spoonful of soft sherbet. She let the sweet, cool fruity flavor slide down her throat. It was good.

"You think I can get the abortion this week?"

"I doubt it. Doctors have to schedule operating rooms in advance, except in an emergency. Of course, it will have to be soon, you're almost two months. I'll make some calls tomorrow. And while we're at it, we'll get you tested for VD."

"Oh, God, I—"

"Trena, calm down. It's just better to know. Hopefully, you're okay. I may get tested myself." Arnell saw the look of confusion on Trena's face. "Hey, better safe than sorry." She began eating her sherbet again. She noticed Trena watching her. "Would you like some?"

Trena nodded.

"Help yourself," Arnell said, mindful of not pampering Trena. Trena was going to have to start growing up and being responsible for herself. "There's another mug in the first cabinet on the second shelf."

While Trena scooped out her sherbet into a plain white mug, Arnell continued to eat hers. She hated having to go behind Trena's parents' backs to get Trena an abortion. Boy, if they ever found out, she would be in as much trouble as Trena, but someone had to give Trena a second chance. If it had to be her, then so be it.

Once again seated, Trena ate a spoonful of sherbet, rolled it around on her tongue before swallowing. She immediately scooped another spoonful into her mouth. Arnell watched Trena enjoying the sweet, cold dessert. It was obvious that her appetite was returning, or at least that baby inside her was begging to be fed.

"There's some orange sherbet in the freezer, if you want it," Arnell said.

Trena went right away to the freezer. "I like to mix them," she said, wasting no time opening the new container of sherbet.

Smiling to herself, Arnell wondered what it would be like for her if she were to get pregnant. She watched as Trena scooped mounds of orange sherbet into her mug atop the softening raspberry. "Trena, I'm going into the living room, bring your sherbet in there."

"Okay." Trena left the half-empty container of sherbet open on the counter. In the living room, she sat on the floor at the coffee table. "Arnell, can I ask you a question?"

"Sure."

"Do you like your mother?"

"That's an interesting but odd question. Why do you ask?"

"See, I love my mother, and a lot of times I even like her. Since I ran away, I had time to think about my mom and I guess I know now that all that bitching she was doing was for my own good. Even my sister was only thinking about what was best for me. But your mother, Queen Esther, she don't seem like a normal mother. Did she ever get on you for . . . you know being with men?"

Arnell almost laughed. The only time Esther had bitched at her was when she didn't want to sleep with the men she was set up with. How funny was that?

"My mother is far from normal, Trena. She's on a planet all her own."

"Do you like her the way she is?"

"To tell the truth, Trena, if I had to choose a mother, Esther would not have been my choice, but since she's the mother fate gave me, I deal with it. I know Esther's not your typical mother, and I would have been scared to death if she had been stranded on a deserted island when I was born."

"How come?"

"She probably would have eaten me at birth."

"That's whack."

"Trena, my mother has always been out for self and I understand that, because now, I'm out for self—without her."

"I guess I'm lucky to have the mother I have, then."

"I would say so."

"So you don't love your mother?"

That, Arnell did have to think about. "I wouldn't say that I don't love her. I guess I do. I just don't like her very much."

The sound of a car could be heard pulling up into the driveway outside the living room window. Arnell rushed to the window. She knew the car. What she didn't know was why that car was in her driveway.

Thirty-Five

Big Walt's muscular body filled Arnell's doorway, dwarfed her living room chair, and filled Trena's eyes with fear. Trena had not eaten another spoonful of sherbet since she heard Arnell say that Big Walt was their unexpected visitor. Trena had tried to run to the bathroom to hide, but Arnell wouldn't let her—Big Walt was not going to force Trena to go back to The Honey Well—not in her presence. Trena stayed seated on the floor, but she was no longer relaxed. She started playing with her sherbet—lightly jabbing the frozen dessert with her spoon. She really thought Big Walt was there to take her back.

Arnell wasn't afraid of Big Walt, he had never been a threat to her. In fact, Big Walt had always been especially protective of her. Still, there was no doubt in her mind that Esther had sent him.

"So what does Esther want?"

"Arnell, how come I can't just be stopping by to see you? I miss seeing you at The Well."

Arnell smirked. "Yeah, right, tell me another."

"C'mon, Arnell. Why you wanna play me like that? I thought we were friends."

"Big Walt, in six years, you've only been out to my house three times and all three of those times was because I was having car trouble and you brought me home. So cut the bull. What does Esther want?"

Big Walt settled back. "Your mother misses you."

"I'm sure she does," Arnell said, looking at Trena who was sitting back on her heels, her head down. "However, I'm in the process of cutting that apron string she's been choking me with."

"Ah, c'mon, Arnell. The queen means well and you know it. When she—"

"Big Walt, you don't know—"

"Arnell." Big Walt put up his huge hand to silence Arnell. "I know I don't know your mother like you do. No one does. But I'm not fooled by her, either. She can be cold, and she can be a, pardon me, a bitch. But the queen is a fighter. She's done whatever she had to do to survive. Nothing was ever given to me, so I can understand that. I had to fight for everything I got—me and my brother both. My mother left us with our grandmother when we were barely walking."

"Did you ever see her?" Arnell asked.

"Sure, when she was in between men and needed a place to sleep."

"Was she an addict?"

"Not that I know of. She was just a woman that couldn't be without a man and the men she got, didn't want her with kids on her back."

"Her children should have come first."

"Damn skippy," Big Walt said. "Now, the queen? Arnell, she thinks the sun rises and sets on your head. That woman loves you to death. All she wants from you is your love and respect."

"Love? Respect? Big Walt, you sound like Melvina."

"That's cold. Melvina's a serious snitch. I'm nothing like that, but—"

"No you're not, but you believe my mother's lies about loving me. The truth is, she doesn't know the meaning of love or respect."

"You're wrong, Arnell. Queen Esther really loves the hell out of you."

"I thought you said you knew my mother."

"I did say, not as well as you, but I know that you're probably the only person she's ever loved on this earth. I know that her and Tony were tight, but when it comes to you, the queen would slay the devil to keep you safe."

Arnell just looked at Big Walt. Most people didn't know that he was only twenty-six years old. He looked at least four years older, but that was because of his size and the clean-shaven head he proudly sported. Just like his head, Big Walt was always clean—he always wore a suit. Dressing down for him was wearing a sports jacket with a pair of sharply creased jeans. But the tie was always there, no matter how hot the weather. When Big Walt was on the job, his size alone was intimidating and when he growled, he could stop a heart from beating. Yet, he wrote songs that could make a heart sing. It would surprise many that Big Walt was a songwriter. When he was on the job at The Honey Well and there was no trouble for him to deal with, he often sat scribbling in the little notepad he carried tucked in his jacket pocket. As much as Big Walt loved writing lyrics, it wasn't for himself he wrote, he couldn't sing a note. He wanted to hear a real singer sing his songs the way he was hearing them in his head. Arnell had seen the words he had written, and realized that Big Walt's heart was as big as his body. His songs were beautiful. If any of the clients ever guessed that Big Walt was a teddy bear and not a grizzly, they might no longer fear him.

The one other person who knew that Big Walt had a soft side was Esther. She really liked him and that was because she could easily manipulate him into doing anything she wanted. Of course, having a trump card up her sleeve helped a lot when it came to Melvina and Big Walt. Only one year after he started working for Esther, she gave him a twenty-thousand-dollar loan so that he could purchase the studio equipment he needed to produce his music. He paid her back by working off the debt salary free for ten months. Every since that loan, Big Walt did whatever Esther wanted him to, without question.

"Why are you bothering me about that woman?" Arnell asked. "Trena, I know you're on my side."

"I am, but she's your mother."

Big Walt looked at Trena like he had only just noticed her. "You're the little girl who just moved into The Well, ain't you?"

Trena slipped her hands down between her thighs as if she were trying to warm them. Her head was rigid as she stared at Arnell.

"You got that wrong," Arnell said. "This is the little girl who escaped The Well. Trena, eat your sherbet, it's melting."

Trena scooped up a smidgen of soft orange sherbet, just barely enough to taste on her tongue.

"You had no business being in The Well in the first place, little girl," Big Walt said. "The Well's not a playground."

"She knows that now," Arnell said.

Trena wouldn't look at Big Walt.

"By the way, Arnell. Guess who I saw the other day on the A train coming into Brooklyn?"

Arnell thought about it. If Big Walt was asking her that question, it had to be someone from The Honey Well. "Don't know and don't much care."

"I figured you'd say that, but it was Kitt."

Arnell never liked Kitt—too much of a whore. The girl really liked prostituting. Arnell remembered trying to talk to Kitt about getting out of the business before she even got started good, but Kitt said, "You don't want me around because you're jealous. I get more clients than you." Arnell left her alone after that.

"That's the girl whose room I was in, right?" Trena asked.

"That's her," Arnell said, noting that both Trena and Kitt had gotten pregnant in that room by the same man.

"Yeah," Big Walt said, "Kitt wants to come back to The Well. She begged me to ask the queen to let her come back. She said she had an abortion, and that she hates walking the street."

"My heart aches for her," Arnell said cattily. "Big Walt, can we please stop talking about Kitt? I'm really not interested in anything about her. Now, you came here for a reason, and I believe that reason is my mother. What does she want from me besides my blood?"

"Okay," Big Walt said, adjusting his tie. "Queen Esther asked me to drive out here to make sure you were all right since she couldn't reach you by phone. She's been worried about you. And . . ."

Arnell pursed her lips cynically.

". . . she said to tell you—no, ask you—if you would please come to see her . . ."

"Not a chance in hell."

Trena's head swiveled from Big Walt to Arnell.

". . . She said she had something very important to tell you. That you had to hear it from her first."

"*It* being?" Arnell wasn't convinced that *it* was important.

"That, I don't know," Big Walt conceded. "But I do know that something strange is going at The Well."

"Like?" Arnell felt herself growing wary. Esther was summoning her again but she wasn't going to allow herself to fall into that trap.

"There's this old dude that's staying at The Well. He's staying in this little girl's room," Big Walt said, pointing to Trena.

"It's not my room," Trena said under her breath.

Now that was strange. Arnell had never known a man, besides Tony, to ever stay at the mansion. "Who is he?"

"Don't know."

"How long has he been there?"

"Melvina said he came last Monday."

Arnell's brow shot up. "And he's been there all this time? A whole week?"

"That's right."

"Maybe she's found a replacement for Tony."

"Come on, Arnell, it's not like that," Big Walt said. "The queen's been staying in her suite—by herself. At first I thought she was hiding out because she was hurting behind Tony, but I think it got something to do with that dude."

"What's his name?"

"Kesley something or other."

That name seemed . . . Arnell gasped. She remembered Esther mentioning that name just months ago. From what little Esther had said, it could not be a good thing that this man was back in her life. "Kesley Hayden?"

"Yep, that's his name."

"My mother said he was dead."

"Then he's a ghost," Big Walt said. "Do you know who he is?"

Arnell shook her head.

"Well, I got this bad feeling," Big Walt said. "Arnell, this dude's walking around The Well like he's the man of the manor. The other night, he took the money from the clients and I don't know if he gave any of it to the queen."

Arnell's jaw dropped.

"Now, Arnell, you know that's bad. You know how the queen feel about her money."

"Who doesn't know?"

"Well, that dude is messing with her money big time."

Oh, damn. This is bad.

"And I'll tell you something else that's strange," Big Walt continued. "You know the queen's always checking out everything—the girls, the music, the house, the food. Everything."

"To the tiniest detail," Arnell agreed.

"Well, she don't check a damn thing anymore, that dude does. As sure as I'm sitting here, I know this dude got something on the queen."

"Like what?"

"I don't know, but whatever it is, it's making her sick. The other night, she had one of those heart episodes."

Arnell wasn't a bit concerned about Esther's heart condition, she knew that Esther was a faker. Arnell waved her hand.

"That's cold, Arnell," Big Walt said with a chuckle. "But for real. I think the queen's in serious trouble."

Arnell was reminded of what Tony had told her. *Things done in the dark will come out in the light.* Esther's past—the past that she didn't want to talk about—had caught up with her. The man from thirty years ago that Esther thought dead, was staying in her precious mansion. This had to be driving her mad.

"Too bad Tony isn't here to help her."

"That's for damn sure," Big Walt agreed, "but you're here."

Arnell began shaking her head no. "I can't help my mother. Whatever her troubles are with this Kesley person, they're too much trouble for me. I have battle scars on my behind, on my mind, and on my soul from dealing with my mother's troubles."

"But she has no one else, Arnell. Tony is gone. You're her blood."

"Arnell," Trena said, "maybe you need to go check on your mother."

"Damn it!" Arnell fell forward with her elbows on her thighs and her forehead resting on the balls of her hands. "I can't do this," she moaned. "Every damn time I try to wrench myself out of my mother's clutches, something comes up and flings me back into her grasp like I'm a goddamn boomerang with no will of my own. Why the hell can't I get free of this damn woman and her problems?"

"I know why," Trena volunteered.

Arnell waited for the answer that she knew would be too simplistic to be ignored.

"Maybe it's because you do love your mother."

Arnell slumped back against the cushion. "I don't need my mother's kind of love—it's robbing me of my sanity."

Thirty-Six

Once again, because of Esther, Arnell was on her way back to The Honey Well. There was nothing sweet there for her—only misery and shame. Big Walt insisted on driving her and Trena into Brooklyn, and he also promised to bring Arnell back home no matter what time it was. Arnell was planning on holding him to that, or she swore she'd kick his ass and make him pay for a car service to take her back to Garden City. She had no intention of spending another night in Esther's mansion. They dropped Trena off in Bushwick on Broadway, two blocks over from her house—Trena didn't want to be seen getting out of Big Walt's car by her mother or sister. It was going to be hard enough as it was to keep her pregnancy a secret.

"Don't forget to make that call," Trena reminded Arnell before getting out of the car.

Arnell promised that she would. By the time she was walking in the front door of the mansion, Arnell was hyped. She was excited for reasons she couldn't comprehend, other than possibly because she was getting ready to meet a man from Esther's past who might tell tales—dark, ugly tales—that Esther had always been mum about yet were powerful enough to render her powerless. Why else would she allow this Kesley Hayden to force her to cower inside her suite, while he collected her money? Something was definitely wrong. Big Walt was right about that.

A few feet inside the parlor, Arnell stopped. The music stopped

her. It wasn't classical, it wasn't jazz, it was rhythm and blues—
Cloud Nine? The Temptations? Their smooth, finger-popping
sound seemed so out of place. Across into the living room, far off in
the corner, Arnell could see Jeanette and a man talking intimately.

"This is Monday," Arnell said to Big Walt. "Why is there a client
here?"

"That old friend of Esther's made some changes."

"In a week? I guess I need to speak to—"

Kesley suddenly appeared out of nowhere to greet Arnell. "Well,
well, well. Little Arnell." Grinning, Kesley sized up Arnell. "You're
every inch your mother when she was your age. But I should have
figured that, you were a looker when you were a baby."

In turn, Arnell sized up Kesley. She was slow about it. Kesley
Hayden was quite a bit older than her but not quite as old as Esther.
Not bad to look at, not a bad dresser, but obviously bad news—that
cocky smirk on his face said so, and so did Big Walt who whispered
in her ear, "Trouble."

"You seem to know me, Kesley Hayden. Why is it that I don't
know anything about you?"

"You mean your momma didn't tell you about me? She must
have told you something, you know my name, or," Kesley glanced
up at Big Walt, "did the big man here tell you about me?"

Melvina stuck her head out from the dining room.

"Oh, I know your name," Arnell said, "but that's about all I
know. However, I get this feeling that whatever I find out, I'm not
going to like."

"Little Arnell, don't say that," Kesley said. "We could be real
good friends. In fact, I could be like a daddy to you."

Arnell glowered. "Let's get something straight, Mr. Hayden . . ."

"I like that—Mr. Hayden," Kesley said, smiling.

". . . Whatever your plans are for my mother, for this house, or
even for me, cancel them. Nothing here is up for sale or available to
be stolen. Therefore, I suggest you pack your bags and leave."

"Not possible," Kesley said.

Melvina scooted away.

"Anything is possible," Arnell said flatly. "If you need some
help packing, Big Walt is an excellent packer. In fact, I might help
you myself."

Looking at Big Walt, Kesley rubbed his clean-shaven chin. "Maybe we should speak to Esther before we start packing."

"We don't have to speak to Esther," Arnell said, "I'm speaking for her."

"Arnell," Esther said, hurrying into the parlor. "I didn't know you were here. I'm so glad to see you."

"Esther," Kesley said, "I was just about to go get you."

Right off, Arnell could see the stress on Esther's drawn, unmade-up face.

"Mother, what's going on here? Why is this man acting like he's the lord of the manor?"

"Kesley's an old friend."

"Esther, that's what I was trying to tell your girl. I told her I could be like a daddy to her," Kesley said, his voice dripping with sarcasm. He went and took Esther's hand.

Arnell saw Esther's eyes grow cold and dark, she saw the set of Esther's jaw tighten, she saw Esther snatch her hand away from Kesley and step a foot away from him, but that was all Esther did. Her mouth wasn't spitting out foul words or threats, which was so unlike her.

"I don't know what's going on here," Arnell said, "but Mother, you had better tell me something. I know you. This is not what you would want—some fast-talking pimp from your past crashing in here running your show. Who is this man? More importantly, what the hell does he have on you?"

"What makes you think Kesley has something on me?"

"Don't play dumb. It doesn't become you."

"I told you, Kesley's an old friend."

"I don't believe that for a minute," Arnell said, now really annoyed. "Mother, you would never allow some jerk—"

"Jerk?" Kesley asked.

"Did I stutter?" Arnell asked, looking pointedly at Kesley. "Like I was saying, some jerk off the street from your past to simply walk in here and tell you when and where to spit. So tell me, Mother, what's going on? Or I will walk out this door and let him continue whatever the hell he's doing to you."

Esther didn't know how to begin explaining. She looked from Arnell back to Kesley.

Kesley easily pulled Esther back to him. "We'd hate for you to stop coming by," Kesley said. "We'd miss you, wouldn't we, Esther?"

Arnell could not believe the silence of Esther's tongue, nor could she understand why Esther was letting Kesley hold her when the look on her face shouted clearly that she couldn't stand the man's hands on her. When Esther dropped her eyes, Arnell knew that this was worse than Big Walt had said.

"This is just too unreal," Arnell said to Big Walt.

"I told you."

"Arnell," Esther said, "Kesley really is an old friend. He's all right."

"If that's the case, Mother, your old friend should understand that he's not wanted here; that he should stay in a hotel. Brooklyn has one now, you know? It's called the Marriott."

"I like it here just fine," Kesley said. "It's so homey."

"Okay, that's it," Arnell said, rushing at Esther. She snatched her by the arm, pulling her away from Kesley. "We talk. Now!" Arnell pulled Esther down the hall to her suite. Before she could even close the door, Kesley put his foot in the door and stopped it from closing. But Big Walt was right on him, holding him back from entering.

"Let them talk, man!"

"Get your hand off me, boy! You don't know me. I'll shoot you—"

"Let him go!" Esther ordered. "Let him go." She sat heavily in her chair.

Big Walt did as he was told. Kesley smirked at Big Walt and walked on into the suite. Big Walt stepped inside behind him. Melvina found a comfortable spot in the doorway.

"You want him here? Fine," Arnell said, "but I'm going to speak my mind. Mother, I am not stupid, and neither is Big Walt. What does this man have on you? Tell us, before it's too late."

Esther's fear of Kesley outweighed her contempt for him. "It's nothing."

"Mother, you'd better cut the crap and tell me the truth or this leech will suck you dry, and believe me, poverty is not very pretty in old age."

"Arnell, you're not needed here," Kesley said. "I can take care of Esther."

"This is absurd," Arnell said, dismissing Kesley with a flip of her hand. "Mother, everything you've worked for—this house, your money, even this disgusting business, which you should definitely close down, everything will vanish before your eyes. I refuse to stand by and let that happen. As much as I want to stay out of your business, I can't. I can't let this man do this to you. Whatever it is that you've done, you need to tell me. We'll deal with it together and get this . . . this man out of your life."

"I wouldn't be so sure about that," Kesley said.

"I am not talking to you!" Arnell snapped.

"You got some attitude, girl."

"Mother, how much can the past hurt you?"

"It can hurt her a hell of a lot," Kesley said. "In fact, it could hurt you more."

Arnell cut her eyes at Kesley. Maybe she should be afraid of the dark secret he held over Esther's head that he was now threatening her with, but Arnell was so angry she saw him solely as the enemy she needed to confront. Arnell moved slowly toward Kesley.

"How dare you presume that you could come in here and blackmail my mother. Whatever she's done, she could never be as disgustingly vile as you."

"Are you sure about that?"

"Oh, I'm sure," Arnell said. "Mr. Hayden, you're a user, a leech. Get out of this house before I have you thrown out."

Big Walt took a step forward. His nostrils were flaring.

Kesley glanced at Big Walt. He took a step back. "Esther, I think you'd better talk to your girl and your enforcer here."

"Mother, put him out or I will."

Esther searched for something to say that would make Arnell back down, but nothing she thought of made sense. "Kesley, maybe you should—"

"Maybe. H'm," Kesley said pensively. "That's a good word, Esther. Maybe I should start talking about how your husband died."

Gasping, Esther covered her face.

Arnell knew that she had heard right, she just didn't think the words were right. She looked at Esther and saw that her hands were covering her face. There was a soft moan coming from her. Now Arnell was scared.

"What about you, Arnell?" Kesley asked. "Don't you want to know the truth about how your daddy died?"

Big Walt was disgusted. "Man, you're foul."

"I've been called worse, big man, I ain't upset, though. I play the hand I'm dealt and Esther just forced it. So," Kesley said, turning back to Arnell, "can you handle the truth?"

"My father died in a car accident. What's so damning about that?"

"Is that what Esther told you?" Kesley asked, looking at Esther. "That's a big lie, Esther."

"You know something different? Tell it," Arnell said, daring Kesley. "I'm listening."

"No! Kesley, no!" Esther exclaimed. "Arnell, leave this alone. Please."

Esther's desperate plea piqued Arnell's curiosity. She turned back to Kesley. "You're leaving this house, I guarantee you that. So if you have something to say, say it."

Kesley looked to Esther. "Am I leaving this house, Esther?"

Esther sighed her acceptance of the situation. She wanted Kesley gone. If the truth would release his hold on her, then the truth had to be told. She had to take her chances that Arnell wouldn't hate her.

"I'll tell it," Esther said, unable to look at Arnell. "Arnell, your father was murdered. Kesley killed him."

Thirty-Seven

It wasn't unusual that the house was quiet, the house was usually quiet when Trena wasn't there to blast Mary J. Blige's or
Usher's pulsating jams from the stereo in the living room or her
"gutter rap" as her mother called it, from her boom box in her bedroom. What was unusual was that Cheryl and Maxine were sitting
together in the living room with no other sounds in the house surrounding them—no television, no music, and when Trena walked
in, they stopped talking and stared at her. Right away Trena knew
that something was wrong.

Trena's knees were quaking. "What's up?"

"Where have you been?" Maxine questioned.

"Nowhere." She started up the stairs.

"Trena, come in and sit down."

"I need to go up to my room. I'll be back," she said, hoping to
delay the inevitable.

"No, Trena," Maxine said firmly, "we need to talk—*now.*"

There was a nervous little flutter in Trena's stomach as she went
on into the living room. She headed for the single chair closest to
the door.

"Sit next to me," Maxine said.

Definitely not wanting to, Trena went anyway to sit on the sofa,
but she didn't sit next to her mother—she sat on the end, as far
away as she could get. She glanced at Cheryl and saw that Cheryl
was looking at her stomach. Trena's heart thumped. *They know!*

"Where were you?" Maxine asked, still not raising her voice.

Trena eyed first Maxine and then Cheryl. "Why?"

"Don't answer me with a question, Trena," Maxine said testily. "Where were you?"

"Dang! I was visiting a friend. Man!"

"Girl, you better watch your mouth," Maxine warned.

Trena set her jaw firm and folded her hands in her lap.

"Trena, we called all of your friends," Cheryl said. "No one had seen you. At least that's what they told us."

"They were telling the truth. I was visiting that lady that helped me at the shelter. She said I could talk to her whenever I wanted to."

"I see," Maxine said. "Is there anything you need to be talking to us about?"

"No."

"Trena, we're your family," Cheryl said, "if there's something you need help with, you should tell us."

They know. Fixing her eyes on the pink and white silk floral arrangement sitting atop the entertainment unit, Trena suddenly felt sleepy. "I don't need help with nothing."

From between the seat cushion and the armrest of the sofa, Maxine pulled out a small crushed up blue and white box. She held it up for Trena to see. Trena immediately recognized the box. How could she be so stupid? She had taken the pregnancy test kit and thrown it out in the public trash bin, but the box, she had thrown away in her own small garbage container in her room.

"Was it positive or negative?" Maxine asked.

Trena couldn't bring herself to answer. When tears slipped from her eyes, she felt betrayed by them.

"It was positive," Cheryl said sadly.

The tears wouldn't stop.

"Oh, Trena," Maxine said, disappointment clear in her voice. "How could you? You made me a promise. You've messed up your life."

Trena could no longer hold in her anguish. She cried as she had done at Arnell's—loud and hard

"Dad is going to be so upset," Cheryl said. "Mom, maybe we shouldn't tell him while he's on the road. Maybe we should wait until he comes home again."

"No," Maxine said, "we'll tell him tonight when he calls. He should know."

"No!" Trena tried to get control of her crying. "Mom, please . . . please . . . don't tell Dad. I don't want him to be mad at me."

"Well, Trena, it's a little late to worry about that. You should have thought about that before you broke your promise and gave up your virginity."

Crying again, Trena looked to Cheryl. "I wasn't tryin' to get pregnant."

"You're a young girl, Trena. You could damn near get pregnant if a guy spits on you. The question is, what are we gonna do about it?"

"Nothing," Maxine said. "Trena is going to have this baby."

"No . . . no. I can't."

Maxine wasn't moved by Trena's tears. "You *will* have this baby. That's all there is to it."

"No, Mom, please. I can't have this baby. I have to get an abortion."

"You can forget that. You won't be killing babies in my house. Having this baby will teach you that a hard head makes for a life-long hard lesson learned, and you *will* take care of this baby on your own. It's your responsibility. Not mine, not Cheryl's, and certainly not your father's. Speaking of your father, who is this baby's father?"

Trena hid her face behind her arm.

"It's Omar, isn't it?" Cheryl asked.

"It's not Omar."

"We called him," Cheryl said, "and—"

"No! No! You didn't call Omar!"

"We most certainly did," Maxine affirmed. "He's going to be just as responsible for this baby as you are."

"Oh, God!" If Omar knew, then, by now, all her friends knew. Trena could imagine all the bad things they were saying about her. She wasn't going to be able to ever look Omar in the face again. Trena began to cry so hard her chest, her neck, and her back ached. She broke out in a cold sweat. She began to feel weak, her stomach churned.

"Mom, she's gonna make herself sick," Cheryl said.

"She'll stop crying when she's tired, but she'd better get use to the fact that she will be having this baby, and if Omar doesn't do what's right, I will take his hot ass to court for rape."

"I swear to God, Mom, it's not Omar. He didn't get me pregnant."

"That's what he said, too, but you're both lying."

"No, Mom, it's the truth! I swear. I can't believe you told Omar that I was pregnant."

"I don't see why not," Cheryl said. "Trena, you and Omar were always messing around. You were gone for more than a month. You and Omar were free to do whatever you wanted."

"But, it wasn't Omar. I never saw Omar the whole time I was gone."

"Then who in God's name was it?" Maxine asked.

Trena's crying tore at her throat. She felt like she was tearing herself up inside.

"Trena, I don't wanna hear that you don't know," Maxine said, "because that would mean that you were whoring out there on the street like a common tramp. Is that what you were doing?"

Unable to stop crying, Trena knew that she could never tell where she stayed or what she did.

"I think it's Omar,"Cheryl concluded.

"Me, too," Maxine agreed. "If they won't tell the truth now, they will when the baby is born and I get a DNA test done."

Trena couldn't let that happen. She suddenly bolted for the front door.

Maxine jumped to her feet. "Trena, get back here!"

"I'm sorry, Mom." Trena unlocked the door. "I'm sorry I caused you so much trouble."

"Trena! Where are you going?"

Cheryl rushed to the door just as Trena yanked it open and ran out. "Trena, come back here!"

Trena kept running. She was never going back. She was never going to have this baby. She just couldn't.

Thirty-Eight

Still as a stone, void of any emotions, Arnell sat with her back stiff, her eyes closed, her hands prayer-like to her lips listening to the sounds around her. She could hear Big Walt breathing hard, like he couldn't wait to get his hands on Kesley Hayden. Melvina had managed to worm her way into the suite, and from her came soft "humph, humph, humphs." Kesley Hayden had taken a seat minutes after Esther started her horrid tale of lust and betrayal. He made not a sound, but Arnell could imagine that he was still sitting with his legs crossed and a smug grin on his face while he quietly rubbed his chin. Next to her sat Esther, her mother, her albatross, the woman who, even back then, needed lots of money to feel secure, and plenty of sex to feed her sense of poor self-esteem—at least that's the conclusion Arnell had come to after trying for years to figure her mother out. Why else would Esther do all the ugly things she did? Arnell didn't have to hear a peep from Esther to know that she was close. She felt her. It was as if Esther had her arms around her, embracing her, closing her up in a dark, windowless room where the air was musty and dense.

"Arnell," Big Walt said, "are you all right?"

"Can I get you tea or water, child?" Melvina asked.

Arnell responded to neither. She had begun to think about the father she never got to know. His death had to be horrible, but his marriage to Esther must have been much worse. If he had not been killed by Esther's lover, he might have lived and saved her from a life of degradation and shame.

"I know you're upset, sweetie," Esther said, "but please, please understand that I was young and foolish. I didn't know Kesley was going to beat your father to death. I tried to stop him. I—"

"Liar!" Kesley said. "You did nothing. You—"

"Shut up, you bastard! You murdered my husband! You kept kicking him. You kept punching him in the head. You wouldn't stop until Bryant was dead."

Slowly Arnell opened her eyes. She lowered her hands to her lap. Her chest was tight with anger at Esther, but she despised Kesley Hayden just as much.

"Damn right," Kesley said. "I was defending myself. I wasn't going to stand there like a punk and let him beat me down. It was him or me."

"Bryant was no match for you, Kesley, and you knew it. You wouldn't stop. I told you to stop."

"Liar!" Kesley spat.

"You're the liar!" Esther screamed. "I—"

"Mother!"

Esther immediately turned to Arnell. "It's the truth, Arnell, I tried to make him stop. You believe me don't you? I loved your father. He—"

"Mother, if you loved my father so much, you would not've cheated on him."

"I made a mistake. I—"

"I do not want to hear your excuses."

Esther looked beseechingly at Arnell. "Sweetie, I'm sorry you had to find out about how your father died from this lowlife bastard."

Arnell felt like she would throw up at the sound of Esther's voice. Refusing to look at her, Arnell shut her ears to her and set her sight on Kesley Hayden. "I need to understand something."

"And what would that be?" he asked.

"You were a number's runner, right?"

"No, I had territory. I was a number's banker, not a runner. I made hundreds of thousands of dollars a month."

"So what happened? You lose all your millions?"

"I didn't lose nothing. Everything was stolen from me when I was locked up."

"How unfortunate," Arnell said. "So you were a number's banker. How is it that you supplied my mother with the cocaine she used to set her uncle up with?"

"Connections, baby, connections," Kesley said, remembering. "Esther, that was that scum of an uncle that molested you, right? Sure, I plunked down some big bucks to score those kilos. Esther, you never paid me for those two kilos. You owe me for that too."

"You go to hell. I—"

"Shut up!" Arnell snapped. Esther did. "It looks to me, Mother, like you'll be walking into hell, hand-in-hand, with your lover for planting drugs and getting my father killed."

"Wham!" Kesley said, punching the palm of his left hand.

"Arnell!" Esther's feelings were truly hurt.

"I like you," Kesley said to Arnell, "you're my kind of woman."

Such a thought repulsed Arnell. "Believe me, I'm far from being your kind of woman. Your kind of woman is the queen here. You really, truly deserve each other, and as old as you both are, you should be ashamed of your damn selves. You're too old to be playing these games."

Kesley chuckled.

"You seem mighty pleased with yourself, Mr. Hayden," Arnell said. "It must feel really good to get revenge on your lover for not coming to your defense in court. Did you lie awake every night in your cell dreaming about ways to destroy my mother?"

"Hey, it helped pass the time, but I had more pressing business to take care of when I got out of the joint," Kesley said. "So I'm a little late in collecting on this debt."

"Humph," Esther said, "and that's probably because you couldn't find me," Arnell ignored Esther. "You're a wretched soul, if you lived with revenge on your mind all these years."

"A nice payday could clear my mind up in an instant."

"You can go fuck yourself," Esther said, "you're not getting another dime from me."

Arnell hated that Esther was trying to profile. "Mother, if you could have handled this, I wouldn't have to be in the middle of this crap. So would you please shut the hell up and let me deal with your mess?"

Esther's fingers were trembling but she managed to light a cigarette.

Arnell glared daggers at Esther, but she had to deal with Kesley Hayden before she could get to her. "It seems to me, Mr. Hayden, that you're going away empty-handed."

Kesley lurched forward. "No the fuck I'm not! I didn't spend all those years in jail because of a bitch to end up with nothing. You owe me, Esther! You owe me!"

"I don't owe you a goddamn thing! You killed Bryant! You owe me, you bastard!" As angry as she was, Esther saw Big Walt and Melvina staring at her but she didn't care what either one was thinking. Only what Arnell thought concerned her. "Arnell, your father was a good man, I always told you that. Remember? He—"

"Please shut up."

"But, Arnell, you have to know that I didn't set out to cheat on your father. I was . . ."

"Mother."

". . . young. I got caught up. I . . ."

"Mother!"

". . . made a mistake. I—"

"Esther!" Arnell shouted. "Goddamn it, shut up!"

Esther froze. She stared wide-eyed at Arnell. As angry as Esther was at Kesley and James, she didn't want to completely alienate Arnell. Esther began puffing on her cigarette, while her right leg went to shaking harder.

Kesley was impressed. "I see you know how to handle the queen. Good girl, I could use you around here to help me manage this place."

Arnell marveled at the audacity of the man. "You are so full of yourself. Use me? Around here? I don't think so. For one thing, you won't be here. Not in this house. If what my mother just told me is the big revelation that you came here to blackmail her with, then you made the trip for nothing. I am not the least bit surprised."

Melvina started clapping. "You tell 'em, Arnell!"

Big Walt flung his hand out toward Melvina, stopping her from clapping, while Esther covered her own mouth to keep from cheering. She hadn't been wrong—Arnell did love her.

"So I'm supposed to believe," Kesley began, "that you don't care that your father caught me banging your mother in his garage or that he died behind my beating his ass?"

"Oh, don't get me wrong, I care, but not in the way you'd expect," Arnell said. "The way I see it, you have no leverage to blackmail my mother with. If you were betting on me to be your ace, you lose, because unless you're telling me that she physically killed my father, or that she solicited his death, then any discussion between you and me is finished. As for my mother, the queen . . ." Arnell looked at Esther. This scandalous revelation really didn't surprise Arnell. It was just like Esther to disrespect the man she married by allowing another man to make love to her under the roof that her husband provided for her and his child. But to stand around and watch her child's father murdered at the hands of her lover, was unforgivable.

Esther waited anxiously for Arnell to say what she was going to do to her.

". . . the queen and I will have our discussion in private," Arnell finally said. "You, Mr. Hayden, could have E-mailed me or sent a postcard and saved yourself the trip."

"Damn, Esther, you've done yourself proud," Kesley said, amazed. "Arnell's a cold-hearted bitch just like you."

Big Walt barreled down on Kesley before Kesley had a chance to turn his head and see him coming. Big Walt yanked Kesley up out of his chair as if he weighed no more than a five-year-old. "You don't talk to a lady that way!" Big Walt yanked Kesley's left arm up behind his back.

"Get your fucking hands off me!" Kesley's struggle to free himself was futile, Big Walt's hold was like the jaws of a pit bull. Kesley's face was twisted from the pain in his arm and shoulder, but he refused to be removed from the room. He grabbed onto the heavy mahogany-framed chair he had been sitting on with his right hand and straining, tried to pull back from Big Walt.

But Big Walt wasn't letting a chair stop him from his task. Grunting, he doggedly dragged the chair and Kesley—inch by inch with him.

Buzzzz! The front doorbell rang.

Melvina glanced toward the suite door. "Is anybody out there?" she asked, not wanting to leave the suite and miss anything.

"You get it, Melvina," Arnell said, wanting to get Melvina's nosy ass out of her sight, while she herself couldn't pull her eyes away from the battle of wills before her.

Melvina didn't budge.

Buzzzz!

Esther stood. "Melvina, get the door!"

"Yes, ma'am," Melvina said, hurrying off.

"Well, Mr. Big Shot," Esther said snidely. "Didn't work out like you planned, did it, you trifling bastard?"

"You're a whore, Esther! That's all you'll ever be."

"That's fine, but what will you be? An old, deadbeat ex-con, trying to blackmail a woman into supporting you."

"Yeah, but I won't be a used up, ugly ass old whore."

Esther squared her shoulders. "Baby, I'm far from used up. You know that. Just last night you begged me for some, but I wouldn't sleep with your sorry ass to save my own life."

"Bitch, I don't want your old ass."

"That's because you want my money, you son of a bitch. Plus, you thought you could steal my daughter's love from me, but you were wrong. Arnell loves me. Scum like you wouldn't understand that. You could never destroy the love me and Arnell have for each other. No one can. Especially a bum like you."

Esther was so into telling Kesley Hayden off, she wasn't aware Arnell was watching her.

"You're an uninvited guest in my mansion," Esther said, posturing, reemerging as the grande dame of the mansion. "Big Walt, get him out of my face!"

Big Walt put more effort into hustling Kesley toward the door to the suite.

"No!" Melvina said. "This is not a good time." Arnell and Esther both could hear Melvina out in the hallway. They both wondered who she could be talking to.

"Let go of me!" Kesley shouted. "You can't put me out. I got my things upstairs."

"We'll put them out on the sidewalk." Esther couldn't believe she had been afraid of this bum for nothing.

"I'm not going anywhere!"

"No! Queen Esther is busy," Melvina could be heard saying just outside the suite door.

"I can hear that," the visitor insisted, "but I need to speak to her. It's important."

Arnell recognized the voice of the visitor. She rushed around Big Walt and Kesley struggling closer to the door. She made it out into the hallway just as Melvina was pushing James away from the suite door.

"Melvina!" Arnell exclaimed. "What are you doing? Are you crazy?"

Startled, Melvina snatched her hands off James's chest. Arnell saw the frantic look on Melvina's face, but it was James's shocked expression that stumped her.

"What's going on?" Arnell asked.

Esther could hear Arnell speaking out in the hall. She wondered what was going on out there.

Melvina gawked at Arnell while James, also staring, looked like he was caught in the blinding headlights of an oncoming car.

"This place is insane," Arnell said. "James . . ."

Oh, my God! Esther's heart fluttered.

". . . why are you struggling with Melvina?"

James didn't answer. Arnell could see James's Adam's apple yo-yoing in his throat.

"James, I've been calling and calling you. Where have you been? Why haven't you returned my calls?"

Esther didn't know which way to turn. She started trying to pry Kesley's hand off the chair. "Big Walt, take him into my bedroom and sit on him."

"Your bedroom?" Big Walt asked, perplexed. "I thought you wanted him out of here."

Esther's heart was pounding. "Look, I can't explain it right now. Just do as I say." *God, if I'm going to have a heart attack, let me have it now.*

"Hold up!" Kesley shouted. "I'm not going in there."

Big Walt started trying to push Kesley toward the bedroom.

James began walking on leaded feet toward Arnell. Melvina backed into the dining room. Arnell noticed the beads of sweat on James's forehead as he got closer. It was hot outside, but not in there.

"I've been out of town," James lied. He pecked Arnell on the cheek.

At Esther's bedroom door, Kesley caught hold of the door frame and thwarted Big Walt from pushing him inside. "Somebody call the police!" Kesley shouted to whoever the visitor was out in the hallway.

James stepped back from Arnell. "What's going on in there?"

"You really don't wanna know," she said, taking James's arm and turning him away from Esther's suite.

Kesley suddenly twisted his body around in the direction of his left arm thrusted up behind his back and dropped to the floor, pulling himself out of Big Walt's hold. Quickly rolling away from the bedroom, Kesley sprang up off the floor and hurtled madly for the open suite door. Esther reached out for him but Kesley sidestepped away from her. Big Walt gave chase. Kesley plunged through the open door and rammed into the wall opposite the door, startling James and Arnell who turned and saw Kesley rebound and head toward them.

"Get him!" Esther shouted. *God, please don't let him see James!*

Kesley collided with James and Arnell, knocking Arnell against the wall. James quickly grabbed Kesley.

"Are you all right, Arnell?" James asked, holding onto Kesley until Big Walt snatched him and flung him into the wall. He put his massive arm up against Kesley's throat, penning him against the wall. Kesley couldn't breathe, but he struggled to get a look at the guy that had his arm around Arnell.

Rushing out into the hall, Esther saw in James's eyes that he recognized Kesley from the morning after they made love. Worse of all, she saw in Kesley's expression that he recognized James. Esther felt weak in the knees. This was not how this was supposed to play out. Especially not after Arnell had stood with her against Kesley.

"I don't know what's going on here, and I don't care to know," James said. "Arnell, let's get out of here."

Arnell wanted more than anything to get away from Esther and her mess. Besides, she needed to tell James about her life out of earshot of so many people.

"Take him out the back door," Esther whispered to Big Walt.

Big Walt dropped his arm from Kesley's throat and was about to force him down the hall when Kesley pulled back.

"Hey, man!" Kesley shouted to James's retreating back. "I remember you. You were the naked guy wearing the towel in Esther's bedroom a week ago."

On the other side of the wall in the dining room, Melvina covered her mouth.

"Arnell, this your man?" Kesley asked.

Big Walt tightened his grip on Kesley but he was no longer pulling Kesley toward the back door. He looked questioningly at Esther, who had turned away and was quietly wishing that she could black out.

"What's he talking about?" Arnell asked James.

"I need to speak to you alone," James said. "I can explain."

"Yeah, man, explain to all of us how you was wearing only a towel in Esther's bedroom the day I came here. Esther was wearing her robe but I know she wasn't wearing a damn thing underneath. That was a thin robe, Esther."

"Screw you, Kesley," Esther said.

Arnell searched Esther's defiant face. The fear she saw there confirmed Kesley's story. "Oh, God." She shook James's hands off her.

Melvina sneaked back into the hallway.

"Arnell," James said, trying to take her back into his arms. "I can explain."

Arnell threw up her hands and began backing away from James. As much as she wanted to believe that Kesley Hayden was lying, that he was trying to get back at Esther for betraying him, for not sharing the wealth, she could not convince herself that nothing had gone on between James and Esther. Their eyes were shouting at her that they had done something they weren't supposed to. From the moment Kesley told on them, neither could look the other in the eye, as well they couldn't look at her. Arnell was glad for that.

"Damn," Big Walt said, releasing Kesley. He looked disgustedly at Esther.

"Damn, is right," Kesley said, grinning. "Esther, you've been up to your old tricks, haven't you, old girl? But with your daughter's man? Damn. Aren't there any lines you won't cross?"

Arnell felt like she was sinking in a cesspool of quicksand. "You're supposed to be my mother, damn it!"

Esther slumped back against the wall in the hallway. Suddenly, grimacing, she clutched her chest and began to slide slowly down the wall to the floor. Only Melvina rushed to Esther as she pretended to struggle to catch her breath. There were no sharp pains in her chest—her heart was beating just fine, but she cried out in pain anyway. The pain she was experiencing was in her mind. For the first time in her life, she was scared that she really could lose Arnell. Admittedly, she had seduced James to get back at Arnell for taking Trena out of the house, but never in a million years would she have thought that she'd have to face her past and Arnell all in the same day. It wasn't supposed to happen this way. It just wasn't.

Thirty-Nine

There was something so pathetically sad and ironic about Esther having sex with James, that Arnell simply wasn't amazed. Oh, it threw her for a moment and it disgusted her totally, but it was just so ironic that Esther's deeds of the past and present would come full circle and smack Esther in the face and give Arnell a helping hand in ending her relationship with both Esther and James. She almost wanted to laugh, but couldn't; she was hurting too bad. Besides, Kesley Hayden laughed enough for himself and her as Big Walt roughly jostled him through the kitchen and out the back door of the mansion. Kesley Hayden may not have gotten his money, but he did topple Esther. She had fallen hard from her throne and certainly wasn't so high and mighty with the back of her head kissing the floor. Only Melvina, forever loyal to Esther, hurried off to find Esther's tiny white pills which she quickly returned with. She stuck one under Esther's tongue. Arnell lifted not one finger to help. She didn't care if Esther lived or died.

Arnell turned to leave. James caught her by the arm.

"Please give me a chance to explain," he said.

Arnell cut her eyes down at James's hand on her arm. She glared at his hand and then at him. James released her. She began walking away just as Melvina helped Esther to her feet and into her suite. Esther instantly recovered.

"Arnell, please," James said. "You have got to hear my side of this."

Inside her suite, Esther and Melvina stood at the door, listening to Arnell and James.

Arnell turned back. "There is nothing in the world you can say that will make me understand how you ended up in my mother's bed."

"It meant nothing to me, Arnell. It was not what I wanted."

Scowling, Esther balled up her fist. *Bastard!* Then she realized that Melvina was taking in everything she did and said, "Get out!"

Melvina scooted out of the suite and hurried back to her kitchen.

"Then how is it that you got *it* in the first place?" Arnell flipped her hand. "Forget it! I don't need to know." She started again for the front door.

"Goddamn it, Arnell, you have got to listen to me! Please!"

Arnell stopped walking but she stood with her back to James. She had told herself she wasn't going to listen, yet she was morbidly curious about how and when Esther and James had come together as lovers, and at the same time, she realized how perfect this was. She wouldn't have to tell the secrets of her life to James, they were hers to keep forever. There would never be another man she'd let get that close to her again.

"I've been tearing myself up inside trying to make sense of what happened," James said. "Yes, I got your messages, every last one of them. There were times when I was even sitting by the telephone when you called, but I was too ashamed to answer. For God sake, I had slept with my future mother-in-law! Arnell, I couldn't look myself in the mirror. I certainly couldn't look you in the eye, much less talk to you. I was disgusted with what I had done. Sure, I could blame it all on Esther, and maybe I should. She seduced me with all the wiles of Jezebel. My father would cane me if he knew I was so weak of flesh that I could not control my wanton desire for the mother of the woman I love . . ."

Esther smirked smugly. *That's right, you wanted me just as much as I wanted you.*

". . . Yes, I could blame it all on Esther. She was doing things to me that made me forget who we were to each other. But in truth, I must share in the blame. I let myself be seduced when I knew better. I knew the minute the seduction started that it was wrong and I didn't stop it. I'm guilty of that and much more, but I realized upon opening my eyes that I loved only you and wanted only you. The sex that I indulged in with Esther was evil, and I pray God forgive me for it."

Evil! Esther was beside herself. She began to pace. *That was the best goddamn sex you ever had. How dare you damn me to hell when you fucked me harder than I fucked you.*

"Oh, sure, God may well forgive you, James, it's me that won't," Arnell said, turning her hand over. She looked at the diamond she had been so happy to receive as James's promise to love only her.

Esther was pleased. *Good. He wasn't good enough for you anyway.*

"Arnell, we can get through this. We can't let this break us up."

Again, Esther smirked. *Oh, it's breaking you up, buddy. Deal with it.*

Arnell slipped the diamond off her finger.

"Please, don't take off the ring," James said.

Arnell studied the ring. It was beautiful. "I never told you, but this ring fell into a toilet full of shit. Isn't that ironic?"

James paused. He didn't know if Arnell meant that literally or not. "Arnell, we don't have to let this break us up."

"James, we were broken up even before we came together. Neither one of us knew that then, but our whole relationship has been mired in shit from the moment I met you." Arnell held the diamond out to him. "To tell you the truth, I should have never accepted this ring. I'm sorry. And believe me, that apology, I truly owe you."

"I don't want the ring."

Esther wished that she could go out into the hall. *Give the damn ring to me! I'll pawn it.*

"Take it," Arnell insisted."

"I want you to be my wife."

She dropped the ring to the floor at James's feet.

James didn't let the ring he'd paid so much for pull his attention away from Arnell.

"Arnell, please give me another chance. We can go to counseling. We could use my father. He—"

"I be damn. Not if he was the last minister on earth." Arnell pivoted and started walking away. Oops. She forgot something.

"What is that supposed to mean?" James asked.

"And mother," Arnell called, "I know you're listening. You and I? We're through also."

Esther stepped quickly out into the hall. "Are we, sweetie?"

James picked up his sparkling diamond from the burgundy scalloped carpet. He stared into its maze of faceted brilliance.

"Without a doubt," Arnell answered.

"Are you absolutely *sure* about that?" Esther asked, pushing, trying to give Arnell every opportunity to rethink what she was doing.

Arnell began walking away.

"Well, since you're sure," Esther said, raising her voice, "James, how would you like to hear about Arnell's life as a prostitute?"

Arnell stopped dead in her tracks. The bitch was leaving her with not a shred of dignity. Just as Esther had betrayed her father and Kesley Hayden, Esther was betraying her—her stupid, stupid child. But hadn't Esther deceived her all of her life? This was but one more incident in a slew of betrayals. Turning and facing Esther, Arnell saw not her mother before her, but the devil herself, hell-bent on destroying her. No wonder she had always felt like a motherless child. No wonder at times she questioned why she was even born, and sometimes wondered if she killed the woman that gave her life, if she would cease to be or would she be reborn.

Forty

While James stood slack-jawed, Esther's vicious tongue spun a tale of Arnell as a promiscuous teenager who couldn't wait to prostitute herself at the age of sixteen with the landlord when Esther wasn't home. Arnell had gasped time and again, calling Esther a liar and pointing an accusatory finger at her for forcing her to do what no true, loving mother would ever ask of a daughter. After a while when she saw how useless it was to keep trying to defend and explain herself, Arnell stood silent and let Esther spin her vicious lies. After all, what did she have to lose? It was over between her and James, and she was done with Esther. The only reason she stayed and listened to Esther's lies was so that she'd know, firsthand, how far Esther would go to decimate her character. And looking at James's stunned expression, she couldn't tell whether he believed the absolute worst about her or not.

James was crestfallen as he meandered around Esther's suite. "I can't believe this."

"Believe it," Esther said, pleased with herself for getting a measure of satisfaction. She wasn't about to let Arnell walk out on her without suffering, without knowing what it was to lose the one she loved.

"All this time," James said, looking at Arnell, "you were a prostitute, in this house, and I never had a clue?"

Arnell tried to still her shaking hands by balling up her fists. She didn't answer James because her voice might sound shaky and really, she saw no need to answer.

"I'm sorry, sweetie, I thought James should know the truth. You let him think you were scandalized because we slept together, so I figured he should be let off the hook."

James moved anxiously about the room.

"You are a pathetically sad liar," Arnell said to Esther. "I almost feel sorry for you."

"Sweetie," Esther said in a syrupy-sweet voice, "I know you're mad at me for telling on you, but I thought it was for the best."

"You are so full of shit! You do nothing for the best of anyone but yourself. Weeks ago when we had dinner with Tony, I had planned on telling James about my life, but you faked that heart attack to stop me."

"I remember that," James said, "and I asked you later at the hospital what was going on between you and your mother. Why didn't you tell me then?"

Arnell looked steadily at Esther. "Because I wasn't as brave as I should have been. I was afraid to lose you, yet I wanted to tell you to put a stop to her blackmailing me. Every time I tried to pull out of the business, she kept reining me back in with threats to expose me."

"Don't use me as an excuse, Arnell," Esther said. "When I wasn't around, you could have told James a million times over about your secret life."

"Perhaps, but you know as well as I that it wasn't such an easy thing to do."

"So I've made it easy for you. I've told James for you, and believe it or not, James, I've been kind. There is so much more you would definitely find interesting—if you get my meaning."

Arnell angrily flounced around the room. "You got something more to tell? Goddamn it, tell it! You have James's undivided attention. Personally, I don't care anymore. Do you understand that, Esther? I don't give a good goddamn about anything you have to say. You can no longer make me dance to your music. You can no longer use or abuse me." Arnell felt her heart racing, she felt like her lungs were about to burst. "You can't hurt me anymore."

"We'll see about that," Esther said, not the least bit outwardly perturbed.

James stood slump-shouldered, looking at Arnell.

Arnell's anger was burning her up. Her face was flushed. "Oh, we will see. I suggest you unblock your damn ears and let what I've told you bore into your thick, conniving little skull. Yes, we're through. You can bet your manipulative ass on that. You're out of my life—for good."

"Sweetie, you will always need your mother."

"Not the mother that you are." Arnell advanced on Esther. "Hell, how did you become the mother, the woman that you are? You have no soul, no conscience. Was it what Slick did to you?"

"Who the hell is Slick?" James asked.

"Fuck Slick," Esther said, "I hope he's rotting six feet under."

"God," Arnell said, "if Slick is the reason you're this heartless, this vicious, I hate him too. He is just as responsible as you are for making my life a living hell."

"Sweetie," Esther said, hoping to dispel some of Arnell's anger, "I know you might not believe me right now, but I love you with all my heart."

"You don't have a heart."

"Being bitter isn't good for you," Esther said.

"Being your daughter has never been good for me." Arnell raised her trembling right hand. "I swear before God you are dead to me."

Stone-faced, Esther stared at Arnell. She grew angrier the farther Arnell pulled away. "Everything I've ever done has been with you in mind. Melvina's right, you are an ungrateful child."

Arnell's hands wouldn't stop shaking. "No, Esther, you're an ungrateful, mean-spirited, nightmare of a mother who emotionally and psychologically abused her child. You never cared about me. You used me to get what you wanted. You only cared about the almighty dollar. As long as I helped you rake in the dollars, I was your 'sweetie,' your baby. But when I started rebelling, wanting out, and that's been since day one, you threatened me. Woman, you ruined my life, but I won't let you ruin my future. You got that? I will not let you ruin the rest of my life. I'll put my hands around your neck and choke you first."

Cool as an autumn breeze, Esther blew out a ring of smoke. "It's a sin to kill your mother, isn't it James?"

"My God, Arnell," James said, ignoring Esther's question. "Why didn't you tell me about this when we first started seeing each other?"

"What would your response have been, James, if I had said, 'by the way, I'm a prostitute and my mother is a scorpion queen running a brothel?'"

"I . . . I would—"

"You would have kept walking. In fact, you would have stopped using my editing service. You would have avoided me at all cost, that is, unless you wanted to have sex with me."

"That's how men are," Esther said. "Sex is their god."

"Arnell, I was never like that."

"Oh, no?" Esther asked, raising her brow. "Then how did we end up in bed?"

Arnell wished she could slap that self-satisfied smirk off Esther's face. The woman had no concept of the magnitude of the wrong she had done.

"You set a trap." James pulled his shoulders back. "Stupidly, I dove in and lowered myself to the level of a snake's belly."

That self-satisfied smirk Arnell had just seen on Esther's face flashed from a hurt look to a disgusting sneer as she glared at James.

"But that's not how I met or first made love to Arnell." James went and stood a foot in front of Arnell. "We started seeing each other and fell in love. I still love you, Arnell. I know the kind of heart you have. I know the kind of person you are. You're nothing like your mother . . ."

Esther scoffed by flipping her hand at James.

". . . You've been telling me all along that Esther manipulated you all your life. I believe that now. I didn't believe it completely before, but you never told me all that she had done to you. I don't believe for a minute that you prostituted yourself of your own free will at such a young age. In my heart, I know that's not you. If this house is a brothel, and your mother is the madam, then I know what the truth is."

Arnell was hearing James's words, but she couldn't believe—didn't want to hope—that he was prepared to forgive her.

"Arnell, I'm not so sanctimonious that I can't see we've both made regretful mistakes. Neither one of us is perfect and neither one of us can throw stones. I'm asking you to, please, forgive me for what I did with your mother."

Esther was pleasantly surprised. James was proving to be much more of a man than she thought he could be. How come he couldn't want her the way he wanted Arnell?

Arnell was stunned. "But, James, I—"

"Arnell, I was caught in your mother's web, just as you've been all your life . . ."

"That's right," Esther said, "blame me. It's all my fault."

". . . I can only imagine what it's been like for you." James continued, "In all fairness, you don't owe me an apology, your mother does. She owes us both one."

"Hell will freeze over first," Esther said, lighting her fifth cigarette. She needed to do something to make sure that Arnell and James stayed apart. "Hey, Mr. Magnanimous, you seem to be so forgiving of Arnell at my expense, are you willing to forgive her for fucking your father?"

Arnell felt like a vat of acid was dumped into the pit of her stomach. The pain was awful. She clutched her stomach.

"What the fu—" James rushed at Esther sitting on the love seat. He towered above her. "Do you ever quit?"

Esther took a long, slow drag on her cigarette.

"What kind of woman are you? Were you sent up from the bowels of hell to destroy good people? My father is a minister! He's a good man."

"He's a man who likes to fuck prostitutes," Esther said coldly. "Don't believe me? Ask Arnell. In fact, ask the Right Reverend Stanton yourself. I'm sure, being a minister and all, he won't lie to you."

James turned away from Esther. To Arnell, James looked like he had just come face to face with the grotesque, foul-smelling, fire-spitting demon of the damned. His shocked eyes were wide, his forehead was deeply creased, his mouth was open, his face was drained of his golden bronze complexion. He was red and blotchy.

Quivering to the very core of her being, Arnell knew there was no turning back. "It's true. Your father—"

James grabbed Arnell by her shoulders and violently shook her, making her head whip back and forth. "You're lying! Goddamn it, you're lying!"

"Oh, no, she's telling the truth," Esther quipped.

Arnell tried to pry James's hands off her, but again James shook her. "How could you fuck my father? He's my father! Goddamn it, he's my father!"

Arnell struggled to catch her breath and to steady her head. Her neck was killing her, her head was hurting, and James's fingers were digging into her shoulders. "Let go of me!"

After a painful heartbeat, James released Arnell. He began to sob.

"Humph, humph, humph," Esther said. "I see you can get pretty violent."

Arnell tried to rub her achy neck. "You are a contemptuously bitter, evil old woman. How could you be so cruel? So vindictive? You knew this would hurt him."

"Sweetie, that's not my problem. I just simply told the truth."

"Then tell him that you also fucked his father."

James almost choked. He started coughing.

"You want the whole truth, James?" Arnell was now hell bent on freeing herself of all secrets. "Esther and I both had sex with your father, together and separately."

"What?" James roared.

"It's called a ménage à trois," Esther informed James. "It's all the rage."

"You are truly vile," Arnell said. "You're sick to be enjoying this. James, you should know how that came to be."

Whether James wanted to know more or not, he said nothing as he gawked in disbelief at Esther and Arnell.

"Money truly is my mother's god, James. Five years ago, at your father's request, for a fee of five thousand dollars, my mother manipulated me, her own personal hand puppet, into having a ménage à trois with her and your father."

"You didn't turn down your share of the money," Esther said.

"I was a prostitute. Isn't it about the money?"

James's mouth never opened, as he was frozen in stunned silence.

"When this is all over, sweetie, remember it was you that told this part. I would have never told him this."

"No, you would have held that over my head until the day I died."

"Sweetie, you really do think so little of me. I would not've hurt you that way."

"Oh God, woman! What planet are you on? You have always hurt me! You've cut my heart out. And this is about more than James. It's about my entire life. It's about you being the worst kind of mother ever imagined. That umbilical cord that attached me to you didn't just give me life, it poisoned my life, it took my life's breath every time you pimped me to another man."

Stubbing out her cigarette, Esther lit another. "I need a drink," she said, looking at the bar on the side wall where James stood with his hand covering his mouth. She couldn't get her drink just yet—she didn't want to go anywhere near James.

"You're just like your lover Kesley, you are disgustingly vile," Arnell said. She realized that no other words fit Esther more perfectly. "Are you happy now that you've destroyed so many lives?"

"I'm getting a little tired of all these names you're calling me." And just so you'll know, whatever I did, I was always looking out for you."

"Stop lying! You didn't sleep with James for me. Am I supposed to be so stupid that I'd believe that? Are you insane?"

"Arnell, you've never had a realistic thought in your head. Shit happens. The sooner you both realize that, the better off you'll be."

"You are a nasty bitch," James finally said.

Esther widened her eyes at Arnell. "You're gonna let him speak to me that way?"

"Oh, I believe he has earned the right to speak to you any way he wants. As for myself, I second his sentiment."

Esther shrugged. "Fine. I'm not mad at you, Arnell. I know how you are when you're upset, but none of this changes the fact that James isn't good enough for you. He—"

"Who are you," James bellowed, again rushing at Esther, "to say whether I'm good enough or not?" He had his fists balled up. "You, of all people, can never sit in judgment over me or any human being."

"I wouldn't say that, James. You had sex with me. It didn't take twenty minutes to get you into bed. You're just like your father."

James raised his fist, knuckles popped, threateningly at Esther. Arnell held her breath. Esther held James's gaze. She was daring him to hit her. It would give her so much pleasure to call the police on him. The moment was still, the air was tense. Not even the music that was just starting up again far off in the living room penetrated their thoughts. James's fist was squeezed so tight he began to feel the muscles in his arm spasm.

Esther taunted, "Show us the kind of man you really are, Mr. Magnanimous."

James struck out at Esther, but he pulled his punch at the very last second. His fist stopped within an inch of Esther's face. She choked on the smoke she had just inhaled. Arnell gasped. James worked his jaw as he lowered his fist and began backing away from Esther. He backed into a table. Turning, he looked down and suddenly swiped a small white porcelain figurine from the table and flung it across the room, hitting the wall behind Esther. The figurine shattered and exploded into tiny pieces.

Arnell understood perfectly well James's rage. She was feeling that same rage herself.

"You will pay for that," Esther said, trying to sound threatening although her insides were quivering. She wasn't so much afraid that James had been aiming at her or that he would have hit her, he had better not. It was her angst that Arnell was never going to forgive her that was scaring her.

"If anyone pays," James said, "it will be you." His eyes were wild as tears filled them and spilled over. "My father is a goddamn minister. He—"

"He's an adulterer!" Esther shouted, flicking her cigarette ash onto the floor. "He's the worst kind of hypocrite. He's a—"

"Stop it!" Arnell warned, "Or I swear, I will make you pay for this myself. And you know I can."

Esther huffed and flipped her hand at Arnell, but she did shut up.

James anxiously rubbed his forehead. His tears flowed. "Arnell, please don't lie to me about this. Is this the god's honest truth? Did . . . did you really have—"

Inhaling deeply to keep from crying herself, Arnell pressed her hand over her heart, but her voice cracked anyway. "It's all true."

"Oh, God," James moaned, lowering his head. "I feel so dirty. This place ... it—"

"Oh, grow up!" Esther spat. "This is a brothel, not a damn church."

"She's right about that," Arnell said. "Nothing clean, nothing moral, and certainly, nothing religious goes on here."

"I beg your pardon. I think the Right Reverend might disagree about that."

"Leave my father out of this sordid mess! He's nothing like you."

Esther sucked her teeth. "Spare me! Boy, let me enlighten you about your father, the great man. The Right Reverend was face-down, deep in this *sordid mess* as you call it. In fact, he couldn't get enough. He liked having two and three girls at a time," Esther said, remembering the money he had paid for that privilege which in turn, over the years, paid for her roof and her new kitchen.

James went to storming madly about the room. "This can't be true. This just can't be true."

"James," Arnell said, following behind him, "your father started coming here five years ago. At first we didn't know he was a minister, but Esther found out soon enough. That was five years ago, James, I didn't know you then. I didn't even know that you existed. In fact, when I met you, I didn't connect you by name or avocation to your father, and really, you look nothing like him."

"Thank God," Esther quipped.

"How fortunate was that?" James asked, breathing hard from moving nonstop and from being so upset. "Would it have made a difference if you had known I was his son?"

"Nope," Esther said, with the kiss of a devious smile on her lips.

"I wasn't talking to you!"

"Well, I—"

"Shut the hell up!" Arnell glared at Esther.

"You stay out of this!" James shouted at Esther. "You're ... you're—" He clutched his head and stormed over to the window. "Goddamn it! What the fuck have I gotten myself into?"

"Yes," Arnell said, wanting to go to James to comfort him, but daring not, "it would have made a difference if I had known who your father was. I would have never started seeing you. James, if you remember, it was more than six months before I went to church with you and met your parents."

"Yes, but I told you about them soon after we met."

"No, you didn't. You told me about your father three months after we met and by then I didn't know what to do. I tried to stop seeing you, remember? But you kept coming back and I let you because I had fallen in love with you."

"You should have told him anyway," Esther said, lighting another cigarette.

"Shut up!" James and Arnell shouted in unison.

"Damn. Excuse the hell out of me," Esther said, taken aback. This conversation wasn't going the way she expected. James was supposed to be damning Arnell to hell and Arnell was supposed to be disgusted by James's whining.

"James," Arnell said, emotionally drained, "we can go on forever about this. For me, it's not necessary. Yes, your father was a frequent visitor to The Honey Well—"

"The Honey Well?" James asked, perplexed.

"That's what men call this place," Esther said, "the place where they come to have sweet, honey licking sex."

Arnell put her hands on her hips. "If you don't stay the hell out of this conversation, I am going to duct tape your vicious mouth shut."

"And I'm supposed to let you?" Esther questioned, her brow raised.

"You won't have a choice," James said, joining in, "and I won't need Arnell's help to do the taping."

Arnell and James both glared bitterly at Esther.

Although she didn't like that Arnell and James were ganging up on her, Esther concerned herself only with the ugly sneer on Arnell's lips and the hateful glare in her eyes. Maybe she had pushed Arnell too far.

"Does my father still come here?"

"No," Arnell answered. "He stopped after he saw me with you that time you took me to the church."

"Oh, God." James was incredulous. "You knew each other that day and never said a word?"

"What was I supposed to say? I knew your father from The Honey Well. There is no way to introduce that kind of information to you or your mother in any setting."

"Oh, God." James said, his eyes wide. "My mother."

"I'm sorry," Arnell said.

"My mother will die if she ever found out about this."

"She sure—" The threatening look Arnell gave Esther halted her words. Again, she looked away.

"James," Arnell said, "I'm sorry for keeping the truth from you about me. Your father? He has to answer to you and your mother, and, I guess, ultimately to God. As for myself, I'm going to do us both a favor and walk, no, run out of your life." She felt the tears welling up. "I wish for you the absolute best."

James and Arnell held each other's painful gaze but a handful of seconds, but it was more than enough time for their eyes to tell the other what both knew in their hearts. It was over. It was James who looked away first.

Arnell didn't glance Esther's way as she left the room.

Esther rushed behind Arnell out into the hallway. "Arnell, you and I aren't finished. We have more to talk about."

Abruptly about-facing, Arnell was on the verge of hurling every obscenity she'd ever heard in life at Esther, but an instant calm came over her when she saw the panic in Esther's eyes. It was a welcome sight.

"Sweetie, I know you're angry with me and you have every right to be," Esther said, wringing her hands, "but, please, please don't leave just yet."

Arnell suddenly felt that maybe she did have something to say. "Actually, Mother, or should I say Esther? Yes, Esther is more appropriate, don't you think?"

Esther searched Arnell's face. Nothing about her seemed familiar. There was no glimmer of forgiveness or love or pity in her eyes or in her voice. Arnell had closed herself off from her. Esther felt cold. She could feel Arnell's hatred cloaking her like a bone-chilling frost on a frigid winter night. She needed to stoke the smoldering ashes of their once close relationship. If Arnell walked out on her now, Esther knew that she would be all alone. With Tony gone, there would be no one to care if she lived or died.

"Well, Esther," Arnell said, "leaving is the best thing I can do for myself. From now on, I'm doing what you do best—I'm looking out for number one. Besides, I've stayed longer than I should have by some sixteen years."

"But, sweetie, I am so sorry. You know I'd never do anything to really hurt you."

"Geez, Esther, will you always be a liar?"

"But—"

"Everything you've ever done has been engineered specifically to hurt me."

"No, not to hurt you, sweetie, but to keep you safe from men that were only going to hurt you in the long run. They're all nice and loving in the beginning, but after they get you fooled into trusting them, they turn on you. They lie to you. They hurt you."

"My," Arnell said musingly, "but that sounds so much like what you've done to me since I was child. And correct me if I'm wrong, Esther. You're the one that put me in the hands of these very men that you say will hurt me in the first place. See, this is my point, you've always been my worst enemy."

"That's not true. I'm the only one that loved you, sweetie."

Arnell was aware that Esther was getting closer to her. "You call what you have for me, love?" She chuckled bitterly. "Geez, Esther, your kind of love is lethal. And would you, for God sake, stop calling me sweetie. I hate that name. In case you don't know, it's supposed to be a term of endearment, not condescension."

"You don't have to be hateful, Arnell. You're going to need me one day."

"Dream on."

"You can't just throw me away," Esther said. "No one in your whole life, besides me, has ever been there for you. No one, besides me, has ever sacrificed a thing for you. I am the only one that has ever truly loved you."

"Oh, well, poor me. How did I get to be so fortunate. Oh," Arnell said, "I know. I didn't have a father. I guess if my father hadn't been murdered by your lover, I just might have had the opportunity to experience love the normal way."

Esther felt the muscles in her chest tighten. "I swear to you, Arnell, if I had it to do over, I would have never had that affair with Kesley. It is my fault that your father was taken from you, but that's why I've spent my whole life try—"

"No!" Arnell threw up her hand. "Do not let another lie slither from between your lips. I couldn't bear it. In fact, we have nothing more to say to each other."

"Arnell, please." Esther's nose was starting to sting. "Please don't hate me."

"That's just it, I don't." Arnell saw James finally come into the doorway. He had been hanging back, listening. Before he could say anything to her, she walked out the front door.

"You'll be back!" Esther shouted as tears rolled down her cheeks. "Mark my word, you'll be back."

Not on your life. Arnell felt the unbearable weight of Esther's control lift off her shoulders as she exited The Honey Well. She was finally free.

Forty-One

Big Walt was a man of his word. He was waiting in his car for Arnell when she walked out of The Honey Well. He blew his horn. Arnell had never been so happy to see such a strong, friendly face in her life.

"Are you all right?" Big Walt asked after Arnell had settled back in the passenger seat.

"I will be." Exhausted, she let her head fall back against the headrest. "Please, take me home."

"You got it." Big Walt started to pull out. He glanced in the side view and then the rearview. He stopped the car. "There's your man."

Arnell quickly looked back. Under the darkening sky, James was standing on the sidewalk looking back at the mansion.

"You wanna talk to him?"

Facing forward again, Arnell lay her head back against the headrest.

Wasting not another minute, Big Walt headed toward Ocean Parkway. He nor Arnell spoke until he merged with the heavy traffic entering the Belt Parkway, which would take them out onto Long Island.

"I drove that fool, Kesley, to the subway station on the other side of Prospect Park. I made sure that he got on the train heading for the Port Authority. He should be able to get a bus going somewhere, anywhere out of New York. He was a pissed off brother. He said—"

"Big Walt." Arnell rolled her head wearily from side to side on the headrest. She didn't need to know nor did she want to know anything about Kesley Hayden. He was none of her concern.

"No problem." Big Walt drove on five minutes more in silence. "What are you gonna do about your mother?"

"I'm going to see the Brooklyn District Attorney tomorrow."

"No shit?"

Arnell closed her eyes. She was ready to shut Esther down—permanently.

"That's deep," Big Walt said. "Do you want me to go with you?"

"I need to do this alone."

Again they drove on in silence.

"Do you remember my friend, Ace?" Big Walt asked.

"I'm trying to not remember him."

"Oh, snap. Why's that?"

"Big Walt, be for real. I hate to say it but you and your friends stormed Tony's funeral like you were some tactical goon squad. I didn't like that scene at all, so believe me, I'm trying to forget anything and everyone involved."

"That was the queen's idea."

"Like I didn't know, but I don't wanna talk about her, either." Arnell closed her eyes.

"Then let's talk about Ace. He's not a bad guy and he's real interested in you."

"Tell him not to be, because I am not interested in any friendships, relationships, partnerships, fellowships, in fact, no kind of ships. I'm not in the game anymore."

"That's too bad," Big Walt said, his eyes fixed on the road ahead.

"Believe me, I would never be interested in a guy named Ace."

"Well, Ace isn't his real name. That's his nickname. His name is Clifton Jameson. He's an electrician, he owns his own business. I think he has about twelve guys working for him."

Confused, Arnell looked hard at Big Walt. "So . . . why would he—"

"He was watching my back. He's my brother. We do that for each other."

"Do you mean brother as in blood?"

"My name is Walter Jameson, remember?"

"To tell you the truth, I've been calling you Big Walt for so long, I forgot that you had a real name."

"That name was part of the job. The day of Tony's funeral, I had a job to do and it wasn't one that I was comfortable with, so I pulled in my boys. The Hammer, or rather Roy, which is his real name. He's a cop."

"Are you kidding?"

"He was off duty."

"But did he know who Esther was? Did he know about her brothel?"

"Yep."

"And?"

"Arnell, a lot of cops know about The Honey Well. Some have even been there. Didn't you know that?"

"Well, yes, but Roy—"

"Yeah, he could have gotten into trouble, but he didn't. No one knew who he was."

"That was so sick," Arnell said. "Why would he risk—"

"For me," Big Walt said. "Look, we played it so that no one would get hurt."

"Excuse me, but big guns more than hurt people."

"True, but we had dummy bullets. We knew better than to go in there with live ammo, and we knew that just seeing the guns would make people back off, which they did. If you noticed, the boys out front never came inside. They were scared of their own shadow."

Arnell was amazed. "Damn. Big Walt, ah, can I just call you Walt?"

"My family calls me Walter."

Tears threatened, but Arnell held strong. "You should have everyone call you Walter. Walter, don't you think you need to get another job?"

"After today, no doubt. I was just doing this until my music hit anyway. I just sold six songs to a singer who's about to burst on the scene. He's gonna be large, and so am I."

"That is really great. I hope it all works out for you." Arnell meant that.

"So, what about my brother? Can he call you? He's thirty-five. He's really a good man. He won't do you wrong. I'd kill him if he did."

Glancing up at the road sign, Arnell saw that they were exiting onto the Southern State Parkway. "Give me some time," she said. "I have to nurse my soul for a while."

"I hear that."

Arnell closed her eyes. "Wake me when we get to my house." She felt the car pick up speed. It was nice to be going home.

Big Walt shook Arnell first gently then a little harder when she didn't stir. He had cut the engine before Arnell finally opened her eyes.

"You have company," Big Walt said, looking toward Arnell's house.

Still sleepy, Arnell slowly focused on the lone figure of a girl sitting on the steps to her house. "Who is that?" she asked, wondering why the porch light hadn't come on.

"It looks like that young girl, Trena."

And it was. Trena had made her way back to Arnell's. She didn't know where else to go. She stood when Arnell began to climb out of Big Walt's car.

"Do you want me to take her back to Brooklyn?" Big Walt asked.

Arnell closed the door. "No. She needs me."

The bathroom lights were off. Only candles—eight large white ones—illuminated the room in a dreamy, fantastical glow. Esther lay back in her bathtub filled with lavender scented oil and big white bubbles. The stereo in her suite was turned up loud so that she could hear it clearly in her bathroom. Yanni was soaring on the wings of flying violins. The music filled the large bathroom. Esther closed her eyes and let the hot water relax her muscles while the beautiful music embraced her and carried her away. She really needed to unwind after all that drama. As soon as Melvina brought her martini, she'd relax even more and maybe stop, for a minute, thinking about Arnell. The others—James, Kesley—she didn't give a damn about. Arnell might be angry with her right now, but she'd get over it. She always had before. This was no different. Arnell would pout, and she might not call for a few weeks, but she'd eventually call and they'd forgive each other and then they'd go on. They had to, they only had each other.

Warm tears eased down Esther's cheeks. She really hated that she'd hurt Arnell so badly. Why in the world would she set out to seduce James to get back at Arnell when she knew that Arnell would hate her? And all for a man that was a nothing. Arnell had to know that James wasn't right for her—he was weak. Arnell should be thanking her for breaking them up instead of being angry with her. Arnell needed a strong man, a man who didn't get a hard-on the minute the scent of a new woman drifted up his nostrils. One day Arnell would realize her mother was right and forgive her. Hopefully soon.

Esther let unwanted tears flow unchecked, unabashed. *Damn.* She brought her fist down on the side of the tub. An overwhelming feeling of loss consumed her, but the hell with that. She never lost anything, not anymore, not since she had gotten on her feet and lived her life as Queen Esther. That's who she was, Queen Esther, and no one would ever take that from her. Tony understood that. He was the only one who allowed her to be herself without condemnation or reproach, but he was gone now. Poor Tony. She was really missing him. In her heart, she knew that he had been murdered and the way things stood with his family, she would probably never learn the truth.

Esther was alone, but she was going to be all right. She was Queen Esther, after all. No one got the better of her. Hadn't today proven that? Kesley was out of her life and Arnell wasn't going to marry James. Oh, Arnell was upset right now, but she'd be back and they'd be friends again.

Esther scooped up a handful of bubbles. She blew them and watched a few float in midair. Like those bubbles, she should have been feeling as light as air. She had come out on top. Why wasn't she feeling some measure of satisfaction? Why was she feeling so terrible? It could only be because she had hurt Arnell—her baby. What she had done with James, what she had done with Kesley all those years ago, was too much for Arnell to deal with. There had to be a way to make it up to her. Damn, but she was too tired to think about that right now. She would figure it out tomorrow. That's what tomorrows were for.

Behind Esther the door to the bathroom closed. "Melvina, don't close it. I wanna hear the music." She slid lower into the water, up to her shoulders. Closing her eyes, she let the warmth of the water relax her muscles and soothe her troubled mind.

Esther could feel Melvina standing over her. "Just leave the drink on my bath caddy."

No glass was set down. Curious, Esther opened her eyes. She opened her mouth to scream, but hands, big, strong hands, the same hands that killed her husband, suddenly gripped her head and began pushing her below mountainous clouds of bubbles. Esther kicked wildly, she clawed frantically at those hands, those arms, but her scratching didn't stop Kesley Hayden from forcing her head under the scented water. Esther thought of Arnell. She wasn't ready to leave Arnell, they hadn't made up yet. Esther kicked harder, splashing water and bubbles against the wall, onto the floor, and onto Kesley Hayden. She tried to scream but the water that filled her lungs choked her, burned her throat, stung her nose, and finally, took her life.

Forty-Two

The tears wouldn't come. As hard as Arnell tried, she couldn't pull a tear from her heart. She sat in front of Esther's open casket wondering if she had died knowing that a part of her—that little girl inside her who had yet to be hurt—still loved her. On that ugly day that Arnell had last seen Esther, she had planned to never see her again, although she didn't think for a minute that her last good-bye was to be so final, so soon. That urgent telephone call from Melvina would forever sound in Arnell's ear. "That man! He kill Queen Esther! Arnell, your mother, she dead!" At Esther's funeral, Melvina and Jeanette were the only ones that cried.

Arnell couldn't say that she ever mourned the woman that birthed her into the world—the tears she finally shed after burying Esther were more for herself than for Esther. She truly felt like she was all alone in the world, although being alone was what she needed after all she had been put through, but Sharise would not allow her to be by herself to welter in the dark, dreary pit of depression she had let herself sink into. Sharise left her children to their father and the nanny to stay with her for two weeks, proving to Arnell that she was not alone. To Sharise, Arnell was able to admit that she was glad she was now a motherless child for she was forever free of the voice that stifled her words, and free of the arms that encaged her. She thought often of Esther—the good and the bad—but she didn't miss her. Any love she had for Esther came only from that little girl, Sweetie, but Sweetie had ceased to be when a price was put on her vagina. What she had been feeling all these years for Esther, was a daughter's obligation, and her death freed Arnell of that.

A month after burying Esther, Arnell was sorting through Esther's papers and came across letters from her brother Matt. Some were dated as late as the year before. Arnell was stunned. Esther never mentioned that her brother even knew where she was, or that he had been in touch. The fact that Esther kept the letters or even read them was mind-boggling in itself. There were twenty-seven letters in all, most pleading with Esther to straighten out her life and to come back to the Lord. Back? Was Esther ever with the Lord? Arnell doubted if she was even with the Lord now. Surely, Esther must have scoffed at that suggestion from her brother, but nothing could have prepared Arnell for the letter that read, "Sister, we were born in the Church. We were both baptized as babies. Our father was a minister, he taught us at his knee to be righteous and clean. Sister, you live an unclean life. Your greatest sin is that you washed your only child in the smutty waters of fornication and degradation, and not the holy waters of redemption. I should have fought harder to take her from you, I am sorry that I did not."

Those words brought tears to Arnell's eyes to know that someone, at one time, had really cared about her. Although Esther had mentioned that her brother had tried to take her from her at one time, Arnell didn't remember it herself. But just the thought that he had wanted to rescue her from Esther was comfort enough. What Arnell hadn't known, was that her grandfather had been a minister and that Esther had been brought up in the Church. How could a person veer so far off track? How was it that Esther never told her anything about her upbringing? But then, Esther never told her anything on her own. Everything was always pulled from her. Arnell had to know more.

Setting her manners aside, Arnell didn't call the telephone number she found in several of the letters from her uncle; she took a chance and drove to New Rochelle in upstate New York on a cool October afternoon. It was a Saturday so she prayed that her uncle would be home. Uncle Matt opened the door, and only after a moment of looking in her face, he opened his arms. Arnell closed her eyes and let her uncle's arms do for her what no man's arms had ever truly done—touch her soul. She cried for all the hugs she had missed and when she realized that her Uncle Matt was crying, and that there was woman, who had to be his wife, who had come up behind him and was also hugging her and crying too, Arnell knew that she had found her family.

"Esther was a loving child who grew up to be an angry woman," Uncle Matt said. "Esther was twelve when Daddy died and about seventeen with Momma died. She had changed even before then, but she became another person after Momma died. She started smoking and drinking, and going around with young people that were up to no good. I thought I understood why, but Esther always said that I was wrong. I guess I just never knew."

Arnell told her uncle about his Uncle Slick. His gasp of alarm filled the room and his tears for Esther were long overdue.

"I should have protected her, she was my little sister and Daddy always said, 'Take care of your little sister.' I failed to do that."

Arnell realized that there was so much Uncle Matt did not know about Esther. Too much for Arnell to tell on her first visit, much of which she would never tell—some things just ought to be buried with its owner. Esther never answered Uncle Matt's letters after the first two, so whereas Arnell thought her uncle's letters meant that he knew about Esther's brothel or even about Esther pimping her, he didn't. He just thought that Esther was living a loose life around her child. Arnell let him continue to believe that. It was for the best.

She stayed the night and the next morning met Gary, one of her three cousins. Over time, she would meet them all, but none had to know.

EPILOGUE

Arnell admired the ring of frosted pink rosettes she'd designed along the border of Ashley's two-layer vanilla-frosted birthday cake. The sounds of high-pitched squeals and laughing children sailed through the open kitchen window. There was a yard full of toddlers being entertained by a cherry-nosed, big-footed, chalky-faced clown. Arnell could not believe that Ashley was three years old today. It seemed like only yesterday that she and Cliff were bringing Ashley home from the hospital, but Ashley's size and her boundless inquisitiveness confirmed that the years had indeed slipped by. She was the most talkative child Arnell had ever known, not to mention smart and unbelievably adorable. Of course, it was disconcerting that Ashley was every inch a look-alike for Esther. But Arnell didn't let her baby's resemblance to Esther taint her love for her. She would never harm her baby girl as Esther had done.

Esther would no doubt adore Ashley, but even if Esther had not been murdered, she would not have been allowed within a mile of Ashley. Arnell was serious about being a good mother—she would teach Ashley morals and principals, and she would protect her from the lechery of men and women who sought only their gratification. She would see her baby girl safely into adulthood.

It took six months for the police to track down and capture Kesley Hayden in Dallas. This time, he was sentenced to twenty-five to life without the possibility of parole—Esther would have loved that. Somewhere on the other side, Esther was probably mad as hell that she couldn't laugh in Kesley's face. But that wasn't all that Esther would be spitting fire over. Arnell was certain that Esther turned over in her grave ten times the day her precious mansion sold for nine hundred and fifty thousand dollars. Again Melvina cried—after all, her home had been sold right from under her. Arnell had no use for the house where only bad things had happened to her and perhaps many others. It wasn't a place that she could ever lay her head down in again.

"Hey, babe, the cake looks good," Cliff said, sticking his finger in the bowl that the vanilla frosting had been made in. He licked at the frosting on his finger. He frowned. "This stuff is too sweet." He looked around for something to wipe the rest of the frosting on.

Arnell took Cliff's finger into her mouth and sensuously sucked it clean of the frosting.

"Behave yourself. There are fifteen innocent children outside."

"They're not in here." Arnell pressed her body into Cliff. She licked his lips.

"Now, I like this sugar better." Cliff took Arnell into his arms and tongued her deep and long.

This was just one of the many stolen moments since Ashley was born, and Arnell relished each as if it were the first. She could never thank Walter enough for pushing her to give his brother a chance. It had been the last thing she wanted to do, especially after getting out of the relationship with James. She never heard from James again, and that was a good thing. They would have never been able to look each other in the eye and not see Esther or the ugliness of Arnell's past. When she did finally take that call from Walter's brother, Clifton, a whole year had passed, Trena had delivered a son, Chad, and Arnell had begun to take classes toward her master's. It wasn't so much that she was eager to start dating; she did it to silence Walter. Like Sharise and Trena, he was driving her insane. Sharise had been checking on her, Trena had been leaning on her, and Walter had been calling under the pretext of asking how she was doing to see if she was ready to go out with his brother. The funny thing was, she and Cliff hit it off right away—the truth up front helped, although Cliff knew a lot about her already. They had just celebrated their fourth anniversary that past May—two months ago. It was a good marriage, Cliff was as good a man as Walter had said. Cliff was very patient in the first year they dated. He didn't push Arnell when she held back sexually. That period of celibacy strengthened their relationship and allowed Arnell to see the man who came to love her with no strings attached. Cliff never brought up her past, not even when heated words between them pulled them a foot apart—but they never let that foot become a mile. The ring Cliff gave her had never fallen into the toilet and Arnell didn't expect that it would—she never took it off in the bathroom. Why tempt fate, when her life was so right?

Arnell was in her fourth year of teaching high school English at Francis Lewis, and loving it. Trena was in her junior year at St. John's University and doing quite well—she wanted to be a child psychologist. After Chad was born, Trena never made plans to move out and Arnell never suggested that she should. Time healed Trena's womb and her mind. She was going to make it, that Arnell was sure of. The Honey Well didn't steal either one of their dreams, it only stole an ounce of their dignity.

In Cliff's arms, Arnell forgot about cake frosting.

"Y'all cut that out!" Trena said, entering the kitchen. "This is supposed to be a kid's party."

Arnell and Cliff ended their long passionate kiss, but they didn't leave each other's embrace. "What are you up to?" Cliff asked. "I thought you were supposed to be outside helping to oversee the activities."

"I was—darn near by myself. Only Arnell's cousin, Gail, is helping me. Michael's asleep and Sharise isn't a bit of help. She's sitting in the chaise with her feet up."

"Now, Trena," Arnell said, moving away from Cliff. "I know you remember what it's like in the last month of pregnancy."

"I wasn't lazy."

"Yeah, right." Arnell said. "I remember differently."

Cliff teasingly pulled his T-shirt away from his stomach and arched his back. He took a few ponderous steps with his hands pressed into the pit of his back.

Trena picked up the dishcloth from the table and threw it at him. She laughed in spite of being sensitive about how big she had gotten when she was pregnant.

Arnell punched Cliff in the shoulder. "That isn't funny. You try carrying a fifty-pound watermelon in your stomach for several months and see if you laugh."

"Man," Cliff said, straightening up, "women have no sense of humor."

"Certainly not pregnant women," Arnell said. While she had relished every moment of her pregnancy with Ashley, Trena didn't enjoy one day of her pregnancy.

Chad was now six years old and a big brother to Ashley. Trena agreed to go through with the pregnancy only if she could live with Arnell and give the baby up for adoption, but as fate would have it, Chad became Arnell's baby the first time she felt him kick inside Trena's stomach. Trena, along with Sharise, was godmother to Chad and Ashley, and had no hangups with being around Chad. She coddled him just as much as she did Ashley, but she didn't want Chad for herself. Trena's mother and sister wanted her to bring Chad around, but Trena never would; she didn't want Chad to be a part of their lives, and that was because she could never bring herself to tell them how Chad came to be. As it was, it took some time for Trena to feel good enough about herself to be a part of their lives again. Her father still hadn't forgiven her for giving Chad away, but Trena didn't see it as giving Chad away. She saw it as giving Chad a chance to be loved without memories of his conception blocking that love.

Andrew Peebles never knew that he had a son; he was killed trying to rob a bodega. Turns out he wasn't a producer after all. He was just a thief stealing from others to pay for his visits to The Honey Well.

The real producer it seems was Walter. Walter was now *the* Walter Jameson, one of the most sought-after songwriters and producers in rap music. He did himself proud and made Arnell and Cliff even prouder when he agreed to be godfather to both Ashley and Chad. Arnell had her own family now, and took not one of them for granted.

Trena stuck the third pink candle into Ashley's birthday cake. "Let's do this."

Just as Arnell picked up Ashley's cake, she was kissed ever so gently on the right cheek. "I love you too," she said to Cliff, "but what was that for?"

"What was what for?" Cliff asked.

"The kiss."

"I didn't kiss you."

"Yes, you did."

"No, I didn't."

Arnell looked at Trena.

"Don't look at me, I didn't kiss you."

"I swear," Arnell said, "it felt like someone kissed me on the cheek."

"Oooo!" Trena said, "we have ghosts."

The fine hairs on Arnell's arm stood up. "Don't joke. I believe in ghosts."

"I think we should join the party," Cliff said. "You lead the way."

Feeling full and warm in her soul, but uneasy in her mind, Arnell led her family out into the backyard to sing happy birthday to her baby girl.

THE HONEY WELL

GLORIA MALLETTE

ABOUT THIS GUIDE

The suggested questions are intended to
enhance your group's reading of
Gloria Mallette's THE HONEY WELL.

DISCUSSION QUESTIONS

1. As a teenager Arnell was manipulated by her mother, Esther, into prostituting herself in order to keep a roof over their heads, but as an adult, why is it that Arnell is still allowing herself to be manipulated by Esther? Why can't Arnell break the ties that bind them together? Does not having any other familial connection make Arnell cleave to Esther even more?

2. It has been said that individuals hurt most the one they love. Do you believe that Esther truly loves Arnell? In fact, is Esther capable of really loving anyone?

3. Esther was molested by a close relative, an uncle, as a little girl. This is more common than not. How has this molestation affected Esther psychologically and how has it affected her relationship with men?

4. Arnell is engaged to be married and she has somehow managed to keep her past from her fiancé. Was she right to keep this secret so long? Was she foolish to get engaged in the first place when she knows that Esther will use that engagement to control and manipulate her?

5. Arnell wants desperately to be rid of Esther and plans on leaving The Honey Well for good, but once she sees Trena, the teenager who has run away from home, Arnell decides to help her. Why?

6. Trena is like so many young girls who are eager to grow up and be out on their own. Was Trena's home life so bad? Is it unrealistic for a young girl to hold on to her virginity until she is eighteen? Until she is married?

7. Is Trena's first sexual encounter in The Honey Well all that she thought it would be? Why not?

8. Arnell's last encounter at The Honey Well is technically a rape. It's understood why she didn't report it, but why would she not fight back?

9. As time goes by, Arnell appears to be getting stronger in her determination to break away from Esther, yet she drops everything to be by Esther's side when Tony dies. Why? And why would she be her defender against Tony's family when she feels that Esther is wrong to barge into Tony's funeral?

10. Esther seduces Arnell's fiancé, James, to get back at her. Is it true that some mothers see their own daughters as competition?

11. James is obviously not as strong a man as Arnell needs. Does she need a man at all to get where she needs to be in her life?

The following is a sample chapter from
Gloria Mallette's upcoming novel
DISTANT LOVER.
This book will be available in October 2004
wherever hardcover books are sold.

Hordes of people—some strolling, some shopping, others hurrying about their own personal business—were rudely brushing past Tandi Crawford, irritating her, making her move out of each square foot of sidewalk she claimed while she waited for Brent. She couldn't get mad at Brent, he was only four minutes late. She was the one that was early—twenty-seven minutes early. Of course, if Brent was allowed to come to her house to see her, like other girls' boyfriends, she would not have had to sneak and meet him on the corner of Jamaica Avenue and 164th Street, one of the busiest commercial street corners in Jamaica, Queens, on a Saturday afternoon, when she was supposed to be bowling with her girlfriends up on Hillside Avenue. If her father had an inkling, he'd put a dog collar around her neck and let her out only when school was in session. Her father didn't like Brent and the truth was, grumpy old Glenn Belson didn't like her either. But that was all right, his disliking her didn't bother Tandi, at least not anymore.

All that mattered to Tandi was that she had Brent and that they were in love. And it *was* love, although puppy love is what Aunt Gert called it; a hot ass is what her father called it. Of course, neither was right. She wasn't a starry-eyed kid and she wasn't hot to lose her virginity. She was truly in love, and while losing her virginity wasn't uppermost in her mind, she would not hold back nor would she regret it if it were to Brent Rodgers. He was to die for. Sometimes Tandi felt like she couldn't breathe until she could see

Brent again; until she could touch him and know that he was real and not a figment of her imagination. Oh, but Brent was very real. Hadn't he, just yesterday, behind the bleachers in the school gymnasium, tongued her deep and long while feeling her breasts under her gym shirt, rendering her weak in the knees and moist in a place where she had not yet been touched? Soon enough, that's for sure.

Oh, God! There he is! Brent was coming. Tandi's heart leaped. Her pulse quickened as she watched Brent's long muscular legs bring him closer. The funny thing was, she must have seen him walking down the street hundreds of times, yet each and every time she saw him was like seeing him for the very first time. He still took her breath away just as he did to a lot of girls in their high school. She knew of three in particular who would scratch her eyes out to get with Brent, but who could blame them? Brent was all that and more. He was definitely something to look at. The skimpy muscle shirt and mid-thigh shorts he wore exposed his sculptured biceps, his touch-me pecs, and powerful runner's thighs. Brent truly must have been a beautiful baby because he was so fine now, and he was all hers. Tandi couldn't wait to be in his arms; to taste of his lips; to feel his hardness against her softness. Her entire body throbbed with a yearning so strong she trembled. She wanted Brent to—

"Mommy! Are you sleeping in there?"

Tandi's eyes flew open. She yanked her hand from between her thighs. She quickly sat up, splashing the tepid bath water up against the wall and over the side of the tub onto the floor. "Damn," she whispered, hating that the bath mat was probably soaked, and most likely the rug, too. She looked down at her legs through the clear water. There wasn't a single bubble left.

Knock . . . knock . . . knock.

"Mommy! Can I have some ice cream and cookies?"

Glancing at the door, Tandi sighed heavily. Back to reality. She was no longer that carefree seventeen-year-old girl whose every thought was of Brent. She was a wife to Jared, who no longer noticed her, and a mother to Michael Jared, who was the light of her life. Secretly, she ached shamelessly for an eighteen-year-old boy from way back in the day when the lazy hazy summer days of her sexual awakening, combined with soulful love songs whet her appetite for Brent and filled her head with erotic fantasies, making her reality even sweeter when he became hers.

"Mommy!"

"What!"

" 'Bout time! Can I have some ice cream and cookies?"

"Did you finish your homework?"

"Yeah. Can I have some ice cream and cookies?"

"Michael Jared, you had cookies when you got in from school this afternoon."

"Mommy, that was hours ago and you only let me have three."

"That's because you ate a whole package of cookies yesterday."

"It was a small pack. Mommy, we got cookies, why can't I eat 'em?"

"Boy . . . Michael Jared, you're wearing me out. Take three more cookies and let me finish my bath in peace." She knew that he would ignore her and eat darn near the whole package again. But what could she do? He was a growing boy with a big appetite.

"Mommy, one day you gonna drown in there."

"I'm sure you'll break down the door and save your drowning mother, won't you?"

"That's gross! I don't want to see you in no bathtub. I'd call 911."

"By that time, I could be dead."

"They'll bring you back, just don't let them see you naked."

Tandi smiled to herself. "Boy, go get your cookies and ice cream before I change my mind."

Michael Jared was her heart, her baby, but he was a boy at the awkward crossroads of still being a little boy and the awakening of his own sexuality. He had a hissy fit when she told him that she use to bath him along with herself, and sometimes along with his father when he was a baby, which wasn't all that long ago, and now that he'd had his first wet dream and, most likely, compared notes with his equally horny finger-playing buddies, nudity and sex went hand-in-hand despite what she told him to the contrary. Michael Jared thought it gross to even think of her and Jared as either nude or sexual.

Knock . . . knock . . . knock.

She had thought Michael Jared had gone. "What?"

"Mommy, can I watch TV?"

"You know the rules."

"Can I, please. I finished my homework. One hour. Please, Mommy."

She wasn't up to a long drawn-out debate. "Thirty minutes, Michael Jared, and no more. It's almost nine o'clock."

"Thanks!"

Tandi could hear him running down the stairs. "And don't make a mess!"

Whether Michael Jared heard her or not, he'd still leave melted chocolate ice cream spots on the coffee table in the family room and his empty bowl in the sink without a drop of water in it. Too many times she had tried to get him to clean up after himself, but Michael Jared seemed to prefer emulating his father. There wasn't much she could do about Jared, his mama had already raised him, but Michael Jared, he could still be taught. Tandi wasn't about to saddle her future daughter-in-law with a man who expected his woman to do everything for him except for maybe picking his teeth. That is, not if she could help it.

She often wondered what kind of father Brent Rodgers would have made. God, she had to stop doing that. Drawing her legs up, she planted her feet solidly on the bottom of the tub, gripped the sides and heaved herself up. Water cascaded down her body back into the tub like a waterfall. Plucking the towel off the rack alongside the tub, she began drying herself. Lately, more and more, Brent was constantly on her mind. If she wasn't comparing Jared to him, she was wishing that he'd call or show up at her door. She hadn't seen him in twenty years so she didn't know if he was alive or dead, married or single, or if he was a bum in the street or president of a company. They had only gone together that one unforgettable last semester, but she could still feel what it was like to be kissed by him, and, in her mind's eye, she could still see him walking down the street like it was yesterday. The more she thought about Brent, the more she ached to see him; for that she blamed Jared. If her life with him were any good, if he hadn't cheated on her and left her doubting her own ability to keep him interested, she wouldn't be dredging up memories of Brent Rodgers and relying on those memories to feed her emotionally anemic love life.